THE CRUEL COAST

Books by William Gage
Appointment with Dishonour
The Cruel Coast

William Gage
THE CRUEL
COAST

 The New American Library

For General Philip S. Gage, U.S. Army (Ret.)

THE CRUEL COAST

OVERTURE

Early on the last Tuesday of May, 1944, some five hundred sea miles west of Ireland, a German submarine was slicing through the fog in pursuit of an Allied convoy. The fog was a thick white quilt that extended from mid-Atlantic to the Western Approaches, and from the Faeroes to the Scillies. It hamstrung shipping from Minches to Milford Haven and grounded most aircraft in Ireland, Wales, and the west of England. It caused innumerable accidents. It was also directly responsible for the ramming—and near-sinking—of the German submarine.

Unterseeboot 324—her crew called her the Shark Boat—was making eighteen knots, her best surface speed, that morning. At 0700 hours, the convoy was estimated to be fifteen miles distant, but, urged on by the young officer of the watch, U-324's sound and radar operators were eagerly searching ahead. They did not pick up the enemy corvette abeam, closing them on a collision course, until it was too late.

Dawn Action Stations had sounded in the U-boat over an hour before. But the fog was so thick that the commanding officer, Lieutenant Commander Ludtke, had not kept his crew alerted for more than a few minutes. He was confident U-324 would not raise the convoy until 0900; in the meantime, his people could do with another hour of sleep. Ludtke gave the order, went to his stateroom, and was almost immediately asleep. So, within minutes, were all the U-boat's officers and men, save only those on watch.

Just at 0700, then, U-324's defenses were down. The captain slept like a drugged man. Immediately forward of his stateroom, the first lieutenant, Lieutenant Reigel, and the engineer officer, Lieutenant Hoffman, snored softly in their wardroom bunks. A few feet forward of them, the cook and his yawning messman were boiling porridge and slicing black *Kommissbrot*. In the next compartment, the forward torpedo room, the bunks were full of sleeping men. A couple of leading hands assisted the torpedo officer as he tinkered with a troublesome magnetic pistol in one of the spare torpedoes.

Astern, in the engine-room compartments, three ratings stood by their diesels and electric motors, thinking dully of breakfast. Amidships, the duty electrician's mate and planesman brooded over their dials, and the radar, sound, and radio operators watched and listened. Above them, in the conning tower, the helmsman flexed his fingers, shifted his feet, and minded the binnacle. Above *him,* on the bridge, the officer of the watch stared into the greasy coils of fog. A boatswain's mate, a messenger, and two lookouts stared hard too, although they could see only a few yards and were bored and thinking of other things. The officer of the watch was an eighteen-year-old midshipman, making his first war patrol in

I

the North Atlantic and determined that the convoy be found on his watch.

It did not work out that way. A British corvette, sweeping well astern of the merchantmen, made radar contact and closed U-324 at flank speed. When the Britisher burst through the low-lying fog, four-inch gun crashing and twenty-millimeter cannon hammering, the midshipman jabbed the Action Stations klaxon and shrieked for an emergency turn. It was too late.

At the first sound of the klaxon, Captain Ludtke vaulted from his bunk into the companionway and shot up the ladder to the bridge. Coming out of the hatch was like entering a lurid, noisy nightmare. The mountainous bow of the corvette was rushing down on them like an express train. Slugs screamed and ricocheted across the bridge, and three of the five watchstanders had been hit as they tried to man the Oerlikon guns. The boatswain's mate, Ludtke saw from the tail of his eye, was already dead.

When the corvette rammed them, striking the U-boat about thirty feet from the bow, it was with stunning, shocking impact. Everyone on the bridge was knocked to the deck. On his knees, the captain saw the corvette's bow had ridden up on his fo'c'sle.

Ludtke scrambled to his feet, shouting orders and defiance. The Action Stations bridge watch streamed out of the hatch and the U-boat's twin Oerlikons began to clatter. The range was so close they could not miss. Within a few seconds, the corvette's port twenty-millimeter cannon—the only gun she could bring to bear—was silenced and smoke poured from her pilot house.

Less than sixty seconds had elapsed since the grinding crash of the collision, but Ludtke acted promptly. He could not know the extent of damage to his boat. U-324 might sink if he backed away, even assuming he could disengage. But the alternative was clearly disastrous: within a matter of minutes the Britisher would board and overpower him by sheer weight of numbers.

"Both engines, astern full!" he shouted down the voice pipe. And a moment later, to his first lieutenant in the conning tower, "Number One, send a couple of hands up here and get the wounded below."

There was no acknowledgment from Lieutenant Reigel and the captain swore. Then U-324's diesels thundered and her screws made a milky froth of the slate-colored water. The boat shuddered and vibrated and finally moved astern with a tearing, grinding rumble. As she wrenched free of the corvette, the submarine listed heavily to starboard and went down by the bow with sickening abruptness.

Ludtke ordered the after ballast tanks flooded to correct the boat's trim. Again there was no response from Lieutenant Reigel—it was the chief quartermaster who acknowledged the order. But there was no time for the captain to wonder about his first lieutenant. Smoke floats were rushed to the topside and thrown overboard to provide a screen of sorts. U-324 continued to back down, Ludtke maneuvering her so as to keep abaft of the arc of fire of the corvette's four-inch bow gun. Simultaneously, the corvette was turning, so as to bring the four-incher to bear, and her automatic weapons were again pumping tracer at the U-boat. As Ludtke opened the distance, taking full advantage of the smoke floats, he presented a progressively more obscure target. Still, casualties mounted on the bridge and gun platform of U-324. The chief quartermaster was hit as he helped the wounded below. The leading signalman, struck as he launched a smoke float, disappeared over the side. The captain himself sustained a splinter wound in the right leg. One Oerlikon jammed, but the other remained in action, and, just at the end, the thirty-seven-millimeter Bofors gun was manned and got off a few rounds. When Ludtke last saw the corvette, flames were licking brightly at her pilot house. She was moving slowly forward, with full port rudder on, still trying to bring her four-inch gun to bear. But her bow was smashed, her forepeak flooded, and the turning was very difficult.

The white, swirling fog closed between the two ships and there was a sudden, clangorous silence. The U-boat captain's voice crackled metallically down the voice pipe again, and this time the first lieutenant answered.

"We've lost her for a bit, Number One," said the captain. "Send two men to help clear the bridge of the wounded. Rig the boat for diving and have the Damage Report ready soon as you can."

They got the wounded below, and threw the shattered body of the boatswain's mate over the side. Ludtke took extra seconds to put an inflated life belt around the corpse so it would float. He came down the ladder last, his right leg soaked with blood and agony lining his face, and the hatch was closed and locked. The captain sat down on the blood-smeared deck of the tiny conning tower and tried to keep from blacking out.

"Why didn't you acknowledge my orders, Number One?" he growled. "What's the matter with you?"

Lieutenant Reigel was a big, dramatically handsome man, but his face was twisted with pain.

"It's my ankle, Captain. I think it's broken. That little Jew, Oberteuffer, was late down the ladder and knocked me off it. I'm putting him on a charge, Captain——"

"We haven't time for your troubles," Ludtke cut in. "What's the Damage Report?"

"Pressure hull is ruptured, sir. Forward torpedo room flooded and sealed off. Battery compartment is partly flooded and chlorine gas escaping. It's also sealed off. We're trying to pump it out, but the main pumps are out." He paused, with a grimace, and looked at the engineer officer.

"All main electric power is gone, Captain," Lieutenant Hoffman said quietly. "The boat can't run submerged."

Ludtke grunted. "What about casualties?"

"Torpedo officer and ten hands lost in the two forward compartments, sir," Hoffman said. "We brought five wounded down from the bridge. Two more hands were injured when the limey rammed us."

Ludtke remembered the boatswain's mate and the leading signalman floating in the slate-gray swells. That meant twenty casualties out of a ship's company of forty-eight. Yet outwardly the captain seemed completely unruffled. He remained on the deck of the conning tower, staring at the circle of white, blurred faces above him as he croaked his questions and instructions.

"Radar operating? Can you find the enemy by sonar?" And when the replies were negative, "Very well, come to one hundred eighty degrees. Both engines half ahead. Unbutton the hatch and set Surface Action Stations. You take the conn on the bridge, Number One. Clear the stoppage in the starboard Oerlikon and keep the gun crews closed up. Radio in commission? No?" The captain shrugged. "Perhaps it's just as well. They'll be waiting to D/F our transmission."

Despite the cramped space in the conning tower, there was no confusion. Orders were given, the hatch was opened and Lieutenant Reigel slowly ascended the ladder, favoring his ankle. The helmsman was frightened when he realized the gyro compass was out, but, without question, he steered a magnetic course. Everyone was frightened, but there was very little noise. Directly under the conning tower, in the control room, it was different. From below they could hear the sobs, curses, and long, dreadful groans of the wounded. It was dark down there, except for flashlights and emergency battle lanterns. With the main power gone and the smell of chlorine gas in the boat, Ludtke knew panic could spread—even among a well-disciplined crew. He spoke sharply to a petty officer:

"Lay below, Schiller, and get those people into their bunks. Tell the quack to give them what's necessary to stop that flaming music." (The quack was the sick berth attendant or medical petty officer. Most U-

4

boats carried a doctor in 1944, but the midshipman, borne for training purposes, had displaced U-324's regular medical officer.)

"Chief," the captain said to the engineer officer, "carry out the standard decoy procedure. Pump out twenty tons of fuel oil and get the usual stuff over the side—crates, furniture, bedding, uniform caps. You know the drill. Maybe that, and the bodies, will fox them."

"Aye, aye, sir," said Hoffman. He looked at the captain's bloody trouser leg. "I'll send the quack up to look at that leg, sir."

"*After* he stops that damned music," the captain said. He leaned his head back against the bulkhead. He was faint and drenched with sweat. He had hoped, at first, to submerge to periscope depth, stalk the corvette, and finish her off with his stern torpedoes. But surfaced in the fog, with no radar, was like playing a game of blind man's buff. Ludtke did not care for games of chance; he liked to have the odds in his favor. If the enemy found him, he would fight. Under the circumstances, he was glad to break off the action. The captain glanced at the eight-day chronometer mounted on the bulkhead. It was only 0725 hours.

Within minutes, the groans and curses below stopped. Auxiliary lights came on and emergency repairs were effected. The near-panic disappeared and the crew went quickly about its duties, with discipline and precision. After all, the crew remembered, this was the Shark Boat— the ace of the Second Flotilla. "Don't worry, mate," Lieutenant Hoffman heard one stoker reassure another, "the Old Man'll take care of us."

Busy with the rigging of portable pumps, Peter Hoffman smiled to himself. The ship's company did not like Ludtke, but it respected him mightily. The Old Man had brought them out of tight spots before. Ludtke had driven the Shark Boat for nearly four years, remarkably long for a U-boat skipper. He was cautious, crafty, a fighter who rarely fought without supporting odds. It was that quality of cunning, so the story went, that won U-324 her name. At La Spezia, in 1942, an inspecting Italian commodore had paid an elaborate Latin compliment. This submarine is like a shark, the commodore reportedly said, ferocious but not foolhardy. From that day, U-324 *was* the Shark Boat, and, among his fellow captains, Ludtke was often called The Shark. The holder of the Knight's Cross of the Iron Cross, Ludtke had no ambition other than to be decorated with the Oak Leaves, an award held only by one or two living captains. Ah, he'll deserve it, Peter Hoffman said to himself, if he brings us out of this one.

At the same time, on the bridge, Lieutenant Reigel was straining his eyes against the fog. Around him, the Action Stations bridge watch, gunners, loaders, and lookouts, glared anxiously about. Even in the fog, they knew they were not safe. The corvette and others of her escort group were close at hand, and, at any moment, a radar-controlled salvo might bracket them. The U-boat was making twelve knots, her best speed considering the weakened bulkheads and hundreds of tons of water in her two forward compartments. Her radar antenna was shot away, and her underwater sound gear was good only for a few hundred yards. She was like a sitting duck, Reigel thought bitterly, cursing his ankle, Seaman Oberteuffer, and the carelessness of the midshipman. Like a blind sitting duck. He heard one of the ratings make a low, pessimistic comment and the encouraging reply of Schiller, Boatswain's Mate, Second Class, and now the senior deck petty officer: "Don't worry, Anton, the captain knows what he's doing. He'll take care of us, my boy."

Reigel swiveled around in the splinter-torn conning chair, his face dark with anger. "Silence on the bridge," he snapped. "You're at Action Stations—to listen and look." Damned fools, he thought irritably. They think the Old Man will take care of us. Well, as long as he does, the son-of-a-dog can have his Oak Leaves.

Lieutenant Commander Gerhard Ludtke thought briefly of the Oak Leaves as, still sitting on the deck of the conning tower, he permitted the sick berth attendant to minister to his leg. Ludtke was thirty-five, old for a U-boat captain, but he was convinced that only in the U-Waffe could a former Merchant Mariner win recognition. He was starved for recognition. He was the senior captain in the Second Flotilla, but he wanted more than that.

Ludtke had commissioned U-324, nearly four years ago, in the Blohm and Voss yard in Hamburg. She had never had another captain. Under his command, she had fought from Tobruk in the sun-flecked Mediterranean to the icy Denmark Strait. She was a tough and wily fighter, with a British destroyer and 120,000 Gross Registered Tons of Allied shipping to her credit. To be sure, other skippers had sunk more than 120,000 G.R.T., but in 1944 those skippers slept on the bottom while the Shark Boat kept the sea. Ludtke lit a cigar and exhaled noisily. They were hunting him now, but if this fog and his luck held, he'd bring the Shark Boat back to Lorient. He and she would be famous together, the most famous team in the U-Waffe.

Although Ludtke did not know it, the corvette that had rammed him had lost her radar and was almost equally helpless in the fog. She called up reinforcements and two destroyers joined in mid-morning, but the weather prevented the use of aircraft. The destroyers made a box search and shortly after noon, one reported the slick of fuel oil, bits of wreckage, and a floating body. The commanding officer of the corvette permitted himself modest thoughts of an investiture at the Palace. At Liverpool, in the underground headquarters of the Commander-in-Chief,

Western Approaches, staff officers recorded a probable kill. The staff officers were cynical about oil slicks and wreckage, but it wasn't likely a five-hundred-ton U-boat could be rammed squarely and still survive.

At 1100 hours, U-324 was still undetected, and Ludtke altered his course to 090 degrees. Barndt, the sick berth attendant, administered morphine, picked out scraps of steel and bone from the wounded leg, dusted it with sulfa powder, splinted and bandaged it. After an hour's fitful sleep, Ludtke felt better. He drank some broth, smoked another cigar, and felt tough and confident when the engineer officer, Peter Hoffman, came up to make a detailed report.

Hoffman was a slightly built man in his late twenties, with close-cropped wheat-colored hair. His features were regular, almost ordinary, but he had a way of smiling, a shy, tilted smile, that was somehow endearing. People liked Hoffman—the deckhands and torpedomen who professed disdain for all engine-room snipes, even the French dockyard navvies from whom he wheedled and stole. Ludtke wasn't endeared to Hoffman by his smile, but he recognized him as a competent engineer and a born leader. Hoffman had been in the Shark Boat fifteen months. Almost from the beginning, the sailors would follow him anywhere. He did not bray his orders as Reigel did, like some SS *Gruppensfuehrer;* in fact, he almost never raised his voice. It was a quiet, flat voice, yet the crew strained to catch its meaning and to carry out his wishes.

Lieutenant Hoffman made his report, not smiling, and while Ludtke knew most of the facts, the details weren't good. The radar was permanently gone, the radio incapable of transmitting or receiving. Limited auxiliary power was available, Hoffman said, and they would soon have most of the water out of the battery compartment, the second forward of six watertight compartments in the boat (the first—the forward torpedo room—was ripped open to the sea, and nothing could be done about it). But, Hoffman continued in his quiet voice, the chief damage had been done in the battery compartment. Enough seawater had entered it to short-circuit the cables leading to the electric motors in the maneuvering room. The storage batteries were awash, generating clouds of chlorine gas. With the boat surfaced, the gas was not dangerous, but until the water was completely pumped out, the cables replaced, the battery plates dried, and fresh acid added, there would be no main source of power in U-324. The Shark Boat could not proceed submerged.

"Jesus," Ludtke said bitterly, "these damned VII-B boats."

Hoffman knew what the captain meant. In most submarines—Axis and Allied alike—there were two battery compartments, one forward

7

and one aft of the control room. Had U-324 been of this conventional design, only the forward batteries would have been knocked out. She would have been able to proceed submerged—very slowly, of course, and for limited periods. In that case, Ludtke could have made for Lorient. But the VII-B class was unique. There was only one battery compartment—forward. In U-324, all the batteries were covered with seawater, and every discussion of the intelligence, patriotism, and antecedents of the responsible naval architects was academic. The Shark Boat could not proceed submerged.

Hoffman knew what that meant, too. In the month of May, 1944, the U-boat that could not submerge was almost certainly doomed. There were hundreds of enemy aircraft whose radar could pick up a surfaced submarine fifty miles away. Against them, the U-boats were almost defenseless. They had to surface to recharge batteries, yet they had no radar able to give sufficient warning of a plane. Very often, Hoffman knew, a Coastal Command bomber or a carrier-based fighter-bomber would dive out of a cloud to kill a U-boat. Even worse were the night attacks, when a boat's bridge watch would be suddenly blinded by an aircraft's searchlight and simultaneously bombed and strafed. Inexorably, Hoffman told himself, the Battle of the Atlantic was being lost. There were too many escorts, too many planes and hunter-killer groups, and too much scientific technology arrayed against the U-Waffe. During the last fortnight, the engineer lieutenant knew from the radio traffic, there had been less than a half-dozen boats in the Western Approaches. The hunters had become the hunted.

"It depends on the fog, then," Ludtke said. He only repeated words that had been uttered a thousand times in U-324 since the ramming. Only if the fog persisted was the U-boat relatively secure. Not just the fog around them, at sea, but the fog over the airdromes in Northern Ireland, Wales, and southwestern England. No man aboard the Shark Boat knew how far the fog extended, or to what degree Coastal Command was operational. Each man could only hope or pray, according to his lights, that it was thick, low-lying, and widely spread.

"Yes, sir," said the engineer lieutenant. "There's one more thing, Captain. The galley's gone. Equipment's ruined and a lot of the food."

Ludtke morosely regarded his cigar. "We can't dive, we can't ask for help, we can't even get a decent meal. Is that it, Chief?"

"Yes, sir."

"And when the fog lifts, or even before it lifts, the R.A.F. will be after us." The captain swore, with fluency and imagination, and Peter Hoffman and the helmsman listened respectfully.

Ludtke presently fell silent and Hoffman spoke again. "The cook, sir, and his messman. They're sewn up now, ready for burial. Permission to pipe hands to service?"

Ludtke grunted a sour affirmative. A little later, after Boatswain's Mate Schiller had roused the off-duty hands from their bunks and fallen them in abaft the conning tower, the captain struggled up to the bridge, and was assisted aft, onto the Bofors gun platform. Below him, a straggly double line of sailors stared glumly at two lumpy mounds of canvas, each on a stretcher and covered by a naval ensign.

The boatswain's mate called the sailors to attention, and Lieutenant Reigel limped aft from the bridge onto the gun platform. "Ship's company," he roared belligerently, "off caps!" He glowered about him, at the bareheaded gunners, loaders, and lookouts, at the sailors at attention on the afterdeck, and then handed U-324's prayer book to the captain.

Ludtke began to read the burial service in a voice devoid of emotion. "Oh most powerful and glorious Lord God, at whose command the winds blow and lift the waves of the sea and who stilleth the rage thereof. . . ."

From where he stood, beside the two corpses, Hoffman could scarcely make out the words. He watched the two officers above him, the chunky, clean-shaven captain and the tall, powerful, bearded Reigel. Both stood at attention, yet both grasped the rail for support, Ludtke favoring his leg and the first lieutenant his ankle. The tiny gun platform on which they stood was called the Winter Garden, for some obscure reason dating back to the Kaiser's service. A curious name, Hoffman reflected. In other navies, he understood, they called it the Cigarette Deck, which made sense. But in the U-Waffe, it had always been the Winter Garden.

Finished with his reading, the captain snapped shut the prayer book. Three riflemen fired three ragged volleys, and Ludtke looked at his first lieutenant.

"All right, let 'em go!" Reigel boomed, and Hoffman stiffened with sudden, outraged anger.

"Belay that!" he snapped at the two sailors who stood inboard of the stretchers. "Wait for the pipe," Hoffman said savagely and turned to the boatswain's mate. "Now, Schiller," he ordered.

As Schiller trilled the wavering, mournful notes, the crew stood at rigid attention. A burial ought to be done properly, Hoffman thought irritably; any officer, even a Party member, ought to know it's important to the men. Then he nodded to the two sailors, and one after the other, they raised the stretcher ends and slid the shrouds out from under the ensigns into the gray, fog-covered sea.

Lieutenant Reigel dismissed the formation, glaring at Hoffman. Hoffman was the senior, by a few numbers, but as a member of the Engineer

Branch, he rarely interfered with the first lieutenant's orders. Captain Ludtke, sardonically amused by Hoffman's indignant interruption and Reigel's scowling counterreaction, heard snatches of the ratings' conversations as they went down the hatch.

"A good thing Mr. Hoffman stepped in at the end, there."

"*Ja*, Number One wasn't going to let Cooky have his farewell pipe."

Ludtke stared at the fog and reflected on his two surviving officers. Both Hoffman and Reigel knew their jobs and did them well, but there the similarity ended. The engineer officer had an innate sense of the proper thing to do; the crew liked and respected him. The first lieutenant, on the other hand, was harsh and demanding. Hoffman knew the first name of every rating, his home town, and the names of his children. Reigel barely knew the last names—his interest in the ship's company did not go beyond that. A good officer, Ludtke admitted, but he often thought Reigel would have been more successful in the Waffen SS than in the Navy.

For the rest of Tuesday afternoon and evening, and all through the night, U-324 steamed eastward in the fog. Hoffman and Reigel stood watch-and-watch on the bridge, the latter's ankle giving him pain and making him more irascible than usual. Ludtke remained in the conning tower, plotting his dead reckoning positions with the help of the patent log. The rest of the ship's company stood their watches, slept, and ate cold rations. On the bridge, the sailors peered vainly into the fog; below decks they speculated endlessly about it—its extent and probable duration. Some of the crew were fatalistic about the fog, others were alarmed when the wind freshened by as much as a knot.

There was another funeral the next morning. The unfortunate midshipman had died of his wounds during the middle watch. This time the dreary little ceremony on the afterdeck was performed with due propriety; the engineer lieutenant was officer of the watch and the first lieutenant did not stir from his bunk. The enlisted men were apathetic about the burial. They didn't know the midshipman well and were more interested in the fog. Ludtke noted, however, that they moved smartly at Hoffman's commands. Ship's company, off caps. On caps, hand salute. Saluting detail, present arms. Prepare to fire. Aim. Fire. The orders were obeyed, Ludtke thought, almost as crisply as if his sailors were Brandenburg Guardsmen.

Later in the morning, the first lieutenant came up to the bridge and saluted the captain.

"Sir, request permission to convene a Deck Court."

Ludtke wanted no part of administrative detail, but he could not easily refuse. Presently, the accused, the plaintiff, and the master-at-arms were ranged before him. Ordinary Seaman Oberteuffer was thin, nervous, and incredibly young. Lieutenant Reigel was massive and truculent. Boatswain's Mate Schiller, a stolid Saxon, carried the log-book, so as to record the proceedings of the court. Around the little group, the Cruising Stations bridge watch simultaneously stared outboard and strained to hear the testimony.

"Very well, Number One, what's the charge?"

"Desertion of post in the face of the enemy, sir."

"Go on."

"Yesterday morning, sir, when Action Stations went, I was going up the ladder to the conning tower. This little kike—" he gave the accused a malevolent stare—"this Oberteuffer, sir, came down the ladder, crashed into me, and knocked me off the ladder. Sprained my ankle. What happened, sir, is plain. Oberteuffer didn't wait for the Action Stations watch to relieve the bridge. He bolted. He deserted his post, Captain, in the face of the enemy."

Aboard any man-of-war, there are rules governing rights-of-way for personnel during an emergency. This is particularly important in a submarine where the companionways and ladders are few and small. In the U-Waffe there was a basic rule, drilled into ship's companies by thousands of exercises: the Action Stations watch relieves the Cruising watch, starting with the bridge. That is to say, a cruising detail lookout waited until the entire Action Stations complement was on the bridge before going below.

Everyone, of course, knew this. It was one of the first things taught aboard training ships. Ludtke glowered at Oberteuffer, a soft-mannered, smooth-cheeked deckhand, and invited him to speak.

The accused was frightened but articulate. "I'm no coward, sir. I was properly relieved before I went below."

"Who relieved you?"

"The leading signalman, sir."

The captain frowned and rubbed his chin. The leading signalman was dead and could contribute no testimony. Ludtke knew Oberteuffer had a good record and that the first lieutenant disliked him. Still, this was a serious charge. Ludtke growled in his throat.

"Begging the captain's pardon," Lieutenant Hoffman interrupted. As officer of the watch, he had been close to the conning chair during the proceedings. "Sir," Hoffman said, "I was in the control room when the limey rammed us. Right after that most of the Cruising watch came down from the bridge—Koenig, Heinz, Schirmer."

"This was before Number One started up the ladder?"

"Yes, sir."

"That's not true, Captain," Reigel broke in furiously. "The kike left his station——"

"Don't use that word, damn it," Hoffman flared. Oberteuffer, he knew, had had a Jewish grandmother, but the boy was a Lutheran.

"That's enough, Chief," the captain said coldly. "You've not been appointed to defend this man." He sat very still, fingers drumming on the arm of the conning chair. He looked at his two lieutenants, who glared angrily at one another, at the accused, who stood with his heels together and shoulders squared, and at Boatswain's Mate Schiller, also at attention. The lookouts and gunners of the watch stared out at the fog, obviously waiting for the decision.

Everyone knew what the decision had to be. The evidence was that Lieutenant Reigel had been tardy in going to his station in the conning tower. It was natural for men on the bridge, when relieved, to assume reliefs had reached the conning tower. Young Oberteuffer had a good record. But a commanding officer had a duty to his first lieutenant; that was the most important concern.

"The accused is found guilty as charged," Ludtke said. "In view of the accused's good record, sentence is commuted to ten days solitary on bread and water, sentence to be served when we reach Lorient. Court dismissed."

The little group saluted him and broke up. Reigel was displeased—the sentence was a minimum one. Oberteuffer was very unhappy—he was barely eighteen, proud to be in the U-Waffe, and he hated to see his record fouled. Hoffman was coldly furious. He understood the system and regarded Ludtke as a good captain. Once the court was convened, the Old Man had done what he had to. It had been Reigel who should have been accused, Hoffman told himself, Reigel who had been late in going to his station. Under his breath, the engineer officer ground out a string of blasphemy. Schiller laboriously wrote the verdict into the log and relieved his feelings by spitting to leeward. The watchstanders stared at the fog.

After the Deck Court, the day was uneventful. All repairs possible while underway had been accomplished. There was little to do except worry about the fog and speculate on the submarine's destination. One of the helmsmen reported the Old Man had been studying the Coastal Pilot for the west coast of Ireland, and that set off a riot of rumor. The captain, as usual, kept his own counsel and not even the officers presumed to inquire about his plans. As Wednesday afternoon wore by, the Shark Boat steamed eastward and the men fretted about the fog.

During the second dog watch, Reigel reported the wind was freshening and the captain struggled up to the bridge. The first lieutenant was right. There was a sharp quartering breeze and the fog would soon be dissipated. U-324 had been shrouded for nearly three days by the thick blanket—opaque, oppressive, and blessed. Since the ramming thirty-six hours before, it had been almost the sole topic of conversation in the boat—the subject of anxious questions when men awoke and of muttered prayer when they went to their bunks. Now the fog was lessening perceptibly and the bridge watch looked apprehensive.

"Just in time, too, Number One," Ludtke said with brisk confidence. "We can't be more than fifty miles from the Irish coast and we'll need a star fix this evening." He looked about him, noting that the worried frowns were disappearing. The news that they were so close to shore would travel fast, he thought to himself, and would be good for the lower deck's morale.

"Let's see," Ludtke went on. "Vega and Denebola will be early stars tonight, Number One. We may see them in a couple of hours and have a horizon, too. Let me know when they're visible."

"Aye, aye, sir." Reigel came to attention and saluted, and the captain slowly went down the ladder.

Midway in the evening watch the star sights were taken. There were a few minutes of labored computation and then the helmsman heard the first lieutenant's report.

"We're here, sir," Reigel said, circling a cross on the chart. "Seventy-one miles from the mouth of the Shannon. It bears oh-nine-five degrees magnetic."

The captain hitched himself painfully to the chart table and considered the fix at some length. Then he blew into the voice pipe and spoke: "Bridge? Bridge, I'm altering course to one hundred five degrees. That's right, one hundred five degrees. Call me at midnight."

The helmsman shifted to the new heading and Ludtke composed himself for sleep. Reigel went below to his bunk and, on the bridge, Hoffman stared at the sky and the gently rolling stars. Both officers wondered about the change of course. There was a graving dock, they knew, at Limerick, up the Shannon. And Galway, eighty miles or so to the north, was a major port. But the Shark Boat was steaming east by southeast, on a course, Hoffman judged, that would take her to Bantry Bay. That seemed odd to Hoffman, but he stifled his curiosity. The Old Man had brought her 450 sea miles since the collision, and he'd take her the rest of the way. For the remainder of the watch, U-324 steamed steadily on her new heading.

THURSDAY

It was a little past midnight by the brass chronometer on the conning tower bulkhead. In the first few minutes of the new day, the three surviving officers of U-324 were gathered about the chart table. Hoffman had just come down from the bridge, cold and tired. He grunted a good morning to the captain and Reigel and made a brief entry in the log. When he straightened wearily from the logbook, Hoffman spoke slowly and economically, as though too many words might exhaust him.

"We're steaming as before, Kurt. Course one hundred five magnetic. Speed one hundred twenty turns—just under twelve knots. There's a Force Three wind following us from the port quarter. Fog's almost gone. Moon is down. Pretty well overcast, only a few stars. We've sighted no lights during the watch."

Lieutenant Reigel listened thoughtfully, his blue eyes still clouded with sleep, his fingers absently tugging at his curly blond beard. Reigel was twenty-five years old and acknowledged to be the handsomest man in the Second Flotilla. Some of the younger ratings said he looked like a movie star.

"The midwatch is set throughout the boat," Hoffman said. "Boatswain's Mate Schiller is P.O. of the watch. That's all, except at about 0300 hours, we'll raise Tearacht Light, off the coast of Ireland. It's an occulting light, four ten-second periods to the minute. Right, Captain?"

The commanding officer, slumped in his chair by the chart table, grunted an affirmative. His right leg, heavily bandaged, rested before him on a crate padded with kapok life jackets. Where Hoffman was slight and slender, and Reigel tall and handsome, Lieutenant Commander Gerhard Ludtke had a chunky body, a thick neck, and a brutally ugly face, permanently yellowed by atabrine. His nose, broken years before in a Panama bar, was a twisted lump of cartilage and tissue. His mouth was straight and uncompromising, with colorless, very thin lips. The irises of his lashless eyes were a light hazel, so pale as to be almost yellow; they had a trick, when Ludtke was displeased, of sharpening and hardening so that they glinted like cold quartz. His head was shaven to the skull bone in the old Prussian fashion, with just a patch of hair, always impeccably parted and plastered flat at the crown. Listening to Hoffman's remarks, he chewed a dead cigar; now he picked up a pair of dividers and jabbed at the chart before him. "Here's our 2400 position by D.R. You got a pretty good sight last evening, Number One, so we can't be very far from this position. If we hold present course and speed, we ought to raise Tearacht Light by about 0330."

"Yes, sir, 0330," Reigel said.

The captain stared at the chart for fully half a minute. In the cramped conning tower, his officers waited, watching him. There was no sound above the creaking ship noises and the steady *thrum thrum thrum* of the diesels. Finally the captain spoke again.

"It's necessary, gentlemen, that we put into an Irish port to make repairs. We must be able to dive. So far, what with the poor weather, we've been very lucky. But, even with a hurricane, we couldn't cross the Bay of Biscay on the surface."

Hoffman and Reigel agreed. A German submarine wasn't safe anywhere in the North Atlantic. The chances, they knew, were even worse in the Bay of Biscay, where enemy antisubmarine patrols, hunter-killer groups, and aircraft concentrated. The Bay was a funnel between the ports of western France, where the U-boats based, and the ocean. In the spring of 1944, it was also the graveyard of the U-Waffe.

"From what you tell me, Chief," the captain said to the engineer lieutenant, "we could repair the boat in a few days at a port like Galway. I know the Irish have no love for the limeys. But the limeys would learn of our presence and they'd have half the ships in the Western Approaches waiting for us to come out. So, gentlemen, we must reach an Irish port where we can get help and where news about us won't leak out. Where would that be, eh?"

Hoffman and Reigel stared at him blankly. In the last two days it had been apparent U-324 would have to seek refuge in some neutral Irish port. With the radio out of commission, the submarine could not rendezvous with a U-tanker and effect repairs at sea. But Hoffman and Reigel had not asked questions. Ludtke was not fond of being questioned, and, like the rest of the ship's company, they instinctively trusted the captain.

"I don't know, sir," the first lieutenant said finally.

"An island, Number One, an island." The captain permitted himself a thin smile. "That's the solution. An island where we can repair the boat—a place where we can get the spare parts we need from the mainland."

"An unoccupied island," Reigel said with sudden excitement. "There must be scores of them along the Irish coast."

"Not unoccupied, Number One," the captain said. "Remember, we must have help from the natives. Someone who can go to the mainland for us. We could never get the parts ourselves without giving the show away. There's another thing, too. We need a protected harbor and some sort of quay to come alongside. We won't find those on an unoccupied island."

Ludtke looked at his officers but they made no response. After a few seconds, the captain brought the closed dividers carefully down on the chart. They stared at the dot he had indicated, saying nothing.

"*This* is our island, gentlemen. Spanish Island. About nine miles off the Kerry coast. There's a harbor there, and a quay built by smugglers in the nineteenth century, according to the Coastal Pilot. Fishermen live there. That's all I know about it."

"How much water in the harbor, sir?" Reigel asked.

"I don't know, Number One. The Coastal Pilot doesn't say. The tide tables don't even list the place. So, we'll go in when it's high tide at Dingle, the nearest port that *is* listed. That's at 0610—just before sunrise."

He paused again, looking from one to another for comment. But neither Hoffman nor Reigel said anything.

"When we pick up Tearacht Light this morning, we'll be only six or eight miles from Spanish Island. Call me then, Number One. Chief, you be prepared to go ashore with five hands when we close the island. I can't send the first lieutenant. His ankle wouldn't be much good ashore. I'll need help from ashore in berthing the boat, Chief. And it's important to take the natives by surprise; if one of them gets away to the mainland and starts talking about us, we'll never get back to Lorient."

"Aye, aye, sir," the two officers said.

"Very well, gentlemen," Ludtke said. "Goodnight."

They bade him goodnight. Hoffman went down the ladder into the control room and picked his way forward to his bunk. Reigel took his Zeiss binoculars off the bulkhead peg, slung them around his neck, buttoned the sou'wester under his chin, and climbed up the ladder to the bridge. Ludtke put a pillow behind his head and stretched out in his chair, careful not to move his wounded leg. If his luck held, he would get a good three hours' sleep. Sunrise would be at 0613. By that time, the Shark Boat should be in the harbor of Spanish Island, safe from the probing radars of Coastal Command. It was fortunate, he thought, that three persons aboard U-324 could speak English—his two lieutenants and himself. Not many boats were so well equipped for a visit to an Irish port. He dropped the cold cigar butt on the deck and cushioned his head, permitting himself a short, humorless smile. He closed his eyes and was asleep almost immediately.

Above him, on the bridge, Lieutenant Reigel stared at the eastern horizon. For the benefit of the watch, he kept his voice harsh, but he smiled to himself. Only a few more hours, now, and they would be safe. There'll be women on Spanish Island, he told himself, and he could do with a little fun. The first lieutenant had a prodigious reputation as a ladies' man. He was proud of it and tried to maintain it. Behind his back, the sailors called him the tomcat and he was secretly pleased. When he had his own boat, he told himself, a tomcat would adorn its superstructure, just as a slavering shark's head was painted on the conning tower of U-324.

Reigel had been almost irresistible to women for ten years, ever since he put on the uniform of the Hitler Youth. He had been tall and good-looking even then, and wherever he had gone, he had conquered. In Berlin, at the Naval Academy at Lübeck, in London, where he had been on the Naval Attaché's staff, in Norway, on the Riviera, and, most recently, in dingy Lorient, he was triumphant. He was extremely vain about his physique and was given to daily periods of exercise with a barbell he kept in the wardroom. He was pleased with the prospect of women, happy he did not have to go ashore in the dinghy, and, in spite of himself, impressed with the captain's plans. He had not liked Ludtke since the day he reported aboard and the Old Man had eloquently established there would be no Nazi salutes in the Shark Boat. On the other hand, Reigel admitted, Ludtke was a highly competent skipper. Twenty-four hours ago, the first lieutenant had been positive the boat was doomed. Now it appeared her luck was holding. He was scornful of the ratings' commonplace, "the captain will take care of us," but he had to acknowledge the Old Man had a plan for hiding and repairing the boat.

Reigel realized there was a good reason for the comparative longevity of U-324. A submarine is only the extension of one man's ingenuity, resourcefulness, and will. A submarine captain can carry a green, timid crew to great victories, or he can destroy the coordinated efforts of veterans. U-324's successes, her ability to stay at sea, and her reputation for wiliness and luck all reflected her commanding officer's character and experience. Ludtke, Reigel knew, was a reservist, a man without influence in high places or aspiration to shore duty. More than once the first lieutenant heard him say he had joined the Navy to fight and the place to fight was at sea. So far as Reigel could tell, the Old Man thought only in terms of an efficient boat, G.R.T. sunk, and the Oak Leaves.

Ludtke was an iron-hard captain, surprisingly so in view of his Merchant Navy background. The answer, as Reigel vaguely understood it, was that Ludtke's father had been an officer in the old Imperial Navy, a veteran of the High Seas Fleet. Ludtke had grown up in the depressed years of the Weimar Republic, with his mother forced to take in laundry. He had been refused an appointment to the Naval Academy as a boy, but when, in 1937, he obtained his Reserve Commission, he was determined to let nothing interfere with recognition.

The captain was feared by his men, and with reason. Once, in the Mediterranean, he had thrown overboard a torpedoman who was behaving irrationally. Again, when a gunner's mate failed to hit a powerless little coaster, he had disrated the man on the spot and ordered him sent to the Eastern Front as of the day they returned to port.

A tough, self-centered captain, yes. The German service always was a hard one. But oddly enough, U-324's people were ready to fight for Ludtke. On one notable occasion, at the Hotel Pigeon Blanc in Lorient, they fought with wine bottles and chairs against other sailors of the Second Flotilla who had made sneering references to The Shark. The crew, while they did not like him, had a deep-seated pride in Ludtke. They respected his knowledge of the sea and stars. They admired his understanding of the boat—how sharply she would dive or how deeply she would lie. Most of all, they appreciated his reputation. He was lucky and the Shark Boat was lucky. It followed that they were lucky.

For Ludtke, as for any other commanding officer in the Battle of the Atlantic, three hours' continuous sleep was a hard-bought luxury. This time there was no alarm, but in less than two hours the captain was jolted awake by his wounded leg. Stabbing spasms of pain reached up to his thigh and made him grind his teeth. He cursed under his breath until the breath was short and the sweat glistened on his forehead. The helmsman noticed his distress and was solicitous. Ludtke snarled for Barndt, the sick berth attendant. As he waited for him, the captain clenched his teeth and glared around him. The chronometer on the bulkhead read 0215.

Within two minutes, Barndt was in the conning tower and preparing a syringe of morphine. His little eyes were sunken and bloodshot with lack of sleep. Nine officers and men, including the captain, had been hurt or wounded in the battle with the corvette; up to now, Barndt had lost only the midshipman. Lieutenant Reigel was fast recovering. Of the six hurt or wounded ratings, two were in critical shape, three were resting comfortably and likely to recover, and one, a serious leg wound, was completely unpredictable. There was little Barndt could do for his patients beyond keeping them comfortable with sedatives and changing their dressings, but his duties had exhausted him.

While he administered morphine to the captain, cut away the tape and gauze, sprinkled sulfa powder on the shattered leg, and rebandaged it, Barndt reported as best he could on the condition of his other patients. Normally, the sick berth attendant wouldn't have dared to ask a question of the commanding officer, but the mounting strain of his responsibilities was more than he could contain.

"They're saying we'll reach Ireland during the morning watch, sir. Is that right?"

And when Ludtke had grunted an affirmative, "Will there be a surgeon there, sir? We must have a surgeon soon, sir, or there'll be more work for the sailmaker."

"We'll have a surgeon to help you as soon as we can," Ludtke said. "In the meantime, quack, you'll have to carry on."

Barndt finished his work and went below, mumbling and shaking his head. The captain drank coffee and, as the pain in his leg deadened, stared at the chart. He had finished a second cup when Lieutenant Reigel's report of Tearacht Light, its bearing and estimated range, rasped down the voice pipe. Ludtke plotted his position, worked rapidly with dividers, parallel ruler, and protractor, and gave his orders to the bridge.

"Come to oh-nine-oh, Number One. Reduce your speed to eight knots. Give me bearings on the light every two minutes." He turned to the helmsman. "Pass the word for Mr. Hoffman."

Presently, the engineer officer was in the conning tower, rubbing his eyes. He studied the chart with the captain. They agreed U-324 would be off Spanish Island at 0445, less than ninety minutes before sunrise.

The captain brought out a sheet of paper. On it, he had drawn a crude outline of Spanish Island, enlarged from the Hamburg Hydrographic Institute chart. The island was nearly three miles long, and perhaps a mile and one-half across at its widest. It was shaped like an inverted pear, round at the top and with a tail tapering off at the bottom. The harbor was indicated and this, Hoffman thought, gave the island a slight resemblance to a seahorse. On the paper an arrow indicated magnetic north and a circle represented U-324's probable position when the landing party left.

Ludtke's instructions were simple. Once ashore, Hoffman must reconnoiter and insure a safe mooring for the boat. He would report back to the submarine, and, when the boat had proceeded in accordance with his signal, Hoffman and his people would stand by to help berth it. All the Coastal Pilot reported about Spanish Island was that a harbor existed on its eastern side. It would be dangerous to take U-324 into it if she were completely sound. As she was, down by the bow, listing ten degrees to starboard, and with only the diesels for power, it became almost reckless.

There was an even more important reason for sending an advance party ashore. No word of the U-boat's arrival must leave the island by radio, telephone, or signal. No native must leave the island.

"Is that completely understood, Chief?" the captain asked finally.

"Aye, aye, sir," Hoffman said. He folded the crude map carefully and stowed it away in an oilskin wallet.

Ludtke glanced at the bulkhead clock and at his wristwatch. He whistled into the voice pipe and spoke to Reigel.

"It's 0345 now, Number One, one hour to launching. Call all hands to breakfast, and at 0415 go to Action Stations. I'll come topside now and take over the deck."

"Aye, aye, sir," Reigel said, and in a few moments, Hoffman heard the word being passed. With the galley wrecked and the cook dead, he thought fleetingly, breakfast would be another meager meal—coffee, sausage, black *Kommissbrot*, and jam. It would be different, he told himself, when the boat was safely moored at Spanish Island.

The engineer lieutenant went below to eat, and Ludtke struggled out of his chair and into his oilskins. He put on dark goggles to precondition his eyes for the blackness above, slung his glasses around his neck, and hoisted himself, one rung of the ladder at a time, up through the hatch to the bridge. For the next hour he and Reigel were busy with their navigation. They had only the indistinct flashes of Tearacht Light to guide them. With the failure of the power, there was not even the help of the fathometer.

Presently, alarm gongs sounded and the Surface Action Stations were manned. It was 0415. The captain gave instructions to the new watch.

"Pay special attention to the surface sector Red two-oh to Green three-oh. Watch for surf, boys, watch for surf."

At 0430, Ludtke reduced speed to six knots. On the afterdeck, Hoffman briefed his landing party. He had carefully chosen his five sailors, and had included Ordinary Seaman Oberteuffer as a public affirmation of his faith in the man. Hoffman could not guess at his reception on Spanish Island; he hoped there might be an opportunity to recommend Oberteuffer for an Iron Cross. That would give Ludtke a reason to rescind his Deck Court sentence. Hoffman told his people that he and two hands would go in the ten-foot aluminum dinghy, towing the three others in individual rubber rafts. U-324 had two larger rubber rafts nested on the fo'c'sle, but they had been riddled by the gunfire of the corvette.

At 0440, U-324 was close to the estimated launching point, according to the bearing on Tearacht Light. But there was no sign of surf, no sound of breakers above the throb of the engines. Ludtke, worrying about the set of the Gulf Stream, began to sweat.

Five minutes dragged by as the submarine continued eastward. Ten minutes. With impenetrable blackness ahead, the captain ordered all engines stopped. For a moment the muffled thunder of the diesels stayed in his ears. Then there was another sound, the blessed booming of surf, and simultaneously a confused, happy babble of reports.

"I hear surf, Captain!"

"Breakers on the port bow!"

"Surf bearing Red two-oh, sir!"

"Very well," Ludtke sang out, and he grabbed the voice pipe to issue new instructions. Once he had made the landfall, he lost no time in bringing the boat to the approximate launching point. As he did so, Hoffman came forward and reported.

"Ready to cast off, sir."

"That is good," Ludtke said. "All engines, stop," he barked into the voice pipe.

The U-boat rolled heavily in the Atlantic swells and it was not easy to get the rafts and dinghy launched and manned. It was 0520 by Hoffman's waterproof wristwatch when they finally began paddling for the black mass with the fringe of white water at its base. Hoffman, Boatswain's Mate Schiller, and Able Seaman Kramer were in the dinghy, towing Able Seaman Heinz, Signalman Koenig, and Ordinary Seaman Oberteuffer in the three rubber rafts. The boatswain's mate had a Schmeisser nine-millimeter machine pistol and a heaving line for testing the depth of the harbor, the signalman had his lamp and a first-aid kit, and all had pistols and electric torches wrapped in oilcloth.

They paddled hard, for there were dim, grayish streaks in the eastern sky. In the dinghy, Lieutenant Hoffman's muscles were tense with excitement. He kept reminding himself he must not appear to be frightened. But this was frightening work, landing at night on an unknown island with orders to capture its inhabitants. There might be five persons living on Spanish Island, or there might be five hundred. They might be friendly or hostile. They might be armed. With an effort, he forced himself to stop these useless speculations. The first job, he told himself, was to get ashore safely.

Hoffman had hoped to find a stretch of beach, but the darkness made this impossible. He tried to find a place where the white-backed surf was less violent, but he had no luck. With increasing strength, the swells carried them in, and there was no chance to reconnoiter. When they were a hundred yards from the shore, the big froth-edged combers swept them forward remorselessly and the paddles could only be used to steer. Not until they were twenty yards from the shore did Hoffman realize the extent of the danger. Ahead of them, massive boulders rose ten to twenty feet; one moment they would be half covered with black water and huge fountains of booming spray would erupt above them; in the next, cascades of water would be draining from them and boiling seaward, producing a sort of countercurrent which, in turn, would be overcome by the next breaker.

For the last few terrifying yards, the four tiny craft were completely out of control. The line that joined them parted. The dinghy was hung up on a jagged rock and the following breaker hurled its occupants into the sea and smashed them against the shore. Both of Schiller's legs were broken, but with the help of Hoffman and Kramer he dragged himself to safety. In a shallow eddy, all three collapsed, completely spent. Koenig and Oberteuffer landed nearly a hundred yards away, terrified and exhausted, but without injury. The sixth man, Able Seaman Heinz, simply disappeared.

It took valuable minutes for Hoffman to regroup his forces. The blackness and the thunder of the surf made it difficult for the survivors to find one another. Then they spent time searching for Heinz and the dinghy, and making Schiller comfortable with an ampule of morphine. Presently, Hoffman issued his orders. The two petty officers—the signalman and the crippled boatswain's mate—would stay where they were. The two seamen—Kramer and Oberteuffer—would follow the shore to the left, going clockwise, and he would go to the right. When they met, the seamen would report on the number and location of boats and buildings, berthing facilities that might accommodate a U-boat, cables leaving the island, wireless antennae, and anything else of particular interest. If they encountered any natives, they were to capture them and bring them along. No shooting, if it could be avoided. The password would be Shark Boat.

"Understood?" Hoffman asked sharply. The two deckhands mumbled affirmatives. They were cold and wet, afraid of the black, alien island, and shocked by the loss of a messmate.

"Shove off, boys," Hoffman said. "Go as fast as you can. It will soon be light."

As they moved cautiously away, he turned to Koenig.

"Make this signal to the boat: 'Commencing recco.' " It would do no good, he thought, to report his losses. Ludtke couldn't help him now. As Koenig began to call up the U-boat, the engineer officer started to pick his way over the rocks to higher ground.

For the first time in over two months, Hoffman was completely alone. Although he had not shown it, he had been badly shaken by Heinz's death and Schiller's accident. The lieutenant was excited, a little afraid, and worried, too, about the two sailors groping their way in the opposite direction. They were very young—neither Kramer nor Oberteuffer was yet twenty—and badly frightened.

At first it was hard going for Hoffman. On his left was a wall of rock and to his right the booming surf. There were brief stretches of beach, where he could dogtrot, and clusters of boulders that he had to climb over. Twice he was drenched with icy spray and that served to accelerate his speed. The faster he went, he kept telling himself, the less chance there was of Kramer and Oberteuffer getting into trouble.

It was characteristic of Hoffman that he think of his men. He was quite unlike the captain, who regarded his crew as a set of reasonably competent automatons, or Reigel, who held everyone, except the chiefs and leading petty officers, in complete contempt. Hoffman knew the sailors of the Shark Boat—not just his own engineering gang, but all of them. He not only knew the sailors—he worked for them. He helped prepare the crew for rating advancement tests and supported it in arguments with the cook. He chose recordings for its music programs, judged its chess tournaments, smelled its socks, and listened to its marital problems. He drilled his people hard, and he was not afraid to punish them, but mostly he worked at expounding one thesis: the U-Waffe was the hope of the nation; the Second Flotilla was the elite of the U-Waffe; the Shark Boat was the ace of the Second Flotilla. Hoffman did not think of medals, like Ludtke, or dream of his own boat, like Reigel. Inwardly, he was somewhat cynical of victory and of his chances for survival. Promotion never occurred to him. All his loyalties—since he had no family—were centered in the crew of U-324. And because he worked at this every day, the crew respected and admired him. The crew trusted Ludtke. It detested Reigel. It would have followed Hoffman anywhere.

Wading, climbing, scrambling, and running, Hoffman made his way along the rocky shore. After a bit, the sky grew lighter, his visibility improved, and progress was easier. He was able to cut across the southern promontory of the island, the tail of the seahorse the captain had drawn, and he turned northward. Some forty-five minutes after leaving his men, the engineer officer clambered over one last limestone outcrop, and, in the pale gray light, discovered what he had come for—the harbor of Spanish Island. The morning fog still opaqued it, but he could see it was more cove than harbor, with a narrow mouth—barely a hundred yards wide—and well protected from the sea. Though it was small, there was searoom to spare for a U-boat. Best of all, a stone quay, crudely but solidly built, extended forty meters or so into the cove. There were a handful of black fishing boats beached near the quay, turned over so that they resembled small, sleeping beetles. No other craft were in sight.

The rocky heights of the island swept down to the cove on three sides. Spanish Island's greatest elevation was at its north-center. There seemed to be a plateau there, as though the island were a truncated cone. On the eastern edge of the plateau, about a mile from the jetty, was an ancient stone tower. From the tower, twisting down to the quay, was a rude path, and, flanking it, Hoffman counted a dozen cottages of mud or stone, each with an outbuilding or two. At least half the cottages looked abandoned, their thatched roofs fallen in. But from the chimneys of others, wisps of blue-gray smoke were curling. The island was coming awake and Hoffman fretted at the slowness of his sailors.

Close to where he stood, next to the quay, there was a small stone building. The door was open and he looked in, using his torch. It contained a broken dory on crude wooden sawhorses, narrow-bladed oars, cordage, lobster traps, spherical crayfish pots, and bronze-red seine nets hanging from the beams. Obviously, it was the communal storehouse for the island's fishing gear. He walked out of the musty sea-smell of the building and saw Kramer and Oberteuffer picking their way along the shore of the northern arm of the cove.

The engineer officer walked out on the quay and tested the water's depth with a fishnet weight at the end of a length of line. He was gratified to find it over three fathoms. Plenty of water to moor the Shark Boat, and the tide still flooding. Coming back, he studied the eastern slope and the cottages scattered along the path. They were low-set buildings, hugging the lee of the island to escape the wind. Their roofs were thatched with straw or reeds. Their windows, glinting in the early light, were high and narrow, so that they resembled eyes under the shaggy brows of the thatch. One of the closest had a radio antenna. Spanish Island was a harsh, inhospitable-looking place, Hoffman decided. There were no trees and only patches of coarse, closely cropped grass. Up near the cottages, there appeared to be several little gardens, carefully tended and protected by stone walls.

Kramer and Oberteuffer trotted up, flushed with excitement and exertion. They had nothing to report.

"Very well, then," Hoffman said. "We've got to work fast. You, Kramer, go back to Koenig as quickly as you can. Give him this signal for the Shark Boat: 'Enter harbor.' Got it?"

Kramer repeated the message and left at a run. Hoffman turned to Oberteuffer and said, "Let's go." Then he walked up the hill toward the cottage with the radio antenna.

It was nearly sunrise and behind them the eastern sky was aflame. There was no sound except for the crunch of their boots on the shale and pebbles. When they came to the first ruined cottage, a sheep dog appeared and barked at them. They went quickly by and came to the building with the radio antenna. Hoffman knocked sharply on the door and loosened his pistol in its holster. They heard voices inside, one of them loud and querulous, and Oberteuffer licked his lips nervously.

Abruptly, the upper half of the door creaked and swung open. A middle-aged man stood before them, his trousers pulled over long woolen underwear, rubbing sleep from his eyes. When he saw his visitors he lowered his fist and stared at them, his annoyance gone. He was not alarmed, only surprised and curious.

"Good morning," he said in Gaelic, and then in English. "Welcome to Spanish Island."

"Good morning," Hoffman said in heavily accented English. It was the first time since the university he had spoken English and it seemed awkward. "May we come in, please?"

"Come in, pray, and welcome to this house." The islandman opened the lower half of the door and stood aside as they crossed the threshold, two dirty, bearded strangers in heavy sweaters and trousers stuffed into stained sea boots. They had lost their caps in the surf and wore nothing to identify themselves as German sailors.

"Come in, come in," the islandman said again. "God stay with you. You're after being torpedoed then?"

Hoffman gave a short humorless laugh.

"No," he said, the English coming slowly. "No, we've not been torpedoed. We do the torpedoing. I am an officer in the German Navy. My U-boat is about to enter your harbor."

"Mary, Mother of God," a woman's voice said. In the dim light of the interior, Hoffman made her out, a matter-of-fact middle-aged woman in a rusty black dress. Behind her, against the far wall, he noted a bulky radio-telephone set, its speaker, and a microphone.

"Would you gentlemen be wanting some tea?" the woman asked.

"Thank you, ma'am," Hoffman said. "We would like tea." He watched the woman move to the hearth and lower the kettle two notches on a crane over the flickering turf flames. Then she went to a dresser and began to transfer cups and plates to a heavy rectangular table.

"It will be ready in just a moment, gentlemen. Just a moment," she said, smiling at them.

The head of the house said excitedly, "From a U-boat now! Mother of God! Sit down, gentlemen. Draw up, draw up, I pray you. The tea will be ready directly."

He lit a kerosene lamp, fumblingly, and put it on the table. Hoffman found a chair and Oberteuffer a stool. The lieutenant smiled.

"This is a nice cottage you have, sir." His eyes swung around the kitchen. "I see you have a radio."

"Yes, yes, the wireless," the islandman said. "We can get the news and weather forecasts from Radio Eireann, and the music from the B.B.C.——" He stopped with the sudden realization that he had said something tactless. "Just the music, of course. Operas. Light operas."

"What about the microphone? You can talk to the mainland?"

"Indeed we can. We can talk directly to Ballykerry Village with the radio-telephone. We use it to order things and in emergencies."

"Does anyone else on the island have a radio-telephone?" Hoffman asked.

"Och, not a bit of it. This is the only R/T set on Spanish. The only radio. You see, they don't belong to me. The post office put them here, because I'm the postmaster."

"Is there any other way to send a message to the mainland? A telegraph cable, for instance?"

"No other way, I fear, saving the curraghs—the fishing boats. But you're more than welcome to use the R/T."

"No." Hoffman smiled. "No, thanks."

There was a silence, broken only by the bubbling of the kettle on the hob. The woman unhooked it and filled the teacups.

"There now," she said. "There's your tea, gentlemen. Good, strong red tea. Dermod, you'd best be washing and putting some clothes on. I'll fetch some bread and marmalade for the gentlemen while you do."

The islandman was suddenly embarrassed and disappeared into another room. Peter Hoffman grinned. The scalding tea tasted good to him. He ate two slices of freshly baked soda bread, liberally spread with marmalade.

"May I ask your name, ma'am?"

"It's Beg, sir. Brede Beg. My husband's name is Dermod."

"Your breakfast is very good, Frau Beg."

She smiled and insisted they have more. With apologies, she also produced some salted bream. The Germans accepted large portions and were eating greedily when Dermod Beg rejoined them.

"How many persons live on Spanish Island?" Hoffman asked him casually. About now, he thought, the Shark Boat would be receiving his signal.

Dermod Beg wrinkled his forehead.

"Och, it would be twenty-five maybe——"

"Less than that, now," his wife said determinedly. "There'd be only twenty, twenty-one. There used to be many more," she said apologetically to Hoffman. "But the young people keep leaving for the mainland —for Tralee and even Limerick."

"Well, now, let's tally them," Dermod Beg broke in. "There'd be the O Ŕuiarcs—Sean and Kathy O Ŕuiarc. Then there'd be the Mors. There's four of them and the three little ones. That's seven. There'd be Eamon Og and his wife Peigeen and their babbies. Five more. There'd be Lady Maudie Wynne and Kelly and ourselves. How many is that, now?" he asked, turning to his wife.

Brede Beg's lips moved silently. "Eighteen," she said, "but you forgot Nora. Nineteen with Nora."

"Nora is Lady Maudie's granddaughter," her husband explained to the Germans. He was silent for a moment, his face screwed up in thought. "Only nineteen." Dermod shook his head. "I declare to God, I thought there were more."

"Any firearms on the island?" Hoffman asked. "Rifles, pistols?"

The couple looked at one another blankly. The islandman shook his head again.

"I've been living here for nigh sixty years, sir, and I've never seen a firearm."

"Very well, Herr Beg," Hoffman said, swallowing the last of his breakfast. "Now, I want you to go and bring all the inhabitants of the island to this cottage. All of them. Yes, right now. Our U-boat will be entering port shortly and I want to tell them about it. I don't want anyone to become frightened." He turned to Oberteuffer and spoke briefly to him in German.

"Go with him. I want all the natives down here. Don't let anyone get near the fishing boats."

Dermod Beg looked bewildered.

"All of them? The children, too?"

"The babies, no. Children who can walk, yes."

Brede said slowly, "Lady Maudie is too ill to come. She's crippled with the rheumatism."

"All the rest, then." Hoffman stood up abruptly and the others rose with him.

"I think they'll come along without any fuss, Oberteuffer," he said in German. "They'll be curious rather than frightened. Never mind the babies and one invalid woman. If anyone tries to get away, shoot him. Keep them together and don't waste any time. Shove off, now."

The seaman saluted and escorted Beg out of the cottage. Almost immediately he was back.

"The Shark Boat's coming around the point, sir."

Hoffman swore. "Hurry up with those people, then. We need them to moor the boat." From the doorway, he could see U-324, her conning tower canted drunkenly to starboard, coming through the early morning haze into the harbor. The bullring and serrated net-cutter at her bow gave the U-boat a slightly reptilian appearance.

He looked around him at the buildings of the tiny settlement. A hundred yards up the hill, a woman was carrying water toward her lime-washed cottage. She stopped and waited curiously for Beg and Oberteuffer to reach her. A dog barked at them, and Hoffman saw a donkey cropping grass behind the woman's cottage. Farther up the hill he saw a boy leading an emaciated cow toward a shed. Milking time, he said to himself.

He remembered the radio-telephone, and asked the Beg woman to come outside. Mildly perplexed, she obeyed, and for ten minutes they waited while her husband and Oberteuffer rounded up the islanders, while the Shark Boat lay just inside the cove, her engines idling and a leadsman in her chains.

The people of Spanish Island straggled down to the Beg cottage, exchanging good mornings with Brede and alternating curious stares between the submarine and the German officer. Even before they had assembled, Hoffman saw that one of the group did not belong to it. She was a girl in her mid-twenties with bright blue eyes and coal-black hair that brushed her shoulders. Unlike the other women, she had no shawl. She wore a hand-knit cardigan and a tweed skirt instead of a dark dress, and brogues instead of cracked black shoes. Unlike the others, she did not smile at him.

"Who's the young lady?" Hoffman asked.

"Och, isn't she the darling, now?" Brede Beg asked in reply. "That's young Nora Berkeley, who visits us now and again from Dublin. She's Lady Maudie's grandchild."

Hoffman did not stare at Nora Berkeley, but, as the group formed about him, he was highly conscious of her presence. She chatted with everyone, including the children, and once or twice he heard her laugh. It was a very pleasant laugh. The lieutenant stood as tall as he could. He was watching a glowing red rim of sun work its way over the pearly mist when Oberteuffer saluted and reported:

"All present, sir, except one old lady and two babies."

Hoffman looked around the semicircle. His first impression was that except for Nora Berkeley, the people of Spanish looked very much alike, and that they were a shabby lot, their clothes poor and patched, with a salt-stained patina of age. The women wore black, and the men rough, homespun trousers with cordlike seams, dark jerseys, thick-soled boots, and tweed caps with the bills unbuttoned.

Almost immediately, Hoffman saw that two of the islanders were physically different from the rest. Where the other adults were lean and dark, or lean and gray, according to their age, these two—a man and a woman—were red-haired and of impressive dimensions. The man was powerfully built, with huge arms, and was freckled and grinning. The woman was big and full-blown, with a wild mane of fiery hair and a vague, bemused expression on her face. They were both in their late twenties, Hoffman judged, and obviously brother and sister.

Including the two redheads, there were thirteen adults facing him. Four children were also part of the semicircle, one a boy of about eight, the others still clutching at their mothers' skirts. From time to time, the boy, or one of the adults, would turn and look at the U-boat in the cove. All of them were curious but completely unafraid. All but the girl in the cardigan were smilingly expectant.

"Ladies and gentlemen," Hoffman said loudly in English, "that is a U-boat of the German Navy. I am its engineer officer. It is necessary that we put into a neutral Irish port for a day or two. Our boat has been damaged and we need time to make repairs."

There was a warm, friendly buzz from the islanders. His thumbs hooked in his gun belt, Hoffman waited until it had died. "While the boat is here," he went on, "you will not be permitted to use your fishing boats or to communicate in any way with the mainland. That is an order—to be obeyed, on pain of death."

The smiles faded from the faces around him. "If you obey that order, you have nothing to fear," Hoffman continued. "Now, my first request is that you—the men at least—go down to the quay and help the U-boat to moor."

"Why should we help to moor your ship?" cried the girl in the cardigan sweater. She came into the center of the semicircle. "We didn't ask for Nazis on Spanish Island—ordering us about on pain of death!"

"Now, then, Nora," said the oldest of the islandmen, "these men are in trouble. We can't send them away."

"We don't intend to order you about, miss," Hoffman said earnestly. "But we must have a place to repair the U-boat and we must do it secretly."

Nora Berkeley was not a beauty in the classic Irish sense. She was good-looking because of her black hair and blue eyes, her sparkling smile, and the proud lovely way she carried herself. A critic would have said her nose was too snubbed, her mouth too wide, and her chin too determined. As she faced Hoffman, her eyes flashed, her mouth was clamped in a stubborn horizontal line, and her chin was outthrust. Hoffman thought her the prettiest creature he had ever seen.

30

"You see, miss," the lieutenant said, his voice loud enough so all the islanders could hear, "the English are hunting us now. They're all around us, dozens of destroyers and corvettes. If they catch us while we're helpless——" He snapped his fingers dramatically.

"The war is none of our doing," Nora said sharply, but it was obvious to Hoffman that most of the islanders were for the underdog and against the Royal Navy.

"There are wounded men in our U-boat," he continued. "We have medicine, but those men need fresh air and nursing—care for which we'll gladly pay." The engineer lieutenant looked around the semicircle and saw nothing but friendly smiles and nods. Whether motivated by curiosity, sympathy, Anglophobia, or a sense of fair play, the islanders wanted to help.

Nora Berkeley sensed the feeling of her friends. She turned and spoke to the old man.

"Very well, Sean, let's not be beastly to the Germans. But remember, Sean," she went on, "a warship can spend only three days in a neutral port. That's all they allowed the *Graf Spee*. That's international law."

"I think it's right to help them," Sean O Ŕuiarc said. He turned to the islanders and a chorus of approbation went up.

Lieutenant Hoffman didn't like the reference to international law, but he smiled his thanks. "Take them down to the quay," he said in German to Oberteuffer. "I'll stay here by the R/T set."

In a matter of minutes, Oberteuffer had his line-handlers ready, and U-324 came alongside the stone quay, her diesels snorting and snuffling. The lines were thrown and made fast, the engines were stopped, and sailors spilled out of the conning tower. Hoffman could hear the faint babble of excited voices from the Irish on the quay. A gangplank was rigged, and the captain came ashore, seated in a chair formed by the interlocked wrists and hands of two of the biggest stokers. Hoffman could not see his face, but he could identify him by his white cap. By long tradition, only the commanding officer of a U-boat wore a white cap cover. The engineer lieutenant went halfway down the path to meet him.

Ludtke was in a jovial mood. He congratulated Hoffman and allowed himself to be carried into the Beg kitchen. Seated before the fireplace, his wounded leg propped before him, he listened to Hoffman's report and asked several questions. Brede brought him tea and he smoked a cigar. Occasionally, he asked a question of Dermod Beg in English. Dermod, he quickly found, was voluble and anxious to please. The post-

_ities, with a broad, flattish face. He was nearly bald,
iron-gray hair that ran over his ears and around his
ows were permanently arched, so that even in repose,
was quizzical and slightly mischievous. If Dermod was
_lined to garrulity, and looked slightly intemperate, his
_sinesslike and matter-of-fact. There was a brisk, no-nonsense
_about her that Hoffman liked. When the captain thanked her
_ea, Brede bobbed him a curtsy and went on with her cleaning.
_it an hour after U-324 had made fast to the jetty, Ludtke sum-
_d Lieutenant Reigel and the leading petty officers to meet with
_ and Hoffman. Soon they were all present—Albrecht, the chief ma-
_inist's mate, Dietrich, the petty officer telegraphist, Kreisler, the
_lectrician's mate, Muller, the leading torpedoman, and Brandt, the sick
berth attendant. All their faces were split with toothy grins. Ten weeks
of ill-weathered patrol in the North Atlantic, climaxed by two interminable days of complete vulnerability, had built up a high degree of
tension—even in the phlegmatic Albrecht. Now, the grins seemed to
say, we are safe. We can see the sun and breathe the sweet, clean air.
We can smoke when we want. We can be alone when we want. The captain has brought us in safely. The captain will take care of us.

Ludtke wiped the grins away with a few harsh sentences: "This is no
liberty port, boys. We're here to work—to repair the Shark Boat. I'll
shoot the man who chases the women, or goes swimming or fishing, or
puts his head down when he should be working. Understand? Now,
then. We'll set three regular watches, Number One. The first in this
room, to make sure that no native uses the R/T set. The second a lookout watch in that stone tower at the top of the ridge. They call it Norseman's Tower. The third the regular port bridge watch.

"Now, I want two men billeted in each of the cottages that are occupied. Let's see. There's the Wynne cottage, the Ogs', the two Mor
cabins, the O Ŕuiarcs', and this one. That's six. I'll want an officer or
P.O. in all but this one. I'll stay here. This will be my Command Post.

"Move all the wounded into the building by the jetty, quack. The
Begs say the women will help with bedding and blankets. They'll make
bandages, too."

The captain drew deeply on his cigar, thinking hard as he gave his
orders.

"This evening, Number One, at high water, I want to move the boat
forward along the quay, right up on the beach. I want to sally ship to
port, so as to get as much of that hole as possible above the waterline.
That means shift all possible weight aft and to port.

"After that, we'll open up the forward torpedo room. Get the bodies

out and ready for burial. Pump out the compartment and make it watertight."

"Aye, aye, sir," said Reigel, furiously making notes.

Ludtke blew a long plume of cigar smoke and turned to Lieutenant
Hoffman.

"Chief, give me a full damage report as soon as you can. There are
two priorities: patching up the hole in the pressure hull and getting the
electric motors running. Let me know what equipment we'll need to
make Lorient and how much time you'll need to make the boat ready
for sea.

"I'll want a report on the radio, too, Dietrich," he said to the P.O.
telegraphist. "We've got to put that right.

"Muller, take all the fishing boats—curraghs, they call 'em—and put
them where the bridge watch can keep an eye on them. Another thing.
It isn't likely, but we could be spotted from the air. Break out some
canvas and prepare to camouflage the boat as best you can, after we
move her."

"Aye, aye, sir," said Leading Torpedoman Muller. With Schiller's
injury, he was the senior able-bodied petty officer of the deck force.

The captain stared at the turf fire, wondering if anything important
had been omitted.

"Oh, yes. Number One, break out what we can spare from the pro-
vision locker and spread it around among the natives. You know—
sausage, navy beans, bacon, stuff like that. That will help take care of
our people billeted on the beach."

Ludtke threw his cigar butt into the fire.

"We're safe here for a day or so. Time to get the boat in shape to
return to base. But we'll have to work hard—harder than we work at
sea." Ludtke looked at the expressionless faces about him. "Work your
people until they drop and then keep them going. There's to be no
liberty, no skylarking, no sniffing around the women. Remember, the
natives will help us—so treat them as allies. They have no use for the
limeys.

"Very well. You all know what you have to do. I'll be right here"—
he smiled bleakly—"awaiting your reports."

The petty officers began to shuffle out of the cottage. Barndt gathered
his courage and asked, "Captain, sir, what about a surgeon? Can we
get a surgeon, sir?"

"We'll get one shortly, quack."

"I've a new stretcher case, Captain. Boatswain's Mate Schiller. Both
his legs are broken and I'm not sure I've set them properly. We need
help, Captain."

"That's enough, Barndt," Ludtke said. "You'll get your help." He sent Dermod Beg out to bring the men of Spanish Island together and told his two lieutenants to remain with him.

"We three are the only ones who know English. We'll have to handle all the communications between our people and the Irish. So I want you to hear what I have to say to the peasants."

Soon the males of Spanish Island were gathered around him—Dermod and four others—with smiles on their lips and questions in their eyes. One of them had a full thatch of white hair. He was a good deal older than Dermod Beg, but very erect. Ludtke estimated he was in his seventies. The other three were younger than Dermod, two of them thin and dark, the other a huge, redheaded, barrel-chested man with a wide grin. Dermod introduced them—the older one was Sean O Ŕuiarc, the two dark ones Eamon Og and Padraig Mor, and the redheaded giant was Tomas Mor. Ludtke acknowledged the introductions, lit another cigar, and spoke earnestly in English.

"Men of Spanish Island. On behalf of the German Reich, I thank you for your generous hospitality. We will be here a day or two before we put to sea again. We intend to respect the neutrality of the proud Republic of Ireland. In return, we ask you not to signal the mainland or in any other way call attention to our presence. We ask you to suspend your fishing while we are here. We will billet our men in your homes. Do not be afraid. We are your friends. We will share our food with you, and if you help with our repairs, you will be well paid in Reichsmarks—worth their weight in gold."

There was a silence in the low-ceilinged room. The two lieutenants warily studied the islanders, and four of the islanders looked at one—the white-haired old man. He had a craggy, windburned face, the color of mahogany and cross-hatched with wrinkles. The color of his skin accentuated the whiteness of his hair, his heavy brows, and the tufts of white hair on his cheekbones.

"Sean," Dermod said to him in a low voice. "It's for you to reply."

"I am Sean O Ŕuiarc," the old man said, addressing himself directly to Ludtke. "I am the oldest man on Spanish and the man who speaks for all of us."

He paused and looked around him. The four other islanders nodded assent.

"You are in trouble, Captain, and we will do our best to help you. We do not think too kindly of the English, ourselves, but we must remain neutral. We cannot permit you to stay longer nor six tides—the three days allowed by international law. In that time, however, you have our sacred pledge that no one on Spanish will report the submarine."

"Thank you, Herr O Ŕuiarc," Ludtke said gravely.

"What about the fishing?" one of the younger islanders asked. He was a tall, dark, angular man, with a long, bony nose. "The bream are running heavy these days, Sean. Surely out on the ocean we won't be seeing anyone to talk to. . . ."

"I'm sorry," Ludtke said firmly. "The curraghs are not to be used. We need your help here on the island, and we can't take chances. Those are my orders and they will be enforced."

"After all, Eamon, it will only be a day or so," Sean O Ŕuiarc said to the tall, dark man.

"That's right," said the captain.

"What is it you'd like us to help you with?" asked the burly red-headed islandman. Ludtke briefly explained the tasks ahead of them—moving the wounded, opening up the forward torpedo room, burying the dead, camouflaging the boat, and repairing the hull.

"Arra, it sounds like a month's work," old Sean said finally. "Best we get started." He stood up and with dignity shook hands with each of the German officers. The other islanders awkwardly followed suit, and they filed out. The three German officers looked at one another with undisguised pleasure.

"They mean to help us," Reigel chortled as though he hardly believed it. "This is great luck."

"Yes," said Ludtke with his thin smile, and then, paraphrasing the old islander, "Best you get started, gentlemen."

The lieutenants saluted and, still grinning, they went out into the bright sunshine, leaving the captain and his aching leg alone by the fire.

For the first time, Ludtke had the opportunity to examine his Command Post in detail. There were three rooms in the cottage, with the central one—the kitchen—twice as large as either of the others. It was, Ludtke judged, some twenty feet long by fifteen feet wide. The walls were whitewashed, and the floor was of smooth, hard-packed clay, broken by a couple of small rope rugs. The door and a small window were on the south side of the room, and there were two other windows on the north side, with bits of stiff sailcloth for curtains.

The kitchen furniture was extremely simple. There was a crudely made, generous-sized table with a kerosene lamp between the northern windows, and a big, open dresser against the east wall, its shelves filled with china. There was a bench under the southern window, the rocking chair that Ludtke had preempted, a straight chair, and a couple of three-legged stools.

Next to his chair, on the west side of the room, was a huge open hearth, with a simple wrought-iron crane and adjustable pot-hangers.

Some utensils were ranged beside it—trivet, griddle, and three-legged oven pot. Above them, from pegs, hung a row of implements—a ladle and a knife, a huge fork, and a potato masher. Across the room, in the northeast corner, a whitewashed ladder led to a loft; on one side of it stood a wooden churn, on the other, the chest bearing the radio-telephone set.

There was little to alleviate the functionalism of the kitchen. On the mantel stood a framed oleograph of Christ displaying a bleeding heart. Flanking it were a heavily retouched photograph of Eamon de Valera as a young man and a postcard view of the shrine at Lourdes. Further along were some seashells and another photograph—of a popeyed young man in a high-collared uniform. Later, Ludtke learned the young man was Dermod's only son, a policeman in Philadelphia.

Across the room from the captain's chair, a wall niche contained a small crucifix; below it, there was a tiny brass lamp with a candle that gleamed steadily through its red windows. This was the light of perpetual adoration. A few feet from the little shrine a row of pegs held oddments of clothing and a canvas bag with the letters G.P.O. stenciled on it.

The smaller rooms of the cottage, Ludtke discovered, were even more utilitarian. The bedroom to the west butted snugly against the side of the hill. The Begs called this their "best room." It contained a huge lumpy bed, a chest, a stool, and a basin that rested on a cask. Dermod and Brede had given this to the captain and moved to the loft.

Ludtke grunted and savored his cigar. Not much of a cabin, he thought, but it was clean and, despite its austerity, had a certain cheeriness. It was comfortable before the turf fire. As he waited for the watches to be set and the repairs begun, Ludtke felt the weariness and long-stored tension begin to drain out of him.

Sean O Ŕuiarc was not a man to call a meeting casually. The last time he had summoned the people of Spanish together had been in 1935, when the government considered moving all the island's population to the mainland, and its representatives visited Spanish. It would be safer, the government had said, if the island were abandoned. Sean had argued that the real purpose of the scheme was to bring Gaelic speakers into a land that was supposed to speak Gaelic but resisted it. The islanders had met, refused, with rare unanimity, to budge, and sent the bureaucrats back to Dublin.

Now, nine years later, Sean called all the island to another conference. He held it in Lady Maud's kitchen because it was the biggest on the island, and so that Lady Maud, who was virtually bedridden and very inquisitive, could hear all that went on. When everyone was there, Sean stood with his back to the mantel and its framed photograph of Lady Maud's late husband, Sir Laurence Wynne, D.S.O., shown wearing a Kitchener mustache and the ornate turn-of-the-century dress uniform of the Royal Dublin Fusileers. He was homely, stern of countenance, and in his befrogged, aguletted tunic, somehow absurd-looking.

Briefly, Sean told the people in the crowded kitchen of the submarine's problems, his pledge not to report its presence, and how the islanders could help.

They were obviously glad to help. Dark, sharp-featured Eamon Og was still gloomy about the fishing, but the Mor brothers were philosophical.

"It's only a day or two, Eamon," said the burly, redheaded Tomas.

"Aye, Eamon, that's the truth of it," said Padraig. Padraig was dark-haired and much smaller than his younger brother, but he had an undeniable facial resemblance. He was the only man on the island to wear the Pioneer badge, a heart-shaped bit of enamel that proclaimed his total temperance. In comparison with Tomas, he said very little. He said even less than Eamon. When Padraig did speak, he was usually right, and he enjoyed a reputation for sagacity exceeded only by old Sean himself.

"They have asked me not to tell a soul of their being on Spanish," O Ŕuiarc said. "I have given my word that we'd not breathe word or wind of it."

"You did the right thing exactly, Sean," Dermod Beg said with conviction. "They need the chance to repair their ship and get on with their war with the Tommies."

"Aye, let's help them," boomed Tomas Mor, and the others agreed, Eamon with no great resentment about the lost bream, and Padraig with a characteristic little duck of his head.

The men having spoken, Sean looked around the kitchen and waited to hear from the women. In a small, primitive society like that of Spanish, women were not apt to contradict their menfolk, but there were at least two old and independent enough to dissent. These were Maura Mor, known as the Widow, and Lady Maud Wynne, propped up in bed in the adjoining room.

The Widow was the mother of Padraig, Tomas, and Shelagh. She sat near the chimney place, gloomily regarding the speakers. Although her husband had been dead for many years, Maura Mor wore her years heavily, as though she were in perpetual mourning. She had a long skeletal face and rarely smiled. Dermod often said he was afraid of her, and, although he spoke in jest, there was some truth in it. Maura Mor preferred to keep her own company, and as a rule the islanders left her alone. Now, when Sean looked at her, the Widow nodded lugubrious assent.

Unlike Maura Mor, Lady Maud Wynne was the soul of sociability. Despite her arthritis, she was gay and voluble. Although he could not see her, Sean knew she would be perched up in her big four-poster, a wizened, wrinkled little person, her china-blue eyes snapping with excitement as she listened, her maidservant, Kelly, and her granddaughter, Nora Berkeley, beside her.

Lady Maud had come to Spanish with her husband and Kelly in 1920. An officer in the I.R.A., the baronet had returned to Cork the next year and was killed by the Black-and-Tans, but his widow had remained on the island. For the last decade she had not left her cottage. The islanders were very fond of her, and Lady Maud was enchanted with them. Informed on a variety of subjects, she had an encyclopedic knowledge of Spanish Island. She knew its history and folklore better than Sean himself. Chiefly through the O Ŕuiarcs and Kelly, she knew almost everything about its daily life, whether it be the size of a litter or lobster catch, the appearance of a baby's tooth, or the price of a new pair of boots. This interest in her neighbors and their workaday lives, according to the islanders themselves, was the force that kept Lady Maud alive. They did not resent the old lady's gregariousness, curiosity, and love of gossip. Instead, they were proud of everything about her.

"What say you, Lady Maudie?" asked Sean, raising his voice.

"I say you are right, Sean," piped the little voice from the bedroom. "I say we should help them."

Sean looked at the other women of Spanish. His own wife smiled agreement. Kathy O Ŕuiarc was a gnarled little creature, who spoke only Irish and was addicted to snuff. She was the same age as Sean, but where he appeared to be in his early seventies, Kathy looked ten years older.

Sean turned to Brede Beg. In her fifties, with iron-gray hair and a lined, undistinguished face, she was serious, hard-working, and universally respected.

"I do think we should help them," Brede said slowly, and Sean smiled at her, considering his decision approved.

"And what do the young ladies say?" he asked courteously. "Peg, Maeve, Shelagh? Do you agree?"

The young ladies of Spanish, at this particular gathering, were ranged on the other side of the kitchen, beside the big dresser with its open shelves of crockery. Peigeen Og was nearly thirty, dark and homely.

She was Sean's granddaughter, but she had none of the old man's vigorous good looks. She was so devoted to her husband and children that she seemed almost uninterested in the rest of the community. Maeve Mor was Peigeen's contemporary and, like Peigeen, dark and nondescript looking. The daughter of Dermod and Brede, she was aggressive and articulate—characteristics sharpened by domestic service in Tralee a dozen years before.

The third of the young women was five years younger than Peigeen and Maeve, much bigger, and with nubile good looks that made them insignificant by comparison. Shelagh Mor was a spinster, tall, well-padded, and crowned by a mane of gorgeous auburn hair. Her features were regular, but there was little animation in her face. Her eyes were expressionless and her mouth usually slack, almost as though she were drugged. Now, as Peigeen and Maeve gave their approval, she beamed vaguely, almost uncomprehendingly.

"That settles it then," said O Ruiarc. He was about to conclude the meeting when Nora Berkeley spoke from the bedroom door.

"Excuse me, Sean. What will happen when the steamer comes next Monday?"

"Och, Nora, they'll be far gone by Monday," O Ruiarc said. "International law says a man-of-war cannot stay longer nor six tides in a neutral port. You said so yourself."

"And what if they don't leave then?" Nora asked. "That's only Sunday."

"They're honorable men, child. They know they've to leave by Sunday."

"Honorable men?" Nora asked, her voice hardening. "How can they be honorable, and torpedo defenseless merchant ships?"

"That's the only way submarines can fight," Sean said.

"Indeed, Nora, enough of that," Lady Maud said, surprised and irked that her granddaughter would interrupt Sean's meeting.

But the girl stood her ground. "Ah, gran, I don't mean to be rude," she said. "But we're making a mistake." She turned back to Sean. "These Germans know nothing of honor. They're hard, crafty men who'll take advantage of your kindness."

As the youngest present, Nora's viewpoint was quite different from that of the men and women of Spanish. As a Dubliner, she was the best informed about the war. She regularly listened to the news, read the *Irish Times,* and had formed some opinions of her own as well. In the last few years, for instance, she had known several young Irishmen who had joined His Majesty's Forces; she maintained a sporadic correspondence with some. At dances and parties, she had occasionally met

Allied naval officers. They slipped down from Belfast in civilian clothes to sample the steaks and prawns and bright lights of the capital. Nora found them good company, as distinguished from the sour types of the German Embassy.

Sean O Ŕuiarc knew little of this. He did not believe what Nora had said, but he was too gracious to argue with her. On the other hand, Lady Maud was not so polite. "Indeed, Nora, one would think you wanted to help the English!"

On the kitchen mantel, Nora could see Sir Laurence Wynne's photograph in its frame of peeling gilt, and her temper rose.

"Now why would I help the people who murdered my grandfather?" she shot back.

"Come back here, Nora, and sit down!" snapped Lady Maud. "Sean, I think the meeting is adjourned."

This was all the islanders needed. They got to their feet, talking with animation, and trooped out of the kitchen. If they were a bit embarrassed to witness a family argument, this feeling was lost in the general excitement. Everyone was eager to start helping the Germans.

Kelly slipped unobtrusively out and Nora went obediently into the bedroom, sat down, and stared at the floor. In a moment, her irritation had cooled.

"Ah, gran, I'm ashamed to be so hotheaded."

"Hotheaded you are indeed, Noreen." The old lady's use of the diminutive meant her granddaughter was forgiven.

"I'm no Anglophile," Nora said. "You know that. It's just that I don't like these Germans telling us we can't leave the island, even to fish, and putting their sailors in our houses."

"But we want to help them, Nora," Lady Maud said equably. "We can clean up the submarine and take care of the wounded."

"Yes, I suppose so," Nora said. Since her parents died when she was twelve, Nora had visited Spanish Island once or twice a year. She had grown up to love Spanish and its simple, pious primitives. She brought them books, fruit, tools, and toys. She taught the children, helped with the sheep-shearing, and fished with the men. Now, she felt, these decent, unworldly people needed her protection. She had tried to warn them, but they had paid no attention, although, she admitted to herself, there had been nothing specific about her warning, nothing but a vague premonition of trouble.

"Well, then," said her grandmother after a moment. "Fetch Kelly and carry me into the kitchen. I'll watch the submarine with my telescope. Then you and Kelly can go down and help the wounded sailors."

．　．　．

By mid-morning, the military routine that was to govern Spanish Island was established. Watch bills were drawn up, and the first watch-standers took their posts—at the round stone tower, in the Beg kitchen, and on the bridge of U-324. The rest of the ship's company began cleaning themselves and the boat (the first lieutenant had warned that a Captain's Inspection was likely that afternoon). A shower was rigged in the after torpedo room, and as the men bathed, their filthy clothes were brought onto the quay where some of the island women took them away to scrub and iron with hot flat stones. (Later in the day, they did the same for the blankets and blue-and-white checked sheets.) Kathy O Ruiarc led her ass down from the well with casks of fresh water. The water was heated over fires built on the quay and the sailors shaved— many for the first time in two months. As the sun mounted, the men of U-324 began to look and feel better. They still had pale faces and deep-set, red-rimmed eyes, but the tangled, matted beards disappeared and they wore fresh clothing. The pungent smell of cheap eau de cologne, used by the bridge watches to remove encrusted salt, was washed away, along with bodily odors. The stench of a U-boat long at sea lingered below decks, but it was dissipated as mattresses and pillows were aired and lockers and compartments scrubbed.

Ludtke had warned his officers against the crew's fraternizing with the women of Spanish. He need not have concerned himself that first morning. When Shelagh and Nora appeared on the quay there were stares, earthy ribaldries, and a few long drawn-out whistles. But that was as far as it went. The sailors were grateful for the chance to bathe, to stretch their arms, and to breathe the fresh air. They were pleased to stand on a level, steady platform, happy to look at the cottages and outbuildings huddled against the hill, to see the sky and smoke their pipes and Gold Dollar cigarettes. Most of the crew came from small towns and farms; the sight of the sheep and scrawny cattle pleased them. The men seemed to realize they were suspended between two worlds. They were not at sea under a rigid discipline that extended to the amount of time spent in the heads. Nor were they in Lorient, ready for leave, careless of authority, and confidently accepting the prestige that attached to U-boat sailors. They were surprised and delighted by the hospitality of the Irish, but discipline still prevailed. The memory of the last two days, when they had been completely vulnerable, was still with them, and no one could forget that fifteen shipmates were dead and eight more hurt or wounded. Above all, they were impressed with the gravity of the situation. The boat had to be repaired—and even the youngest seaman realized it was a major job for a naval dockyard.

The people of Spanish Island knew little of this. What they did know was exciting enough. A German submarine lay against their jetty. The submarine had a cruel, gaping hole in her side and many of her people were killed or wounded. Sean O Ŕuiarc had said the Germans could stay six tides and the islanders were eager to help. All of them, except Lady Maud and the babies, were trying to be of service.

Back in Lorient, as Signalman Koenig reminded Electrician's Mate Kreisler, civilians obeyed orders grudgingly, with a furtive hand out for *le pourboire,* as though they knew time was running out on the U-Waffe. At Spanish, on the other hand, the crew of U-324 were regarded as conquerors. It was remarkable enough to have their clothes and blankets washed by the island women. It was astounding to see other islanders on their knees, scrubbing the interior surfaces with strong disinfectant. The language barrier proved no handicap. It was surmounted by grins, signs, and a general air of good fellowship.

Pink-faced Dermod Beg was the man most responsible for this genial atmosphere. The postmaster was everywhere in the boat, grinning, chuckling, and careful to avoid any strenuous work. Mostly he followed the officers, embellishing their requests to the Irish, adding refinements of his own, and contributing comments on a variety of subjects.

"Come now, Paddy," he would say with great good humor. "You've missed getting under those wee pipes in the corner. That's where the rats like to nest. You're not wanting rats on this lovely ship, are you, Paddy?"

Then, while Padraig Mor lay on his belly and scrubbed some minute, nearly inaccessible area, Dermod would tell Hoffman or Reigel about the torpedoing of a liner in the old war; two bodies, he would say, and sometimes four, were washed ashore on Spanish. Or he would speak of his son, a policeman fighting the gangsters in the States. Once, injudiciously, he told of the great moment in 1927 when Lindbergh came over Spanish on his historic flight.

"The *St. Louis* flew so low," he beamed confidentially, "even the goats were frightened. They had never seen an airplane before."

"Och, Dermod, it was *The Spirit of St. Louis,*" said Peigeen Og, stolidly scrubbing a locker. "And, from what I've heard tell, you were as frightened nor the goats."

"Not at all, girl, not at all."

"Brede says you took one look at the airplane, went into your best room, and hid under the bed," Peigeen said inexorably.

"Och, not at all, not at all," Dermod said again. His cheeks were flaming red. Amid the laughter, Hoffman translated the exchange for the benefit of the sailors. More laughter followed and Dermod, protesting good-naturedly, swaggered into the next compartment, where within seconds he was exhorting his neighbors to scrub faster and harder.

All the islanders were happy to help that morning. Everything about the submarine was exciting—the deck guns, the huge engines, the gleaming torpedoes, and the bewildering array of dials and gauges and valves. The great hole in the hull was fascinating and so was the strange language of their visitors. It was almost as if the U-boat had come from the moon; not quite, because they knew the U-boat was an ally, dedicated to the war against England. Most of the islanders had never seen an Englishman, but that made no difference. The English were their enemies. The Germans were their friends and these Germans needed help.

Warmed by the sun, refreshed by showers and shaves, the submariners were in equally high spirits. The awful tensions of the past two days were receding. They were safe for the time being, and when the Shark Boat left Spanish, it would be submerged and headed for Lorient. The sailors were impressed by the islanders' unflagging industry. They were amused by Dermod and intrigued by Shelagh's ripe curves and Nora's smart good looks.

"Look how these Irish work," one rating said to another. "They want to help us, all right."

His mate agreed. "Sort of like the Frisian islanders, ain't they? You know, tough, wiry, wind-beaten——"

"Nothing wiry or wind-beaten about that redhead," grinned a stoker, "or the brunette, either."

"Which do you figure the Tom Cat'll go for first?" the first rating asked, and they chuckled together. At the time, it was a casual joke for the German sailors.

Lieutenant Reigel had, of course, seen Shelagh Mor and Nora Berkeley when the U-boat docked, and had figuratively licked his lips. Later in the morning, he had made conversational overtures to Shelagh, but the girl only smiled shyly and went on with her scrubbing. Nora was different. She wanted no part of the Germans and she had a temper. Only two years before she had seen a Dublin cab driver beating his horse; she had attacked the surprised jarvey with her umbrella, and with such ferocity that she broke his nose and was found guilty of damages in Police Court. There was nothing shy or dissembling about Nora. When Reigel approached her, she was distant and coldly sarcastic.

The lieutenant came up to her as she talked with Sean O Ŕuiarc on the quay.

"Ah, Herr O Ŕuiarc," he boomed jovially, "you didn't tell me about this lovely young lady."

Since he had had no words whatsoever with the lieutenant, the old man was mildly surprised.

"This is Miss Nora Berkeley from Dublin, sir. Nora, may I present——"

"Kurt Reigel, first officer of U-324, at your service, miss." He clicked his heels together and gave her an elaborate salute. "I might have known you were from Dublin. Your clothes stand out among these rustic costumes."

Irritated, the girl gave him a cool nod. "I must be getting back to the storehouse, Sean," she said. "There's still lots of scrubbing to be done." She paused, looked directly at the first lieutenant and added, "It's not terribly clean around here either."

She walked up the jetty, Reigel accompanying her with his exaggerated limp and trying to make conversation. He spoke of visiting Dublin before the war, although he had never been there, and of his high regard for the Irish. The girl answered in unsmiling monosyllables. Her temper was simmering.

"Who are you visiting here, Miss Nora?" he asked as they came to the door of the ancient building at the head of the quay.

"Lady Wynne, my grandmother," Nora said. "Now, I've lots of work to do. I'm sure you do, too, if it's only to supervise the rustics. Please excuse me."

Reigel saluted again and smiled. He went back to the boat, not greatly concerned with his rebuff. In his rather extensive experience, he had learned there was no need for him to chase women. Sooner or later, the women were chasing Kurt Reigel. He was supremely confident neither Shelagh nor Nora would be an exception.

The petty officers drove the crew hard that morning. Shortly after noon the storehouse was ready and the wounded were brought out of the boat and made comfortable there. One of the ratings had a broken ankle and another a brain concussion, both as a result of the ramming. Neither appeared to be in serious condition and Boatswain's Mate Schiller's broken legs were routine fractures. On the other hand, the two seamen who had been hit on the bridge were suffering, and Chief Quartermaster Haas, with a bad splinter wound in the abdomen, was in critical condition.

Brede had organized the women so there would be nursing assistance for Barndt around the clock. Lieutenant Reigel, inspecting the casualties in what the Germans called the sick bay, noted the watch list she had tacked up on the door—Peigeen, Maeve, Nora, Kathy O Ŕuiarc, and Brede herself—and idly asked why the red-haired girl was not included.

"Och, we couldn't have Shelagh," Brede told him. "The poor thing is not—not quite responsible, Lieutenant." Her forefinger jabbed at her temple, and she shook her head sadly. "She's a fine girl, mind you, but nursing's a dead tricky job."

Reigel pursed his lips and said he understood. Shelagh might well be half-witted, he thought, but she was young and ripe-bodied. He could think of other things for her to do besides coddle the wounded.

For the moment, however, he was not concerned with Shelagh. Alongside Nora Berkeley, she was a cow. A little later, when he made up the list of shore billets, he thoughtfully assigned himself to Lady Wynne's cottage.

After the first lieutenant had thumbtacked the billet list on the control room bulletin board, he went ashore again. He was standing at the head of the quay, watching the activity on U-324's topside, when a small, shy voice at his elbow said, "Pardon, sir, have you killed many Englishmen?"

Reigel looked down at eight-year-old Timmy Mor and laughed.

"Plenty, my boy, plenty. And there'll be a lot more, too."

"With the cannon, sir," Timmy asked, pointing to the deck guns, "or with your revolver?"

Reigel laughed again. "Oh, both of them," he said. "The guns boom, and the pistol bangs, but the end is the same for the limeys."

The boy considered this information gravely. On an impulse, the first lieutenant unholstered his Walther seven-millimeter automatic pistol, made sure of the safety, and handed it to Timmy.

"I've plugged a lot of them with this," Reigel said with a grin. "Look it over."

Timmy inspected the pistol carefully. His eyes were round with excitement and wonder. He pointed it at a boulder and said "bang" in a hushed voice.

Reigel laughed again and retrieved the automatic. He agreed to Timmy's shy proposal that they shoot some rabbits later.

"Sure, lad, sure," he said and went up the path to report to the captain. The islanders were friendly, he thought, and helpful. The women were good-looking. Even the brats were polite. Spanish Island would be a good port, after all.

● ● ●

Late in the morning, Hoffman, Leading Torpedoman Muller, and Albrecht, the dour chief machinist's mate, began to study their initial problem—the patching of the pressure hull. First, they sent a diver down to determine the extent of the hull damage. From the man's reports, it seemed almost hopeless to try to repair the boat. There was a jagged, transverse slash in the pressure hull, about fifteen feet long, where the corvette's prow had smashed the submarine. The slash began at the weather deck, over the forward torpedo room, and ran down to about seven feet below the waterline. The plates of the pressure hull were bent cruelly inward; at their point of rupture they were less than a yard apart, but the concavity extended a good ten feet along the side of the boat.

Squatting on the jetty beside the huge, ugly wound, Hoffman and his petty officers listened to the diver's reports, drew sketches on pads of paper, and asked for more details. The diver, wearing the regular escape gear of the U-Waffe and armed with a waterproof electric lamp, went down again and again to give them their answers. When he was through, Albrecht and Muller were pessimistic.

"Looks like a drydock job," Albrecht clucked dolefully. Muller grunted an agreement.

Hoffman shook his head. After long deliberation, he gave his orders. The starboard fuel and ballast tanks would be emptied, the portside tanks filled and flooded. The auxiliary pumps were to be rigged, removing as much seawater as they could from the forward torpedo room. At the same time, everything heavy and portable—stores, ammunition, torpedoes—would be shifted aft and to port. The anchor was to be manhandled onto the jetty and carried, with all its chain, up onto the beach. As a result of all this effort, the boat would be careened to port, and its stern weighted down until the propeller guards struck bottom.

It took several hours to transfer the fuel oil, the heavy stores, and the torpedoes. The men were tired and the petty officers had to drive them. Getting the fourteen-hundred-pound stockless anchor onto the jetty was a long, back-breaking job. Hoffman wanted it inland for two reasons—to lighten the fo'c'sle and later, by using the windlass, to move the boat farther up on the beach. The islanders produced a two-wheeled cart and the O Ŕuiarc ass. The cart's bottom collapsed, but the animal, urged on by the switches of Kathy, dragged the anchor inland, and they embedded it in the rocks above the sick bay.

Watching the work proceed, Lieutenant Hoffman was impressed by the complexities of the task, by his own responsibilities, and then, by his extremely limited training to meet them. Of all the officers and men of U-324, none was more inadequately prepared for the Navy than the engineer lieutenant. Peter Hoffman was the only son of a Bavarian schoolmaster. He grew up in the little market town of Wasserburg, east of Munich, pampered but not entirely spoiled by his middle-aged, middle-class parents. When Hitler came to power in 1933, he was a studious youth of seventeen, bespectacled, a passable violinist, and passionately fond of Goethe. He entered the University of Munich that autumn, and for four years devoted himself to physics, with time out for the violin and for skiing in the Austrian Alps. His parents died during his first year in the university; as a result he spent even more time at his books, his music, and his sport. Whenever he looked back at his undergraduate years, Hoffman was mildly surprised that he had been so completely isolated from the turbulence of contemporary Germany. Outside the university walls, there were torchlight parades, Party rallies, and street brawls, but he did not concern himself with them. Jewish professors were dismissed or retired, but he was not close to any of them, and he did not consider it his business. He was vaguely concerned when Einstein, Franck, and other great physicists fell into disrepute, but he knew it was a dangerous topic to discuss, and, in the end, did nothing. He was graduated in 1937, and in March of the next year, the month of *Anschluss,* he was married to the daughter of a history professor, a man whose lectures closely followed the precepts of National Socialism and the Ministry of Education.

The marriage was a happy one. Erika had two miscarriages, but these tragedies seemed to knit Hoffman and his young wife more closely together. He was no longer immured in his books and experiments, and he began to take more interest in the world about him. He was worried by the insistence of the authorities that only German physics mattered, but no one he knew seemed to share his concern. A few mistakes were made, his father-in-law admitted once, but they were inevitable in the emergence of a strong new nation. Hoffman considered himself a patriot, and he did not argue the matter. As Germany went down the road to war, he tried to concentrate his energies on being a good husband and a good instructor. That was an ostrichlike mentality, he once confided to Chief Quartermaster Haas, and it availed him nothing. When war came, he was called up and sent to Midshipman School. He served in a cruiser during the Norwegian campaign, and then as torpedo officer in a coastal U-boat. He was shy and reserved at first, but more and more he came to like the rough camaraderie of the U-boat service.

In early 1943, he was posted to U-324. Erika was killed that spring in an air raid, and her death served to harden Hoffman. After his first patrol from Lorient, he did not take his violin to sea and rarely wore his spectacles. By the fall of 1943, Peter Hoffman was a tempered veteran. He did not like Ludtke, but he respected him greatly and he was proud to be in the Shark Boat. He was not hard-voiced, like the first lieutenant. He gave orders in quiet, flat tones, and he never looked behind to see if he was being followed. He obviously considered the sailors of the U-324 to be the best in the Navy and, in return, they gave him unquestioning obedience. So far as the crew could tell, he had no outside interests. Koenig, the mail orderly, said he never received a letter. Apparently he no longer thought of music, or physics, or the ski slopes of Garmisch. In their place, it seemed, the guns, torpedoes, and engines of the Shark Boat, and the men who served them, made up his conscious life.

Up in the Beg cottage, the captain spent the late morning drowsing in front of the fire. He was tired and his leg ached. Behind him the radio-telephone set sputtered sporadically—mostly in Irish—and the enlisted watchstander listened without comprehension. His standing orders were simple: If he heard the English words 'Spanish Island,' he was to tell the captain; if anybody but the captain tried to use the set, he was to shoot to kill.

Ludtke tried to sleep, because he knew it was good for him. But thanks to his leg, he was mostly awake—and thinking. Below him, he knew, they were well along with the cleaning of U-324. Eventually, they would sally ship and repair the gaping tear in her side. But they had to do more. The batteries must be recharged and cables connecting them to the dynamotors replaced. How best could that be done, he asked himself, staring at the flickering turf.

The quick, easy answer, he knew, was to radio for help. The boat's radio was still out of commission, but Telegraphist Dietrich had assured him a jury serial would be rigged soon. An appeal meant a rescue U-boat would be dispatched with the necessary cables, circuit breakers, and battery acid. Still better, the gear could be parachuted to him by the Luftwaffe.

It sounded quick and easy, but it wasn't. It required breaking radio silence and that was what Ludtke dreaded. Even in code, the signal would be recognized as German by the British RDF stations. If they got a fix, Coastal Command aircraft would be over Spanish within two hours, and, even camouflaged, U-324 could not stand close investigation from the air. The captain deliberated the pros and cons and considered there were too many of the latter. His signal would have to be a long one, and its point of origin would be less than two hundred miles from a dozen RDF stations. It would be hard to miss.

The alternative, of course, was the Irish mainland. He considered, and rejected, making a signal to the Embassy in Dublin. Using low power and the diplomatic wavelength, he could reach Dublin with little danger of a fix. But Ludtke was wary of civilians on principle, and, from Von Ribbentrop down, he actively distrusted the foreign service. They were not people to keep a secret.

That left sending one of his officers to find the gear on the mainland. Hoffman or Reigel could go by curragh—with Dermod Beg, for instance. The cable and sulphuric acid should be available at an electric utility warehouse or a chemical wholesaler's. When Dermod and Brede came back to the cottage for the noon meal, he asked them where the cable and acid might be found.

Dermod was reluctant to display his ignorance. He scratched his bald head and mulled over the question. Finally he answered. There was no chance of getting the supplies in Ballykerry, he said, with conviction. Possibly in Dingle. Probably in Tralee. There was a big chemical works there, and a distributor for electrical parts as well. He could ask Sean O Ruiarc.

"Begging your pardon, sir," Brede Beg said quietly. "There's someone who'd know more than Sean about these matters. Young Nora Berkeley, Lady Maudie's grandchild."

"Nora's a wee girl," Dermod snorted. "She's not be knowing about such things."

"Och, a girl can find a chemical works quicker nor some booby of a fisher," Brede retorted. "Nora's a mainlander, she knows the way about. I'm saying naught against Sean, but himself or you or the Mors would be lost in Tralee."

Dermod protested, his face reddening. Ludtke considered and decided Brede's suggestion was a good one.

"Thank you, Frau Beg," he said, "perhaps when we've finished our meal, you'd bring the young lady to see me."

A half hour later, Ludtke interviewed the girl alone. A good-looking piece, he decided, but far less cooperative than the islanders he had met.

"Indeed, I'd not be knowing about that class of stuff," Nora Berkeley told him positively. "I'd be no help at all to you, Captain."

Ludtke repeated his conviction that the gear was available. All he wanted from the fraulein, he said, was her help in locating the warehouses. She knew Dingle and Tralee, he pointed out, far better than any of the islanders.

Nora remained adamant. "I'm glad to help with the scrubbing and nursing, Captain, but not help repair the submarine so it can go back to sinking ships."

Ludtke was not accustomed to argument, but he smiled and said: "I respect your sentiments, fraulein. If you don't help us, I can always radio France for the equipment. I can get it that way, but it will take longer. It could take as long as a week, and there might be trouble. My sailors haven't seen women for nearly two months. When they're idle and get to drinking, they'll be hard to control."

The girl flushed. "A week? Why, that's impossible," she said hotly. "The Ballykerry steamer will be here Monday, and besides, international law——"

"I'm the law here, fraulein," Ludtke said coldly. "And I mean to take my boat back to Lorient. If I have to, I'll blow the Ballykerry steamer to little bits."

Nora's temper bubbled and she started to speak. Then, as she stared at the unblinking yellow eyes of the German, she suddenly felt queasy. Something forced her to turn away and she knew the battle was lost.

"Very well," she said in a tiny voice. "When will we leave?"

"Probably tonight, fraulein. I'll let you know. Thank you for your cooperation."

For a long time after the girl had left, Ludtke sat and stared at the fire, still weighing the alternate courses of action. In mid-afternoon, he sent for Reigel and Hoffman. The first lieutenant reported the radio was in commission, and Hoffman gave the captain a list of equipment essential to restore full electric power. The three officers sat on an outcropping of rock beside the Beg cottage and watched the work on the U-boat through binoculars. They consulted the tide tables, drew diagrams, and computed ballast weights and degrees of list. The tide began to flood in at five, and the lieutenants went back to the jetty, encouraging the sailors and islandmen to redouble their efforts. The tide would be high shortly after six; at that time U-324 must be careened and her wound entirely exposed.

Ludtke hobbled back to the fire. Referring to Hoffman's list, he slowly wrote out a signal to Headquarters:

ADMIRAL COMMANDING U-BOATS FROM U-324. TEMPORARILY SAFE SPANISH ISLAND OFF KERRY COAST. UNABLE PROCEED SUBMERGED. REQUIRE FOUR CIRCUIT BREAKERS TYPE B-366, SIX LITERS CONCENTRATED H2S ACID, FOUR LITERS DISTILLED WATER, FOUR FATHOMS 32 CM. ELECTRIC CONDUIT CABLE. ALSO MEDICAL ASSISTANCE. ADVISE IF PARACHUTE DROP AND/OR U-BOAT HELP POSSIBLE. LUDTKE, COMMANDING.

He considered the excited surprise and jubilance the signal's receipt would create at Headquarters and was briefly amused. If it were sent now, the Admiral Commanding U-boats would do everything possible to send a U-tanker or drop the equipment and a parasurgeon. But it was a long message, easily D/F'ed and quickly recognized as sent by the fist of a German radioman. In the unlikely event the bombers of Coastal Command did not penetrate the camouflage he planned, the British would be alerted and demand the Irish investigate every harbor along this coast.

Ludtke considered his message for a long time, chewing a cigar and thinking hard. He had to make his decision soon. He wanted to send the signal—by morning the signal could bring help; the equipment and technicians to install the equipment, a surgeon to tend to his leg and to his chief quartermaster. But the signal could also bring disaster. It could mean surrender, either to the British or to the Irish authorities, and Lieutenant Commander Ludtke was almost pathologically opposed to surrender. From the age of fifteen, he had associated surrender with his father, and whenever he heard the word, or even thought of it, it stirred a deep-hidden sense of personal shame. For Ludtke's father had surrendered a battleship to the Bolsheviks in the naval mutiny of 1918, and the son never allowed himself to forget it.

Gerhard Ludtke was born in Emden, in a modest brick house less than a mile from the North Sea Shipbuilding Works. His father was a career officer in the Imperial Navy, mentioned in dispatches for his conduct at the Skagerrak—the action the British call Jutland. In the last year of the war, the elder Ludtke was executive officer of S.M.S. *Hannover* of the Third Battleship Squadron of the High Seas Fleet. He died that November, in somewhat mysterious circumstances, leaving almost nothing to his widow. The Ludtkes were a proud, patriotic family and the years after the armistice were filled with misery and depression. The Navy scuttled itself and Germany was humiliated. Frau Ludtke's two youngest children died of pneumonia in the winter of 1919–1920, and Gerhard himself had memories of scavenging from garbage pails. Even in those bitter days, he had too much pride to beg. In 1922, when he was fifteen, the boy visited his father's last captain to enlist his help in obtaining a Naval appointment, and the whole world crashed down upon him. Old Von Schoenhausen told him, bluntly and terrifyingly, how his father had surrendered *Hannover* at Wilhelmshaven to the local Soldiers and Workers Committee, when he, Captain Von Schoenhausen, had been ashore. Commander Ludtke had been a traitor—a mutineer. No Ludtke, Von Schoenhausen told him savagely, would ever be commissioned in the Navy again.

It was a devastating experience for a fifteen-year-old. After twenty years, Ludtke could still see the fierce blue eyes and bristling beard of

Captain Von Schoenhausen and hear his stinging words. From that time on, with complete singleness of purpose, he concentrated on joining the Navy and redeeming his father's name. Redemption, he decided, could be accomplished best by his own achievements in the Navy. In 1923, through the offices of an old family friend, he went to sea as a cadet in the North German Lloyd Line, and for fifteen years, followed the merchant service as cadet, midshipman, and mate. He became a Naval Reservist in 1935 and was called to active duty three years later. Von Schoenhausen was long dead and no one remembered Commander Ludtke of *Hannover*, but Gerhard soon realized a merchant sailor had little chance to advance in the surface Navy and he achieved a transfer to the U-boat Arm. He spent two years in the Baltic and several long months ashore. Then came the appointment to U-324 and acceleration of his struggle for recognition. They began to recognize him when the Italian commodore dubbed his command the Shark Boat. Ten war patrols later, Ludtke wore the Knight's Cross at his throat; if he brought the Shark Boat home this time, he would be in line for the Oak Leaves and promotion. He would be an authentic hero, the most famous living skipper in the entire U-Waffe.

He wrenched himself from his train of thought and returned to his problem. Should he go to France or Ireland for help? It appeared that the latter held less immediate danger. He was still struggling with his dilemma when, exactly at six, two stokers came to carry him down the hill and aboard U-324. A few minutes after the hour, Ludtke was on the bridge of his ship.

Careened nearly fifteen degrees to port, her stern just under water and her bow upthrust above the jetty, U-324 was a grotesque sight. A dozen German sailors and Irish fishermen manned her mooring wires, and other sailors her capstan bars. Presently, on the canted bridge, Ludtke shouted, "Both engines, ahead slow," and she inched forward along the quay. Ten feet, twenty feet. He felt the hull grinding on the rocky bottom, at a point just aft of the forward torpedo room, and stopped the engines until reassured there was plenty of water under the propellers. Then he brought her forward another thirty feet, until the rocks grated solidly under the wardroom. With the capstan, they dragged the boat a few yards further inland.

"All engines, stop," Ludtke ordered, and a minute later, "Finished with the engines. Secure the watch below."

U-324 was jammed up on the rocky shore as far as she would go, heeled over to port at an alarming angle. There was maximum exposure of the ugly slash in her side. The wound was ready to be bandaged. But before that could begin, the bodies of eight shipmates had to be removed from the forward torpedo room.

At a quarter to seven, Reigel gave the dreaded order and the circular watertight door leading to the smashed compartment was opened. During the afternoon, wheezing pumps had brought tons of seawater out of the forward torpedo room, but hundreds of gallons had been left and now spilled aft. The dirty water that gushed into the petty officers' quarters and the wardroom country was a filthy, nauseous flood. To the characteristic smell of a U-boat long at sea—compounded of bilges, stale food, diesel oil, unwashed bodies, and excrement—was added a new and indescribably revolting odor. There was still a trace of chlorine gas in the boat, but this, like all the other smells, went unnoticed when the forward torpedo room was opened. The new odor, cloying and contaminating, was the sweetish stench of death.

One officer and seven ratings had been in the forward torpedo room when it was sliced open by the corvette's bow. For three days the sea had ripped the corpses, smashing them against the bulkheads. The sea had shattered bunks and lockers and broken a torpedo from its chain hoist, and these had assisted in the churning, battering, and shredding of the eight bodies. The corpses were mangled and dismembered and in an advanced state of decomposition. Stoker Scheutze, a tough-stomached Bavarian, was the first sailor to enter the compartment. He was violently sick and staggered up on deck, retching horribly. Reigel ordered diving gear broken out for the others of his detail.

The sweetish-sour odor of decay permeated the boat, but the men wearing the diving helmets weren't affected by the smell. The sight of the tortured and bloated remnants of their messmates was another thing entirely. Two other ratings were overcome by nausea and forced to go topside. Like Scheutze before them, they crouched numbly by the rail, struggling with the convulsions of their stomachs, cursing, and thoroughly unhappy.

Slowly, though, the work was done. The shattered bodies were brought up and out to the jetty in tarpaulins, where they were transferred to eight oblongs of canvas. Trying to assemble the eight corpses was like working some hideous jigsaw puzzle. Heavy stones were placed at the foot of each shroud and the canvas sewn shut by the island women. Since U-324 carried only three flags, the large battle ensign was cut into eight squares, and each square was stitched on a shroud, approximately over the heart of its occupant.

It was dark before the melancholy chore was over, and kerosene lamps were brought down to the jetty from the cottages. Below decks, portable battle lanterns glowed somberly as the work of cleaning up the forward torpedo room began. First, there were the torpedoes themselves. The German sailors called them "eels," although in every other navy they are known as "fish." There were four eels in the tubes and three spares in the compartment. Two of the spares were in bunkers below the deck and one had been in the chain hoist, ready for loading. The force of the collision had distorted the tubes and jammed the torpedoes in them so that they could not be removed. The eel in the hoist had been dislodged and had rolled adrift in the compartment, back and forth, grinding the corpses with each motion of the boat. The torpedo in the starboard side bunker had taken the full force of the corvette's bow and was twisted and flattened.

Under the direction of Reigel and Muller, the only surviving torpedo petty officer, the chain hoist was repaired and two of the spares brought out through the forward hatch onto the fo'c'sle. They weighed close to a ton apiece and it was not an easy job. Nothing could be done with the third spare, and it was left in the starboard bunker. Then with the oxyacetylene torch, the twisted, crumpled wreckage of bunks and lockers was cut loose and carried up through the hatch. Shortly aften nine o'clock the forward torpedo room was hosed down; it was empty of the tangled wreckage of steel and human bodies, but, oddly enough, the sweet-sour stench of death remained.

Reigel did not delay in setting his men to work closing the gaping wound in the submarine's hull. The plates that had been forced inward by the collision had to be hammered back into place. The strongest stokers and seamen, torsos glistening with sweat, pounded with sledges, urged on by the snarls of the first lieutenant. Reigel was undoubtedly the strongest man in U-324. He worked with his barbell assiduously, as proud of his muscles as he was of his Nordic good looks. Now, this pride in his strength asserted itself obliquely.

"Come on, Kramer, where's that muscle you've bragged about to the tarts in Lorient?" he would ask sarcastically, or more directly, "Damn you, Schirmer, get your back into it, or you'll get five days of bread and water."

The sledgehammers crashed against the plates, and relays of ratings grunted and swore, against a background noise of gurgling pumps. Almost from the start, everyone but Reigel could see it was no use. The sledges dented and dimpled the plates but they could not force them back into place. After fifteen minutes the hole was as big and ugly as ever.

"Christ, what a bunch of weaklings," Reigel snorted scornfully and went up to the bridge to report to the captain. It was obvious Ludtke did not like what he heard. His leg ached badly and he had just heard that the barometer was falling. In the pale glow of the gangway lantern, his face was lipless, harsh, and deeply lined.

"Very well, Number One," he said at length. "Dismiss the working party, and send two hands to carry me up the hill. Seal off the forward torpedo room and secure the pumps. When you're done, get the Chief and report to me."

Reigel went below and gave his orders. Soon he and the engineer lieutenant trudged wearily up the rocky path. The two officers did not exchange small talk. They were both bone tired. Hoffman's normal dislike for the first lieutenant was compounded by his recent discovery that Reigel had billeted himself with Lady Wynne and her granddaughter. Hoffman told himself that was foolish—that Nora Berkeley deserved what she got. But he could not put the girl completely out of his mind.

They found the captain smoking a cigar in front of the fire, with Dermod Beg hovering solicitously near him, Brede knitting, and the radio-telephone watchstander alert in the background. Ludtke told his officers to sit and consulted his wristwatch. It was a few minutes after ten. When he began to speak, it was with implacable decision.

"It's too dangerous to break radio silence, gentlemen. We'll have to go to the mainland for our gear. The stuff should be available, and not too far inland. Chief, I want you to get it. You'll leave at midnight, in a curragh. Fraulein Berkeley will go with you as a guide."

Hoffman nodded. He calculated he had had three hours of sleep in the past twenty-four, perhaps a dozen in the last three days.

"Aye, aye, sir," he said. He was so tired that the thought of Reigel's loss of Nora Berkeley did not amuse him.

"Sir," the first lieutenant protested, "the chief won't know where to go—I doubt these rustics know what a circuit breaker is. We have no money, not so much as an English pound. And they'll never get that gear back in a stinking curragh."

Ludtke stared at him during this outburst but said nothing.

"Captain," Reigel said hoarsely, "a signal will do the trick. We can have the Luftwaffe here tomorrow morning."

"Herr Beg," the captain said with such grimness that Dermod blanched and stood erect. Ludtke did not take his eyes from Reigel. "Whom, Herr Beg, do you recommend for the rowing?"

"Well, sir," Dermod said tentatively, "there's Eamon Og and Padraig——"

"There's a blow coming up, Dermod," Brede said in her matter-of-fact voice. "The lieutenant will need the strongest oars. Tomas is more powerful nor Paddy Mor."

"Very well," said the captain. He took his eyes off Reigel and looked at Hoffman. "Number One has raised some interesting points. First, money. We can't pay for the gear, Chief, so you're to write chits, payable by the Embassy in Dublin, for what you bring back. Second, it may be impossible to bring the gear back in one curragh. Get another boat at Ballykerry, Chief, and tow it back. You'll have no problem."

He leaned back, seeming to wipe his hands of the entire project of invading the mainland.

"First thing tomorrow, Number One, we'll bury the dead. Bury them at sea, Number One, like sailors. Use the curraghs. Then we'll have to find some sheet steel and patch the hole. If we had some hydraulic jacks, we could force those plates back, but that's impossible. No, the patch is best."

"Yes, sir," Reigel said numbly.

Ludtke surveyed his audience. "That's all, gentlemen. Herr Beg, let the fraulein and Eamon and Tomas know our plans. Chief, get yourself a nap, and shove off for the mainland at midnight. Number One, inspect the watchstanders and the sick bay and report back to me. Thank you."

The two lieutenants saluted and Dermod touched his temple. They left the cottage and plodded up the footpath. There were only a few lights to be seen. The wind whistled and the surf grumbled.

"The Old Man's crazy," Reigel snarled. "It's like hunting a pin in a haystack. He could send a signal and have all your cable and circuit breakers here tomorrow."

"Not so crazy," Hoffman said. "If this weather keeps up, no curragh will make the crossing tomorrow, and no aircraft will fly."

"Aye, it's old man winter having his farewell crack at us," Dermod Beg said. "He'll make the trip that much faster for you, Lieutenant."

Reigel muttered a choice obscenity. He was still furious when Hoffman left them at the O Ruiarc cottage and when Dermod turned in at Lady Maud's. The first lieutenant felt he deserved to be going into the comfort of the Wynne cottage to drink a cup of tea and talk with intimate innuendo to Nora Berkeley. Instead, he must painfully pick his way to the top of the island, inspect the watch set at the Norseman's Tower, go down to the U-boat and the sick bay, check the watchstanders there, report to the Old Man, and then come back up to Lady Maud's. He did not answer when Dermod Beg bade him good night.

Inside the Wynne cottage, Dermod's message produced sharply different reactions. Lady Maud, preparing bandages before the kitchen fire, squealed with excitement and delight. All day she had hoped to help the German sailors; now, her own granddaughter had been chosen to guide them on the mainland.

"Och, this is lovely news, Nora," her Ladyship cried. "We'll be doing something to help the sub, not sitting on our backsides like a pack of feeble-wits." She disdainfully tossed the muslin in her lap into a basket of bandages.

Nora said nothing, but her face was dark with anger. She had expected the summons, but she hoped the gathering gale might delay it. She had said nothing to her grandmother about her interview with Ludtke; there was no point in needlessly upsetting Lady Maud.

Dermod saw Nora's face cloud over and was wary. He liked Nora very much, but he knew that she had a temper, and he had no desire to be caught in an extension of the morning's argument. Fortunately for him, Lady Maud Wynne held the floor. She wanted to know who was going to Ballykerry and was pleased with the choice of oarsmen. She wondered why they were leaving at night, and when Dermod told her, she asked for details of the weather. Then she began making suggestions to Nora—to take money and sandwiches, Kelly's old duffle coat, the map of County Kerry, and Her Ladyship's own cable-stitched scarf. Dermod was relieved to see the girl agree to the various recommendations. He felt sorry for her—it was no night for a young girl to be making the crossing—but it was obvious Lady Maud did not mind. He declined the offer of a cup of tea and said good night to the old lady. "They leave at the midnight, Nora," he cried cheerily. "God stay with you, child."

The girl gave him a solemn little smile and thanked him. Dermod went out, thinking she was not so upset, after all, about helping the Germans. She had looked angry at first, but she seemed ready to go. It did not occur to him Nora had decided she could fight Ludtke best by guiding his expedition to the mainland.

When Hoffman turned in at the O Ruiarcs, he found Sean playing checkers with Signalman Koenig at the kitchen table. He declined a bottle of stout and told them he was off for Ballykerry at midnight.

"Are you away, now?" said old Sean in a surprised voice. "Who are the rowers?"

"Tomas Mor and Eamon Og."

"Och, well," said the old islandman, "I'd best be dropping in on them. Peigeen and the Widow will want to know if I approve."

"I hope you do, Sean."

"Indeed, indeed." The old man's smile gleamed in his saddle-colored face. "I'll visit Peigeen and the Widow as soon as I massacree your sailor at draughts."

Hoffman grinned and asked Koenig to call him at a quarter to twelve. He climbed the ladder to the loft and was asleep immediately.

Seconds later, it seemed, Koenig was shaking him awake. Hoffman made his final preparations. Along with his pistol, he took a knife, a pocket compass, and a flashlight. In the kitchen, the O Ŕuiarcs waited for him. Kathy, smiling and mumbling shyly, gave him a packet of sandwiches.

"May God and Mary be with you, Lieutenant," she said, but she spoke in Irish and Hoffman was not sure of the exact words.

"Here is some money, Lieutenant," old Sean said, giving him seven pounds in crumpled pound and ten-shilling notes. "You'll need it now," he said when Hoffman protested. "It's a dear land, is Holy Ireland."

The old man insisted on escorting him to the quay and they set off down the path, Hoffman still arguing about the money.

"Och, you'll need every penny of it, Lieutenant," Sean said. "There'll be food and drink to buy, and petrol——"

"Petrol?"

"You'll be needing a car to bring the electrical parts back to Bally-kerry," Sean said. "We've a good friend in Ballykerry. He has a fine wee lorry. I'm sure you can borrow the loan of it."

Hoffman realized he had not even thought of transportation—essential though it was. "You're right, Sean, money is important. When I get back, we'll work out a fair exchange—clothing, flashlights, compasses, what you want."

They walked down the path together, Hoffman aware that the wind had freshened considerably. He was impressed again by the friendliness and generosity of the people of Spanish. They had worked hard today for the crew of the U-boat—with the cleaning and repairs, the shifting of heavy gear, the nursing of the wounded. They had shared their food and drink. Two of them were going with him on what could be a hazard-ous expedition. Although they had almost nothing, they were ready to give him money. Hoffman could not believe this would happen in most parts of the world.

A little knot of men and women awaited Hoffman and Sean on the quay. Tomas Mor and Eamon Og stood next to their curragh. With them were Padraig and his wife and sister, Peigeen Og, and—pale and unhappy in an old duffle coat—Nora Berkeley.

By the fitful light of a kerosene lantern, old Sean observed the amenities.

"You know Tomas and Eamon, Lieutenant. No finer oars ever worked these waters."

Hoffman shook their hands. "I'm honored to cross with you, gentlemen. This won't be an easy expedition. But, with the Lord's help, we'll find the equipment we need."

The two islanders grinned at him.

"And you've met Nora, of course. Nora knows the mainland as I know the back of my hand."

Hoffman bowed. "You'll be of tremendous help, I know. Thank you for joining us."

"Don't thank me, Lieutenant," the girl snapped. "I'm not here of my own free will." She swung away impatiently to ask if the curragh was ready.

Hoffman grimaced and Sean looked distressed by her rudeness. But there was no time for apology in the flurry of blessings and good wishes. Peigeen Og kissed her husband very formally and Shelagh embraced her brother. The petty officer of the watch came down from the U-boat's bridge with an armful of life belts. Both Hoffman and Nora took one, but Eamon and Tomas declined. They picked up their curragh and put it in the water. It was made of tarred canvas, stretched tight over wooden frames, and Hoffman noted it was as light as a canoe.

"Not very substantial, is it?" he asked Sean. There was a note of apprehension underlying his wryness, and the girl in the duffle coat gave a short laugh.

"Ah, you're brave enough to torpedo unarmed ships, you can take this little joyride to Ballykerry," she said and scrambled into the bobbing bow. Swearing under his breath, Hoffman gingerly got into the sternsheets, the two islandmen took up their narrow-bladed oars, and the curragh started for the mouth of the cove and the dark, wind-tossed sea.

FRIDAY The new day was overcast and ominous. Ragged clouds scudded across the lead-colored sky and the sea was an angry gray. At seven, when Lieutenant Reigel left the Wynne cottage, the islanders were already at work. Padraig Mor and his son, Timmy, were securing the curraghs with heavy stones. Along the shore and on the hillside, Sean, Dermod, and many of the women were covering stacks of turf and kelp with canvas, and then securing the ricks with ropes and pegs.

The first lieutenant was in good spirits as he went down the path. The frustrations of the night before had left him. He had slept well, breakfasted well, and his ankle hardly bothered him. He was resigned to the temporary loss of Nora Berkeley. Shelagh Mor would, he considered, prove an adequate substitute.

When Reigel reported at the Command Post, Ludtke envied his fitness and exuberance. His first officer was cleanly shaven, a luxury for submariners. At sea, there was no fresh water for shaving, and salt water was too painful for most. Ludtke was normally an exception to this; he used his razor daily, as though to demonstrate his superiority in the smallest degree over his officers and men. This morning, however, the captain had not shaved. He looked exhausted and unwell and said little as Reigel reported on the worsening weather and made recommendations for the new day's work. There were two matters of primary importance—burial services and the hull repair. The captain agreed with Reigel's plans for the service and scheduled it for 0900. Then they considered the best way of patching the hull. It was necessary to take some steel plating from some nonessential location on the boat and weld it over the slash. Reigel suggested they use sections of the outer hull— the thin layer of steel outside the pressure hull, which protected the fuel and ballast tanks and streamlined the boat. Ludtke vetoed the idea. The thin-gauge metal, he said, would not stand up under pressure when U-324 dived.

For a few minutes they considered other areas. Finally, it was decided to rip up the platform deck abaft the conning tower—the Winter Garden—and use layers of that as the patch. In the Mediterranean, Ludtke recalled, with an awning rigged, the Winter Garden had been a pleasant place, almost like a veranda on a North German Lloyd cruise ship. If they tore up the Winter Garden the thirty-seven-millimeter gun would have to be jettisoned, but, as Reigel pointed out, they'd have little use for it on their way to Lorient.

The captain grunted approval and sipped his morning tea, well laced with brandy. His leg ached with dull persistency and it was hard to concentrate on his problems.

There was, for instance, the building of a cofferdam, or caisson, around the hole in the hull to permit the welding of the patch. Here, Reigel pointed out, the thin plates of the outer hull could be used effectively. They discussed this at length, the lieutenant describing his plans, drawing a sketch, and the captain commenting briefly and generally assenting.

Shortly before nine, Sick Berth Attendant Barndt entered and made a brief inspection of the captain's leg. When Ludtke questioned him about his patients, he gave a guardedly optimistic report. The chief quartermaster, it appeared, had spent a restful night; after breakfast he had called for his accordion and rendered a few old drinking songs. The chief was too weak to sing, but his tunes had pleased the men and the two Irish women who were helping with breakfast.

"Ah, that is good," Ludtke said, momentarily forgetting his reserve. "Old Pressure-Proof can't be in bad shape if he's playing his music box and charming the ladies."

Reigel laughed and Barndt smiled dolefully. Chief Quartermaster Haas was known as Pressure-Proof throughout the Second Flotilla. He had acquired the nickname two years before, off Iceland. The Shark Boat had had to crash-dive in heavy weather and Haas, lashed to his bridge station, had been unable to free himself. The boat was six fathoms below and gaining depth fast when his absence was reported to Ludtke. Most captains would have shrugged off the loss. Probably Ludtke would have, had the missing man been a lookout—even a watch officer. But, without hesitation, he had ordered the planes reversed. The boat surfaced, not far from an angry but inaccurate corvette, and the unconscious, half-frozen Haas was cut loose from his station and hustled below. U-324 dived again and eventually evaded the attack. Pressure-Proof Haas survived, and his endurance and Ludtke's loyalty became staples of mess-deck conversation. It was, perhaps, the most important episode in the somewhat apocryphal legend that Ludtke took care of his men.

Reigel was still chuckling about Haas and his accordion when a messenger knocked and reported that the burial party was ready. Ludtke put on his uniform blouse and the white cap. The messenger and Barndt made a chair of their hands and wrists and, escorted by the first lieutenant, carried him down the hill to the jetty. The eight corpses lay there in a precise row, each in his clean canvas shroud and each wearing his scrap of battle color. The entire ship's company, except the wounded and watchstanders, was fallen in on the jetty. Behind the sailors stood the able-bodied population of the island.

Chief Petty Officer Albrecht called the crew to attention and handed

U-324's prayer book to the captain. In the sudden silence, Ludtke heard one of the women whisper, "Sure, there's no priest for the poor dears."

"Ship's company," Reigel thundered in his best parade-ground manner, "off caps!" All the Irishmen followed the example of the sailors, although not so precisely. Ludtke, his white cap tucked under his left arm, standing on his good leg and leaning on Barndt, read the burial service in a hard, emotionless voice. The wind ruffled the pages of the prayer book and ruffled his hair. Once, as he paused, he heard a muffled sob from one of the island women. Why should she be grieved, he wondered with brief irrelevance, and remembered that the Irish were notorious sentimentalists—weak sentimentalists.

The prayers and rifle salutes concluded, the eight bodies were carefully placed in curraghs and rowed out into the cove by Sean, Dermod, and Padraig. The sailors of the burial detail tried to be reverent in their committal of the bodies, but the water was choppy and the curraghs bobbed and slithered disconcertingly. Under the circumstances, the heavily weighted shrouds had to be unceremoniously manhandled overboard.

The sailors were relieved when the job was done and the fragile-seeming curraghs beached and secured. As they scrambled ashore, the island women were still clustered on the jetty. They were watching the beginning of the construction of the cofferdam.

As soon as the last body had slid into the cove and the captain had gone back to his Command Post, Reigel had gathered the key petty officers about him and explained the task ahead of them. He had conceived the cofferdam as a semicircular shield of steel that would be sunk between the punctured hull and the jetty, and then pumped dry so as to permit welding the plates over the slash in the hull. Only lightweight steel for the shield was needed, Reigel explained, and ordered Albrecht, the chief machinist's mate, to cut away sections of the saddle tanks of the submarine. These, he explained, were to be fabricated into a curved section eight feet high and ten feet wide across the chord. To anchor the shield, he ordered four twelve-foot lengths cut from the handrails that ran the length of the hull, just above the waterline. These rods, he told the petty officers, would be pounded into the rocky bottom of the cove in a half-circle around the gash in the hull. The shield would then be spot-welded to the four uprights and to the hull itself. Scraps of burlap would be packed at the bottom of the shield to prevent its leaking. If all went well, the crude cofferdam would be reasonably watertight and the deck plates of the Winter Garden could be welded over the slash. Reigel said he wanted the cofferdam to be in place by noon—the time of low tide.

"We're in for a gale," he added, although no one needed to be reminded of that unpleasant fact. "I want to get this in place before it hits."

All did not go well, of course. The cutting and shaping of the shield itself went smoothly, but the sinking of the four pilings—the four sections of handrail—was another story altogether. The rods were of brittle carbon steel and they had to be pounded into rocky beach. It was a difficult job for Stoker Schirmer, a powerfully built man who could wield the sledge as though it were a tack hammer, and even tougher for the pairs of sailors who held the rods. They stood on improvised ladders, waist-deep in the water, and every time Schirmer's sledgehammer fell, they were jarred to the soles of their feet.

They started to sink the four shafts at half past ten. Each of the rods had to be driven at least one yard into the rocky bottom. The first was nearly that depth when Schirmer's sledge missed by a fraction of an inch and bent it so badly that it was worthless. After a half-dozen blows, the second rod snapped—at about four feet from the top—and the upper section smashed down on the left wrist of Ordinary Seaman Oberteuffer, nearly cutting his hand off.

There were a few seconds, then, of shock and horror. The force of the blow had knocked Oberteuffer off his ladder into the water. The blood spurted from the severed wrist arteries and stained the water an ugly frothy pink, churned up by the thrashing of the terror-stricken seaman. When they had recovered from their initial paralysis, three or four sailors jumped in after Oberteuffer and struggled to get him up onto the jetty. They would get his head above the surface, and then he would scream with fear and pain, swallow seawater, and go down again. Finally, with much difficulty and cursing, they got him up on the jetty, put a crude tourniquet above the elbow, and carried him into the sick bay. Barndt applied another tourniquet and punched morphine into the wounded man. Muller gave him artificial respiration, emptying his lungs of most of the seawater. Kneeling beside Oberteuffer and surrounded by most of the crew, the sick berth attendant and the first lieutenant examined the smashed wrist.

It was a sickening sight—the oozing, clotting blood, the splintered bones protruding, the hand dangling limply. Oberteuffer writhed and groaned piteously. Two men held him down on the mattress and big Schirmer was crying like a child. Kneeling beside the mattress, Reigel, with great difficulty, got Oberteuffer to take a swallow of cognac. Oberteuffer gulped, choked for a bit, and lay back, still groaning.

"It's bad, isn't it, quack?" Reigel asked, and inwardly cursed himself for asking the question. Anyone could see it was very bad.

"God in heaven, yes," Barndt said heavily. He glanced at the other wounded men, ranged on mattresses around the room. There were six of them, three hurt so badly he didn't know what to do for them. The island women assisted with the nursing, it was true, but they couldn't do much more than change dressings and sponge the patients. They didn't understand German, and they rattled their beads and prayed when he most wanted help.

"It's bad, all right," Barndt said. "We need a surgeon, Mr. Reigel, if Oberteuffer's going to make it. That goes for some of the others. The chief quartermaster, for instance."

He looked up at the first lieutenant, his little eyes desperate. "I'm a pill-pusher, Mr. Reigel. I can handle colds and diarrhea. But this sort of thing——" His voice trailed off and he shook his head helplessly.

"We need a surgeon," he said again.

There was a stir and a scrape of feet at the doorway, and the captain was carried into the sick bay. The yellow eyes were pale and the lips set in a thin line. Reigel got to his feet and saluted. The others stood at attention, Schirmer still sobbing and trembling.

Ludtke stared at the smashed wrist and then spoke to Barndt. His voice was as icily contemptuous as if he had looked at an underdone chop.

"This looks bad, quack. What's to be done?"

"We've got to get a surgeon, Captain," the sick berth attendant said lugubriously. "He's nearly lost his hand."

Ludtke had himself brought closer and carefully examined the wound. Around him the circle of sailors looked stunned and nauseated. Oberteuffer groaned softly. The pupils of his bloodshot eyes had been reduced by the morphine to tiny dots that stared up blankly. His face was cold and gray. After a few long seconds, the captain spoke.

"Amputate."

The circle looked at him blankly, and he repeated himself.

"Amputate."

Barndt protested. He didn't know how to perform an operation like this. A surgeon was necessary——

"I'll perform the operation." Ludtke cut him off. The captain's eyes were like yellow agate. He sent for Brede and Dermod Beg and gave crisp orders. He wanted boiling water, lots of it. He wanted sharp knives and shears. Schirmer was sent for the carpenter's small handsaw, Barndt for his surgical chest. Reigel ordered additional battle lanterns brought in and rigged around Oberteuffer's mattress. He saw that a fire was built outside and water boiled in kettles from the U-boat's galley. Barndt administered more morphine to the wounded man and sterilized the instruments. During these preparations, the captain sat near Haas's pallet, coldly aloof. When all was ready, he scrubbed his hands with disinfectant and put on rubber gloves. Barndt held Oberteuffer's shoulders down and Reigel his legs. Brede Beg attended the instruments and dressings. Dermod had been sick, it seemed, and Padraig Mor stood by the door, waiting to bring more boiling water.

The captain ordered all the rest outside. He spoke quietly but with such grim intensity that in seconds the room was cleared.

First, he carefully sponged the wound and cleaned it with disinfectant. Ludtke had no surgical clamps and he tied off the veins and arteries with sutures. It was a slow, laborious job, made more difficult and awkward by the captain's wounded leg. He had to kneel beside the mattress, and his leg ached badly. He could not be sure the sutures would hold when the tourniquet was loosened, and that called for extra thread. In minutes, Ludtke's rubber gloves became slippery with blood and he fumbled with the thread. His leg pained him with fierce spasms and his face began to glisten with sweat. Watching him, Reigel was increasingly alarmed. Obviously the captain was in pain. But the first lieutenant was completely ignorant of surgery and it did not occur to him to volunteer to relieve Ludtke.

Suddenly, Padraig Mor spoke, in a surprisingly firm voice: "Give over, Captain, and let me do it. This is too hard a job for a sick man."

"Och, yes, Captain, let Padraig do it," Brede said.

Glancing over his shoulder, Ludtke only grated an obscenity.

In less than a minute, though, he had dropped the blood-greasy scissors three times. The savage imagery of his cursing appalled Brede, but Padraig Mor said again, "Give over, dear man, give over. You can't do the work with such a terrible pain in your leg."

Ludtke glared about him. He looked at Reigel but the first lieutenant did not meet his eye. With a strangled, despairing oath, the captain pulled off his gloves.

Padraig was deliberate. He scrubbed his hands, put on the gloves, and knelt beside the captain. With Ludtke directing, and Brede assisting, the little islandman took up the task of tying off the veins and arteries. Eventually, Ludtke was satisfied and Padraig began the sawing of bone and the cutting of tendons and muscle. Oberteuffer writhed in agony and the captain swore at Reigel and Barndt who held the patient in place. Oberteuffer shrieked once and Ludtke ordered him gagged. Brede deftly pushed a bandage into the wounded man's mouth and tied it in place. White-faced, Padraig went on with his work and finally

Oberteuffer's hand was off. Barndt stared at it for a moment as it rested on the mattress. A few seconds before, it had been part of a living person; now it was a bent-fingered claw, curiously shrunken and hideously discolored. Barndt shuddered and was suddenly and violently nauseated; Petty Officer Dietrich was brought in to replace him. After a moment, Padraig picked the claw up and put it under the mattress. Then he began stolidly and meticulously to remove tiny bone chips and shreds of skin and tissue. Ten minutes more and the flaps of skin were sewn down over the untidy stump. There was a pause.

"Ah, that may do the trick," Ludtke said slowly. "Loosen the tourniquet, Sparks, and we'll see."

Dietrich looked at the tourniquet sunk deeply into the flesh of Oberteuffer's upper arm. It was impossible to know if the crude sutures would hold when the tourniquet was loosened and the blood came pumping down into Oberteuffer's forearm. He was afraid to do it, but more afraid of the captain. He slowly turned the toggle of the tourniquet and waited. Amid the bluish edges of the wound, bright bubbles of blood appeared, oozing thickly, but there was no sudden spurting of blood. The sutures were holding. Dietrich laughed, a little light-headedly, and everyone else smiled with relief.

Padraig Mor finished the job then, applying a light tourniquet to Oberteuffer's arm, padding and bandaging the stump, and taping it to the patient's chest. Oberteuffer's pulse was stronger, very fast, and his flesh was burning hot. He might not live out the day, but everything possible had been done for him.

"A shipshape job, Herr Mor," Ludtke said, showing no emotion. "We are grateful to you."

He offered cognac but Padraig refused. He was deathly pale. The others accepted some refreshment and began to chatter.

"A fine job, Captain, a fine job, Mor," Reigel grinned. "A surgeon commander could not have done better."

"Och, wouldn't it put your heart crosswise in you to see that poor lad's face?" Brede asked.

Padraig suddenly swayed and nearly fell. He was close to collapse and Ludtke ordered Dietrich to help him out of the stuffy building. Then the captain turned back to the patient. Oberteuffer's face was gray. His jaw was set but he groaned softly. Barndt, recovered from his nausea, came in and examined the sailor. He seemed dazed and distracted as he removed the gag.

"Captain, Captain," he said slowly, "when are we going to get a doctor? This man is in extreme shock. And there are others, too. The chief quartermaster is dying, sir. We must get help from the mainland."

"Soon, quack, soon," Ludtke said. "Keep the boy comfortable now, with plenty of sedation. This afternoon, get a volunteer to give him a pint of blood. Don't let him move. Tonight, perhaps, we'll take the tourniquet off."

He turned to Reigel and said with his acid, thin-lipped smile, "Now, then, Number One, you've had a nice stand-easy. Get your gang together and set those pilings in place. We'll miss the noon low tide, but we're not going to miss the one at midnight. Remember, there's a gale building up."

The first lieutenant saluted, the captain was carried back to the cottage, and work resumed at the jetty. Schirmer was too unnerved by the accident to be helpful and Stoker Scheutze replaced him at the sledgehammer. This time the sailors used pipe wrenches to hold the rods. As the wind grew in force and the surf boomed louder and louder, Scheutze hammered at the pilings. The islanders stood around him, groaning in sympathy when the big Bavarian missed a stroke and bent a rod, applauding when he hit one squarely. The work went slowly, but by mid-afternoon, despite the rapidly deteriorating weather, all four uprights were securely embedded in the rocky bottom.

When Ludtke returned to his Command Post from the sick bay that morning, he was very angry. He slumped before the fireplace, somberly staring at the tiny blue flames, his strong teeth clamped on a cigar. After a very few minutes, he snapped at the watchstander to fetch Dermod Beg.

Ludtke was glad to be alone. It gave him an opportunity to groan when the pain in his right leg became unbearable. Ludtke did not indulge himself in the luxury of suffering in front of others. He was still irritated at his inability to complete the operation on Oberteuffer. He was furious at poor Barndt. A trained sick berth attendant sick to his stomach! The captain spat against Brede's whitewashed wall. He thought of Reigel, and his face contorted with rage. "The pride of the National Socialist Party," he said aloud with heavy irony, and ground his teeth. Damn and blast them both. They had stood by while a scrawny, banty Irishman, ready to puke, had done the job. Ludtke swore bitterly, and this time his anger was self-directed. Of course, he told himself, his officers and men would not follow him if he betrayed his pain or asked for relief. With a vicious oath, he pulled the cork out of the cognac bottle and took a searing gulp.

Then, for a few minutes, Ludtke concentrated on his problems. There were two of them, really, although one was subordinate in importance.

The main problem, of course, was the repair of U-324. The minor one was getting some sort of medical help for his wounded. There were seven now, in addition to himself. Only Reigel, Hoffman, and twenty-three enlisted men were left to repair and work the boat. Twenty-six men, including himself. Four days ago, there had been a complement of forty-eight.

Ludtke's leg began to throb and he grunted with exasperation and helped himself to the brandy. There was little he could do at the moment about the first problem. It was up to Hoffman to provide the acid, cables, and circuit breakers. But the second was becoming more critical. Even if Hoffman brought back the gear and repaired the batteries, barely half the crew was available for duty. There were only three who could navigate—Reigel, Haas, and himself. The chief quartermaster was seriously wounded. As for himself . . .

As though to underscore his concern, an excruciatingly painful spasm struck him, extending to well above his knee. He rocked with the agony, groaning and shredding the cigar with his teeth. As the pain subsided, giving way to a dull ache, Ludtke cursed softly, but with bitter vehemence. Outside, the wind whined and whistled, and behind him, the radio-telephone set gurgled and squawked with static and intermittent snatches of conversation. Ludtke twisted around and gave it an ugly stare. He didn't like the idea, but he was going to use the radio-telephone.

The watchstander knocked and entered, Dermod Beg behind him. Dermod's face was pinker than usual, thanks to the wind and the exertion of the climb.

Ludtke offered him a drink of brandy, which was instantly accepted.

"Watching them pound those stakes puts a terrible drought in a man," Dermod said in mock apology, but the captain did not smile.

When the drinks were poured, Ludtke and the islandman toasted a safe, speedy return to France for U-324. The captain lit a fresh cigar. "Tell me, Beg," he said, "the old lady who is bedridden in the farthest cottage. Does she have a doctor from the mainland?"

"Och, yes, Captain," Dermod beamed. "There's an extremely good man near Ballykerry who treats Lady Maudie. Doctor FitzGerald. I'd liefer have Doctor Fitz looking after me dying than some Limerick specialist watching me healthy." He chuckled and studied his empty glass.

"How often does this doctor visit the island?"

"Well, now, it's been months, sir. You see, the only soul on Spanish that isn't the better of herself is Lady Maudie, God save her. But she has her drugs and medicines and Kelly to do for her, so Doctor Fitz doesn't come so often as you might think."

Deliberately, Ludtke poured two more brandies. He gave Dermod a cigar.

"My sailors are dying," he said. "We've got to get Doctor FitzGerald out here. I'd like you to call him up on the R/T and tell him the old lady needs help. Would he come?"

There was a raffish, conspiratorial gleam in Dermod's eye. "Of course, he'd be coming, sir. He'd liefer be coming on Monday in the steamer, the *Kerry Queen*, but he'd come today if he had to."

"We need a doctor before Monday," Ludtke said shortly.

"Aye, Captain. We do indeed." Dermod scratched his pate thoughtfully. "I could go after him in the curragh, but I doubt we could get back. This old devil—" he eloquently lifted his eyes—"will be blowing a blue murder by nightfall."

Ludtke scowled. "Can he get a boat at Ballykerry for the trip?"

"Och, aye, he can that, Captain. There'll be plenty of fishers who can row him out."

Ludtke nodded his head at the set and gave directions. Dermod switched on the sending button and, very shortly, made contact with Ballykerry. Lady Maud Wynne, he reported, had taken a bad fall and broken several bones. There appeared to be complications. Could Doctor Fitz come to Spanish as soon as possible? Unfortunately, there were no curraghs available at Spanish to make the trip. Could the doctor get someone to row him over? Ballykerry acknowledged the message, invoked the Almighty's blessing on Lady Maudie, and promised to report as quickly as possible.

Ludtke thanked Dermod, dismissed him, and looked at the fire. The watchstander made him a little meal, but there was little else to do but wait for Ballykerry to reply. The captain studied the signal to Headquarters he had drafted and put it back in his pocket. There was little point in sending it now, he told himself—no aircraft would fly in this weather. He listened to the wind rattling the window panes of the cottage and speculated on Hoffman's progress. If the girl behaved herself, Hoffman ought to locate the gear. She was far from trustworthy, he told himself, but the engineer officer was smart enough to keep an eye on her. He wasn't a damned fool about women, like Reigel. Had he sent Reigel, the captain was convinced, the expedition would be captured by now. Ludtke recalled how agents had been landed by U-boat in 1940 on this very coast. Theirs had been a well-conceived plan to aid the I.R.A. in an invasion of Northern Ireland. But the *putsch* had failed dismally; the agents had been seized, almost before they were out of their rubber rafts.

He was still mulling over his problems when Sean O Ŕuiarc knocked and entered. The old islander was courteous and deferential. He inquired after the captain's leg and told him three of the four cofferdam stakes were in place and that both Haas and Oberteuffer rested comfortably.

Ludtke offered him a cognac and Sean graciously refused. They talked briefly about the weather and agreed that all signs pointed to an extremely filthy blow.

"I suppose you get plenty of this, Herr O Ŕuiarc?"

"Och, aye, from October to May, it's one gale after the other, with neither stop nor stay."

"It's a hard life," Ludtke said. "I'm surprised people stay on the island at all."

"Well, it's like this, Captain," the old man said slowly. "On Spanish, you're one with the wind and sky and ocean and you're free. You're conscious of great things, Captain, of your utter dependence on God. You're close to God. Do you know what I mean, now?"

Not completely knowing, but impressed in spite of himself, Ludtke grunted. There was a moment of companionable silence. Sean was about to speak again when the watchstander interrupted.

"Captain, Captain. They're calling us up, sir."

"Come in Spanish. Come in, Spanish Island," crackled the radio-telephone receiver, and Sean O Ŕuiarc got swiftly to his feet.

"Stay where you are," Ludtke flashed at him, and, over his shoulder, "Get Herr Beg up here, on the double. *Raus!*"

The sailor departed precipitately and there was a long silence in the Beg kitchen, broken only by the noise of the radio-telephone. Most of the time there were scratchy, unintelligible rasps of static, occasionally broken by a crackling question ("How d'you hear me, Spanish?") or a plaintive statement ("This is Ballykerry calling Spanish Island. Hullo, Spanish"). Sean O Ŕuiarc stared at Ludtke. He was certain Ballykerry's message was about Lieutenant Hoffman's trip to the mainland and he was puzzled by Ludtke's refusal to let him answer.

Dermod Beg entered the kitchen, puffing, a few minutes before two. The captain waved him to the radio-telephone set, and very shortly a new voice, high-pitched and querulous, crackled into the room.

"Spanish Island. Spanish Island. This is Ballykerry calling Spanish. Are you there, Dermod Beg? Come in, Dermod."

The islandman answered eagerly. "Aye, Doctor Fitz. Dermod here. Go ahead, now."

There was a volley of squawks and screeches and then, again, the querulous voice.

"They say the sea is too rough for the trip to Spanish today, Dermod. We're in for a bit of a nor'wester. Tell me, Dermod, how is Lady Maud?"

Dermod repeated the essential facts of the old lady's alleged accident. There was a broken leg, he reported, a broken hip, and a fractured wrist. Now, it appeared, Lady Maudie had some internal injuries. When he hesitated, Ludtke would prompt him, confident that the atmospheric interference so distorted the transmission as to eliminate any suspicion at Ballykerry. All this time, Sean's saddle-colored face showed increasing comprehension, and then, increasing displeasure.

"She's terrible sick," Dermod concluded. "She's coughing up blood, Doctor Fitz. I'm afraid she can't last long."

There was another burst of static, and then the high-pitched voice came through distinctly: "Tell Kelly to give Her Ladyship some sleeping pills. Two of the red ones every four hours. Keep her quiet and comfortable. Splint up the leg and the wrist, if you haven't done it already. I'll be over as soon as ever I can. Good luck now, Dermod, and God's blessing on Lady Maudie. Over and out."

Dermod acknowledged and switched off the set. He dared not look at old Sean and he had the wit to say nothing to the obviously annoyed Ludtke.

"Och, Captain Ludtke," Sean said, "there was no reason to make up a fable about Lady Maudie. Doctor Fitz would be happy to come out and attend to you and your sailors."

Ludtke ignored this remark and addressed himself instead to the unhappy Dermod.

"What about getting the steamer to bring the doctor out, Herr Beg?"

"Och, the *Kerry Queen* won't be leaving Ballykerry jetty on a day like this one, Captain."

"Why not? Aren't they sailormen, Beg? I've seen a hundred gales worse than this one." Ludtke spat disgustedly into the fire.

Dermod's face flushed and he protested with vigor. "Arra, Captain, they're good seamen, they are. But it will take them eight hours to get up steam——"

Ludtke swore, briefly, but with such violence that Sean crossed himself and shook his head.

"As God is my witness, sir," Sean said, "the *Kerry Queen* will founder. The sea will go down her stack and fill up her hold before she's two miles out."

The captain obviously did not believe him. "Call up Ballykerry, Beg. Tell them Lady Maud is dying. Tell them we need the surgeon now."

"I swear, Captain," Dermod said earnestly, "by the sweet Savior and all the Holy Saints, this sea will be too terrible fierce for the *Kerry Queen*."

Ludtke stared at him, coldly furious. The captain was not accustomed to having his orders discussed. His lips were compressed so as to be nearly invisible. His face was an unhealthy-looking gray, and from it, the yellow eyes burned up at Dermod Beg.

"Damn you," he said slowly, "call up Ballykerry."

Dermod obeyed, shaking his head with disbelief. It took him a full five minutes to make contact, and, with the scratchy rasp of the static, several more to make Ballykerry understand his message. Lady Maud, he said, was close to death. Could not Doctor Fitz make the trip to Spanish aboard the *Kerry Queen*?

There was no answer for nearly a minute, and Dermod repeated his question.

There was an answering fusillade of crackling and screeches and then, clearly heard—

"—a chance, Spanish, not a chance. The crew is in Dingle and it'll be blowing a blue murder by night. God's mercy on Lady Maudie. Over and out."

Again Dermod switched off the set. Neither he nor Sean said anything, and Ludtke sat very still, staring at the fire. After a minute or so the two islandmen excused themselves and went back to the quay.

With the last of the four cofferdam supports firmly in place, Lieutenant Reigel dismissed the working party. It was five o'clock in the afternoon and very dark. Fierce gusts of wind made it an effort to stand erect on the jetty. Earlier, Reigel had taken some pleasure from the wind as it blew Shelagh's glorious red hair away from her head and molded her clothes to the curves of her body. She left the jetty about four, but Reigel did not dismiss her from his mind. She might be simpleminded, he told himself, but she was ripe for the taking. With her brother Tomas gone, only her mother was in the first lieutenant's way.

He was still thinking of this when he looked in at the sick bay. Except for the noise of the wind, it was quiet inside the musty building. With his sailmaker's palm and needle, Boatswain's Mate Schiller was creating a doll for one of the little Ogs out of rope, buttons, corks, and scraps of cloth. Barndt was asleep among his patients and Maeve Mor was darning a sailor's stocking. All the wounded, she reported, were resting easy. Haas was quiet. Even Oberteuffer seemed comfortable. Reigel acknowledged the information and fished around in Barndt's medicine chest until he found a bottle of pills used for sedation. He put a half dozen in his pocket and went up the path to the Command Post, struggling in the face of the wind.

Ludtke was still glowering over his failure to get the doctor. He heard his first lieutenant's report and grunted.

"Very well, Number One. See that you complete the cofferdam at the first low tide."

"Aye, aye, sir."

"How's the barometer now?"

"Still dropping, sir."

Ludtke swore, slowly and with feeling. "We can't expect any help until Monday, Number One. No doctor, no Hoffman, and no use in breaking radio silence. Nothing could fly in this soup."

He stared malevolently at the fire and said no more. When, after a bit, Reigel excused himself, the captain did not respond.

At the time Lieutenant Reigel left the Command Post, Peter Hoffman was urging an ancient Chevrolet pickup truck over an even more ancient mountain road between Dingle and Tralee. It was very windy, the sky was dark and threatening, the road strange, unmarked, and tortuous. Hoffman was tired and depressed. He had failed in Dingle and the chances, he feared, would be little better in Tralee. His companions were equally weary and disheartened. Tomas Mor and Eamon Og were unhappy at being so far from Spanish, and Nora Berkeley was sullenly hostile.

It had already been a long, frustrating day for them. The day had begun at midnight when they left Spanish Island. To Hoffman, in the cramped cab of the wheezing little truck, that seemed a century ago.

In itself, the journey to the mainland had been uneventful. The wind behind them had been strong and gusty, and the sea very black. It was a quartering sea, with long, rolling, white-crested combers coming out of the northwest that shot the curragh along like a Polynesian surfboard. It was very dark, but Hoffman could still admire the oarsmanship of the two fishermen. Their long, rhythmic strokes—sixteen or so to the minute—never seemed to slacken. Nobody talked much. Twice Eamon, the stroke oar, asked for a heading from Hoffman's pocket compass; once, with a look at the scudding wisps of cloud overhead, he commented pessimistically on the weather.

Nora sat forward of the oarsmen, tending a small, heavily patched sail. Although the wind was strong and erratic, she handled the rusty canvas with a mechanical competence. Desperately unhappy, she had time to think. She was frightened for her grandmother and the rest of the islanders. They were people she loved and they were in danger.

Nora's intimates in Dublin—even the girl she lived with—were hard put to understand her annual visits to Spanish Island. They knew, of course, that her only living relative, a hopeless invalid, lived there. But they could not conceive of the Nora Berkeley they knew, gay, attractive, civilized, fond of dancing, horse shows and the theater, spending her holidays with a handful of rough fishermen and their families. Nora could never make them understand. It was hard to explain how kind the islanders had been to a small orphan on holiday from a convent. How they had taught her to knit and weave, to fish and milk and dance a *ceildhe*. From them she had learned about stars and seabirds and the legends of ancient Ireland. And, as she grew older, the girl found herself reversing the educational process. It was not just teaching the children, although she was very fond of that. It was telling their parents and grandparents of the outside world, of statesmen, scientific discoveries, film stars, and hunt balls in County Kildare. Nora rode regularly on trams and had met Mr. de Valera. She had talked with an American Negro and had been to London. Once, before the war, she spent a week in Paris. For years her letters to Lady Maud had been carefully passed from hand to hand among the islanders; for them she was the chief link with the world that lay beyond Ballykerry Head.

It was hard to explain all this to her friends in Dublin. Once, she wryly recalled, she had protested to her roommate, "Och, it's not a love affair with a man, it's a love affair with a whole island." And the roommate, after some consideration, had gravely pronounced, "You're crackers, Noreen. You're absolutely starkers."

That's what it was, though, the girl told herself, as she watched the sail and the racing shreds of cloud. She had a love affair with the island, and she was not going to see the islanders hurt. Unarmed, unsophisticated, trusting, they were ready to help the Nazis any way they could. Nora thought of the ugly captain and the swaggering first lieutenant and her mouth twisted with anger. As soon as they reached Dingle, she resolved, she would slip away and tell the police. The Guards would go to Spanish and insure that the submarine left there after the three days permitted by international law. Either that, or be interned. It was as simple as that.

Nora saw the dim bulk of Ballykerry Head and began to shorten sail. It would be easy to give Lieutenant Hoffman the slip, she told herself. Sooner or later, she would catch him off guard.

After the curragh had grated on the beach near Ballykerry and they had hauled it up and hidden it behind some boulders, Hoffman's nerves began to tighten. He was on an alien shore, with a packet of sandwiches, trench knife, compass, flashlight, a loaded pistol, and three unpredictable assistants. He lacked even the security of his uniform and that vaguely disturbed him. If the police picked them up, he could be shot as a spy. It had happened before, in the early days of the war, when Admiral Canaris had sent his Secret Service agents ashore on this very coast to stir up the I.R.A.

Eamon and Tomas knew the area well. They led Hoffman and the girl up to the coastal road and along it for half a mile, to the outskirts of Ballykerry. They crossed a rocky pasture and came to a darkened cottage. Eamon roused the owner, identified himself, and the two men shook hands. A few steps behind Og, Hoffman listened to the muffled conversation. He kept his right hand on his pistol, the left on Nora's elbow.

"We've a friend with us, Mick," Eamon said. "He's on the run, poor devil."

"Och, that's bad," Mick said, showing no surprise.

"Could we be having the loan of your lorry, Mick? We must get him to Dingle Town this very night."

Mick's response was quick and unhesitating. Of course, they were welcome to the lorry. He would just go back to the barn and get a bit of petrol for them. It was soft on the petrol.

The lorry was a battered Chevrolet, at least ten years old. They unloaded some bricks of turf from its rear, Mick poured in petrol from a five-gallon can, and they rattled into the night. Hoffman was amazed that no questions were asked. For all Mick cared, it seemed, he might have robbed a bank or murdered a Civil Guard. To a man who had spent his adult life in the Third Reich, it seemed incredible.

As leader of the party, Hoffman took the wheel. (Later, he was surprised to learn that neither of the islanders had ever driven a car.) The right-hand drive was awkward for him and more than once Nora testily reminded him he was on the wrong side of the roadway. There was no moon and the road was dark, twisted and deeply rutted, but there was no traffic and only a couple of sleeping hamlets to pass through. Despite Nora's asperity, there was a certain degree of companionability in the crowded cab of the Chevrolet.

For a good many miles the talk was of fishing. Hoffman's fishing experience was limited, and he was content to ask questions. Tomas told him of the islanders' fishing cycle: mackerel, halibut, and bream in the winter months, lobster and crayfish in summer. Usually they went no farther south than Tearacht, but when the catch was scanty, they would go as far as the Skelligs.

"Even as far as Mizen Head," Eamon interjected proudly.

"Sometimes, when things are terrible bad, we go north for herring," Tomas said, "but the Galwaymen are a mean lot. In summer, thanks be to God, we can set our traps and pots in sight of Spanish."

He told how the lobster trade had fallen off—the French market no longer existed—and Eamon contributed some gloomy comments. Then they collaborated in describing the hunts for the basking shark—occasionally sighted off Galleon's Point and when killed and beached, yielding valuable oils.

Occasionally, the men tried to bring Nora into the conversation. She answered the islandmen with little more than monosyllables and barely acknowledged Hoffman's remarks. Tomas and Eamon were surprised at the girl—Nora was usually gay, full of laughter and stories—but they were too polite to mention it.

After the fishing, the talk was of Spanish itself. The island was named for the Armada, Tomas said, but it had been inhabited since the beginning of history. Saints were on the island once, and long before the Armada, the Norsemen were there. "Frenchmen, too," said Eamon. "They built the jetty for their luggers."

"That was a hundred years ago," Tomas said. "Spanish was a brave place then. Hundreds of people lived there—they had farms, a shop, a school, and a church."

"And a public house," said Eamon.

They all laughed at that, even Nora. Hoffman felt immeasurably better when he heard her. When the two islandmen fell silent, thinking of the past glories of Spanish, he inquired about her life in Dublin. He asked several questions but learned only that she was a secretary to a firm of solicitors and that she enjoyed it. Hoffman gave up and for a mile or two there was silence in the cab of the Chevrolet. At length, Tomas Mor spoke.

"Och, we've been going on for hours about the fishing and all. It's yourself, Lieutenant, that's doing the mighty things. What's it like, now, on the sub?"

Peter Hoffman found himself suddenly inarticulate. He tried to answer, but it was difficult, with the night air fresh in his nostrils, to describe life in a U-boat on patrol. He thought of the icy chill of the dripping, mold-green bulkheads and the stale, inescapable stench of vomit, diesel oil, and unwashed human sweat; he thought of the cold, tasteless sandwiches, the constant noise, the lack of privacy, the unutterable weariness. Above all, he thought of the contagious terror in men's upraised eyes when sonar beams scratched across the hull or depth charges exploded close aboard. He could easily evoke existence in a U-boat for himself—if he lived to be ninety he would not forget it—but it was almost impossible to talk about.

"It's not much of a life, Tomas," he said finally, and rather lamely. "Not much fun. Hard to describe. It's a job that has to be done if the Reich is to survive."

"Is that what you tell the recruits, now?" Nora Berkeley demanded. It was the first time she had really entered the conversation since they left Ballykerry.

"No," Peter Hoffman said dryly. "I didn't consider you a prospect for the U-Waffe, Nora."

Both islandmen laughed at this, and Tomas asked if the sailors liked the submarine.

"I think so—by and large. They're all volunteers for the service, you know. Of course—" Hoffman added, "if they didn't volunteer, they'd be conscripted into the Army."

"I don't like conscription," Eamon said rebelliously.

"There's naught to worry about," Tomas said. "The Republic doesn't have it, does it, Nora?"

Nora confirmed this and the lieutenant told them they were fortunate. "If there was no conscription in the world," he said, "there would be no wars—certainly no big wars."

There was a silence and then Nora spoke again. "And what of your Captain Ludtke?" she asked. "Is he a good man?"

Hoffman considered the question for so long the girl thought he was ignoring her.

"No, I don't think he's a good man," the lieutenant said finally. "I know he's a good skipper. He's gotten results. The men trust him."

"Do you?"

"Of course I trust him."

Nora wondered what this young man would say if he knew of Ludtke's threat. The lieutenant seemed like a decent type. It hardly seemed likely he would let the sailors get out of hand.

The truck crested a hill and a few darkened houses appeared. Beyond them other buildings loomed.

"God and Mary," Tomas Mor cried happily. "We're coming into Dingle."

It was after five by Hoffman's watch as they entered the shuttered, seemingly empty town. Nora directed him to Ashe's Hotel, but it was locked. They drove about briefly, peering at signs, but it was fruitless. With the first signs of life in the streets, they drove north of Dingle, found a remote lane and a sheltering hedge of fuchsia, munched some sandwiches, and tried to get some rest.

It was too chilly for sleep at first. There was a single tarpaulin in the truck but no blankets, and Hoffman was afraid to build a fire. Finally, well after eight, each of them slept a bit.

They drove back into town a little after ten, and parked in an inconspicuous alley. Hoffman felt it better to reconnoiter on foot; the lorry might call attention to themselves. As it was, the men looked like three islanders who had been in the pubs the night long. Somehow, Nora managed to look fresh and well groomed. She seemed so completely different from her three escorts that Hoffman felt even more conspicuous. He reviled himself for neglecting to bring a razor, just as he had earlier cursed himself for not borrowing blankets from Mick.

He was nervous about the girl. She had been hostile when he first saw her, before the Beg cottage, and rude and sarcastic when they left the island. Since they landed, she had spoken very little. The two islandmen, Hoffman felt, were ready to help him. But the girl was not to be taken for granted. Hoffman had little experience with women. That, in itself, worried him. That this woman was attractive, even exciting to look at, that she was different from the islanders and very possibly an enemy, made him apprehensive and unhappy.

Almost immediately, the engineer lieutenant found a green-and-cream telephone kiosk—and a directory for all of Ireland. There were a dozen pink pages in it, listing firms and professional men by classification. Under Electrical Stores, the addresses were all in big cities—Dublin, Cork, and Limerick. It was the same with Chemicals. Hoffman shook his head dejectedly as he emerged from the kiosk. He had a nagging premonition of failure.

It was a market day in Dingle. Despite the freshening wind and ominous skies, the streets were full of townsfolk and countrymen. Many looked twice at Nora and a few glanced curiously at the clothes and stubbled faces of her companions. But there was no suspicion in the glances, and in the crowds it was easy to keep away from the constables. The streets and alleys were full of posters and placards—Cadbury's Chocolates, Drapers, Players Please, Bed and Breakfast, Guinness Is Good for You. By noon, however, there was no sign of an electrical warehouse, and Nora, with the lieutenant in close attendance, went into Ashe's Hotel to make inquiries. Hoffman was afraid of his accent, and the girl asked the questions of an elderly porter. She obtained some addresses and they investigated. As Hoffman feared, the first was an appliance shop. So was the second. The third was the municipal power company. It was several squares away and they took the Chevrolet. When they found its office, the door was locked and the two Irishmen shook their heads. Curbing his disappointment, Hoffman reconnoitered the rear of the building. It had begun to rain gently, and as they stood in the narrow alley, Hoffman felt tired and disheartened. He was simultaneously convinced his mission would fail and determined not to let the others know it. He found a rock, wrapped it in a handkerchief, and advanced on one of the power company's rear windows.

Eamon Og protested. He wanted nothing of a smash-and-grab raid.

"Lord, man, we can't wait until they open up on Monday," Hoffman said, his exasperation showing. He looked to Tomas for support, but Tomas only grinned doubtfully and studied his fingernails.

Hoffman set himself for the blow. Eamon moved close with an arresting arm. "No, no, we can't be breaking in, Lieutenant."

Hoffman stared at him. "Of course we're breaking in, Eamon. We've come a long way. We can't let squeamishness stop us now." He turned, smashed a pane, turned the lock, and shoved the window up.

"Climb in, Eamon, and open the door for Nora and me," he said tensely. "Come on, man. You stay here in the alley, Tomas. Whistle if you see anyone."

The lieutenant was elated to find that the rear of the building served as a storeroom, but his spirits were soon dampened. There were shelves of pipe and wire, cartons of fuses, bulbs, conductors, switchgear, and a considerable assortment of tools. There were a few spools of cable, too, but a few minutes' search revealed all of them to be the wrong size. There were some circuit breakers, but none of adequate voltage. He rummaged through the crates and boxes for a bit, futilely looking for acid, and then said quietly, "This is no good. We'll have to go on to Tralee."

The girl and Eamon regarded him unhappily. Nora's wide-set eyes were as blue as cornflowers, Hoffman thought, somewhat irrelevantly. He found a pencil and after a question about spelling, wrote "For the windowpane" on a slip of paper. He left it on a table, secured by a half crown. Then he ushered his reluctant colleagues into the alley and aboard the truck.

They made one more stop before leaving Dingle. The lieutenant sent Tomas into a shop with a couple of pounds to buy a blanket.

"We'll probably have to sleep out again tonight," he told Nora. "You need more than the tarpaulin to keep you warm."

"That's kind of you," the girl said coolly. "What about Eamon and Tomas?"

"We have to buy food and petrol," Hoffman said. "I've only a few pounds left."

Nora had some money but she said nothing. She would need it, she told herself, when she escaped.

It was raining steadily as they left Dingle and drove northwest into the mountains. The windshield wiper refused to work and Hoffman felt extremely dispirited. All he had achieved in Dingle was a quarrel with Eamon Og. Tomas, he believed, was still on his side, but Eamon was now a doubtful ally. As for Nora, Hoffman was certain she would bolt if she had the chance. Somehow, Hoffman told himself, he must win her over. If she did escape the Shark Boat was lost. He was trying to work out some gambit that might lead to amicable conversation when the girl broke her silence and offered to spell him at the wheel.

It was the first time Nora had volunteered to drive. Obviously, she was competent and Hoffman was glad he had surrendered the wheel. After a couple of miles, he complimented her on her driving. She ignored this, but the Chevrolet gave them something in common and they established tentative agreement on the poor quality of the brakes and springs, and the handicap of an inoperative windshield wiper. Hoffman consulted her on the adequacy of the petrol supply, the probable distance to Tralee, and the size of intervening villages. He commented on the weather, the sharpness of the curves, and the difficulty, for him, of the right-hand drive. He kept talking, even when he got no response. He had the vague, desperate hope he could mollify her, but as the miles clattered by, that was not so important as staying awake. He had a dreadful, nightmarish vision of being roused from sleep in front of a police station.

They had crossed the spine of the Slieve Mish range and were rattling down toward the Bay of Tralee when it happened. Tomas Mor began to snore. The snore began as a purr, mounted to a loud, rude crescendo, and tapered off in a diminishing whistle. Hoffman began to laugh. In one moment, he had been staring at the highway ahead, convinced his mission was doomed to failure; in the next, Tomas' absurd, vulgar snore had pricked some risibility. Hoffman laughed until the tears came, and, remarkably enough, the girl began to laugh, too.

They did not discuss the source of their merriment. Irritated by the laughter, Eamon Og woke Tomas with elbow jabs in the side, but for a mile or two, Nora and the German lieutenant chuckled over the memory. That helps, Hoffman said to himself. We've something in common, if it's only a primitive sense of humor.

Shortly after eight in the evening, they came into Tralee. It was raining steadily and there were few people abroad. They found an open garage where they fueled the truck and Hoffman borrowed tools to fix the wiper.

"Now then, Nora," he said, "drive to the chief hotel, please. We'll make inquiries there as we did in Dingle."

"It's just a few squares ahead," the girl answered. "We're in the High Street now."

They drove on, slowly, and as they passed a building with two green lights gleaming at its door, Eamon said sourly, "That's the place to stop, Nora." The others looked and saw a rain-slicked brass plate lettered *"Guarda Siochana."* Eamon gave a mirthless laugh and they went on to park before the hotel.

Nora and the lieutenant walked up the steps together. There was a feeble electric sign over the door and Hoffman read it aloud. "Bresnahan's Hotel. I should have thought they'd call it The Rose. You know, the Rose of Tralee." He gave Nora his shy little smile, but she ignored his remark. As they walked into the lobby, they looked an ill-assorted couple. The girl was ready to cry out for help. Equally tense, the German walked close beside her, his right hand close to his pistol.

The clerk at the reception desk regarded Nora with admiration and appeared not to notice her escort. He seemed startled by her question and asked her to repeat it.

"Why, no, miss, I'd not know of an electrical wholesale company in the city. But I'll fetch a gentleman from the bar who'll be knowing. Half a sec, miss."

The clerk shortly produced a florid, rotund businessman, complete with mustache, waistcoat, and bowler. He removed his hat and the girl repeated her question.

"An electrical parts wholesaler?" The businessman twisted his mustache, preening himself for Nora and ignoring Hoffman. "To be sure, there's Terence Mulcahy in the Crescent. He's near as big as Coyle and Ryan in Limerick. But he'll not be open this evening, miss."

"We'll visit him on the Monday," Nora smiled. "Terence Mulcahy, you said, sir?"

"Aye, in the O'Connell Crescent," the businessman said, and added, "Would you be too busy to take a dram with me, now?"

Some sixth sense had prepared Peter Hoffman for this gambit. "I'm sorry, sir," he cut in before Nora could speak, "the lady's father is waiting for us outside."

The mustache seemed to droop and the businessman said, "Oh, in that case——" and Hoffman took Nora's elbow firmly and marched her out of Bresnahan's. He was pleased with his adroitness and he thought he heard a stifled giggle from the girl, as they went down the steps. It made him feel like singing. Perhaps, after all, he thought, she's on our side.

The engineer officer was almost gay as he drove to O'Connell Crescent. He broke a window of Mulcahy's warehouse, and, with Tomas, scrambled in. He found a number of circuit breakers of the proper voltage, but not the right-sized cable and no sulphuric acid. Hoffman was badly disappointed. He scribbled a receipt for the breakers, and they returned to the dark, drizzly alley. Eamon Og stood by the truck, looking both unhappy and defiant. There was no sign of the girl.

"Where's Nora?" the lieutenant lashed out, but even as he spoke he knew the answer.

Eamon shrugged his thin shoulders.

"How long has she been gone?" Hoffman felt sick. Earlier, he had been prepared for betrayal, but Nora's cooperation in the hotel had relaxed his guard. He repeated his question, glaring desperately at the two islanders.

"Five minutes, mayhap," said Eamon, smiling weakly.

"God and Mary," Tomas said. "She's gone for the bobbies."

Hoffman swore and looked at his watch. He had been in the warehouse for a quarter of an hour. Perhaps there was time to intercept her.

"Into the lorry with you," Hoffman told the two islanders, climbing into the driver's seat. In three minutes he was back in the High Street. There were a few pedestrians, but he did not stop to investigate them. When he saw the green lights of the police station, he pulled into a side road and braked the truck. Then he got out and walked back to the station. He peered through the windows and saw only a sergeant placidly smoking and reading a paper at a big desk. He stepped into the shadowed entrance, out of the rain and the faint green light, and waited.

For three long minutes Hoffman wiped his sweaty hands on his jersey and cursed himself for not keeping the girl in his sight. Desperately, he wondered if she would come to the police for aid. She might have asked some householder for help. At any moment, he knew, a policeman might come out of the station and discover him, an unshaven, unkempt foreigner with a pistol in his waistband.

The minutes dragged by and then, above the rain, he heard the swift click of a woman's shoes. Hoffman stiffened as the clicking approached. He let the girl come up the steps into the little vestibule and then he took her by the arm.

"Don't make a sound, Nora, or I'll shoot."

She spun around, white-faced, but she didn't scream. Instead, as Hoffman hustled her down the steps and back to the truck, she began to sob. In spite of the clumsy comforts of the two fishermen, she was still softly weeping when Hoffman drove out of Tralee, headed for Limerick City.

After a few miles she checked her tears, but the atmosphere in the cab of the truck continued sullen and unhappy. Once or twice Hoffman tried to make conversation, but only Tomas answered, and he in monosyllables. The lieutenant was irritated and perplexed by their attitude. They had come with him, he thought to himself, with a clear understanding of what he had to do.

Exhausted and depressed, Hoffman tried to think of the job ahead of him. Despite his efforts to concentrate, he kept thinking of Nora. He reconstructed her face, detail by detail. Not really a beauty, he decided. Her nose was too snubbed and her mouth too wide for that. But it was a nice nose and a generous mouth. Her eyes were lovely and the shoulder-length mass of black hair was superb. Hoffman wondered what he would have thought of this girl in other circumstances. If he had met her last fall in Lorient, for instance. It was a pleasant little problem to consider.

The rain fell heavier, and near the village of Carrigkerry on the Shannon, the Chevrolet slowed to less than twenty miles an hour. At eleven o'clock Hoffman decided they could go no farther. They could make Limerick by two, he estimated, but it would not be worth it if he were asleep on his feet. He turned off into a narrow lane, lined with dripping fuchsia, and flicked off the headlights. The truck crawled along for a quarter mile and they made out the dim gabled bulk of a barn. Hoffman found an opening in the fuchsia hedge, parked, and cautiously investigated the building.

Except for a few grunting, inoffensive heifers, the barn was empty. There was plenty of hay and after a few exploratory sweeps of his flashlight, Hoffman gave his instructions.

"Make yourselves comfortable. We'll spend the night here with the cows. Don't try to leave the building, any of you. Particularly you, Nora."

The girl protested a bit, vaguely and unhappily. It was cold in the barn, even with the tarpaulin and blanket over her. The cattle mumbled and grunted and the rain drummed on the roof. Nora was hungry, angry, and afraid. She had failed to turn Peter Hoffman over to the Guards, and he was alert now, and desperate.

The two Irishmen burrowed into the hay. Hoffman made himself comfortable by the door.

"Come here, Nora," he said presently and the girl's apprehension suddenly mounted to near panic. She cowered under her covers until

Hoffman repeated his order and flicked on his flashlight. Dumbly then, she groped her way to him.

"Lie down," he ordered, "with your feet toward me."

Terrified, the girl obeyed and lay shivering. There was an interminable moment and then she realized he had shackled her right ankle to his with his belt, and that nothing more was going to happen. In her relief, Nora began to sob. Don't blub, you ass, she admonished herself fiercely, but it was no use. For several minutes she wept, quietly but convulsively.

Her tears alarmed and irritated Hoffman. He couldn't let her go, and he hardly dared take his eyes off her. She was an enemy. Because of her, Eamon was mutinous—and probably Tomas. Even if they found the gear he wanted, she would be a problem, a very real problem until they were back at Spanish. At the same time, he could appreciate her nervous exhaustion, her terror and uncertainty. Why, he asked himself belligerently, had the Old Man chosen her to guide him? And why had he not refused to take her?

He had no answer for those questions, and eventually he crawled beside Nora, gave the girl a few awkward pats on the shoulder, and attempted to reassure her.

"No fun, I know, Nora, but it's going to be all right," he said lamely. "Nothing to worry about. Try to get some sleep."

Under the tarpaulin, the girl was tense. Occasionally, but with decreasing frequency, she was racked by a shuddering sob. Poor thing, Hoffman thought. The last crying woman he had tried to solace—the only one, for that matter—had been his wife Erika, after she had lost their second son. Hoffman gave a little snarl of self-disgust. You're not supposed to comfort girls, he told himself, your job is to get the acid and cable that will enable U-324 to dive.

Eventually Nora slept. Hoffman listened to her even breathing for a bit. A few feet away, there was a mixture of snores from the islanders. The cattle made their chewing, tail-thumping sounds and the rain rattled on the roof. Very cautiously, so as not to jerk the girl with the belt that bound them, Hoffman composed himself for sleep. The wretched girl will make trouble tomorrow, he told himself. He thought about that for a short time, and then remembered how they had laughed over Eamon's reference to the pub and at Tomas' snoring. She had a lovely laugh, he told himself. He wished she were on his side. Presently, he was asleep.

•   •   •

Shortly after eight that evening, at about the time Hoffman's little truck entered Tralee, Lieutenant Reigel took his ease before the Widow Mor's chimney place. The wind shrieked outside and rattled the shutters, but it was warm and comfortable before the fire and Reigel stretched luxuriously. Shortly before supper, he had had his gear brought down from Lady Maud's and had moved in with the Widow and her daughter. Leading Torpedoman Muller was also billeted there, but Muller was a quiet man who minded his own business. Reigel had requested him to take the middle watch aboard U-324 that night, and the petty officer, asking no questions, had made the necessary arrangements. After supper he had excused himself and now he slept in the loft above them.

Kurt Reigel enjoyed himself as he basked before the fire. He chatted with Maura Mor and admired her daughter. Shelagh sat on a chest against the wall, saying very little but occasionally darting a glance at the German officer. When Reigel tried to include her in the conversation, she would color and giggle and reply in monosyllables. On these occasions, the lieutenant only smiled to himself. Shelagh's mouth was slack and her eyes vague, but her hair, glinting in the firelight, was lovely, and there was a promise of voluptuous femininity beneath the black bodice and the full, wine-red skirt.

Even at fourteen, in the Berlin slum district of Wittenau, women used to pick Reigel up, buy him beer at obscure bars, and rub their legs against his. The outcome was always the same.

In those days, Kurt Reigel had very little future. His father was in Spandau Prison and his mother had disappeared. He himself had a police record for burglary and assaults on drunks in the Tiergarten. In normal times, he was destined for the gallows.

National Socialism changed almost everything for Reigel. The Hitler Youth, and after it, the S.A., gave him direction and purpose. They disciplined him, developed his superb body, and gave him an education. They taught him the finer points of street fighting and how to paint a yellow star of David and the words *Ich bin ein Jude* on an innocent shopkeeper's door. But the Party could never tell Kurt Reigel much about women.

At eighteen, Reigel went into the Navy, and in this most conservative of services, he was not an immediate success. The traditions of the Academy at Lübeck galled him. Staff duties at Wilhelmshaven and the Embassy in London were a bore. The war brought Reigel a degree of freedom, particularly after he joined the U-Waffe. In the U-boat service, he won an Iron Cross and was considered, by 1944, ready for command.

The Navy, however, did not dampen his appetite for women, or diminish his attraction for them.

Even Maura Mor, in her lugubrious way, was voluble in the presence of Kurt Reigel. She worried at length about Tomas, so far from home. She feared he might be out on the ocean that night with the storm coming down on them.

"He's a brave boy," she said. "If Lieutenant Hoffman said row back to Spanish, he'd do it."

"Ah, that wouldn't happen," Reigel smiled. "Hoffman knows this is too rough a sea."

She was unconvinced. "They never know it. Every time they come back safe, they think they're smarter than the sea. Och, I remember my husband. Never worry, he'd say. Then, one day, he was washed ashore at Galleon's Point. He'd been in the sea for three days. He'd swole up so, his legs had burst his trousers."

The Widow began to wipe her long bony nose. Reigel wanted to change the subject, but she told him with clinical detail about her husband's funeral service.

"Och, it was a lovely burial. They all came over from the mainland. Some even brought flowers, and we tucked himself next to his daddy atop the hill, up in the same burial ground where I'll go, and, God willing, Tomas and Padraig and Shelagh, here."

Reigel caught Shelagh's eye and winked, but she did not respond. He tried to change the subject, and, after a bit, the Widow was persuaded to discuss the English.

"Och, those wicked, murdering people," she said harshly, "the terrible things they did in the County Kerry—arrests in the night, shootings, setting cottages and hayricks on fire."

She went on, cataloging the crimes of the Black-and-Tans. "And when they came to Spanish, a dozen or so hulking bully-boys, looking for the Wynnes, they killed one of Sean's pigs and stole my husband's watch."

Reigel smiled at her indignation, and asked if he might have a drink. The Widow produced a couple of bottles of Tomas' stout and joined him in a drink. She croaked:

> Up De Valera,
> The rebels as well,
> Independence for Ireland
> And England to hell!

The lieutenant laughed and responded with the traditional wardroom toast—"We sail against England." A minute later the opportunity he hoped for presented itself. Shelagh's back was turned and her mother was busy at the hearth; it was easy for Reigel to put three of Barndt's sedation pills into the Widow's stout. Three of them, he smiled to himself, should keep her quiet for the night.

They drank their stout slowly and Reigel talked about the war. Thanks to the U-boats, he said, the Third Reich was winning the war. England was slowly being strangled and the Americans were too soft and luxury-loving to help. The Second Front? Reigel snorted derisively. He hoped it would come, so Marshal Rommel could throw the Allies into the sea, but he doubted Churchill had the nerve to try. When he said this, Maura Mor almost smiled.

"The key to victory is the North Atlantic," the lieutenant went on, a trifle pompously. "England depends on her convoys, and lately the convoys have been getting through. The radar in the Allied aircraft keeps the U-boats down. But that will change by summer. They're starting to equip our flotilla with the snorkel this spring. That means we'll be able to run submerged on our diesels—we'll be able to stay down for days."

The lieutenant drank another bottle of stout, although he could not persuade his hostess to join him. Shortly after ten, Shelagh set out plates of jam and soda bread. Once she came close to Reigel's chair and he was acutely aware of her flushed cheeks and swelling bosom. He tried to prod the girl into conversation with questions about her spinning and the island's crops. But Shelagh would only giggle and look to her mother for assistance. Outrageous compliments about her clothes elicited only monosyllables. Reigel couldn't understand it. He finished his Guinness philosophically and listened to Maura Mor drone on about the difficulties of growing vegetables on Spanish.

Presently the Widow announced her intention to retire. "Come, Shelagh, it is near eleven. Let us go down on our knees and say the Rosary."

Shelagh rose obediently. Reigel gallantly protested her departure and the girl smiled at him and gave an inane giggle. Her mother bade the German good night.

"This is a poor class of cotteen, Lieutenant, but you're welcome to all that's in it."

Reigel smiled at the words and tried again to catch Shelagh's eye. He thanked the Widow and watched the bedroom door creak shut behind the two women. He opened another bottle of stout and sat quietly, listening to the wind and the faint sounds of the fire, and indulging himself in delightful speculation concerning the hours ahead. In another forty minutes or so, Leading Torpedoman Muller would get up and depart to stand the middle watch. Reigel would wait another half hour and then, stealthily, he would open the bedroom door and whisper his invitation to Shelagh. The girl was almost certainly a virgin, he decided, and he grinned with anticipation. He closed his eyes and concentrated on conjuring up an image of the creamy, rounded thighs under Shelagh's dark, bell-like skirt.

When the knock came at the door, a quarter past eleven, Reigel hardly stirred. He was sure it was the bridge messenger, come to rouse the oncoming watch. When he saw it was the sailor who had the watch at the Beg cottage, he stiffened with alarm.

"Captain's compliments to the first lieutenant, sir," the man said. "It's just half an hour until low tide."

"What of it?" Reigel snapped, but even as he spoke, he knew the answer. Busy in arranging Muller's midwatch and drugging Maura Mor, he had forgotten an important detail.

"It's the cofferdam, sir," the rating said unhappily. He sensed he brought bad news to the first lieutenant, and no sailor in the Shark Boat liked that. "The cofferdam is to be rigged at low tide, sir, so the hole can be patched tomorrow——"

Reigel slammed his tumbler down on the table and exploded with rage. He kicked the table over and when the tumbler did not break, he smashed it into the fire. The messenger fled. Awakened by the noise, Maura Mor appeared at her door and Torpedoman Muller clattered down from the loft. Frightened by Reigel's violence, the Widow withdrew, but Muller was caught; he stood stoically at attention as the first lieutenant's savage fury broke over him.

Reigel was convinced Ludtke had done this out of spite. The cofferdam could be installed tomorrow, in daylight. But somehow the Old Man had suspected he would be in bed with Shelagh. Reigel could see him, sitting before his fire, his yellow cat's eyes gleaming as he planned this obscenity.

Eventually, the storm subsided. Reigel pulled on his sweater and oilskins, delivered himself of a final vicious description of Ludtke, and stamped out into the windy night.

At the jetty, he found a dispirited knot of sailors huddled around the pilings that circled the gaping hole in the U-boat's hull. None of them had experienced the frustration of the first lieutenant, but all had been summoned from their bunks to work under difficult conditions. The wind tore at their oilskins and they were pelted with volleys of stinging rain. Reigel gave his orders furiously, the petty officers swore mightily, and the semicircular shield of lightweight steel was manhandled down around the pilings. It was welded to the uprights and to the hull, and packing was applied to the bottom of the structure to prevent leaks.

The welding was done speedily, but the caisson leaked, and the calking process took infinite patience and considerable time. Once the cofferdam was relatively watertight, the portable auxiliary pumps were put to work. Leaks developed and were plugged. It was nearly three when the cofferdam was serviceable, and it took another twenty minutes to rig the necessary protective tarpaulins. Then Reigel climbed to the Beg cottage to give himself the dubious satisfaction of waking Ludtke and reporting the caisson installed and watertight.

"Very well, Number One." Even in the darkened bedroom, Reigel thought, the yellow eyes glittered wickedly. Ludtke asked the time, and when Reigel muttered with exasperation, that it was 0330, the captain indicated surprise that the job had taken so long.

"Start the welding operations promptly at eight, mister," Ludtke said coldly. "Don't fail me. I want the hole patched and seaworthy by midmorning."

Reigel started to protest, realized it would accomplish nothing, and left. He told the radio-telephone watchkeeper that all hands, even though they had worked until after three, should be summoned at the regular reveille, and stumbled down the path to the Mor cottage.

When he entered the kitchen, he could hear Maura snoring. Muller was gone, at least for another half hour. But Reigel was exhausted. He peeled off his oilskins, kicked off his dirty sea boots, and crawled wearily into bed. Almost before he could curse his fortune again, the first lieutenant was asleep.

SATURDAY

The full fury of the Atlantic gale struck the island during the morning watch. Fifty-knot gusts of wind tore at the cottages, rattling the windows, wrenching off shutters, and ripping away bits of thatch. Intermittently, there were heavy bursts of rain. At 0630 it was much too dark for work and, after reveille, Albrecht sent the off-duty sailors back to their bunks.

Slowly the visibility improved, and at eight bells, when Able Seaman Kramer went on duty at the Norseman's Tower, he could see a half mile of gray, angry sea. Despite himself, Kramer was a little frightened. The wind shrieked around the tower and the sky was filled with ragged, racing storm clouds, so low they obscured his vision. Sometimes the gusts came at such velocity that Kramer was convinced the tower would be blown down the side of the island; then he would remember it had withstood the hurricanes of centuries and he would grin with nervous sheepishness.

Lieutenant Reigel was shaken awake at seven and ate a hurried breakfast at the Widow Mor's kitchen table. By half-past the hour, he was on the submarine's fo'c'sle, supervising the patching of the hole in her hull. Although U-324 was sheltered from the full force of the wind, the job went slowly. The afternoon before, Albrecht had begun cutting up the deck of the Winter Garden, but the task was only partly done. By eight, though, despite wind and rain, the oxyacetylene torches were hard at work, and within an hour, the thirty-seven-millimeter Bofors cannon had been manhandled below. No one enjoyed the removal of the boat's heaviest gun.

"We may need this baby when we're crossing the bay," a stoker shouted above the wind. His mates agreed, with stolid, monotonous oaths.

"Don't worry, boys," Petty Officer Muller said. "No Beaufighter will see *us* crossing the bay. We'll be twenty fathoms down." And, noting that the stoker looked particularly glum and unconvinced, he added, "The captain knows what he's doing, Willi. The captain will take care of us."

Shortly after that, the first piece of decking was ready for application to the gaping hole in the U-boat's starboard side. During the early morning, rain and seawater had collected in the caisson. This was pumped out and the packing at the base of the shield renewed and recaulked. By nine o'clock, the first section was welded in place; others followed with slow, painfully slow regularity.

As the work went on, the sailors were disheartened by the news that Chief Quartermaster Haas was sinking fast. Shortly after eleven, Reigel was in the wardroom, scowling into a cup of coffee, when Barndt reported dully that the chief quartermaster was dead.

"Very well, Barndt," Reigel said. "Prepare the corpse for burial. I'll tell the Old Man."

"Thank you, sir," the sick berth attendant said gratefully. He had been terrified at the prospect of reporting Haas's death to the captain.

Reigel went up on the windswept deck and inspected the work-in-progress. The sailors of the repair party had heard the news and looked stunned, but the welding was continuing and the boat's side was nearly patched. Still scowling, the first lieutenant left the quay and began to trudge up the path. The force of the wind made him bend forward at the waist until, at times, he had to support himself with his hands. The wind, he thought dispassionately, must be nearly Force Ten. It was powerful enough to dislodge stones the size of footballs and send them rattling down the side of the island. The sky was very dark, with occasional jagged streaks of lightning.

When he reached the cottage and turned, Reigel could see the iron-gray sea, its surface roiled and ugly. He entered and forced the door closed against the wind. The captain, predictably, sat by the chimney place, staring into the flickering flames. He turned, with an effort, and something in Reigel's face made him ask abruptly,

"How is the chief quartermaster, Number One?"

"Haas is dead, sir," Reigel said. "Ten minutes ago."

There was a long pause, the silence broken only by the noise of the wind. Brede Beg put aside her knitting and went up to the little red lamp of perpetual adoration; she knelt, crossed herself, and made a brief, earnest prayer. Dermod stared at the rope ends he had been splicing. The sailor with the radio-telephone watch silently and clumsily began to wipe his eyes. Ludtke fumbled for his cognac bottle and drank directly from it, showing not so much as a wince of reaction.

Reigel, his sou'wester in hand, reported on the progress of the hull repairs. The slash would be welded and the boat seaworthy very shortly, he said, but the captain gave no sign he heard.

"It's a grand piece of engineering your sailors have done, Captain Ludtke," Dermod Beg said tactfully.

Ludtke said nothing. His mind was concentrated on his latest loss. The chief quartermaster, he knew, had been an important factor in the success of the Shark Boat. He had been, Ludtke recognized, the main link between captain and crew, able to transmit an unpopular decision, explain its necessity, and enforce it. Ludtke took a gulp from his bottle. Old Pressure-Proof had been a veteran, seventeen years in destroyers and the U-Waffe. Haas had commissioned U-324 at Hamburg in 1940—

he and Ludtke were the only remaining plankowners—and in the nearly four years of their common service, the captain had come to rely on him more than on most watch officers.

Brede began to sob. Haas had been ashore barely two days, but his accordion and his cheerfulness had made him a favorite of the women who nursed the wounded. The captain, hunched over in his chair, stared at the fire. Once there was a rasp of static from the radio-telephone set and he glowered at it balefully, as though it were responsible for the doctor's failure to appear and the loss of the chief quartermaster. The wind whined outside the cottage and he listened, thinking of it as an enemy. The storm isolated Spanish Island from the outside world and from relief of any sort. It denied them the drugs and medical ability the Irish physician would bring and the equipment and tools Hoffman might produce. Ludtke helped himself again to the brandy and slumped back in the rocking chair.

After a bit, he roused himself and, with an effort, inquired about the weather. What was the barometer doing? When would the wind begin to slacken?

Reigel was not unoptimistic. "The glass is steadying now, sir. The wind is from the west nor'west, and working around to the south'ard. I think it'll blow itself out this evening—by morning at the latest."

"I'm thinking you're right, sir," Dermod volunteered. "This class of a blow usually lasts for only a day or so. It's the old winter having a farewell crack at us."

Ludtke gave them a lowering stare. "Very well, Number One. Get on with your duties. When the repairs are completed, we'll bury the chief quartermaster. That's all."

Reigel clapped on his sou'wester, saluted, and left. He was glad to get out of the cottage. Ludtke was not, at any time, an easy man to sail under. Today, with his senior noncommissioned officer dead and the weather still blocking any chance for help, it was dangerous to be under the same roof with him.

The noon meal aboard U-324 was a gloomy affair. Reigel ate with the crew in the stoker's mess—the after torpedo room. There was hot bean soup and baked potatoes in their blackened jackets—the Mor boy had brought two buckets of them down to the boat. There was freshly baked soda bread instead of the stone-hard Navy *Kommissbrot*. But there was a chill in the submarine and the sailors were depressed. They were young men, for the most part barely out of their teens. At least a third of them were on their first war patrol.

They had come, these sailors of the Shark Boat, from all over the Reich—from Silesia to the Ruhr. For a variety of reasons—extra pay, glory, escape from the Army and the Eastern Front—they had elected to serve in the Navy, the elite of the Wehrmacht, and eventually in the U-Waffe, the elite of the Navy. Life in the U-boats had not measured up to the stories of the recruiting petty officers and the broadcasts of Dr. Goebbels. They had found it a grim, monotonous routine of boredom, discomfort, nausea, and seemingly endless drills, occasionally broken by scalp-crawling terror.

There were compensations in the U-Waffe, of course. They had good food and the extra money. Lorient was a good home port, with a rest camp in the country and the Hotel Pigeon Blanc in town for more strenuous pleasure. They had a skipper with a reputation for taking care of his crew and a good officer in Lieutenant Hoffman. Above all, they had had Chief Quartermaster Haas. Although the war might be going against Germany, the morale of the ship's company had been high until that morning. Now, it seemed, the compensations were running out. They were helpless—and far from Lorient. The captain was badly wounded, Lieutenant Hoffman was gone and might not return, and the chief quartermaster was dead. The young sailors listened to the wind and rain topside and felt the creaking shudders of the hull. They shivered inwardly, ate little, and said even less.

For his part, Lieutenant Reigel ate a good meal. He had long since dismissed Haas from his thoughts. With the pressure hull nearly patched, he could again concentrate on bringing Shelagh Mor to bed. As he carefully deliberated his strategy, he ate three of Timmy Mor's potatoes. The potatoes were delicious after six weeks at sea. For the first two weeks of their patrol, the crew of U-324 had fresh potatoes, but they were usually boiled in seawater—to conserve the fresh—and generally disliked. Since then the potatoes had been canned, and everyone loathed them.

When he had finished, the first lieutenant went on deck and watched the repair party as it welded the last steel plates over the hole in the boat's side. Satisfied, he proceeded up the quay to the sick bay, bending against the force of the wind. He was surprised to find a great many people inside the little building. Most of the ship's company not at work or on watch were there and many of the Irish—Peigeen, Maeve and old Maura, Dermod, Padraig, and Sean. All of them, and the conscious wounded as well, were intently watching Petty Officer Muller and Brede prepare Old Pressure-Proof for his burial.

Peigeen and Maeve were moaning as Reigel entered, and that annoyed him. Maura sobbed as she handed Muller stones to weight the shroud. There was a clicking of rosary beads and crying, too. That irritated him more. Brede was carefully sewing the canvas over the dead man's chest; Reigel could see his face clearly in the light of the kerosene lamps—ivory-gray but perfectly composed. But it was the way he was ignored that infuriated the first lieutenant. He started to call the room to attention and then checked himself. It would do no good to stop this mawkishness. He slammed his way outside. As he left, unnoticed, Brede covered the face of the chief quartermaster and a deep, involuntary groan went up in the sick bay.

Reigel stamped back to the wardroom and angrily smoked a cigar. In less than twenty minutes, Chief Machinist's Mate Albrecht reported the hull was completely repaired. Reigel threw the cigar butt on the deck and ordered the crew fallen in for funeral parade. The sailors were slow in mustering on the quay, and when Reigel discovered the reason, he was irritated again. Without orders, every man had taken the time, as a mark of respect for Haas, to shift from sweater and coverall into dress blues. They stood in two ranks along the quay, the shroud on its stretcher before them, and the Irish clustered on their flank.

Muller called the ship's company to attention and reported all present or accounted for. Reigel grunted and sent two men to fetch Ludtke. He kept the crew at attention while they waited in the wind and rain. He noted U-324's red, white, and black ensign snapping at half-mast, although he had not ordered it, and he spat in disgust.

When the captain arrived on the jetty, he looked briefly surprised at the brass buttons and badges dully glinting, and the cap ribbons whipping in the wind. But he said nothing, took the prayer book from the first lieutenant, and nodded permission to begin the service. The ceremony was short, and, to Reigel, meaningless. In the wind and rain, the captain's reading of the service was largely unheard; the Mausers of the saluting detail cracked rather than crashed. Finally, Ludtke closed the book and Reigel ordered Muller to proceed with the burial. The corpse, with its bit of flag bright against the canvas, was reverently lowered into a curragh, and Muller and Albrecht clambered into the stern-sheets. Padraig and Dermod took the oars and rowed the curragh a few hundred yards into the cove. Reigel watched them stonily. He wanted to dismiss the formation, but he could not as long as Ludtke stood beside him. After a few minutes, the curragh came about, bobbing like a puffin, and, as the oarsmen struggled to hold her head into the wind, the two petty officers gingerly slid the shroud into the water. There was a little murmur from the Irish on the jetty.

"I want to look at the patch, Number One," Ludtke said sharply.

"Aye, aye, sir," Reigel said, and shouted to Kreisler to dismiss the ship's company. He followed the captain as Ludtke was carried toward the U-boat's fo'c'sle. As they went up the quay, they passed the cluster of Irish. Old Sean stood erect and bareheaded in the rain, his lips moving in prayer. The women were praying, too. Their heads were bowed and the black shawls covered them so their faces could not be seen, but their hands moved in crosses. Neither of the German officers paid any attention to them. Ludtke studied the patch for a few minutes and ordered his bearers to carry him back to the conning tower. Then, with some assistance from the two sailors, the captain made his way below and forward. Reigel followed. In the forward torpedo room, Ludtke again studied the repair work. He rubbed his hand along the weldments that fused the Winter Garden decking to the pressure hull. He borrowed Reigel's flashlight and meticulously inspected the welds below the deck gratings.

"Looks like a shipshape job, Number One," he said finally. "My compliments to your welders." He turned to the two seamen. "Now, boys, we'll go back to the Command Post."

Reigel followed them up to the bridge and down to the gangway. The captain stood there a moment, watching the rain beating on the quay. "By the way, Number One," he said, "when the chief comes back with the sulphuric acid, we'll need distilled water to mix with it."

"Yes, sir?"

"Rainwater is the purest water you can get, mister," the captain said with the faintest trace of a smile. "Have some well-scrubbed buckets set out on deck to catch it." He saluted the colors, hobbled off the boat, and the two sailors made a chair and carried him down the quay. Reigel gave the necessary orders about buckets and went down to the wardroom. He relaxed in his bunk and in a few minutes he was asleep.

The first lieutenant awoke at four, just as the bridge watch was changed. He felt refreshed by his nap. It had cleansed him somehow of the irritations that had nagged him in the morning and before Haas was buried. In place of the earlier peevishness, a single brutish instinct dominated Reigel. He was consumed with desire for Shelagh and determined to let nothing interfere with his satisfaction. He shaved and showered, using fresh water brought down from the well by the islanders. He patted cologne on his cheeks and approved his appearance in the mirror. He put on a clean shirt, his uniform and oilskins, and left the boat.

The wind had risen so that it was still close to gale force, and it was raining steadily. The Norseman's Tower at the top of the island was shrouded in clouds and mist. On the slope below it, no man or animal was abroad. Reigel looked in at the sick bay and went up the path, struggling in the face of the wind. He entered Maura Mor's cottage without knocking. The Widow, who had been kneeling by her hearth, scrambled to her feet, nervously brushing back a strand of her lank hair.

"Och, it's you, Lieutenant. Indeed, you gave me a fright. Come, give your heels to the fire."

Reigel took off his sou'wester. "Just making the rounds," he said. "Are you alone, Frau Mor?"

"I am that," she said. "I've been here since the burying. Come, sit down, Lieutenant. Let me give the sods a poke and get the kettle to boiling."

He sat down before the fire and Mrs. Mor adjusted the wrought-iron crane so as to lower the kettle. "Och, it was a sad thing, that poor lad passing," she said mournfully, "and him so cheery and all."

"A good man, Haas."

"He was the same class of boy as my Tomas," the Widow said. "Big and powerful, always laughing and joking." She paused, listening to the sound of the wind and the rattling of the shutters and windowpanes. "Mother of God, I hope my boy is safe ashore this evening."

After a bit, they had their tea, talking casually about the weather and the fierce storms Maura Mor had seen in her lifetime. Eventually, Reigel inquired of Shelagh.

"I've not seen the girl since the burial, Lieutenant. She'll likely be down with the poor sick sailors."

"She wasn't there a little while ago."

"Och, there's plenty of places poor Shelagh could be. A bit more tea, Lieutenant?"

Reigel declined and said he must carry on with his rounds. He put on his rain gear, thanked the Widow, and plodded up the hill. At the Og cottage, Peigeen was busy feeding her two children. In the next cabin, Padraig Mor was concentrated on the repair of a lobster pot. When Reigel inquired about the German sailors billeted with them, both Peigeen and Padraig said they were alone. It was obvious they were telling the truth. In the O Ŕuiarc kitchen, old Sean sat erect in his chair, playing checkers with Signalman Koenig. Another sailor, Able Seaman Kramer, was watching them. They made him welcome and Kathy O Ŕuiarc helped him off with his coat, her Gaelic unintelligible, but unmistakenly hospitable. "She's just after making a fresh cake of bread, Lieutenant," Sean said. "Come and have a sup with us."

Reigel refused, courteously enough, and chatted with the checker players. Although Sean could speak no German and the sailors no English, they were obviously enjoying the competition.

"The old man has got Flags three down, Mr. Reigel," reported

Kramer with a wide grin. "Flags thought he was pretty good before he met this old boy."

Sean put down his pipe with the metal-covered bowl, smiled at them, and asked about the weather.

"Barometer was rising when I left the boat," Reigel told him. "Hard to tell, but maybe we've seen the worst of it." A little later, he asked casually, "Has anyone else been around here lately?"

"No, sir," Koenig told him. "We've been here since the funeral—just the four of us."

Reigel watched the play for a bit and joined in Kramer's laughter when Sean made a double jump. Then he excused himself and went out into the rain and the howling wind. Fifty yards farther up the path, Lady Maud's cottage hugged the lee of the hill. It was the highest of all the homes on Spanish—and the biggest. From its doorstep, Reigel looked back over the tiny settlement and the cove. It was nearly dark and he could barely make out the sea. In the gray patches visible to him, the rain was a solid driving mass that hammered on the waves, flattening them and making them steam with spume and spray.

He opened Lady Maud's door and entered her kitchen. There were no locks on the doors of the island's cottages, and in the gale no one would have heard a knock. When he came in, Lady Maud's maidservant was busy at the fire. She was startled by the sight of the German officer, massive in his dripping oilskins.

"Come in, sir, come in," she stammered. Reigel took off his sou'wester and she recognized him. "Come, sir, let the fire take the wet out of your bones." She made him an anguished curtsy.

Reigel smiled and asked if anyone besides Kelly and her mistress were in the cottage. One poor lad, Kelly told him, one poor lad was asleep in the loft. Would the officer be wanting him, now? No, he said, still smiling, trying to put her at ease.

"Kelly, Kelly!" a tiny voice suddenly shrilled from the next room. "Who is it, Kelly? Who is our visitor?"

The maidservant scuttled away and Reigel removed his raincoat. He was glad to be in this big, warm kitchen, with its floor made of flagstones instead of mud, with its comfortable chairs and enormous dresser filled with china. At the same time, he was irritated at his failure to find Shelagh. He had checked every dwelling from the sick bay to the top of the path and had found no trace of her. He had not been long in any cottage, but somehow the girl had slipped by him. Probably, he thought sourly, she was back in Maura Mor's cottage by now.

Reigel warmed his backside before the fire, angry at his failure and

97

reluctant, for the moment, to take up the chase. As he stood there, he heard a scratch of voices and then the imperious command:

"Don't dawdle, Kelly, don't dawdle. Show the gentleman in, girl." He grinned, in spite of his black temper, and then Kelly was back in the kitchen, curtsying and saying that Her Ladyship would see the lieutenant.

Although Reigel had spent a night under her roof, he had never met Lady Maud. He had been late in arriving Thursday night, and he had left early Friday morning. Now he accepted Kelly's invitation and entered Lady Maud's bedroom.

It was a big room for Spanish, and what with the crackling fireplace, the chairs and bureau, and the huge fourposter bed, Reigel could not, for a split-second, find his hostess. Then he saw her, a tiny creature propped up by many pillows. Her face was as wrinkled and ruddy as a crabapple. She had glistening blue eyes and white hair gathered behind her in a severe knot.

"Good evening, Lieutenant," Lady Maud Wynne said in her high voice. "God be with you and welcome to this house."

Reigel made his way to the outstretched, fragile little hand and uttered the appropriate remarks. He was sorry not to have called before but there had been much work getting the U-boat ready for sea.

"I know, I know," she said. "Pray sit down, Lieutenant. I am delighted to have you come away up the boreen on such a shocking evening. Kelly, bring me the gin bottle and the bitters."

Reigel took a chair. "This is a nice cottage," he said politely. "The nicest on the island. Why, you even have flagstones on the deck."

She thanked him, pointing out that her floor was as uneven as the rest. "That's the way it is all along this coast. That's the reason for so many rockers and creepies—the three-cornered stools."

As is inevitable with strangers, they discussed the weather. Like Maura Mor, Lady Maud had seen many storms lash against the island. "Spanish is a lovely place to live, and I'd not want to leave it, but here death is never very far away," she said. "Every morning the men go out with the tide, but their wives can't be certain sure they'll sup with them that evening. I've lived on Spanish more than twenty years now, and I've seen a lot of good men lost in these sudden storms. They come up, Lieutenant"—she attempted to click her arthritic fingers—"like that."

"It's a bad coast for seamen," Reigel said. "The tides are big and the currents are tricky. We had the devil of a time making our landfall."

"It's a cruel coast, Lieutenant. There have been many wrecks in these waters. When I first came to the island, every cottage was filled with things salvaged from some poor ship—deck chairs, lanterns, kegs, cushions, things like that."

The old lady meticulously made two pink gins and they drank a toast to better weather. The drink warmed Reigel and he relaxed in his chair.

"Where is your home?" Lady Maud asked politely, and he told her Berlin. She had never been there, she said regretfully, adding that she and her husband had spent a month in Baden-Baden in the nineties. Reigel had barely heard of it, and like a good hostess, Lady Maud sought a more interesting subject.

"I'm a bit worried about my granddaughter, Lieutenant. Not that I'm not delighted to have her help the German Navy. When do you think they'll be back?"

Reigel assured her Hoffman and the girl would return directly after the gale was over. He explained the reason for the expedition—something the old lady had never quite understood.

"We need the acid to recharge our electric batteries," he explained. "The same sort of lead storage battery you have in an automobile."

Lady Maud told him she had once had an automobile, a Rolls. That was when she and her husband lived in Cork.

"Och, it was a lovely barouche—the glory of Cork it was." Lady Maud pronounced the city's name as though it were spelled with an *a*. "I'm a Corker, you know, Lieutenant."

Reigel looked blank and she mixed him another drink, giving some thought to her next question.

"The officer who went to the mainland—Lieutenant Hoffman—is he a good man?"

"Very capable, Lady Maud."

"Will he mind his manners with Nora?"

Reigel gave a disdainful laugh. "Ah, Peter Hoffman hasn't the sense to appreciate a good-looking girl."

"He's probably married."

"He was," said the lieutenant. "His wife was killed in an air raid last year."

The old lady looked distressed for a moment. "I'm glad he's capable. And I hope they find the acid. God willing, they'll be back directly this gale blows over."

She dwelt briefly on the dangers of the sea around Spanish, naming the men she had known who had drowned. Paddy O Ruiarc. Seamus Conor. Lorcan and Peadar Mor. Liam Beg and Donal Og.

Reigel was a little bored but the warmth of the fire and the gin were hard to resist.

"Of course," Lady Maud said, "the most famous shipwreck in the history of Spanish was a long time ago—back in fifteen eighty-eight."

Again, Reigel looked blank, and Lady Maud decided he was a rather ignorant young man.

"You know, the Armada, the fleet that gave the island its name."

"Oh, yes, the Spanish Armada."

"The galleon *San Lorenzo de Guadeloupe* was one of the biggest ships in the Armada, Lieutenant. She had near a thousand men aboard her. And her captain, Don Enrique Idiàquez, was one of King Philip's bravest sailors. She was trying to get home, but a storm drove her inshore and she struck a reef just a few hundred yards off the southern tip of the island."

Despite himself, Reigel was interested. "Here? What happened then?"

His hostess busied herself with the loading and lighting of an ancient clay pipe. Between preliminary puffs, she continued in her tiny voice. "A great many lives were lost, of course, but several hundred Spaniards reached the island safely. The islanders fed them and nursed them—they even helped them get a few of their guns ashore before the *San Lorenzo* broke up on the reef. But then, when the Irish Army on the mainland demanded the Spaniards surrender, Don Enrique betrayed the islanders. He declared the islanders were his hostages and if the Irish landed, he would burn them at the stake."

Lady Maud puffed at her pipe and shuddered deliciously. "Exactly how, I don't know, but the Irish did land on the island and surprised Don Enrique. No executions took place—except for the Spaniards. Most of them were killed."

"What about Don Enrique? What happened to him?"

"Och, they took him to the mainland and turned him over to the English. The English took him to Dingle and cut off his head."

Reigel accepted another pink gin and said something uncomplimentary about the English. His hostess heartily concurred. She told him of the Black-and-Tans, and he responded with more modern atrocities, stories of German sailors machine-gunned in their lifeboats and German prisoners slaughtered in the P.O.W. cages of Africa.

"The U-boats will carry on, though," he said, his voice hardening. "This is the only battle that counts, this Battle of the Atlantic. If we strangle the limeys here, there'll be no Second Front, no breakthrough from the east." His face was flushed and his words thickened. "Mark my words, Lady Maud, we U-boats can smash them. At the moment, they've got the upper hand with their aircraft and radar. But the snorkel is operational now, and in a few months there'll be more good news—there'll be a boat that can go twenty-five knots submerged. It's in the

Baltic now for trials. Just think of what that will mean." His voice rose with fierce excitement and he punched his right fist into the palm of his left hand—*thump, thump, thump.* "We'll make a shambles of the North Atlantic convoys."

"Och, that takes me back to the old days, Lieutenant, the old war," Lady Maud exclaimed. Her blue eyes were snapping. "Listen now, whilst I sing you a song of the old war." She leaned back on her pillows, and in her high, unmusical voice, recited these rhymes:

> But now at last, oh God, what joy
> For all who love the Irish green,
> To see the Union Jack go down
> Before a German submarine.
>
> Each Irish prayer's God speed the work,
> May every blow be swift and strong,
> And as each freighted monster sinks,
> We'll shout revenge for Ireland's wrong.

"*Sieg Heil,*" Reigel said loudly, thumping his near-empty tumbler on the arm of his chair. "*Sieg Heil. Wir fahren gegen England.*" He was conscious of a slight giddiness and was suddenly aware he had not found Shelagh and was wasting time. He stood up, knocking over his chair, and explained he was on duty and could not remain longer. Lady Maud gave him a sharp, quizzical look. He was welcome to stay to supper, she said, it was a terrible night. But the first lieutenant declined the invitation, got into his oilskins, and flung himself out into the dark, stormy night.

By God, he said to himself as he started down the path, that old granny is all right. She's on our side. Now, what I need is younger stuff.

When Saturday's first pale light filtered into the barn, Peter Hoffman awoke. It was not a gradual, drowsy awakening. One minute he was asleep, the next tense and listening. The rain still rattled on the roof and his companions were very still. A half dozen cows lay about them, grunting and wheezing in their sleep.

The lieutenant lay very quietly, thinking hard about his chances. He was roughly halfway between Tralee and Limerick, in a totally strange country. The truck was unreliable and so were the two islanders. The only certain thing was that Nora Berkeley wanted to send him to a concentration camp. Actually, all she needed to do was escape and find a policeman. Then the alarm would be telephoned to Dingle and the authorities would proceed to the island and intern the U-boat. He thought desperately of some way he could silence the girl. If there were some deserted cottage where he could lock her up for a few days—ah, that was absurd. His only chance lay in keeping a constant watch on her.

Hoffman unfastened the belt that tied his ankle to the girl's and roused her. In the early light, her face was pale and frightened.

"Good morning," he said quietly. "I'm sorry to have tied you up. Look, Nora, I have a job to do. The crew of the U-boat depends on me and I'm going to get the cable and the acid, if we have to go to Dublin for it."

He was impressed again by the size of her eyes, but he went ahead grimly. "You'd like to turn me in to the police. Very well. I'm not going to let you out of my sight until we're back on the island. I'm warning you, Nora. If you try anything, I'm going to shoot you."

Hoffman expected a violent reaction, tears, denials, or hot accusations, but Nora said nothing. The lieutenant was disgusted with himself and he roughly shook awake the two islandmen.

"*Raus,*" he said angrily. "Rise and shine, you two." My God, he thought, she is very lovely.

Eamon Og awoke sullenly, and Tomas Mor's usual high spirits were dampened by the mood of his companions. They washed at a pump outside the barn, cranked the Chevrolet into action, jammed into the cab, and started east. They stopped, after a bit, at a mean little public house for a breakfast of fish-and-chips. It was a vile meal, even for people who were ravenous, and Hoffman took advantage of it.

"Do you suppose this fish comes from Spanish, Tomas?" he asked, and when the islandman indignantly denied it, "Ah, Tomas, I was only joking. This must be Dover sole, shipped here by the English."

Soon he had Tomas chuckling, in spite of himself, and agreeing that the fish, which none of them could identify, should be called the Black-and-Tans' revenge. At that, Eamon permitted himself a grin. Och, thought Nora Berkeley, this bloody Nazi could charm the snakes out of the bogs.

After breakfast there was a little more talk in the crowded cab of the truck as it rattled through the rain. To their left, the Shannon was murky with fog; on the right, the fields were wet and gloomy. Hoffman asked questions about the countryside, compared it favorably with the Rhine Valley, and, when that failed, with the Loire. Nora maintained a stubborn silence. Occasionally, the lieutenant drew a reply from Tomas —more infrequently from Eamon—but it was obvious the two island-men knew as much of Limerick County as they did of Saskatchewan.

Precisely at two that afternoon, just as Chief Quartermaster Haas was buried, Peter Hoffman drove the little truck into Limerick City. It was raining hard. After a few blocks, Hoffman saw a telephone kiosk and stopped to consult the directory. He remembered the Tralee businessman had mentioned the firm of Coyle and Ryan. As he entered the kiosk, Nora spoke urgently to the two fishermen:

"Tomas, Eamon, we must warn the Guards. Can you help me get away from this man?"

"Och, we can't do that, Nora," Tomas said. "We're here to help the lieutenant."

"Sean pledged us to say naught for six tides," Eamon said slowly.

"Sean didn't speak for me," the girl said. The two islanders looked uncomfortable as Hoffman came out of the kiosk and climbed into the cab.

"Twenty-six Henry Street, Nora," he said briskly. "Know it?"

The girl nodded and the truck rattled toward the center of the city. The rain beat down and the streets were almost empty. Hoffman's confidence returned.

The heavy rain made for hazardous driving, but it also meant few persons would be about, particularly on a Saturday afternoon in the warehouse section of the city. Hoffman began to whistle, and after a few seconds the girl gave him a mildly incredulous look.

"What's that tune, Lieutenant?"

"Why, it's Beethoven," he said. "From the *Eroica*. Do you know it?"

"Yes," she said in a small voice.

As though he'd read her thoughts, he laughed.

"I know. You thought my repertoire was confined to the *Horst Wessel*. Right?"

He looked at her briefly, his whole face alive with merriment, and Nora blushed.

"Turn left at the next corner," she said severely. "Now right. Now you're in Henry Street. Keep straight on until we've passed the Sarsfield Bridge."

It was, she reflected, not really surprising that he knew Beethoven. Despite his appearance, the lieutenant was obviously a gentleman. Everything had gone wrong for him since they landed, but he could still laugh. He had never lost his temper, or his determination. She decided she admired Peter Hoffman and bore him no ill will. If she could only get away from him long enough to alert the police—

The clock at the intersection of Henry Street and the Sarsfield Road read a quarter past two. A few minutes later they were at Coyle and Ryan, Ltd., a huge brick building dripping with rain. Hoffman drove past it slowly, and, after some reconnaissance, parked the truck in the alley at the rear. Coyle and Ryan was guarded there by a brick wall with a big wooden gate, wide enough for the Chevrolet to enter. Across the alley from the gate was a paved parking area that backed up to a warehouse of the Limerick Gas Service. The area was empty except for several long lengths of pipe.

Coyle and Ryan's gate was closed, but when Hoffman rattled it, it seemed to be bolted within, rather than locked. He drove close to the wall and Tomas clambered to the top of the cab and scaled the brickwork. A moment later the gate swung open and Hoffman drove the truck into a little courtyard.

After that, it was easy. A window broken, a door unlocked, and they were inside the warehouse. There was a tremendous variety of gear, neatly stacked and segregated in drawers and shelves and bins. In a little less than an hour, Hoffman had what he wanted—the cable, heavy, lead-lined vessels of acid, and tools and fuses for good measure. He gave directions and Tomas and Eamon brought them out onto the dock and into the truck. He carefully wrote out a receipt and placed it on a prominent packing case. Then they carefully lashed the acid bottles in place, covered the gear, and resumed their positions and drove away. Hoffman was exultant.

"Nothing to it. A piece of cake, Nora."

"You're a ruddy long way from Ballykerry, Lieutenant," the girl said darkly. "A hundred miles at least."

Hoffman laughed. "Nora, my dear, I think we're going to make it."

"I'm not your dear," said Nora, with every icicle she could muster. But Hoffman only whistled as they drove through the wet, deserted streets of the city and into the countryside.

The lieutenant decided against retracing the route he had used that morning. He took the more southerly road, away from the Shannon, and late in the afternoon, the Chevrolet entered Adare.

Adare is a very old village. It includes the graciously decaying ruins of a twelfth-century castle and an even more ancient abbey, tall and venerable oaks and elms, and a main street of thatched, half-timbered cottages. Even in the rain, Adare was delightful and Hoffman was enthusiastic about it.

"Ah, this is lovely," he smiled at Nora. "I'd like to come back here after the war."

"They say Adare is one of the prettiest towns in all Ireland," the girl answered.

Hoffman stiffened. Some two hundred yards ahead a caped figure came into the center of the road and signaled the truck to halt. Hoffman applied the brakes, fumbling for his pistol as he recognized the uniform of the *Guarda Siochana*. He had barely enough time to warn the others to say nothing before the big policeman came to the door of the truck.

"Good evening," the Guard said, smiling. "Are you from Limerick, now?"

"Yes, sir," Hoffman smiled back.

"Would you be knowing the score of today's hurling match?" asked the Guard. "At the Oval?"

"No, sir. Afraid not." Concerned with his accent, the lieutenant clipped his replies.

"Limerick City versus Waterford, it was," said the Guard in an almost wheedling voice. He bent down the better to study Nora's profile.

"Afraid not, sir," Hoffman repeated and Nora shook her head.

The policeman sighed gustily. "On you go, then," he said with a wave of his arm. "Good evening to you."

Hoffman slowly drove down the main street, trembling with relief. He no longer whistled or appreciated the damp tranquility of Adare. Soon, it occurred to him, a beat policeman would discover the unbolted gate and the smashed window at Coyle and Ryan's. The alarm would go out to the surrounding area and the burglary might be linked to the strange truck in Adare. That meant warnings would be telephoned ahead and roadblocks set up. He drove cautiously, bypassing Rathkeale and Newcastle West. This took time. Once, north of Ballymurragh, they were lost for nearly an hour. South of Newcastle West, the country is wild and mountainous, but Hoffman was determined to detour around every village he could.

His passengers said little. Nora was stonily silent, berating herself for her failure to cry out to the policeman. Tomas and Eamon were glum, uncertain where they were, desperately hoping that when they topped the next hill, they would see the ocean.

Close to nine, in the day's last murky light, the Chevrolet was mired in a muddy cowpath north of Abbeyfeale. Hoffman and the two islandmen got out to push. Ankle-deep in the ooze and soaked by the rain, it took them several minutes to rock the truck free. Alone in the cab, Nora discovered the lieutenant had made a mistake: In his irritation, Hoffman had left the key in the ignition lock. It was a nasty thing to do, she told herself, but she didn't hesitate. As the truck finally rolled free, she turned the key and pushed the starter pedal. The engine caught, fluttered, and died. She tried it again—with the same result. In her desperation, the girl had flooded the carburetor and stalled the engine.

She felt sick and unhappy as Hoffman pulled open the left-hand door and got in beside her. In the dim light, she could see he was glistening with mud and rain, so tired his hands were shaking. She expected to be rated and cursed, perhaps even slapped. For a few seconds, the lieutenant sat still. Then, when Tomas and Eamon were seated and the door closed, he spoke.

"Very well, Nora. You want to drive. *You* do the driving and I'll navigate."

She was prepared for anything but mild sarcasm, and she rebelled furiously. "I'm not going to drive, I'm not going to help you," she snapped. "I'm not going to send that submarine back to the war."

"For God's sake," Hoffman flashed, "you offered to help us——"

"You're crackers. The captain forced me to come."

"How could he force you?"

"Simple enough," Nora said bitterly. "Captain Ludtke said if I didn't guide you, it would take a week to get the spare parts from France. He said the sailors would get to drinking and would make trouble. With the women of the island."

There was a moment of sudden, shocked silence. Then Eamon and Tomas, greatly concerned, began to ask questions. The engineer lieutenant tried to dispel their fears.

"There's nothing to it. I know those sailors. Anyway, all the time we've been away, Captain Ludtke will have worked them too hard to think about drinking, or anything else."

He got behind the wheel and coaxed the engine into starting. "There's nothing to worry about," he said heartily. "You'll be home soon." In the faint glow of the dashboard, his face looked old and bleak, and despite herself Nora felt a twinge of sympathy for him.

It was an infinitely long trip across the mountains and down the Dingle Peninsula to Ballykerry. As the truck rumbled eastward into the unending tunnel of rain, there was little talk. They were wet, cold, and uncomfortable, hungry, tired, and depressed. Once Nora offered to take the wheel but the lieutenant curtly declined. A few miles later, he broke the silence.

"Nora?"

"Yes?"

"That was a rotten thing for the captain to do. I'm sorry."

The girl said nothing and they jolted westward. To their right they could hear the booming of the surf. Hoffman fretted at the reluctance of the weather to improve. He had hoped to leave for Spanish as soon as they reached Ballykerry, but he knew the wind and rain would prevent it. He asked the islandmen if they could borrow another curragh tomorrow to transport the gear. Gloomy with worry about his wife, Eamon Og refused to discuss the matter, but Tomas replied shortly that Mick would loan his curragh. Tomas was dubious about the weather, even on the next day, and the weight of the cargo. The ten-gallon acid bottles, he grunted, were very heavy.

Hoffman shrugged his shoulders irritably. "The gale is blowing itself out, Tomas. We'll spend the night at Mick's. Tomorrow we'll see."

It was past two in the morning when they reached Ballykerry. Eamon roused Mick and told him some sort of yarn to explain the delay in returning the lorry and the reappearance of his friend and the girl. Mick bade them welcome and asked no questions. He gave them supper of bread, cheese, and a bottle of stout apiece and bedded them down with blankets in his little barn. Nora had made herself as comfortable as she could, when the lieutenant said, "Your foot, please." At first, she was too numb with fatigue to understand him.

"Stick out your foot, please. For the belt," Hoffman said patiently, and this time, with some muffled bad language, she obeyed. She felt the belt tighten around her ankle and she was also aware of Hoffman retucking the blanket around her foot. He didn't have to tuck my foot in, she thought. Despite her exhaustion, Nora decided he was a very thoughtful person. Probably rather decent, she told herself, before the Nazis and the Navy got him. She snuggled into the hay, and, with the drum-rattle of the rain in her ears, was almost instantly asleep.

When he left Lady Maud's, Reigel was extremely unsteady. It was raining and blowing hard, the rocky path was ink-black and he was glad of his flashlight. By now, Shelagh might be in any one of the cottages he had so carefully checked before. He swore with blurred annoyance. His best plan, he decided, was to return to the Widow Mor's and wait for his luck to change. Perhaps he'd have to drug the old battleship again.

The first lieutenant was almost to his destination when he heard a tiny shout. He waited, probing with the flashlight, until Timmy Mor came panting up the path to him. In the glare of the flashlight, his eyes were big and blinking and his face glistened with rain.

"What do you want?" Reigel asked roughly.

"I was just coming after my da'," Timmy shouted above the wind. "When I saw the torch, I thought you might be himself." He pointed to the south. "We've a sheep with a broken leg down there. We need my da' to carry her to my gran's cottage."

"Who is 'we'?"

"My Auntie Sheel has been down in the old Conor cottage for two or three hours, trying to make the sheep warm. When she didn't come back for supper, my gran sent me looking for her."

"Your Aunt Shelagh?" Reigel exclaimed with sudden elation.

"Yes, sir. Now, I'll be getting after my da'."

"Wait!" Reigel shouted. Excitement welled up in him. "No need to bother your dad. I'll go and carry the sheep back."

"Och, now, you wouldn't be wanting to do that, sir," Timmy Mor said. "The wind and rain are terrible bad."

He would be glad to do it, Reigel said firmly. He explained he was wet already, and he wanted to do a favor for Mrs. Mor.

"I'll show you the way, sir——"

"No, I'll find it," Reigel said sharply. "Just tell me how to go."

The boy protested. "You'd never find them, sir. The Conor cottage is dead hard to find——"

"Take me there!" Reigel shouted, and seeing the sudden fright on Timmy's face, he added, "As soon as the storm's over, we'll go rabbit hunting."

The boy hesitated for a moment. He was a little afraid of the big German officer, but everyone on the island, except Nora, liked the submarine sailors. And the idea of hunting rabbits with a real pistol was irresistible.

"I'll take you," he said, and, with the lieutenant close behind, he clattered down the path. Below Maura Mor's, he struck off to the south, threading his way between stones and boulders. It was hard going for Reigel. The shrieking fury of the gale walloped and buffeted him, deafened him and tore at his oilskins. The footing was unsure and the bursts of wind, catching him off stride, staggered him and came close to knocking him down. But his flashlight helped and after a few hundred yards, young Timmy cried, "We're here, sir. Just ahead now."

"Wait!" Reigel shouted above the wind. His flashlight caught a bit of ruined building ahead, almost indistinguishable from the boulders that covered the slope.

Timmy Mor came back a few steps. In the light of Reigel's torch, his face was perplexed. "It's just ahead, sir," he said again.

The first lieutenant snapped off his flashlight and stared ahead. Directly ahead there was a faint glow and his heart leaped up. By God, he told himself, you've found her. Then he remembered Timmy and the boy's interest in his pistol.

"Listen to me, Timmy," he commanded, squatting and drawing the boy close to him. "I want to surprise your auntie. Just for a joke, understand? Now, I want you to go back and say you couldn't find her. Understand? Also, don't tell anyone you saw me. If you do that, Timmy,

I'll give you my pistol when we leave Spanish Island. Is that a bargain?"

He pulled out the Walther seven-millimeter automatic and displayed it under the flashlight. Timmy's eyes were enormous. As though he couldn't believe them, he leaned forward and gingerly touched the barrel.

"A bargain? Och, of course, sir."

"Very well," Reigel said, "repeat your instructions."

"I'm to go home and say I couldn't find Auntie——"

"Tell them you hunted everywhere."

"Aye, I'll do that."

"And what else?"

"I'm not to say I saw you, sir."

"That is good, Timmy," the lieutenant said, "our bargain must be a secret one. Here——" he fumbled out a clip of ammunition from his pistol belt and gave it to the boy—"here are bullets for the gun—on account. Now, shake hands to seal the bargain."

They shook hands solemnly. Finally, full of excitement, Timmy scampered back toward the settlement and Reigel started for the Conor cottage. He felt like shouting with exuberance. By God, he said to himself, this is what I've been waiting for.

The German was grinning as he covered the last few yards. He paid no attention to the blast of wind and rain. Ahead of him, guiding him, the light was increasingly distinct. He made his way deliberately. It's taken a long time, he told himself, but now you've got the bloody woman.

The Conor cottage, Reigel discovered, consisted of a couple of crumbling walls, at right angles. The roof had long since disappeared, but close to the angle of the walls, and butted against the slope, there was a huge fireplace, a hearth ten feet wide and easily six or eight feet deep. It was, in fact, a small room, covered overhead by the chimney and shielded on all sides except to seaward. Because of the hill's sharp decline, Reigel found, one had to be well inside the old building before one could see into the fireplace. There was a small turf fire there, and he felt his way toward it, his noises muffled by the wind and rain. Eventually, he was close enough to see clearly into the chimney place. A dirty, bedraggled sheep, splotched with bluish dye for easy identification, lay beside the turf fire, and on her knees, Shelagh Mor stroked it and crooned a little song. The first lieutenant entered the chimney place and took off his sou'wester. Abruptly, the sheep bleated and Shelagh, twisting about, gave a little scream.

"Hello," Reigel said, still grinning broadly. "Sorry to scare——"

"Glory to God," Shelagh cried out. She scrambled to her feet, her hand to her mouth and the red hair in gorgeous disarray. "What—what, in the name of all the Holy Saints?"

"Don't be frightened, Shelagh. Timmy sent me," Reigel said swiftly. She stared at him, her hand trembling at her mouth, and he repeated his words, adding, "I'm to help you get the sheep home."

The brute was still whimpering and trying to rise. Reigel glanced down and saw its hind leg was splinted between two bricks of turf, tightly lashed with a piece of cotton.

"Ah, you've set the leg," he said approvingly. "That is good, Shelagh." Taking off his oilskins, he sat by the sheep, carefully examined the splint, and patted the patient. "You're a good surgeon." He grinned up at the girl.

She smiled shyly. "I'm glad the splint looks good. I had to use the turfs—there were no sticks around—and a scrap of my shift to bind them." She blushed—the reference to the binding was obviously inadvertent.

Reigel, still smiling, remained on the floor. It was a basic gambit with him. Standing, one never got anywhere with a woman. He drew Shelagh out, got her talking about the sheep, and, predictably, she was presently on the hearthstones beside him. It was almost immediately obvious she possessed a love and understanding of animals that surpassed that of most human beings. Talking about Mary, the sheep, she was far more coherent than before.

Late in the afternoon, Reigel gathered, Dick, the Widow's sheep dog, had let Shelagh know something was wrong. Dick had led her to where the crippled Mary lay, and with difficulty she had brought the animal to the Conor cottage. There was turf stored there, but she had no matches with which to start a fire. She wrapped Mary in her shawl and lay beside her, giving her warmth and comfort. Later, she heard Timmy shouting above the wind. Dick had fetched *him* to the ruin. Timmy had matches and had built a fire for them, using a scrap of her shift for kindling. Then, in the light of the fire, she had splinted the broken leg, and Timmy had gone for help.

"Och, the poor darling is all right now," Shelagh cried happily. "We'll soon have her down to the cottage. We'll give her some broth and she can sleep with me. By shearing time, she'll be lively as a pig."

She gathered herself to rise. She was disheveled, soot-stained, and half-witted, but she was close to him and her body was superb. The compassion she had shown for the animal probably meant she would be tender in her lovemaking. Reigel took her arm and said urgently, "Shelagh, don't get up."

"Wisha, we can't be spending the whole night here," she said. She was smiling in her vacant, loose-lipped way, until she suddenly sensed the implication of his request. Terror clouded her eyes and she rose quickly. "For the love of God," she said shrilly, "we must be going."

"Ah, no, Shelagh. Padraig and Timmy will be here soon," Reigel said smoothly. "Make yourself comfortable."

"They're coming here?" Shelagh was dubious.

"Of course. If we don't wait for them, we'll miss them in the dark."

The girl saw the wisdom in that, but for a while she remained standing, hugging the shawl around her. Reigel lit a cigarette, stroked the wretched Mary, and made small talk about the weather. Then he began to ask questions about the sheep and other animals of Spanish. Hesitantly, she answered. She told him about Peadar, the ass, and bearded Brian Boru, the oldest ram on the island. She spoke of a pet rabbit she had had as a girl, and of the new lambs. As she talked, Shelagh became more relaxed and animated. Presently, she was again sitting beside the lieutenant.

Reigel kept her talking. Occasionally he reached out and stroked the sheep, as if to demonstrate his fondness for dumb creatures. He was careful to keep the conversation on the animals of Spanish.

"Tell me, Shelagh," he said presently, "have you ever seen the sheep mating?"

The girl gave a hesitant giggle. When he pressed her, she nodded.

"Tell me about it, Shelagh," he elaborated, smiling. If he could get her describing the sexual act of the sheep, she might become excited and more responsive when he reached for her.

Shelagh giggled again and averted her eyes. She said nothing. Reigel talked smoothly of bulls and stallions, watching closely for any reaction. His arms ached with desire, but in a few minutes it was obvious his strategy had failed.

The first lieutenant paused and the smile faded from his face. Something in his eyes warned Shelagh and again she gathered herself to rise. Reigel reached out and caught her by the elbow and pulled her back into his lap. The girl cried out in alarm and tried to regain her feet, but the German locked her in his arms.

"Ah, Sheel, don't be upset," he said. "Give us a little kiss, eh?"

He pressed his lips down on hers, but she tore her head away and began to scream and struggle. The sheep bleated with shrill terror and thrashed about, but Reigel hardly heard the animal. The blood throbbed in his veins. His arms were locked about Shelagh, and as they struggled her bodice was partially torn off. Her shrieks were redoubled at that, and Reigel, in a sudden spasm of fury, slapped her violently. That did not quiet her. He struck her repeatedly until the screaming stopped and Shelagh's entire form was racked with uncontrollable sobs. Sometimes, Reigel said to himself fiercely, a little beating makes a woman more affectionate.

"Come on, *Liebchen*," he panted. "Let me give you a little loving."

The girl continued to sob and shake. Her face, close to his, was bleeding and contorted with fear and shock. She no longer had the power to resist when Reigel's clawing fingers attacked her clothing.

SUNDAY

Ludtke was awakened by a swarm of angry voices in the kitchen. Bothered by his leg, the captain had slept fitfully, and he felt feverish and unwell. Yet he was alert as he listened to the crackle of fury on the other side of the bedroom door. He sat up in bed and looked at his wristwatch. It was a few minutes before eight.

The door opened and the radio-telephone watchstander pushed his head into the bedroom.

"Beg pardon, Captain," he said nervously, "the Irish want a word with you, sir. They won't wait."

Sean O Ŕuiarc pushed his way past the sailor and entered the bedroom. The old islandman's lips were tightly compressed and his face was black with fury. Behind him was the Widow Mor, her face very pale in the frame of her black shawl. After her came the Begs, both greatly agitated. Sitting up in bed, Ludtke glowered at his visitors and rubbed his unshaven chin.

"Well, O Ŕuiarc," he said truculently, "what do you mean, barging in here?"

"It's rape, Captain, rape." Old Sean's voice shook as he spoke. "Your lieutenant has debauched Shelagh Mor. He beat her, he struck her, and she has the marks to prove it. Then he forced himself on her and had sexual knowledge of her——"

"Nonsense!" Ludtke blazed.

"Before God, Captain, it's the truth. It happened last night. He found her in Seamus Conor's old cabin, where she was nursing a hurtened sheep. Poor Shelagh, and she mixed up in the head."

Brede choked and began to sob.

"That's just it, O Ŕuiarc," the captain snarled. "The girl's a lunatic —she doesn't know what she's saying."

"Shelagh is not a lunatic," Mrs. Mor burst out furiously. "She's a good girl, as anyone on Spanish will swear you. She was gone all last evening—from about five o'clock. My grandson hunted for her and then my son. We were up half the night looking for her. Then, a little bit ago, Timmy told us she was in the Conor cottage and that he had told Lieutenant Reigel she was there. When we found her, she was half crazy with shame and fear. She was shaking like she had the fever. She couldn't talk, she was crying and sobbing so. Her face is all cut and bruised where he hit her. Her clothes were torn and half ripped off her."

The Widow paused and there was no sound in the little room but the strangled sobbing of Brede. Mrs. Mor's eyes burned accusingly at Ludtke.

"Aye, Captain, it's the truth she's not said the lieutenant did it. God help her, she's not able to talk sense. But we know he did, as well as there's a God in Holy Heaven. He knew where Shelagh was, and he went after her. I've seen him look at Shelagh before——"

Instinctively, Ludtke knew she was right. Where women were concerned, Reigel was a fool.

"This man has sinned, Captain," Sean said in a trembling voice. "He has committed a great sin."

"What do you want me to do?" Ludtke flared.

"He should be punished, Captain, but that can wait. It's important now to take Shelagh to the mainland where the priest and Doctor Fitz can see her and take care of her. She needs them, Captain Ludtke."

Ludtke made a rude derisive noise. The girl would be all right, he told them, after she had slept for a while. He would tell Barndt to give her a sleeping pill. Later, he would have the ship's company paraded and Shelagh could make a formal accusation. As for taking her to the mainland, that was out of the question.

"The doctor will be here tomorrow, O Ruiarc," he said with grim finality. "And no one leaves Spanish until I do—on the bridge of my submarine."

There was another pause. The Widow said harshly: "May the curse of Christ and Mary be on you, Captain, and on your submarine." She gathered her shawl about her head, turned, and marched from the room.

Ludtke watched her go. When he turned back to Sean, the old man's eyes were unwavering and as hard as sapphires.

"We've tried to help you, Captain, but you've pushed us too far," Sean said bitterly. "We've tended your wounded boys, helped with your burials, tried to get our doctor for you. Our lads have rowed Lieutenant Hoffman to the mainland—we even gave him Irish pounds to aid him. And what's the return of it? Lieutenant Reigel has cruelly raped poor Shelagh, and now you deny her a chance for spiritual comfort——"

Ludtke started to speak, but the old man wouldn't allow him.

"I gave you my word, Captain, we wouldn't betray you. The six tides are up this morning, and the contract is canceled."

He turned on his heel and left the bedroom. Looking frightened, the Begs followed him. The captain watched them go, and produced a rolling volley of obscenities. His anger encompassed the half-witted girl, her vengeful mother, the storm, the cowardly Irish doctor, and U-324's electric motors, but it was mainly directed at his first officer. Reigel was an imbecile. His lust had turned the people of Spanish against the submariners—just at the point where they desperately needed help. If the girl's attacker had been a stoker or a deckhand, Ludtke would have tried and executed him within the hour, but the captain could not shoot the

114

only officer left on the island. He would need him when they left for Lorient; more immediately, he would need him tomorrow, when the steamer from the mainland appeared.

The captain struggled out of bed and pulled on his shoes, trousers, and uniform blouse. Painfully, he crutched himself into the kitchen and drank two cups of tea, laced with cognac. He poured himself a third and dispatched the watchstander to bring Reigel to the cottage. When the man had gone, Ludtke crossed the room, very slowly, opened the upper half of the door, and studied what he could see of Spanish Island, the sea, and the sky.

The wind still blew vindictively, but the rain had almost stopped. The racing, ragged clouds were still low and dark. Outside the cove, the sea was gray and angry, and above the wind, Ludtke could hear the surf booming like cannon. The gale was blowing itself out, he told himself, but he doubted any curragh could live for long in the mountainous waves. At any rate, no curragh was going to try.

Leaning on the bottom half of the door, he inspected his boat through the Zeiss binoculars. U-324 was riding easily beside the quay, well-secured by her tripled-up spring wires. Except for the watchstander huddled on her bridge, there was no one on the topside. Ludtke watched his messenger go aboard and disappear into the conning tower. Then the captain hobbled back to his chair before the fire. He was slumped in it, staring at the flames, when Lieutenant Reigel, looking spruce and fit, came into the kitchen and saluted.

"Good morning, sir. You sent for me?"

Ludtke ignored the greeting. "The day we came on the beach here, mister, I gave explicit orders there was to be no sniffing around the Irish women. Yet the first chance you get, you violate the half-witted redhead. Are you half-witted too?" He spoke in German and the watchstander who had followed Reigel into the cottage pricked up his ears. Ah, this is what the argument in the bedroom had been about.

The first lieutenant grinned. "Begging the captain's pardon, you're mistaken, sir. I never touched the girl."

The captain dismissed this with an ugly monosyllable. "Don't play the innocent with me, mister," he grated. "I want a straight answer or I'll have your guts for a necktie."

Reigel was not intimidated. With a half-smile still on his lips, he said smoothly, "If the girl was violated, Captain, it must have been someone else. One of the islanders, perhaps, or one of the crew. There are a lot of starved sailors in the Shark Boat." His tone was casual, almost insolent.

"By Christ, mister," Ludtke choked, "if we were in Lorient, you'd be court-martialed and sent to a penal battalion on the Ostfront."

"But we're on Spanish Island, Captain, and you need me——"

The kitchen door was flung open and a handful of islanders crowded into the room. Padraig Mor led them in. Behind him was his wife and mother, Sean O Ŕuiarc, and the Begs.

"What do you want?" Ludtke roared. "Get out of this house!" He swiveled to the watchstander. "Throw these peasants out, damn you!"

Before the sailor could obey, Padraig Mor was speaking. His voice was shrill and agitated. "We want to hear what the lieutenant has to say. Here and now, in the presence of God Almighty, we accuse him of attacking and violating my sister."

It was a long speech for Padraig and its end was almost drowned in the clamor of angry voices. The sight of Reigel seemed to infuriate the islanders and they crowded in on him. Ludtke could not see how it began, but there was a sudden flurry of blows. Reigel stepped back so there was a little space between him and Padraig. Both men had their fists knotted. Then the first lieutenant, younger, five inches taller, and fifty pounds heavier than Padraig, crouched and began to weave like Max Schmeling. He feinted expertly, brushed aside his opponent's punch, and smashed Padraig in the solar plexus and then, with both fists, in the face. It was a brutal combination of blows, and the unequal clash was over almost as suddenly as it had begun. Padraig went down in a heap. He tried unsuccessfully to regain his feet and collapsed. His wife, Maeve, knelt beside him and assisted him to a sitting position. Padraig began to retch. He shook his head drunkenly, flexing his jaw and breathing hard. After a moment, he spit a bloody tooth out on the hard clay floor.

"Jesus, Paddy, are you all right?" asked Maeve. Looking up at Reigel, she snarled, "Och, you bloody murdering lecher."

The Widow Mor walked up to the lieutenant and began to curse him, both in English and Irish. When she was spitting and close to raving, Brede pulled her away and Dermod and Sean pulled Padraig to his feet. They helped him out of the cottage and the women followed, Brede weeping and the Mors alternately muttering prayers and shrieking strange imprecations over their shoulders.

The first lieutenant watched them go, massaging his knuckles and still smiling insolently. He accepted the admiring remarks of the sailor and lit a cigarette. "Well, Captain," he said, exhaling a plume of blue smoke, "that's my answer to the rustics."

Ludtke glowered at him. "You son-of-a-bitch," he said. "I can't con-

fine you to quarters. As you said, I need you. But you'll be well advised
to stay near the boat, mister. The islanders won't forget this."

It was close to ten o'clock when Reigel went jauntily down the path
to the jetty. He went straight to his bunk, and, completely free of re-
grets or remorse, enjoyed a long and refreshing nap. The islanders, on
the other hand, were deeply troubled as the morning went by and the
long afternoon wore on. There were long prayers and desperate, im-
practical plans for vengeance. Ludtke, sitting beside the fire, was troubled, too, and as the stories spread through the crew, most of the ratings
were gravely concerned. A few of the younger sailors, of course, relished
the gossip; they were pleased to hear this new evidence of Lieutenant
Reigel's prowess in lovemaking and fisticuffs. This was because they
were bored. After three days of hard work, there was nothing to do.
They would have liked to go swimming or get up a game of football,
even though the weather was poor. But the captain's orders were explicit enough: only men on duty would be allowed ashore; ratings would
no longer be billeted in the cottages.

Gradually, then, as the long day dragged on, the sailors of U-324
came to realize the proportions of the rift between the islanders and
themselves. They became aware of it at noon when the seaman coming
off lookout duty at the tower said the natives would not speak to him;
and when Barndt reported there were no more nurses at the sick bay.
It seemed incredible. Since Thursday morning, the Irish had helped in
every sort of task. They had given up their beds, shared their food, and
reverently assisted with the burials. Now the split was there, deep and
widening. The youngest deckhand could see it hurt the chances of a
safe return to Lorient.

While there was boredom and dull depression in the chilly mess compartments of the U-boat, the prayers and bitter talk continued in the
cottages of the island. During the morning, each of the islanders, except
Lady Maud, visited, in turn, Padraig and his mother. Padraig was
stretched out in bed, half-conscious, zealously attended by his wife. She
put hot cloths impregnated with baking soda and salt over his smashed,
pulpy-looking nose and bruised, discolored lips and cheek. The soda
would reduce the swelling and the salt would heal the wounds. As she
applied the cloths, Padraig would groan piteously, and she feared the
cheekbone was broken. When Barndt came in, instructed by Ludtke to
provide a sedative, Maeve angrily ordered him out of the house.

"Och, the bloody nerve of them," she exclaimed bitterly to Peigeen and Kathy O Ŕuiarc who were in the kitchen. "They beat a man half to death and then try to make up to him with pills and powders."

Barndt had no better luck at the Widow Mor's. When he entered, the Widow was kneeling in front of her candle of perpetual adoration, intoning a Hail Mary. Behind her knelt the Begs and old Sean.

"Holy Mary, Mother of God, pray for us sinners now and at the hour of our death. Amen."

She crossed herself and turned toward the door, angry at the interruption. Barndt stammered his apologies and the purpose of his visit. They could not understand his words but his gesture with the black medical bag was clear.

"He's come to give us a sleeping powder for poor Sheleen," Dermod said. The Widow's deep-set eyes burned at Barndt and she spoke briefly and violently in Irish. The sick berth attendant looked frightened and turned to Sean O Ŕuiarc.

"No, no," Sean said to Barndt, pushing his palms toward the German and the kitchen door. "We don't want any of your medicines. We want you to leave." Barndt went out and the Widow resumed her prayers. After she had finished, Sean said, "The infernal cheek, sending around medicines when the poor girl needs a priest."

"Aye," Dermod Beg said, and turning to Mrs. Mor, "has she taken any food this day?"

"Not a bite, not a drop of tea," the Widow said heavily. Her eyes were dull. For a minute she sat lumpish by the fire, and then she seemed to gather her thoughts. "All she does now is lie in there and cry. You'd think there was not another tear left in her eyes."

Brede made mournful clucking noises, and Sean said again, "The poor girl needs a priest. Father Healy could give her the comfort she's needing."

Dermod reminded them that twice during the winter just passed, when storms had prevented their attending Mass, Father Healy had come the next day by the steamer. Even Mrs. Mor brightened a little at that.

"And Doctor Fitz will be here tomorrow," Dermod added. "He can look after both Sheleen and Paddy."

They were startled by a knock on the door, but it was only old Kathy O Ŕuiarc and Kelly.

"God bless all in this house," Kelly said. Her face looked crushed by the awful news. "How is the poor thing?"

The newcomers were blessed in turn, made welcome, and told there was no change. Kathy and Kelly busied themselves with prayers before the candle. The Begs excused themselves, saying they would see if anything could be done for Maeve. Sean sat on his corner creepie, staring at his hands and occasionally cracking his knuckles in impotence. They were good fisherman's hands, he thought, even if they were over seventy-five years old. Calloused and competent hands, able to steady a boat in a heavy seaway, mend a stone wall or a lobster pot, but powerless against rifles and machine pistols. There were now only two able-bodied men on the island. What could he and foolish Dermod Beg do against two dozen armed and disciplined German sailors?

Sean O Ŕuiarc had considered himself responsible for the island since his father died at sea, thirty years before. It was Sean who argued successfully with the Dublin bureaucrats, Sean who spoke for the island when the archaeologists came to explore the tower and the cemetery, Sean who fought the dog tax and defended the island's fishing rights in Dingle Assizes. But this was different. Spanish was invaded. His people were held prisoner, attacked and cruelly beaten. They looked to him for leadership, but how could he help them?

Perhaps, he thought, the morning tide would bring Eamon and Tomas back to Spanish. Indeed, but what could they do? Of course, if they did come, the other German officer, Lieutenant Hoffman, would be with them. Hoffman was a decent man. It was doubtful he could take over from the sick captain, or arrest and punish the strutting Lieutenant Reigel. Perhaps, though, tomorrow, Hoffman might repair the U-boat and take it to sea, back to the war, and far from Spanish. Tomorrow, too, Doctor Fitz would be on the island, and, God willing, Father Healy. Sean crossed himself and stood up. Nothing could be done for his people today, but tomorrow was bright with promise.

The atmosphere in the Beg cottage that morning had been equally bleak and melancholy. After Reigel left, Barndt had arrived and mournfully performed his daily task of changing the dressings on Ludtke's leg. This completed, the captain had ordered him on his abortive mission to Padraig's and Mrs. Mor's. For an hour after the sick berth attendant had gone, Ludtke sat staring at the fire, chewing cigars to shreds, and concentrating on his problem. He no longer cursed his first lieutenant or promised himself to see Reigel court-martialed. For some minutes he coldly considered faking a confession from some member of the crew —Stoker Scheutze, for instance—and shooting him. He rejected the idea. Everyone on the island, natives and Germans alike, *knew* Reigel had raped the girl. And Reigel's brutal beating of Padraig Mor had amounted to tacit, defiant admission.

Reluctantly, Ludtke came to his decision. If Hoffman were back with the gear and Haas alive and well, Herr Reigel would be arrested, tried, and executed in twenty minutes. If they were here, Reigel would feed the lobsters, the islanders would again cooperate, and the boat would be underway for Lorient. But there was no telling when Hoffman would return, with or without the parts, and Old Pressure-Proof was gone.

Shortly before noon, the captain made up his mind and sent for Dietrich. He dug out the crumpled scrap of paper on which he had drafted his signal two days before, and studied it carefully.

ADMIRAL COMMANDING U-BOATS FROM U-324. TEMPORARILY SAFE SPANISH ISLAND OFF KERRY COAST. UNABLE PROCEED SUBMERGED. REQUIRE FOUR CIRCUIT BREAKERS TYPE B-366, SIX LITERS CONCENTRATED H2S ACID, FOUR LITERS DISTILLED WATER, FOUR FATHOMS 32 CM. ELECTRIC CONDUIT CABLE. ALSO MEDICAL ASSISTANCE. ADVISE IF PARACHUTE DROP AND/OR U-BOAT HELP POSSIBLE. LUDTKE, COMMANDING.

Very deliberately, he pruned the message. He changed the first sentence to AT SPANISH ISLAND OFF KERRY and to UNABLE SUBMERGE. REQUIRE became NEED and AID replaced ASSISTANCE. After more thought, he scratched out the entire phrase ALSO MEDICAL AID. It was important, but it meant more dots and dashes for the English RDF stations, and it was not essential. The Irish doctor would be on Spanish Monday morning. Finally, though it irked his vanity, he deleted the word COMMANDING.

When P.O. Telegraphist Dietrich reported and read the signal, he showed his surprise and concern. "We're going to break radio silence, sir?" he blurted.

"I have to risk it, Sparks," Ludtke said slowly. "I could hang on for a day or two more and wait for Mr. Hoffman to get back with his spares, but I can't take chances with the natives. You've heard what happened?"

"Yes, sir," Dietrich said woodenly.

"They're not our friends any more, damn them. They'll turn us in if they can." He paused and then said again, very quietly, "I have to risk it."

Dietrich saluted and went out. Reflecting on the conversation, the captain cursed silently. He was a weakling to confide his problems and explain his decisions to a rating. Discipline aboard the Shark Boat must be very low when an enlisted man questioned his breaking radio silence. He swore aloud, frightening the radio-telephone watchstander, and poured himself a large peg of brandy. When we get back home, he vowed silently, Herr Reigel will get his reward. Two square feet of flooring in a cattle car bound for the Ostfront.

Ludtke had had no nourishment that morning except tea and brandy. Eventually, in front of the warm turf fire, he dozed, thinking of the return to Lorient. Near the offshore island of Le Croix, they would rendezvous with a small A.A. vessel and be escorted up the long channel. When they passed the little island of Port Louis, with old fortifications, they were safe and the seamen who had been kneeling on the weather decks would get to their feet. Kneeling, according to Second Flotilla's standing orders, minimized serious injury if the boat struck a mine. From Port Louis, there was a scant half hour for the hands to clean up and shift into dress blues. Time enough to send a signal to the Naval Police about Herr Reigel. There would be a band at the quay, Ludtke was sure, and photographers. The Grand Admiral would be there, with his flag lieutenant *and* the Oak Leaves. Or perhaps there would be no ceremony on the fo'c'sle, but instructions to go instead, by big chauffeured Mercedes and special plane of the Fuehrer Flight, to Berlin and an investiture at the *Reichschancellory*.

The commanding officer of U-324 smiled quietly to himself. Absorbed in his dream of revenge and glory, comforted by the cognac and the fire, he slid off to sleep. Outside the cottage, there was the constant whine of the wind and the dull, crashing thunder of the surf. In U-324's wireless office, Dietrich apprehensively sent off the coded groups of the signal that could mean relief—or destruction by the R.A.F. And, in other cottages, the anguished prayers and vengeful planning continued.

Ludtke awoke about two in the afternoon. The wind still whistled and rattled the windowpanes, but it had eased perceptibly. The Begs had not returned, the sailor on watch told him, and Ludtke shrugged his shoulders. He was hungry and the watchstander made him a meal of fried fish and potatoes. The captain ate with evident enjoyment. Since he had moved ashore, he had encountered fish and potatoes at almost every meal. After weeks of canned food aboard the U-boat, he accepted them gladly, enjoying them as though they were served from silver dishes in the Adlon Grille.

His meal over, he belched comfortably and smoked a cigar, studying the fire and thinking. Twice in the afternoon he hobbled to the window and briefly inspected the eastward slope of the island, the cove, the submarine, and the sky. The watch over the radio-telephone set was changed at four. He acknowledged the turnover and watched the turf crackle on the hearth as though he might learn something from it.

As the afternoon wore on, the sun appeared weakly and far to the west. Ludtke did not see it, but he knew the gale was fast blowing itself out. He confirmed this at six, when he switched on the wireless set and heard the static-studded voice of Radio Eireann report the barometer rising and the wind's velocity slackening. From Galway to Bantry Bay, Radio Eireann predicted, there would be clear weather on Monday.

The captain grunted. The steamer from Ballykerry would make her regular Monday crossing to the island. That was good, because the doctor would be aboard it. But plans must be made, the captain said to himself, to receive the trawler. He waited, considering the problem, until he was certain the crew had had its evening meal. Then he sent orders to Lieutenant Reigel and the key petty officers to join him.

When they arrived, Ludtke gave them permission to sit, and they ranged themselves about the kitchen. "Smoke if you want, boys," the captain said, almost graciously. "Tomorrow, the steamer comes from the mainland. I want to discuss with you how we will handle her."

Reigel lit a Gauloise with an air of bravado and the phlegmatic Albrecht began, with painstaking care, to load his pipe. The rest—Barndt, Dietrich, Kreisler, Muller, and Koenig—waited quietly and attentively.

The captain had used the word "discuss," but there was a minimum of conversational give-and-take. As he spoke, it was apparent his plan was carefully thought out; it had all the detail of an Operation Order.

"Tomorrow morning," Ludtke began, "at about eleven hours, the steamer from the mainland will arrive here on her regular weekly trip. From what the natives tell me, it's a dirty little coaster, about fifty tons, called the *Kerry Queen*.

"She carries a crew of three, and tomorrow she'll have a passenger— the Irish physician FitzGerald. Normally, she stays about an hour, to unload fuel, foodstuffs, and other supplies, and to take on fish, lobsters, mail—things of that sort. Our job is to let them do those things without suspecting a German submarine is in the vicinity. We must let them come and go without the slightest suspicion that anything is different on Spanish Island."

The problem stated, Ludtke warmed to the exposition of his strategy. When the *Kerry Queen* arrived, he said, U-324 would be on the other side of the island. The boat would leave the quay by ten o'clock, two hours before the trawler was due to come in sight. He, Ludtke, would be at the conn. Muller would have the helm. Albrecht would be in charge of the engine room. Kreisler, Dietrich, and Koenig the signalman, along with two stokers and two seamen, would constitute a skeleton cruising watch. The Shark Boat would steam on her diesels to the windward side of the island and remain there, hugging the shore, and keeping in visual contact with the Norseman's Tower.

The watch would be doubled at the tower and on the radio-telephone set. Two reliable sentries were to be stationed with Lady Maud; once the doctor had arrived there, he would be held—by gunpoint if necessary—until the trawler had departed. The remainder of the crew would stay in the sick bay, with Barndt and the wounded. Lieutenant Reigel would be in charge. Although the building was only a few yards from the quay, the wounded could not be moved. In case of trouble, Reigel and his men would sortie and capture the *Kerry Queen*.

Now, as to the islanders. The men would be expected to be fishing, especially after the storm. Very well, Dermod Beg, Padraig Mor, and his son would be aboard the U-boat when it sailed. Their curraghs would also be aboard. Only old Sean O Ŕuiarc, the women, and children would be left to welcome the *Kerry Queen*.

"Is that clear now?" Ludtke asked finally. "Are there any questions? Albrecht?"

"Well, sir," the chief machinist's mate said slowly, "I can't see how the people on the trawler will fail to get suspicious. The women may start to bawl."

"Yes, there's that danger, Chief," the captain said. "But we can explain to the women what will happen if we're betrayed. Mr. Reigel will be watching the quay and the trawler from the sick bay. If there's any trouble, he'll start shooting and a lot of people will get hurt. Why, even if they had D/F'd my signal and an English destroyer came in here tomorrow, instead of the trawler, the women would still think twice about betraying us." He noted their questioning looks and, smiling slightly, continued: "So long as Padraig, his son, and Beg are our hostages aboard the boat, the women aren't going to give us away."

There was a little hum of approval, and Ludtke asked if there were any more questions.

"One more, Captain," Reigel said. "I agree the women won't give us away if they can avoid it. But we can't stop the children from talking about a submarine."

Ludtke gave him an annoyed look, but the first lieutenant went on.

"We can capture the trawler, of course, if they betray us, but we can't hold her for very long without some investigation from the mainland. If we have to take her tomorrow, maybe we ought to sail her to France——"

"You mean abandon the Shark Boat, mister?"

"It's a gamble, Captain, whether Hoffman will get back with the cable, the circuit breakers, and the acid. He may not get back at all."

"We're not scuttling the Shark Boat, mister," Ludtke growled.

Reigel knew the captain's views on scuttling, but he plunged ahead recklessly. "The Shark Boat is important to the Reich, Captain, but you and your crew are even more important. If we took the trawler, we could sail for the Lizard without causing any alarm. We'd take some of the islanders as hostages. If we were stopped, we'd be an Irish coaster carrying lobsters to Plymouth. Once off the Lizard, we could slip across to the Channel Islands and Brest——"

Ludtke interrupted with a strangled, deep-throated obscenity. His face was mottled and his eyes glittered.

"We're not giving up that easy, mister. We're going to bring the boat back to Lorient. If the Irish give us away tomorrow, we'll capture the trawler, and we'll wait for Hoffman or for the Luftwaffe. But we're not going to scuttle. Is that clear?"

"Yes, sir," Reigel said sullenly. The Old Man, he thought, wanted the Oak Leaves too much. Perhaps the strain was becoming too much for him.

"Any more questions?" asked the captain belligerently. No one answered. Ludtke waited and then issued some specific orders, to be executed the first thing in the morning. The first lieutenant, he said, would make the assignments for the various watches in the boat and ashore, and see that the hands were properly instructed. Muller would be responsible for dismantling the camouflage nettings and stowing them away. Albrecht would test the diesels. The anchor must be taken in, and the curraghs secured on the fo'c'sle. In addition to all the other steps necessary to make the boat ready for sea, there was the job of policing the quay and its immediate area. Nothing must be left, not so much as an oil-soaked rag or a discarded welding rod, that might cause a curious question.

"That's easy, Captain," Reigel said. "I'll have the Irish do a complete clean-up job."

"You don't seem to understand, mister," Ludtke snapped. "The islanders are no longer our friends, thanks to you. We can't trust them any more. They're as ready to sabotage us as the dockyard workers in Lorient."

There was a knock at the door and the messenger of the watch came into the kitchen.

"Pardon, sir," the boy said excitedly. "The wireless shack has received a signal addressed to us. Priority, sir. They want Sparks to come down and break it."

There was a stir of interest in the crowded kitchen and P.O. Telegraphist Dietrich scrambled to his feet, received a look of assent from the captain, and hurried out of the cottage. In most U-boats, the senior wireless rating was authorized to encode and decode cyphers which, in peacetime, were handled by officers. Aboard U-324, Dietrich was such a rating. He was dependable and loyal, Ludtke thought, watching him go, and much faster at decoding a signal than any of the officers.

With an important dispatch received, the petty officers showed no
inclination to leave the cottage, and Ludtke permitted them to stay. It
was common knowledge, he knew, that he had broken radio silence.
With a perceptiveness not characteristic of him, the captain decided his
leading hands were entitled to hear the answer. Particularly if the answer was encouraging.

The conversation was desultory as they waited for Dietrich to return.
It centered on details of the next morning's various assignments. Nobody wanted to speculate, in front of the captain, as to the nature of
the signal from France. As for Ludtke, he lit a cigar and returned to
the topic that the messenger had interrupted.

"Remember that, mister," he said to Reigel. "The islanders are no
longer our friends. In fact, you'd best warn the watch at the tower to
be alert for a fire. Dermod Beg told me that if the R/T went out and
the islanders wanted help, they'd build a bonfire. If the visibility im-
proves tonight, they might try it."

Reigel acknowledged the order. A little later, Ludtke addressed himself to the entire group.

"One more thing about tomorrow. It will be necessary for me to talk
to the islanders, to tell them of our plans, and to warn them about
giving us away. Tomorrow morning, Kreisler, take a couple of hands
and round them up—everyone except the children and the sick old lady.
Have them all here, sharp at eight. You be here, too, mister."

"Aye, aye, sir," Kreisler said. Reigel grunted an acknowledgment,
and when the captain shot him a furious look, repeated Kreisler's words
with heavy formality.

A few minutes later, Dietrich returned, message pad in hand, and
there was a low buzz of excitement. The captain took the pad and
studied the signal for a long time. The room was very still. Dietrich's
face was wooden but somehow conveyed the impression that the news
was good. Presently, Ludtke cleared his throat and began to read:

PERSONAL FOR LUDTKE. CONGRATULATIONS TO YOU AND SHIP'S COM-
PANY ON YOUR GALLANT FIGHT FOR SURVIVAL. PROMISE ALL HELP AS
QUICKLY AS POSSIBLE. NO BOAT OR U-TANKER YOUR VICINITY BUT
LUFTWAFFE ALERTED AND PREPARING MISSION. DETAILS OF DROP
FORTHCOMING. DOENITZ.

When he looked up, every face in the kitchen was wreathed in a grin.
"That's the stuff," Reigel exclaimed, his earlier sullenness forgotten.
"Now, we'll get out of this hell hole."

There was a happy babble of concurrence. Despite himself, Ludtke's harsh face relaxed in a smile. A signal signed by the Grand Admiral was cause indeed for hope. Doenitz was no longer Admiral Commanding U-boats; he had been elevated to Commander-in-Chief of the entire Navy. His name on the signal meant the Grand Admiral was taking personal charge. Probably the Fuehrer himself was aware of U-324. Ludtke did not think highly of the Luftwaffe; it was no substitute for a proper Naval air arm. But with Grand Admiral Doenitz promising all help, the Luftwaffe would have to make the drop.

"Make sure, Sparks, every member of the ship's company sees this signal," the captain said, thrusting the message pad at Dietrich. "Keep your gang alert for the signal about the drop. Let me know if the limey air traffic indicates anything out of the ordinary—any investigation of this area."

"Aye, aye, sir," Dietrich said, grinning.

It had been a miserable day, Ludtke thought, but help was on the way. The dirty weather was breaking, the doctor would be at work by midday tomorrow, and Grand Admiral Doenitz was taking charge.

"We're not forgotten, boys," he exclaimed almost gaily. "A day or two more and the Shark Boat will be underway."

He dismissed his petty officers and they marched out of the kitchen. They were grinning, pleased at the prospect of action tomorrow, exulting in the promises of the Grand Admiral. Ludtke could hear the excitement in their voices as they started down the path toward the quay.

"Just a minute, mister," the captain said to Reigel.

"Sir?"

"There's one more chore for you to handle this evening." He pointed to the canvas bag hanging on the wall. "That's the island post bag. Tomorrow that bag, full of letters, will be put aboard the *Kerry Queen*. I want the mail censored tonight, understand?"

"Aye, aye, sir," Reigel said dispiritedly. Censorship aboard U-324 was a duty for the junior officers, but the junior officers were dead, and he and the captain were the only ones left who could read English. This, Reigel realized, was no routine job. If the mail was not censored, the police might be landing on Spanish tomorrow night.

"Gather up the letters and bring them here, mister," Ludtke said. A faint smile appeared on his thin lips. "Censor duty will keep you out of trouble this evening."

The first lieutenant saluted and went angrily out of the cottage to find Dermod Beg. He located the postmaster quickly in Peigeen Og's kitchen and spoke bluntly to him.

"All the mail that leaves the island on the steamer tomorrow will be censored tonight. I'll give you one hour to gather up the mail, including any packages, and turn them over to me. I'll be in your cottage. Nothing will be accepted that is not in my hands in one hour's time."

Dermod's broad, pink face was filled with melancholy and frustration.

"Aye," he said heavily, "the post will be there in one hour's time."

Brede began to dab at her eyes and Peigeen gave the German a steady stare of hatred. Reigel turned on his heel and went out, slamming the kitchen door behind him.

The lieutenant had no desire to go back to the Beg cottage immediately. He had had enough of Ludtke for a while. He climbed the path, instead, to the Norseman's Tower and warned the sentry to be alert.

"If you spot anyone moving close by," he said grimly, "challenge them, and if they don't go back to their cabins, start shooting. If they are too far away to challenge, call up the boat for help. Remember, the islanders are against us now, and the skies are clearing. Any signal fires tonight, and you'll be on bread and water for a month."

The sentry repeated the instructions—to be passed onto his relief. Reigel walked down the path to the foot of the hill. He visited briefly with Barndt and the wounded and found their spirits high. Tomorrow, they were confident, the Irish physician would be with them, and probably the parachute surgeons of the Luftwaffe. By Tuesday, they would be on their way home. The lieutenant concurred in this optimism, and went down the quay and aboard the U-boat. He conferred with the petty officer of the watch, impressing him with the need for vigilance, and listening to the routine reports. Satisfied, he made his way back to the Begs', where he found the captain regarding the fire with a bemused expression.

When Dermod came into the kitchen ten minutes later, he had one small package and less than a dozen letters. Reigel lowered the kettle a couple of notches so that it began to boil. He opened the package and found it was a beautifully knit sweater with a variety of stitches, a present from Lady Maud to a cousin in County Cork. Then, one by one, he held the envelopes over the hissing kettle spout, steamed open their flaps, and read the letters. Fortunately for him, Lady Maud was both the island's most prolific correspondent and the possessor of an old-fashioned, extremely lucid hand. Reigel found he could read her elegant copperplate calligraphy in a fraction of the time required for the child-like scrawls of the others.

The lieutenant found one letter, written by Peigeen to a cousin in Ballykerry, that openly referred to the German submarine. Another, from Maeve Mor, mentioned serious, unspecified troubles on Spanish. Reigel dropped both into the fire. Two more, written in Gaelic by Kathy O Ŕuiarc, were similarly consigned. As Reigel laboriously read the others, and scrutinized them for invisible warnings in lemon juice, Dermod rewrapped Lady Maud's package and resealed the letters that had been approved. With an ink pad and a rubber hand stamp, he carefully canceled the postage. Finally, the package and the surviving letters were carefully put in the canvas post bag and turned over for safekeeping to the radio-telephone watchstander.

The task was nearly complete when Brede came into the kitchen, nodded nervously to the Germans, and made her way to the loft. Dermod followed her within minutes and Reigel left shortly after that. The watchstander gave Ludtke some bread and jam and a cup of tea, to which the captain added a generous dollop of cognac. Enjoying his supper, he reviewed his plans for the next day. There was, he admitted to himself, the possibility that the women on the jetty would warn the crew of the *Kerry Queen;* apart from that he could see no loophole in his strategy.

He finished his meal and basked in front of the fire, smoking the last cigar of the day and savoring the words of Grand Admiral Doenitz' signal. PERSONAL FOR LUDTKE. CONGRATULATIONS TO YOU AND SHIP'S COMPANY ON YOUR GALLANT FIGHT FOR SURVIVAL. These days, the Grand Admiral sent very few messages of congratulations, Ludtke told himself. Doenitz was no longer Admiral Commanding U-boats. But Doenitz was primarily a U-boat sailor. The U-Waffe was his first love, and he would do anything to avoid deserting a submarine in trouble.

Ludtke thought briefly of the Grand Admiral as he had last seen him. That had been early in November, 1943, when the Shark Boat returned after its eleventh, and most successful, patrol. Over forty thousand Gross Registered Tons of enemy shipping had been sunk and he had been recommended for the Knight's Cross of the Iron Cross. There had been a band on the quay, Red Cross nurses, skippers of other boats, and all the brass hats. When the gangway had been rigged, the Grand Admiral had come aboard, shaken hands with every member of the crew, and, after a little speech, pinned on the medal. Ah, it had been a fine welcome. But it would seem like nothing when he brought U-324 back from this patrol. This time it would not be just another successful homecoming. It would be the triumphant return of a U-boat that had defeated overwhelming odds; a boat that had been crippled and presumed sunk, one with her captain wounded, half her crew casualties, and her traitorous first lieutenant in irons. Ah, what newspaper stories there would be about the ace of the Second Flotilla! Again, as in his earlier reverie, Ludtke could not decide whether he would be awarded the Oak Leaves by the Grand Admiral on the fo'c'sle or by the Fuehrer in some vaulting, crimson-carpeted chamber of the *Reichs-*

chancellory. In his mind's eye, he could see in photographic detail every movement of the first ceremony. The second was much more vague, based on illustrated magazine accounts and the testimony of long-dead U-boat aces, but for Ludtke, it had a mystic, Wagnerian appeal. The sumptuous furnishings, the clicks of polished heels, the box at the State Opera, the honor guards at present arms, the softly perfumed flanks of expensive trollops—all of these would be strange and wonderful to a veteran of the Fleet. There would be no reference to the Commander Ludtke who had surrendered to the Bolsheviks. But with the Fuehrer's handshake, expiation would come for the Commander's son. In a murky ecstasy, Ludtke debated the advantages of the two alternatives, consumed more cognac, decided in favor of Berlin, and hobbled off to bed.

Sunday was an interminable, aching agony for the men and women of Spanish. For the Germans on the island, it was a day of depression, relieved in the early evening by the radioed promise of help. For Peter Hoffman, Sunday was a day of frustration *and* glorious discovery.

The day began with the lieutenant spitting out bits of straw in Mick's barn and unshackling himself from Nora Berkeley. With their stirring, and the early light, Tomas Mor and Eamon Og awoke. All four mumbled unhappy good mornings. Not until they had emerged from the barn, made their toilets, the men shaving with Mick's razor, and breakfasted, were there any but the barest civilities.

Hoffman did not interfere with the prevailing mood as they ate. As they finished their second cup of tea, he said pleasantly, "The storm seems to be blowing itself out."

Like a good host, Mick agreed. Tomas and Eamon were noncommittal. It had stopped raining and there was a pale, intermittent sun, but the wind still whined and the sea bristled with white horses.

The state of the weather soon became more than casual postprandial conversation. Certainly it would soon be possible, said the lieutenant, to make the crossing to Spanish. There was positive dissent from the two islandmen.

"Och, not at all, Lieutenant," Tomas said. "This sea is far too much for a curragh. Why, the waves are as tall as this house, chimney and all."

"Tomorrow, perhaps," Eamon said. "Today, never."

Hoffman was not satisfied, but he did not argue. He did not object either when Eamon raised the subject of worship, and he accompanied them all to an ancient little chapel. After the service he hurried them back to Mick's where he studied the wind and sky and brooded on the chances of an early return. He did not overlook the possibility of the *Kerry Queen*, berthed, he knew, only a mile away. It was absurd to think of stealing her, but the steamer might be chartered. He suggested this to Mick and was told the crew lived in Dingle. Hoffman scowled. He must get the acid and cable back to Spanish today, he told himself. The R.A.F. could fly in this weather, and U-324 might be discovered at any hour. He knew Tomas and Eamon were superb oarsmen; probably they had made the crossing in far worse weather than this. Nora, he told himself, has persuaded them to delay. She's stalling, hoping the police will track us down. He kept his counsel during the midday meal of cabbage soup and potatoes, but by early afternoon, with the wind slackening, Hoffman determined to go back—by curragh.

When he announced his decision, the two islandmen protested. Hoffman was firm. "You two are old-time seamen," he told them. "You've been in a hundred blows worse than this."

"The leaden bottles are too heavy for the curragh," Tomas said.

"Then we'll tow Mick's curragh behind us."

"Two rowers cannot pull two loaded curraghs into this sea," Tomas argued.

"Then we'll take Mick," the lieutenant said, and touched off another explosion of objection.

"As God and Holy Mary witness, sir," Mick cried earnestly, "I'm no fisher. I've never been out in a sea like this."

Singly and together, they protested. Hoffman was patient but adamant. He coaxed and played on their pride and their patriotic hatred of the English. He promised his life belt to Mick. When he offered them fifty pounds apiece for the crossing, they perceptibly wavered. Fifty pounds was an almost incomprehensible sum—more than a fisherman could put by in a lifetime. Hoffman saw them hesitate and described what the money could do—a better truck for Mick, schooling for the two little Ogs, security for Maura Mor and Shelagh.

Nora Berkeley snorted with disgust but Hoffman's promises carried the day. The two curraghs were loaded—the carboys of acid divided equally and carefully secured to the thwarts, the cable, breakers, and fuses put in the second boat—and they walked them out into the foaming surf. Tomas and Eamon took up the oars in the lead curragh, with Nora steering in the sternsheets. Mick rowed the towed curragh, the most heavily laden, and Hoffman steered.

Almost from the outset, the lieutenant realized the sea was uglier than he'd thought. The great rolling combers came steadily in on them, and the loaded curraghs wallowed instead of riding over their crests. Only a few hundred yards offshore, the bow of the leading curragh shot upward and Nora lost her steering oar. Tomas and Eamon struggled desperately, but in seconds their boat had broached and turned turtle.

Hoffman dropped his steering oar and scrambled past Mick to cut the towline. He dropped his pistol and shouted to Mick to keep the curragh's head into the wind. Then he dived into the sea, striking out for the capsized curragh and the bobbing heads ten yards ahead. The German was not a strong swimmer. In the heavy sea, it took him three minutes to get up to the curragh. His first thought was for the girl. Nora, he saw, had inflated her belt and was treading water easily. Tomas was close to the curragh, dog-paddling frantically, but its slick wet canvas gave him nothing to hold to. Hoffman caught one windmilling arm and showed Tomas how to put his hands under the gunwale and hold on. For a moment the lieutenant stayed with him. Satisfied the Irishman was out of danger, he struck out for Eamon, a few yards closer to shore and struggling crazily. As Hoffman came up to him, Eamon went under for a frighteningly long time. When he came up his eyeballs showed only white and his hands clawed the water with insane fury. Hoffman tried to remember the lifesaving lessons he had taken at the Naval Academy. He closed Eamon and attempted to take him in tow, but the islandman would not allow it. Three times he pulled Hoffman under with him, locking the German's arms to his sides. The lieutenant was as helpless and as frightened as the man he was trying to save. He swallowed seawater and his lungs felt about to collapse. There seemed no escape from the crushing embrace, but with a last frenzied effort, he brought up his knee and caught Eamon in the groin. The islandman went under again, but this time he was too weak to pull Hoffman down.

For a few seconds Hoffman floated, gasping for breath. He took hold of Eamon's hair and struck out for shore. The islander was too spent to resist. He could only choke and feebly groan, and when Hoffman had towed him to shallow water, he was barely able to stand erect.

Hoffman saw both curraghs were drifting onto the beach, Nora and Tomas hanging onto the capsized craft, and Mick guiding the other. The acid carboys in the first boat were still lashed in place. None of the cargo had been lost. Presently, both craft were beached and artificial respiration administered to Eamon. The four men and the girl sat at the water's edge, in various stages of exhaustion, and watched the relentless surf.

It was some time before Eamon Og was able to talk. "You saved my life, Lieutenant," he said huskily. "I'm that grateful. I'll try to repay you."

"Mine, too," Tomas grinned weakly. "My thanks forever, Lieutenant."

"I thought you two could swim," Hoffman said. "When you didn't take life belts back at Spanish . . ."

The two islandmen looked embarrassed and did not speak.

"No one on Spanish can swim," Nora said quietly. "They feel that if a curragh is swamped, swimming only prolongs the inevitable."

Presently Mick and the fishermen left. They were exhausted and needed sleep.

"I must go and freshen up," Nora said. "I've lost my compact. I must look a sight."

"I'm too tired to move," Peter Hoffman said. "Stay with me, please."

Nora could not tell whether this was a request or an order. Unaccountably, she did not care. It was pleasant to sit and watch the restless Atlantic. The wind was steadily diminishing and the late-afternoon sun warmed her. For the first time since her interview with Ludtke she felt almost relaxed.

"This is a beautiful part of the world," Hoffman said after a bit. He regarded the limestone cliffs of Ballykerry Head, the tangled rocks and boulders of the foreshore, and the jade-blue ocean sparkling in the sun. "It's a pity the sea is so dangerous."

Nora smiled. After a bit she said, "You can just see Spanish out there."

"I'd like to go back there after the war," the lieutenant said slowly. "And go along this coast. I'd like to drive along the Shannon again, too, and visit Adare. Even in the rain yesterday, you could tell it was lovely. I guess most of Ireland is lovely, isn't it?"

"Indeed it is," said Nora loyally, and, when she saw he was not going to continue, she spoke again.

"You'll likely be bringing your family after the war."

He raised his head then and stared directly at her. For a second he looked haggard and tortured; then he smiled sardonically.

"There's no family at all, Nora. And I doubt if I'll make the end of the war."

He started to tunnel into the sand in front of him with a stick, saying nothing more, and the girl waited. The tide was low, leaving patches of sand among the rocks, and crabs periodically came out of their holes and scuttled across the patches. The rocks and boulders were bearded with green wrack and studded with barnacles and periwinkles. It was very peaceful, but Nora was no longer relaxed. She wanted him to continue.

After a minute or two, he threw the stick away.

"I'm afraid there's not much future in the U-Waffe. The war won't be over for some time, because Herr Hitler doesn't believe in surrender. But the end is inevitable."

He was silent again, staring at the sand in front of him. "Herr Hitler is a fool, Nora," he said with sudden violence.

"Of course he is!" Nora shot at him. "But the end doesn't have to be inevitable for you. If you get that stuff back to Spanish, and get your ship repaired, what have you gained? A few more weeks of killing, that's all."

"It's not a ship, it's a boat," he said with infuriating irrelevance.

"Och, indeed, it's a boat then," she cried. Irritation and sympathy bubbled in her voice. "For the love of God, walk down the road, past the church, to Ballykerry Village. Ask for Doctor FitzGerald there. Tell him you want to give yourself up——"

"It's no use, Nora." The lieutenant stood up abruptly. "You'll not trick me that way."

"God and Mary!" the girl flashed. "I'm not trying to trick you, you fool!"

"Let's go back to Mick's," Peter Hoffman said quietly. He had confided in Nora, yet he was still not sure whose side she was on. When he offered his hand to help her arise, he saw the tears in her eyes, but he couldn't be certain what they meant.

Supper at Mick's that evening was a pleasant affair. Before the meal, Hoffman offered a few words of thankfulness for their delivery, the three Irishmen punctuating his remarks with resonant amens. There was plenty of potato soup and bread and the men ate heartily. Nora did not eat much, the lieutenant noted, but he was pleased to see there was more good fellowship at the table than since his expedition had begun. When Eamon Og, in his awkward, taciturn fashion, attempted a joke, Hoffman felt he could almost relax. His cargo was no closer to Spanish Island than in the morning, but it was gratifying to know he was no longer feared and hated.

After supper he went down to the beach to inspect the still-loaded curraghs. He was very tired but he felt content and was glad to see the sea was growing quieter. He strolled along the beach a hundred yards or so, smoking a cigarette. When he turned to come back, he was slightly surprised to see Nora sitting on a boulder.

Seeing her excited him, but he walked back slowly and he kept his voice noncommittal.

"A nice evening."

"Yes," the girl said, "it will be fair tomorrow. Won't you sit down?"

Hoffman agreed with her prediction and sat beside her. There was a little pause.

"It's funny," Hoffman said presently.

"What's funny?"

"You've been trying to get away from me for three days. This evening, for the first time, I haven't been standing guard over you, yet you come down to the beach where I am."

Nora bridled. "I didn't come down to see you," she said indignantly. "I just came down to see Spanish." She laughed at her own indignation and the lieutenant smiled.

"It's still there, Nora."

He pointed, and, despite the westering sun, the girl could make out the truncated peak just above the horizon.

"You like the old rock, don't you? You'll be glad to get back."

"Of course. It's really a lovely island, you know. Tiny, but quite majestic in its fashion. I must say I'd like it better if there were trees and grass. It's awfully austere."

"I know. It's like the poet's line 'the common grayness silvers everything.' That reminds me of Spanish."

"What poet?" Nora asked suspiciously. "Yeats?"

"Robert Browning. You know," the lieutenant added, "we give the English credit for some good things—poetry is one of them."

"Och, pull the other one," said Nora.

"Forgive me," Hoffman murmured and gave her a cigarette.

The girl smiled at him after her cigarette was lit. "Actually, it's not the island I like. It's the people."

"I know. Old Sean for one——"

"Ah, Sean's a wizard person. Near eighty he is, and no lovelier, kinder man ever lived."

"He's a gentleman," Hoffman said quietly. "Then there are the Begs——"

"Brede Beg has my love forever. She's the spirit of the island, as much as Sean. She's the nurse, the barber, the tailor, the midwife. She's the one the others confide in. She looks quiet, but when they'd dance a *ceildhe*, with Sean playing his violin, Brede would dance us all into our beds. Would you believe it, now?"

Hoffman said it was hard to believe, and after a pause the girl went on. "Dermod, now, is a lovely man, full of jokes and all. But if it weren't for Brede Beg and the few quid he makes as postie, himself would starve to death."

She touched on most of the other islanders. Padraig Mor was terribly quiet, but a good man, honest with himself and with others. He didn't have much fun, but he was a good father, and a great student of the seabirds. Logically, he would succeed Sean as the island's leader. Tomas, the bachelor, would leave soon, but Eamon and Peigeen would remain, happily raising their children.

"I'm sorry you didn't meet my gran," Nora said. "She's a lovely person. She's barely able to leave her bed, she has arthritis that bad, but she knows everything about Spanish and what goes on there."

The sun slid below the horizon and the twilight deepened as Nora Berkeley talked about Spanish and its people. Nora, the lieutenant learned, had lived there for five years, from the time she was orphaned until she went away to convent school. Since then, she had spent most of her holidays there. She had intimate knowledge of the fishing, sheep-shearing, spinning, and harvesting of kelp. She remembered when the archaeologist from Dublin visited Spanish, and when Tomas and Eamon won the two-mile curragh race in Dingle Bay.

These were mundane subjects, but somehow fascinating for Peter Hoffman. He asked questions, and once he spoke of the islanders' life as a hard one.

Nora agreed. "Indeed, it's a hard life," she said. "Once, three years ago, I brought a friend from Dublin out for the hols." She laughed merrily. "The poor lad couldn't stand it. Uncivilized, he called it, and he left after three days. Uncivilized, indeed!"

Hoffman was interested in Nora's young man. Had he been her fiancé?

"Och, not at all, not at all," she told him, still chuckling. "Desmond Piers is a barrister who wants his creature comforts. We went about a bit in nineteen forty and nineteen forty-one, and we liked one another, but we didn't have enough in common. He married a friend of mine last summer."

The lieutenant smiled, oddly pleased that the barrister was no longer eligible. He sat quietly smoking in the twilight as Nora identified a variety of seabirds for him—black-backed gulls and yellow-billed herring gulls, delicate kittiwakes and soaring, swooping fulmars. A large horseshoe crab inched past them, and Hoffman admitted he had never seen one before. Nora said it was odd, a Naval officer not knowing about seabirds and crabs, and he agreed, adding he had never seen the sea before he went to the Naval Academy. They laughed together companionably.

Presently it grew too dark to see the birds. Hoffman expected the girl to excuse herself, and, hoping to delay her, he asked again about her work. Nora dismissed her secretarial job with a few sentences but she did not go. Instead, she talked of Dublin—of Trinity College, the Georgian townhouses around St. Stephen's Green, and the races at Phoenix Park. She spoke of the swans on the Liffey and of O'Connell Street, the Abbey Theatre and tea dances at the Shelbourne. She described the capital well and with fond enthusiasm, evoking for Hoffman a city of gaiety and friendliness, a city where there were no blackouts, air-raid sirens, or truckloads of soldiers in the streets.

"It sounds wonderful," he said once, wistfully. "It sounds so—" he groped for the right word—"so civilized."

Nora looked at him. A sliver of moon had risen and in its dim light his face looked haunted. The girl felt a rush of sympathy for him. He was a Nazi Naval officer, she told herself, stubbornly determined to let nothing stop his U-boat from returning to France. He was also a brave man, educated, well mannered, with a nice faculty for getting on with people. He must be a good officer, she thought, and it suddenly occurred to her that Lady Maudie would like Peter Hoffman. Then, after a moment, Nora decided she liked him, too. Liked him very much.

As young people will, they discussed their childhood, the dogs they had owned, books read, games played. It was easy to find things in common. He told how he and two friends had frightened a bullying instructor who had the ill fortune to pass a cemetery late at night. Nora gleefully related how the girls in her form would construct mice from bits of fur and pull them with thread across the classroom floor. This, she recalled, invariably caused a nearsighted and cordially disliked teacher to stand on her desk. They laughed together, with the understanding of fellow-conspirators. Things did not seem to have been greatly different at Wassenburg Akademie and the St. Brigid Convent School.

Suddenly the moon was gone and the lieutenant discovered he had only one cigarette. He ceremoniously divided it and they smoked contentedly, enjoying the sound of the surf and the closeness of their bodies.

"That was a grand thing you did today," Nora said slowly.

"What was that?"

"Och, you know. Saving Eamon. And Tomas."

"The sea was too rough. I should have listened to them. They know their boats and these waters."

"I was that frightened when Eamon pulled you under," Nora said. "I was sure neither of you would come up."

"I was frightened, too," Hoffman reflected. Then he smiled. "You mean you were glad I didn't stay under? If I had, your problem would be solved, you know."

"Don't be rude," the girl said hotly. "Just because I don't like your uniform doesn't mean I want you drowned."

"And why don't you like the uniform?"

"You know. Because of the kind of war you fight, sinking defenseless merchant ships."

Hoffman thought of the war at sea as he knew it. On one side, well-escorted convoys, almost-constant air cover, hunter-killer groups, and superior radar. On the other, a pitifully few U-boats, perhaps a half dozen currently in the Western Approaches. But he said only, in his quiet, unemotional voice:

"It's our job, Nora. English submarines sink merchantmen. So do the Yankees. We obey orders, like soldiers and sailors everywhere."

Nora Berkeley felt rebuked, and at the same time she had a strange impulsive feeling about this man. She had a sudden urgent desire to be in his arms and that frightened her. She stood up.

"Forgive me, Peter," she said contritely. "I was the rude one. Now let's go back. We've a lot to do tomorrow."

The lieutenant got to his feet. His heart was singing. For the first time, she had used his Christian name. As they walked across the field to Mick's, he wanted to take her hand but decided that would be presumptuous. They did not speak, but Peter Hoffman felt strong and confident, as though he were ten feet tall.

Eamon and Tomas were asleep in Mick's barn, snoring gently. The sounds set off fits of stifled laughter in Nora and the lieutenant. They made themselves comfortable, still chuckling. Under the circumstances, Hoffman did not shackle his leg to hers. She was not exactly on his side, he thought, but she had called him Peter. He savored that recollection, like a Frenchman savoring an old aristocratic wine. Long after Nora was asleep, he thought about her, recalling her anecdotes, her Irish expressions, how she sputtered when angry, and how her nose crinkled in laughter. For a long time he thought about her, how she looked, and how she had pronounced his name. He was grateful that only once that evening had Nora mentioned the war, and then, he remembered, she had asked his forgiveness.

MONDAY The new day dawned fine and fair at Ballykerry. With the first rays of the sun, Lieutenant Hoffman was awake. For a moment he lay still, listening to the distant murmur of the surf. Thank the Lord, he said to himself, it's going to be a good day. Quietly he got up and went to the door of the barn. The sun was burning away the patches of mist and warming the ground. There was a profusion of wild flowers about the barn, and Hoffman was suddenly aware that spring had returned. The sea was blue, laced with whitecaps, and the salt air good to breathe. He washed at a pump by the barn door stretched himself, grinning, and turned back to wake the others.

Eamon and Tomas still slept but Nora was sitting up under the blanket, her eyes cloudy with sleep and her blue-black hair tangled and matted.

"*Guten Morgen,*" Hoffman said, still grinning. "Believe me, Nora, it is a good morning. It is a beautful day!"

The girl regarded him doubtfully but his enthusiasm was infectious and she began to smile. When she inspected herself in a sliver of mirror, the smile disappeared.

"Mother of God, I do look a sight," she said.

"Mother of God, you look lovely," Hoffman said. He was still smiling but there was something very serious about his voice and his long, steady gaze. He went to rouse the two islandmen and Nora began to comb her hair. She was very conscious of her bedraggled, mud-spotted clothes and her torn stockings. At the same time, and even more disconcerting, she was acutely aware that Hoffman did not seem to mind her appearance. After a moment she got to her feet, and, feeling curiously lightheaded, went out to the pump.

Presently, they breakfasted in Mick's kitchen on bream and soda bread, jam and hot, sweet tea. All three Irishmen felt it would be best to go back to the island by steamer. It would take all day by curragh, they said, and Hoffman did not argue. After breakfast, Mick went down to the Ballykerry jetty to reconnoiter, and within half an hour, he was back to report no policemen about. They collected their curragh and gear and drove down to the quay.

Hoffman was momentarily surprised when he saw the *Kerry Queen.* Subconsciously, he had expected something larger and more in keeping with her name. Instead, *Kerry Queen* was a broad-beamed, deep-chested little trawler with a high prow and a flush deck. She was rust-stained, salt-rimed, and nondescriptly ugly. Before the 1914–1918 war, when she was part of the Galway fishing fleet, her hold could carry a hundred thousand pounds of herring or mackerel. In 1944, the tank fitted below decks rarely held more than a few dozen lobsters. *Kerry Queen* sailed regularly to Spanish on Mondays, to Tearacht Light Tuesdays, and to the port of Tralee on Wednesdays. The rest of the week she lay alongside the Ballykerry jetty, enduring casual maintenance and waiting for infrequent charters. This morning, when Mick's truck rattled onto the jetty, her three-man crew, with the help of a few boys, was loading turf aboard.

"God and Mary, it's Nora back to sail with us," the skipper cried, surprised and delighted. Only a week before the girl had made the same crossing with him. He and his men swarmed about the Chevrolet with greetings and questions. It was the questions that troubled Hoffman. They were so fast and unexpected that he was momentarily shaken and confused.

"What are you doing here, Nora, with Lady Maudie failing so?"

"When did you come back from the island, Nora? Did you not know your granny was dying?"

Climbing out of the cab, Nora put her hand to her mouth, and Hoffman saw the shock in her eyes. He braced himself for trouble.

But there was no betrayal. Instead, the girl choked out, "My gran?" and almost instantly recovered. "Och, my gran *is* very sick, and Tomas and Eamon rowed me ashore just before the gale struck. This is Doctor Hoffman"—she nodded to the German—"he is coming back with us to help."

Oh, glorious lie, Peter Hoffman thought, and said quickly in support of it, "I'm a Swiss. I was on holiday near Tralee, when these gentlemen found me."

The gentlemen in question, Eamon Og and Tomas Mor, looked shocked and baffled by the rapid developments.

"Your granny will be healthy by tomorrow, Nora," the skipper cried with a jubilant clap of his hands. "There'll be two doctors minding Her Ladyship now. Doctor Hoffman and Doctor Fitz."

"Oh?" The girl was very pale.

"Aye, Doctor Fitz has booked passage with us this morning——"

"What in the name of Holy Ireland is all this about, Eamon?" the mate broke in, pointing to the acid bottles and loops of cable in the back of the Chevrolet. Eamon cleared his throat and looked at Hoffman.

"That's electrical gear," Hoffman said swiftly. "With a sick old lady on the island, I'm going to build a little power plant for her. Electrical therapy is good for old people, you know." That seemed to satisfy them, and he added, "Let's get it aboard, Eamon."

"Aye," said the skipper. He gestured at the turf stacked on the jetty. "Let's get at it, boys. We want to be back by teatime."

It was ten minutes to ten by Hoffman's watch. At the hour, he and

Nora were on the afterdeck of *Kerry Queen*, watching the stowage of the acid carboys. Abaft the deckhouse, there was a tangled clutter of freight: the cable and various crates and boxes from Coyle and Ryan's, as well as many unidentified containers; sacks of flour and potatoes, mailbags, bundles of firewood, and stacks of turf bricks; the curragh, and even two small pigs, squealing piteously, their forelegs and hind-legs tied together. In the midst of the tangle Eamon and Tomas were on their knees, carefully lashing down the acid bottles.

The engineer officer satisfied himself that the stowage was proper and shipshape. He was very conscious of Nora's white-faced tension.

"It's going to be all right," he said, giving her elbow a reassuring squeeze. "We'll find out about Lady Maud shortly."

The girl said nothing, but gave him a sad little smile.

"That's the last of the turf, Skip," the mate shouted, and almost simultaneously Hoffman heard the rattle of horse's hooves.

"It's Doctor Fitz," the captain sang out. "Stand by to let go for'ard."

A horse-drawn trap clattered down the jetty, and a little man, encumbered by mackintosh, umbrella, and bag, dismounted, took brief leave of the driver, and came aboard. Hoffman and Nora heard him greeted by the skipper at the gangway and heard the latter say, "I've a surprise for you, Doctor Fitz. Set your bag down now, and come aft with me."

Doctor Fitz was astounded to see Nora. "Great heavens, child," he cried, "what brings you here with your gran so close—so sick?"

The lieutenant braced himself. Beside him, he saw Nora begin to tremble. The girl might lie to casual acquaintances of the trawler crew, but he was not at all sure she would lie to the family physician.

In a weak voice, Nora repeated her story. "Tomas and Eamon rowed me over just before the storm—last Friday. We couldn't find you but we did find Doctor Hoffman here. He's a Swiss physician, on holiday near Tralee."

Dr. FitzGerald looked incredulous. The general practitioner of Ballykerry was a sharp-eyed, sharp-beaked little man, brisk and businesslike, and closer to seventy than sixty. He wore a Norfolk jacket and knickerbockers of rusty Donegal tweed, homespun stockings and buttoned, ankle-high shoes. He nodded to Hoffman.

"You're a physician, sir?" he asked, his voice full of doubt.

"Yes, Doctor, Peter Hoffman of Zurich." Conscious of his dirty, salt-streaked jersey and dungarees, and determined to keep Nora out of the conversation, he plunged recklessly on. "I'm an internist, studied at the University of Munich before the war under Doctor von Brinckman. Perhaps you've heard of him, Doctor?"

"No, I've not," Dr. FitzGerald said crisply. Turning to the girl, he asked, "Did you see my housekeeper when you tried to find me Friday?"

The girl nodded weakly and Hoffman cut in sharply: "The poor girl's worried to death about her grandmother. She ought to lie down. Can't we get started, Captain?"

"Aye, it's high time," the skipper rumbled. "Come up with me to the wheelhouse, Doctor Fitz. You, Nora, can use the cuddy. You'll be comfortable there."

Dr. FitzGerald glared about him suspiciously. Nora averted her eyes and the two islandmen looked at their feet. With a baffled snort, the physician followed the skipper forward. A minute later, in response to a shout from the wheel, the idlers on the quay pushed the gangplank inboard and lifted the hawsers off the bollards. A bell jingled below decks and the engine rumbled. The *Kerry Queen*'s bow swung out from the jetty and she grumbled her way across the harbor. Hoffman watched the little man in knickers climb to the wheelhouse and enter. He realized the palms of his hands were damp with sweat and smiled ruefully. Dr. FitzGerald was suspicious, but other than ask questions of the skipper there was little he could do. There was no radio aboard and if the *Kerry Queen* reversed her course, Hoffman would know it and could take the necessary action. He advised Eamon and Tomas to keep away from Doctor Fitz and escorted Nora to the passenger saloon directly under the wheelhouse. It was a cramped little compartment, with athwartship benches facing one another and a built-in stove. The girl huddled in a corner. Hoffman sat down and tried to relax.

After a few minutes, he discovered relaxation was difficult, even for a U-boat sailor. The vigorous corkscrewing of the *Kerry Queen* as she worked into the chop of the open sea slid him back and forth on the smooth wooden bench. There were disconcerting crashes as the trawler's bow would lift and then smash down into the seas, taking some green water and a good deal of spray over her fo'c'sle. Hoffman was glad he had not insisted on making the trip by curragh. In two hours or so, if all went well, they would be back at Spanish with the gear to restore the batteries and Doctor Fitz to look after the captain and the rest of the wounded. He was confident Lady Maud's illness was only a ruse to get the doctor on the island and he tried to persuade Nora to accept his logic. The girl, he discovered, was weeping softly.

"There, there, Nora," he said. "Your grandmother's all right. It's just a trick of Captain Ludtke's."

She brightened a bit at that, but presently she was crying again.

"Och, these lies of mine," she said unhappily. "I can't bear the thought of lying to Doctor Fitz. I've known him ever since he brought me into the world." She produced a small smile and then began to weep again. It was not the convulsed, panic-stricken sobbing of the barn near Carrigkerry; it was the slow, steady weeping that is inspired by shame.

The *Kerry Queen* twisted and plunged in the choppy sea, but neither of them paid attention to the motion. Hoffman put his arm about the girl and spoke gently. "You told a little lie, a little fib, just to prevent trouble," he said. "If you hadn't, there would have been serious trouble —shooting perhaps."

"He'll find out once we're back at Spanish. He'll think me a traitor."

"Nonsense," Hoffman said. "You've not betrayed anyone. You're simply a neutral helping a sailor repair his ship so as to leave a neutral port."

He took his arm away and she looked at him, her enormous eyes glistening with tears. "I didn't intend to help you, Peter," she said very gently. "When we left Spanish, I was determined to hand you over to the first bobby——"

Peter Hoffman smiled. "But you didn't," he said. "I've a great deal to thank you for, Nora. You helped me make inquiries, you took us to Coyle and Ryan's, you spelled me at the wheel and made conversation with me. Where other women would have become hysterical, you showed nothing but nerve." The girl wiped her eyes and spots of color appeared in her cheeks as Hoffman went on.

"You did try to bolt a couple of times. This morning you could have turned me in with a couple of words. You had a perfect chance to scuttle me and you changed your mind. Why did you do it, Nora? What made you change your mind?"

Nora Berkeley looked at the deck, the color still in her cheeks. Slowly she raised her eyes to the German's. They were, he decided, the loveliest eyes he had ever seen, wide set, very large, very blue.

"I'm not sure, Peter," she began in a low voice. If he doesn't know the reason, she said to herself, I'm not the one to tell him.

The compartment door was suddenly wrenched open and the mate put one foot inside the coaming. "Tea's ready, Nora," he shouted. "How about a cup, Doctor?"

Hoffman grunted irritably, but Nora smiled and said tea would be lovely. Hoffman excused himself and went aft with the mate to fetch it. Eamon and Tomas were sitting with the engineer of the *Kerry Queen*, their backs to the deckhouse bulkhead, drinking tea from thick mugs and discussing the new lobster season.

The mate went down the engine-room hatch to get two more mugs of tea. Hoffman smiled at the others.

"Where's Doctor Fitz?" he shouted above the noise of wind and sea. "Still in the wheelhouse," the engineer answered. "He's that cross with Nora and you."

Cross he would be, the lieutenant thought. He knows something's fishy, but he doesn't know what. Well, he'll find out soon enough.

Braced against a crate, Hoffman felt good. The sun beat down on him and gulls wheeled in the bright blue sky. He could see the sawed-off pyramid of Spanish Island very clearly. The island was less than three miles away. The sun glistened on its rocky sides and picked out the tower at the summit. The lieutenant was quietly exultant. His mission was all but completed, and, considering the gale, in the shortest possible time. There had been no violence, no pursuit. As yet, no one on the mainland knew of the presence of the U-boat.

The mate came on deck with two china mugs of tea, and Hoffman carefully took them forward. Nora accepted hers with a wan little smile of thanks.

"We seem to be right on schedule," Hoffman reported. "The island's dead ahead."

The girl sipped her hot milky tea. A heavy sea smashed into the *Kerry Queen*, spilling some of it, and she said softly, "Damn! What a shocking little boat this is."

Hoffman grinned and they sat together for a bit in silent companionship. *Kerry Queen* still bucked and plunged and rolled, but the lieutenant was certain the sea was moderating.

He put away the tea mugs and presently the girl asked, "What will happen, Peter, when we enter the cove? Do you think they'll fire a shot across the bow?"

Hoffman had been asking himself the same question. "I don't think anything will happen," he said thoughtfully. "There's no reason for the skipper to turn and run when he sees a strange submarine alongside the quay."

"No," Nora agreed, "he'll be curious. And anyway, Doctor Fitz wouldn't let him turn back."

"Is Doctor Fitz so brave, now?"

"Indeed he is," Nora retorted with a flash of spirit. "He's afraid of nothing, and he wants to reach Lady Maudie." She was abruptly silent and Hoffman knew she still worried about her grandmother. He patted her hand and listened to the thump of the trawler's engine.

After a few minutes, the lieutenant asked another question. "Why did you save me, Nora? You were about to tell me when the mate——"

She turned to him, smiling, but saying nothing. And this time Peter Hoffman knew the reason. Slowly, he cupped her chin in his hand and kissed her. He drew back and they briefly regarded one another with grave, delighted wonder. Then he crushed her to him and kissed her again and again, at length and with passion.

They were locked in each other's arms and Hoffman was murmuring awkward endearments into her hair, when there was a deafening close-at-hand blast. It was *Kerry Queen's* whistle, announcing her arrival at Spanish Island. A bell jingled in the engine room and the trawler's engine slowed. From the saloon portholes they could see the rocky cliffs of Spanish sweeping down to the entrance of the cove. Smiling at each other, they disengaged themselves. Nora smoothed her hair. By Hoffman's wristwatch it was exactly eleven forty-five. *Kerry Queen* was right on the dot.

He went out on deck with the girl as the trawler chugged into the tiny cove. For an instant Hoffman was staggered by the absence of the submarine. Had she left them? Was she so well camouflaged? Then he realized what must have happened—she had sortied on the surface and was sheltered on the other side of the island—and he grinned with relief. There was a knot of people on the quay and in a minute they were recognizable. One man—old O Ŕuiarc—and the women—Mrs. O Ŕuiarc, Mrs. Mor, Brede, Maeve, Kelly, and Peigeen Og. There were also children and dogs, but no German sailors. Intuitively, Hoffman knew their dispositions. Some in the sick bay, some at the Command Post. Another in the Norseman's Tower. He stared up at the crumbling stone watchtower and was rewarded, he thought, by a glint that could have been caused by the sun striking binoculars.

Dr. FitzGerald had come down from the wheelhouse and stood by the rail amidships, waving to the islanders. The mate was on the fo'c'sle with a line coiled in his hand; the skipper concentrated on his approach and the engineer waited below. Hoffman took Nora aft where Tomas and Eamon stood.

"Pay attention to what I say," Hoffman said, "and obey every word of it. When we go ashore, act naturally. Greet the women and children. Help unload the ship. Make sure you unload our gear yourselves and leave it on the jetty.

"Remember, there are German sailors with machine pistols in the sick bay—the storehouse. If there's trouble, they'll start shooting. Women and children may be killed, as well as the trawler's crew. Do you understand?"

They nodded, and Tomas asked the inevitable question: "Where's the submarine, Lieutenant?"

"On the other side of the island—I hope," Hoffman said with a wry grin. Then he added, "You've done a great deal in the last few days. Don't be careless now and ruin it."

He turned away to watch *Kerry Queen* go alongside. His hands were sweating. This was the climax of his expedition. If U-324's presence were made known, the Germans could take over the trawler—probably without bloodshed. But by dusk, the little ship would be missed in Ballykerry; there would be questions on the radio-telephone hard to answer, and probably boats from the mainland. By morning there would be many boats and planes. U-324 might be repaired, but the secret would be out and they would have no head start on the R.A.F. Hoffman wiped his palms on his jersey and slipped his right hand under it to feel the cold reassurance of the Luger. With his left, he covered Nora's hand as it gripped the rail. In a little while, if his luck held, the steamer would be done and his mission a success. And even, incredibly, if it were to fail, he had found a girl who was lovely and brave. With amazement, he realized he was in love.

The engine-room bell jangled again, *Kerry Queen* backed down, the yeasty water pounding and frothing under her counter, and the mate tossed his heaving line to Sean O Ŕuiarc.

Monday had begun as a lovely day on the island, but the people of Spanish greeted it sullenly, still shocked by the events of the weekend. Shelagh went about her early-morning chores as mechanically as a sleepwalker. She spoke to no one, not even her mother. Up the path, Padraig gingerly negotiated some tea and a gruel-like mixture of bread and milk. Padraig's broken teeth and smashed nose throbbed with pain, but he was healthy enough to refuse indignantly some brandy (sent to Maeve by Lady Maud) and announced himself ready for the day's work. All Spanish was distressed and vengeful—yet it held hope for the new day. Doctor Fitz was sure to come—Father Healy very likely. Tomas and Eamon were due to return, too, and with them Lieutenant Hoffman, the one German most of them trusted.

U-324's crew, on the other hand, was exuberant. The Irish surgeon was coming, the Luftwaffe was coming—perhaps even Lieutenant Hoffman. Grand Admiral Doenitz was aware of their struggle and was taking personal charge. It was natural, certainly, to be apprehensive about the visit of the *Kerry Queen*. With the steamer alongside the quay, one of a hundred things could betray them. Nonetheless, spirits ran high. By tomorrow, the sailors felt, the Shark Boat would be homeward bound.

From early morning, Germans and Irish alike were busy. There was a great deal to be done to make U-324 ready for sea; the anchor was taken in, the camouflage nettings dismantled and stored behind the sick bay, the curraghs secured on the fo'c'sle, the engines tested, and the various watchstanders chosen and instructed. The caisson used in patching the hull was removed, the boat's ballast was trimmed, and the quay thoroughly policed. It was hard work for the most part, and for the first time since U-324's arrival the Germans worked alone. The Irish were busy enough with their chores. They obeyed sullenly when Petty Officer Kreisler rounded them up after breakfast and herded them to the Beg cottage. All the adults except Lady Maud were there, even Timmy Mor. But when they were assembled, there was an unexpected objection to Ludtke's meeting. Led by Maura Mor and Maeve, the islanders refused to enter the kitchen as long as Reigel was present.

"I'll not be under the same thatch as that wicked man," the Widow said unequivocally. "No more will Shelagh."

"Nor will I enter the house of my birth," Maeve cried out, "until that devil has left it."

At that, Shelagh began to cry and although Kreisler and his sailors pushed and threatened, the knot of Irish refused to move. Finally the captain ordered Reigel outside and the islanders entered the kitchen, tight-lipped. Sean O Ŕuiarc took a chair and glared at the captain. Padraig Mor, returned to the scene of his frightful beating, stood by the dresser. The three older women, Maura, Kathy, and Kelly, found chairs or creepies, and the others ranged themselves against the walls, shuffling their feet on the hard-packed clay. Finally there was silence in the kitchen. Everyone stared at Ludtke in his rocker, and the captain could almost physically feel the hatred in their eyes.

He began, nonetheless, with an elaborate preface. First, he praised the islanders' cooperation and their anti-English sentiments. He stressed the continuing need for secrecy if U-324 was to return to Lorient. Then he confirmed what they all knew—that Doctor Fitz would be aboard the trawler, and why it was necessary to pretend Lady Wynne was critically injured. The women fidgeted at this and glanced at Sean O Ŕuiarc, but the old man's face remained grim and impassive.

Ludtke told them their letters had been censored the night before. Again, that was something they knew, but the irritation showed on their faces. Then he described his plan to take U-324 to the other side of the island, with Dermod, Padraig, and Timmy aboard her. Finally, he cautioned Maeve Mor and Peigeen Og about their children. They must be very careful with the little ones, he warned, lest they innocently betray the U-boat to the crew of the *Kerry Queen*.

"I believe there are normally three men in the steamer's crew. They are probably unarmed. If they are warned there are German sailors on Spanish, or if they seem suspicious, Lieutenant Reigel will attack them from the sick bay with his well-armed men. The *Kerry Queen* will be captured and it's possible that her crew and many of you on the quay will be hurt. Lieutenant Reigel——"

Sean O Ŕuiarc spat eloquently into the fireplace, and there was an angry little murmur from the shawled women against the walls. Ludtke decided further reference to the first lieutenant was not necessary. Instead, he would show his trump card.

"There's one chance in a million the police know we are on the island. It's possible, for instance, they have captured Lieutenant Hoffman, Tomas, and Eamon and Fraulein Berkeley. Suppose the *Kerry Queen* docks and twenty officers of the *Guarda Siochana,* all armed, come ashore. You'll have to persuade them the U-boat has gone, gone for good. If you don't, if the police start searching for us, the signalman at the tower will let me know, and the U-boat will sail for France forthwith—with Padraig, Dermod, and young Timmy aboard."

There was a sudden gasp and then sullen silence. The circle of women stared at him dully, and Maeve began to sob quietly. Ludtke looked from one to another and then directly at Sean O Ŕuiarc. The captain's yellow eyes glinted.

"Any questions?" he asked coldly.

There was only a hostile silence, and he said: "Very well, Herr O Ŕuiarc. We needn't detain these ladies and gentlemen any longer."

They filed out, white-faced and wordless. Kathy O Ŕuiarc, Maeve, and Peigeen went to work gathering kelp, loading it into the cart, and taking the loads down to the jetty. Kelp was a valuable export of Spanish Island. Periodically, the entire population concentrated on the back-breaking harvest of seaweed. When dried and burned to kelp, it could be sold to the iodine plants of the mainland.

Meanwhile, the three men and Timmy Mor went to the jetty where Sean obtained permission to bring in the lobster tank. The tank was a shallow rectangular box, eight feet by four, made of perforated sheets of galvanized iron, and with a hinged hatch. Two metal oil drums, lashed to each end, maintained the tank in submerged buoyancy at its mooring, a half cable's length from the jetty. In season, the catch was emptied into this tank each day to await the *Kerry Queen's* visits.

Under the watchful eyes of the Germans, the islanders unhooked the tank from its buoy and towed it to the jetty. The hatch was opened and the dark green lobsters were scooped up and transferred to kegs stenciled P. HANLON—FISH PIER—DINGLE. The tide was only just beginning to flood, so that the tank was several feet beneath the top of the quay, and it was hard work for Padraig and Dermod to lift the kegs up to old Sean and the boy. The work went slowly. Watching the islanders and seeing their difficulty, Petty Officer Dietrich and a handful of Germans volunteered to help manhandle the kegs up onto the jetty. The Irish refused and it took them nearly an hour to accomplish what would normally have been a few minutes' work. Finally, five dozen lobsters were ready for transshipment. At sixpence apiece, they constituted the main source of income for Spanish Island in the spring and summer months.

The islanders had hardly returned the empty tank to its mooring when Ludtke was carried down to the U-boat's bridge. The captain was in good spirits. The camouflage was off the decks, the sun shone, and it felt good to be aboard the Shark Boat again. He busied himself in planning his navigation and in instructing Able Seaman Kramer as to the ranges and bearings he would require. At five minutes to ten, the chief machinist's mate reported the main engines ready for sea.

"Very well, Albrecht," Ludtke said briskly. He called down the open hatch to the conning tower, "Muller, set the cruising watch."

It was a good feeling to be taking one's own boat to sea again. Ludtke had always loved the sea. As a small boy, he had dreamed of commanding a battleship. Those dreams had been shattered, and, disillusioned and embittered, he had focused his ambitions on the merchant service. For fifteen years with North German Lloyd, he had concentrated everything on becoming a ship's master. War had come before he reached that pinnacle, but for three years he had commanded U-324. The Shark Boat had been his only command. He had built, commissioned, and fought her. He knew her strong points, her weaknesses, and her whims. He had been careless with her, but he would bring her safely home, and they would make each other famous. That was a good feeling, too. He almost grinned as he looked down at Padraig, Timmy, and Dermod on the fo'c'sle and at Reigel and his line-handlers on the quay.

"Signal from the Norseman's Tower, sir," Koenig reported, and added in a few seconds, "Signal reads as follows, sir: Smoke bearing oh-six-oh degrees. End of signal, sir."

"Right on schedule," said the captain, curbing a smile. "Single up all lines," he shouted to the sailors on the quay.

A minute later, he began to sing out other orders, a series of commands that would get the submarine underway. For all his pleasure, Ludtke was concerned about the boat's draught. U-324 had been moved into her present berth at flood tide and it lacked several hours of being high water again. The diesels coughed and rumbled, the wires and gangway were taken in, and the boat moved slowly astern. There was a shuddering, grinding sound as her plates scraped over the bottom. It was slow, anxious going, but eventually U-324 was in a safe depth.

The boat was still down by the stern and listed to port. Ludtke ordered her tanks trimmed, and when she was balanced he waved to the sailors ashore and gave orders to helm and engine room. Slowly the Shark Boat turned, slid out of the cove, and crept south and west, around to the western shore of the island. It was eleven twenty-five by the captain's watch when he turned her head into the wind and ordered the engines throttled down so that the submarine barely had steerageway. He felt naked on the surface, but, as he told himself, there was very little danger. A stray R.A.F. Catalina or Sunderland could appear, of course, or a fisherman from the mainland. But it was not likely. The bridge watch was alert, Koenig with his telescope on the tower, Kramer checking the ranges with a stadimeter, the Oerlikon gunner sweeping horizon and sky with his glasses. On the fo'c'sle below them, Dermod smoked his pipe with resignation. Ludtke lit a cigar. There was nothing to do but wait.

When U-324 left the cove, Reigel, satisfied that no trace of the submarine's presence remained on the quay, took himself up to the vantage point of the Beg doorstep. Quickly, he picked up the steamer—a dirty-looking trawler with a high sheer and a single stack making for the entrance to the cove. He put down his binoculars and noted that it was eleven twenty-five. In another twenty minutes the *Kerry Queen* would be berthed. Trying to contain his excitement, he went swiftly down the path to the jetty. Old O Ruiarc and the women were knotted together there, talking quietly. Shelagh, he noted, was absent, but he knew it would be foolish to inquire about her. The Irish stopped talking as he came up and looked at him sullenly.

"Attention!" Reigel said sharply. "You all know what we expect of you. If the steamer learns there's a submarine here, there will be trouble. Very serious trouble. There's a crew of three on the steamer, all unarmed. I'll have eight sailors in the sick bay with me, all armed with rifles and machine pistols, and all watching you closely. Remember, we want the doctor to come ashore, so he can tend our wounded, so we can leave you in peace and friendship."

He paused, looking at them in turn, trying to ascertain each probable action when the *Kerry Queen* was alongside the quay. Brede's face was stolid and blank, Peigeen Og was frowning, and Mrs. Mor and Maeve looked mutinous. Kelly glared fiercely back at the first lieutenant and old Kathy O Ruiarc had her jaw outthrust and her lips tight. Sean stared at the cove entrance.

There were three children on the jetty and they were no more amiable than their elders. Eamon Og's boy, not quite five, looked defiantly at Reigel. His younger sister fearfully clutched her mother's skirt. Padraig Mor's second son, aged four, wore a solemn frown as he looked from his mother to his grandmother.

Not much peace and friendship here, Reigel thought. He counted the islanders again, took into consideration Shelagh, Lady Maud, and an Og baby in its crib, and decided all were present or accounted for.

"Act naturally, now," he said. The women stared at him without speaking, and he wondered if they realized how nervous he was.

"Ask questions about Ballykerry—about your friends there. Talk about the gale we've had, about fishing, or anything you want to. Smile. And keep an eye on the children. That's important. Don't let them go aboard the steamer. Don't let them out of your sight."

No one said a word. Reigel slapped his pistol holster and said again: "We want nothing from the *Kerry Queen*. We only want the doctor ashore, so we can leave in peace. We want the steamer to leave as soon as possible and suspecting nothing. We put our trust in Irish neutrality."

He turned abruptly and walked toward the sick bay. With every stride, he felt the grim, accusing eyes boring into his back. He had just left the quay when a sudden blast made him want to jump. A second later, he realized it was the whistle of the *Kerry Queen*, just outside the entrance to the cove and trumpeting the news of her arrival.

Inside the crumbling old building, Reigel found an atmosphere of tense expectancy. It was like being in a submerged U-boat, braced for the first pattern of depth charges. Three of the six wounded men were asleep or unconscious, but the others, bright-eyed with tension, were propped up on their mattresses. Barndt and the able-bodied crewmen squatted among the pallets, on buoys, lobster pots, and coils of line, smoking and nervously checking their weapons. They looked at him as he entered and closed the wooden door.

"The smoking lamp is out," the first officer said. "Our friend, the *Kerry Queen*, is outside the entrance."

He had ordered a peephole drilled that morning and he went directly to it. It gave a good view of the quay and the islanders. Although he couldn't see the trawler, Reigel began giving his sailors a running commentary, as though he were a skipper reporting what he saw in the attack periscope.

"They're all on the quay, boys. The old man, six women, and three kids. *Zum Teufel!* They look like mourners at a funeral. They'll give the show away before she's alongside."

Barndt hopefully suggested the trawler's crew might interpret the gloomy faces as concern for Lady Maud. No one really believed him, but they wanted to, and there were grins of approval.

"That's right, quack," big Scheutze said. "If the old lady's dying, her friends aren't going to be happy——"

"Shut up!" Reigel snapped, new excitement in his voice. "I can see her now—a dirty-looking coaster. One stack. They must be burning peat by the look of the smoke she's making. High freeboard. No radio antenna I can see."

He went on with his description of the trawler and her approach. Inside the murky building, his men could hear the jingle of a bell and the pounding of an ancient reciprocal engine as the way came off *Kerry Queen* and she backed down alongside the quay.

"They've got the bowline over," Reigel said, "Sean's making it fast. There are quite a few aboard—God, that's the chief aboard her—Mr. Hoffman. And the girl. Tomas and Eamon Og, too."

He twisted around from his peephole, his voice shrill with excitement. "Maybe they've the gear we need. If they have, we'll get away from this damned island—we'll all get back to France."

There was an animated buzz of approval. "They thought the Shark Boat was gone," someone chortled happily. "Wait'll they see us come into Lorient."

Reigel recovered himself quickly. "Shut up!" he commanded. "We don't know yet what the chief has brought." He put his eye back to the peephole.

"They've rigged a gangway to the quay. That must be the doctor, an old man with knickers and black bag. He's on the quay now, shaking hands with the natives. Here comes Hoffman ashore with the girl. He looks all right. There doesn't seem to be any trouble. . . ."

For the next five minutes, Reigel continued his commentary. His field of vision on the jetty was limited, and, through the narrow aperture, the scene was crowded and confused. Reigel described how the islanders greeted the doctor and Nora Berkeley—and how they shook hands with the two fishermen and the trawlermen. He told of the excitement of the children and the dogs.

"They're coming off the quay," Reigel said sharply. "Silence now. They'll pass close aboard us. There's the doctor walking with Kelly. Mr. Hoffman and the girl are right behind them."

The little group came toward him, the physician asking questions and Kelly looking unhappy. Immediately behind, Hoffman and Nora walked silently. Reigel had only a glimpse of them before they passed from his vision, and he resumed his description of the activity on the jetty. He told how some pigs were brought ashore, squealing with terror, and how Maeve led them away, escorted by laughing children and barking dogs. Sacks of flour were unloaded, he said, and stacks of firewood and bundles of turf bricks. A mail sack was given to Sean, who laboriously receipted for it and, in turn, handed the trawler captain the outgoing post in its canvas bag. Carboys and coils of cable were brought ashore and Reigel's excitement grew. A number of other boxes and crates were brought over the gangway. Some were small, others large and obviously heavy. Reigel did not even guess at their content; they might contain circuit breakers, or they might be provisions and equipment for the islanders. As he squinted through his peephole, he concentrated on some sign that the Germans had been betrayed. There was no such sign. Kathy O Ruiarc urged the ass, with its little two-wheeled cart, onto the jetty. Boxes of freight and stacks of fuel were loaded into it and into the animal's paniers. The old woman led the beast toward them and out of sight. Simultaneously, the loading on of bundles of kelp and kegs of lobsters began.

Reigel's watch said twelve forty-five when the trawler's crew prepared to get their craft underway. There were handshakes and waves, the gangway was taken in, and the engine-room bell jingled. Sean and Peigeen threw the lines aboard and the *Kerry Queen* puffed and panted astern, smoke pouring from her funnel. She saluted the island with a blast from her whistle and slowly turned, making for the entrance to the cove. In a matter of minutes, she had passed out of Reigel's vision, and he stepped back from his peephole.

"She's left the quay, boys," he announced. "We'll give her five minutes to clear the harbor. Then we'll see what they've brought us."

He forced himself to sit down and watch the crawling hand of his watch. By now the doctor would have reached the Wynne cottage and had his little surprise. There was plenty of time for Reigel to visualize his welcome. Kelly would open the door and the physician would walk toward the bedroom, prepared to produce his best bedside manner, and then he would see the two strange seamen with pistols in their fists. He would protest, even think of bolting, but Hoffman would be close behind him, and Hoffman could explain things. Sit down, he would say to the doctor, in his polite fashion. Sit down, please, Lady Maud is perfectly well. We are U-boat sailors and we need your help. In a little while, when the *Kerry Queen* slips her moorings, we will show you what we want.

. . .

In fact, events in the Wynne cottage developed almost exactly as Reigel had foreseen. Lady Maud was sitting before the kitchen fire, wrapped in a quilt and smiling broadly. Two armed sailors were there, too, showing themselves only when Dr. FitzGerald was safely inside. For a few seconds the doctor was shocked, silent, and incredulous. The sight of his face made Lady Maud giggle as she assured him she had never felt better. Nora wept with relief, and Hoffman shook hands with the two sailors and received their embraces, hardly in accord with Naval discipline, but warm and congratulatory. Grinning, the sailors confirmed Hoffman's theory about the U-boat's absence. The captain had taken her to sea that morning; she was off the western shore of the island, in touch by signal lamp with the Norseman's Tower. Mr. Reigel, with eight men, was in the sick bay, ready to storm the trawler if necessary.

Dr. FitzGerald was choleric with anger when he realized he had been hoaxed. His violent reaction amused Lady Maud and distressed Nora Berkeley—especially when he glared at her and spoke darkly of perjury. At that, Lieutenant Hoffman stopped grinning and told the physician to be silent. He peered briefly through a window and assured himself the unloading of the *Kerry Queen* was proceeding normally.

"We'll stay right here," he said, "until the steamer leaves."

"Set out the luncheon, Kelly," Lady Maud commanded. Her eyes twinkled. "Let's make our visitors comfortable."

Kelly shuffled efficiently about the kitchen, setting out plates of cold lobster and boiled potatoes, soda bread and tea. Dr. FitzGerald glowered at the fire. Nora, feeling much better after applying powder and lipstick, brought Peter Hoffman over to her grandmother and presented him.

"Lieutenant, is it now? You don't look much like a lieutenant to me, young man."

Hoffman smiled back at her. "We didn't think the uniform would be helpful on the mainland, ma'am."

"He's ashamed of his uniform," Dr. FitzGerald snapped.

Lady Maud ignored the physician's comment. "Nora tells me your trip was successful—and exciting."

"Quite exciting, ma'am. As to its success, we'll have to wait and see."

"Och, it must have been exciting," said Dr. FitzGerald with heavy sarcasm. "Hiding behind a woman's skirts."

"Doctor Fitz, for God's sake——" Nora began hotly, but her grandmother's shrill voice cut her off:

"Please to remember, Doctor, this gentleman is a guest under my thatch." She rapped out the words coldly, and the physician turned back to the fire. Hoffman, controlling his anger, bowed to the old lady and walked to the other side of the kitchen.

For the next few minutes, Lady Maud asked innumerable questions of Nora. Hoffman stayed by the window, watching the activity on the quay and listening with growing depression to the sailors' report. They told him of Oberteuffer's accident and the chief quartermaster's death. Of the violation of Shelagh and the beating of Padraig. The engineer officer listened grimly. The elation he had known when he crossed Lady Maud's threshold was shattered. Haas was gone. Reigel had played the fool and relations with the islanders had deteriorated badly. It seemed to Hoffman that the U-boat was in even greater danger than before.

They turned their attention to Kelly's luncheon but only the two sailors ate much. Nora learned about Shelagh and Padraig and all the joy of the morning went out of her. Hearing the news, Dr. FitzGerald scowled even more fiercely at his plate. Once or twice Peter Hoffman caught Nora's eye and they exchanged small smiles, but in spite of Lady Maud's questions and comments, the gloom was thick in the Wynne kitchen.

Kelly and Nora had begun to take up the dishes when one of the sailors reported the *Kerry Queen* underway. A moment later they heard the farewell blast of her whistle. Hoffman opened the door and watched the trawler steam out of the cove. At least they now had a chance, a fighting chance, he said to himself. The acid and cable had been landed safely and, apparently, *Kerry Queen*'s crew had not been warned.

The little steamer was hardly into open water before Lieutenant Reigel led his men out of the sick bay. They lit cigarettes, blinked happily in the sunlight, and went to inspect the freight on the quay. Shortly thereafter they were clapping one another's backs and shouting with excitement. Mr. Hoffman had done it. The cable, the bottles of acid, and the circuit breakers necessary for their return to France were there, only awaiting the Shark Boat.

Even before they ripped open the first crate, the recall signal was flashed from the Norseman's Tower to the submarine on the western shore of the island. Ludtke shouted down the hatch for full speed. At the same time, Hoffman emerged from the Wynne cottage and started down the hill to the quay. He met Sean O Ŕuiarc with the mail sack on the path and greeted him warmly. The sunburned old man gave only a grudging nod in reply, and Hoffman went on, perplexed and troubled. When he reached the quay he was greeted with an enthusiasm that partially restored his spirits. Reigel pounded him on the back and the ratings crowded around with grinning congratulations.

"Wait a bit, wait a bit," he said smiling. "I can't be sure this is the right gear. This cable may not be right for our circuits."

They laughed, certain he was only modest, confident in the luck of the Shark Boat. Even Barndt's usually morose face was wreathed in smiles.

"Look, mates," he cried, pointing up the hill. "Here comes the surgeon to take over. Oberteuffer's got a chance now!"

Dr. FitzGerald was picking his way down the path, Nora Berkeley close behind. Barndt's delight in seeing him was dampened when the physician and the girl turned to enter Maura Mor's cottage.

"Hell's delight," Barndt said aggrievedly. "We need him down here in the sick bay."

"He'll be here presently, quack," Hoffman told him. "He wants to examine Shelagh."

Reigel laughed scornfully and changed the subject. "Tell us about your adventures, Chief. Where did you get the stuff? Did you have any trouble?"

The sailors crowded around as Hoffman outlined the main events of the past three days. They were still asking questions when U-324 stood into the cove.

"Stand by to handle her lines," Reigel boomed, and the men dispersed along the quay. The two officers stood watching the U-boat's approach.

"Her trim is good," Hoffman said. "I can see you had to tear up the Winter Garden."

Reigel grunted affirmatively. "How did Nora act on your little expedition, Chief?" he grinned. "Was she cooperative?"

"Very much so. That looks like a shipshape patch, Number One."

"I'm glad she's back, and that she cooperates. Life on this rock will be more interesting now."

"Keep your hands off her, Reigel," Peter Hoffman grated. Long ago he had decided he was not fond of the first lieutenant. Now he suddenly detested the blond wavy hair, the handsome, clefted chin, and the debonair, confident air—everything about Reigel.

His remark only amused the first lieutenant. Reigel was still chuckling when the gangway was rigged and their commanding officer was carried ashore. Both officers saluted. Ludtke had noted the acid bottles and cable on the jetty, and his spirits were high.

"Well, Chief," he sang out, "you finally got back. Have you what you need?"

"I think so, Captain. We'll know pretty soon."

"How long to be ready for sea?"

Hoffman blinked. "Hard to say, sir. We'll start work right away. I'll report as soon as I can."

Ludtke turned to the first lieutenant. "The trawler crew didn't suspect anything, Number One?"

"No, sir, not a thing."

"Doctor aboard?"

"Yes, sir, he's up in the Mor cottage now."

The captain grunted and turned to his engineer officer. He made brief inquiries about Hoffman's trip and nodded at the responses. "This is good, Chief, this is good," he said. He shook Hoffman's hand. "Headquarters will hear of this, Chief. Now, there's nothing to stop us. Will you gentlemen join me for lunch?"

Reigel accepted and Hoffman said he had eaten.

"Very well, Chief," Ludtke said jovially. "I'll send Number One back when we're done." He ordered himself carried up the hill, shouting back at Hoffman to keep up the good work.

Hoffman wearily saluted. He had done a good job, he supposed, but he was conscious only of fatigue and dejection. Thanks to Reigel's cruel lust, the islanders were no longer their allies. He was in love with Nora, and she possibly with him, but the same lust threatened her. With a bitter oath, he went aboard and ordered the cable brought below. They had the cable, acid, and breakers, but he knew it would not be an easy job. Albrecht, Kreisler, and himself were competent to make the usual underway repairs. They knew electrical engineering—but only as it was treated in the maintenance handbooks and operating manuals of the U-Waffe. This would be a major job, one normally supervised by an engineer captain and a staff of civilian experts.

Less than three minutes after Hoffman had gone below, there was an ugly confrontation on the path that led up the hill. Ludtke had to be carried past the Widow's cottage to get to the Begs'. He was abreast of the former, Reigel trudging beside him, when the door opened and Dr. FitzGerald exploded from it, followed by Padraig and Tomas Mor.

"That's him now, Doctor Fitz, the big one," Ludtke heard one of the brothers say, and he told his bearers to stop and put him down. The captain felt good and almost at peace with the world. But the three Irishmen were angry, and the doctor seemed the angriest of all.

"Och, you murdering bully," he spat at Reigel, coming up to him. "You ought to be horsewhipped, you cowardly Hun!" He tried to strike

Reigel but the first lieutenant easily caught his arm and pushed him back on Padraig.

"Watch out, bantam rooster, or you'll get hurt," he grated.

Dr. FitzGerald was obviously ready to risk being hurt, but Padraig restrained him and Tomas stepped forward, his huge fists knotted. "You had sport with my sister behind my back, you dirty, stinking Hun," he cried. "Now take off that pistol and try someone as big as you."

"Silence!" Ludtke roared. "Silence, all of you and attention to what I say! Mister, I forbid you to take off your pistol. That's an order. There'll be no fist fighting here. Now, you, Tomas. There's no evidence as to what man molested your sister. Shut up, damn your dirty eyes—" he snarled as the Irishman tried to interrupt. "If there was proof a member of my crew was guilty, I wouldn't horsewhip him, I'd *shoot* him."

The harsh brutality of his words awed them, and the captain pressed his advantage. "Tomas, Mr. Hoffman tells me you were of great help on his mission. Believe me, you'll be suitably rewarded by the Reich. You, Doctor, are angry because we had to trick you to get you here. Sometimes, sir, the end justifies the means. There are badly wounded men in our sick bay, men who've not had medical attention. They're not responsible for your being tricked. I am. But I pray you, Doctor, don't ignore those dying men. That's your real duty on Spanish Island."

Ludtke clapped his bearers on their backs, was swung into their arms, and resumed his journey to the Begs'. At that moment, Nora Berkeley appeared at the door of the Mor cottage. She had been trying, unsuccessfully, to comfort Shelagh, and had been alarmed by the altercation outside. Reigel greeted her with a salute and a grin—which were ignored—and followed his captain. Doctor Fitz and the Mor brothers were left grumbling on the rocky path.

The incident irritated Ludtke, but he dismissed it as he sat in the rocker before the Begs' fireplace, drank a cognac, and watched Brede scurry about with preparations for the noon meal. As they ate, Reigel described in detail the visit of the *Kerry Queen*.

Despite the unpleasantness on the path, the atmosphere in the Beg kitchen was almost amiable. Everyone was pleased the steamer had come and gone without incident, and that Doctor Fitz was present. Everyone, including the seaman with the radio-telephone watch, was glad at the thought of U-324's imminent return to France. For Ludtke, that meant the Oak Leaves, and for the seaman, precious leave. For Brede and Dermod, it meant a return to their normal lives, freedom to fish or visit the mainland. Exactly what it meant for Lieutenant Reigel, he could not be sure. He told himself it meant his own boat, perhaps one of the new snorkel boats, with a tomcat on the conning tower. The U-Waffe needed new drivers.

Inevitably, the talk swung to Hoffman's adventures on the mainland.

"I wonder how the girl worked out," Ludtke said. "She wasn't too happy to go."

"Nora's a lovely girl, Captain," Dermod said and was ignored for his pains.

"She's happy enough now, Captain," Reigel said. "She's got the chief eating out of her hand."

"So?" Ludtke grunted.

"Yes, sir. I never saw him look at a skirt before. But Hoffman's stuck on this one."

"So?" Ludtke said again, so quietly Reigel had to strain to hear him. "There's a lot of romance on this island, isn't there, Number One? It's a regular Tahiti, isn't it?"

That sounded like a joke and Reigel wanted to smile, but the look on Ludtke's face stopped him.

"No, sir," he said.

There was a long silence. Then the captain, speaking in German, said, "The chief is important to me, Number One. I think I ought to warn this girl he's still married. Eh? That Hoffman is out of circulation. Eh?"

"Yes, sir," the first lieutenant said, smiling to himself.

Brede cleared away the dishes and Ludtke, with a belch, lit a cigar. Dermod waited a moment, saw he would not be offered one, and produced his blackened, taped-up pipe with its metal bowl cover, his knife, and a plug of tobacco. Similarly ignored, Reigel lit a Gauloise. He told the radio-telephone watchstander to go down to the sick bay to see if the doctor was in attendance. If he was, the sailor was to try to make him understand the captain wanted to see him. Reigel drew deeply on his cigarette. The captain's most recent remarks made him feel good. It would take a day to make the repairs—maybe two. In that time, he could amuse himself with Nora Berkeley. She has spirit, that one, he told himself. With her, he could forget his embarrassment over the imbecilic Shelagh.

The atmosphere was chilled by the arrival of a long-faced Dietrich. The P.O. telegraphist brought with him a signal from Headquarters. Continuing bad weather in Brittany, it appeared, had grounded the long-range Focke-Wulf squadrons. The rescue mission was delayed until Tuesday.

Ludtke studied the message and blasphemed mechanically. Then he seemed to recover his buoyancy. "Ah, well, Number One, we don't need the bloody Luftwaffe. We'll get the motors running and go back to Lorient under our own power, eh?"

Reigel agreed with enthusiasm and presently the sailor returned. The surgeon had been in the sick bay and had understood. He would report to the captain in a few minutes. Ludtke grunted and looked at his watch.

"Damnation! It's after two. Get down to the boat," he growled at the sailor. "My compliments to Mr. Hoffman. Tell him he's to keep the engineering gang on the job until the boat's ready to sail. Tell him the first officer will be down shortly to bear a hand. *Raus!*"

The man saluted and scuttled out. Expelling a long jet of blue smoke, Reigel grinned inwardly. Poor Hoffman. Anyone could see he was exhausted. But that didn't matter when you sailed under Herr Ludtke. The son-of-a-dog. How could he understand human frailties, like weariness, or fearing an amputation, or wanting to sleep with a good-looking woman? The answer, Reigel told himself, is that the son-of-a-dog isn't human. He doesn't know fatigue or pain or love. Probably he doesn't know what he's fighting for. His only goals are Gross Registered Tonnage sunk and the Oak Leaves.

"Mr. Reigel," said Ludtke sharply, and the forward legs of Reigel's chair cracked smartly down on the earthen floor.

"Sir?"

"Don't sit there wool-gathering, mister. The chief needs help. Battery acid, for one thing. I think you'll find he needs the rainwater, to mix it with the sulphuric. There may be other ways you can help Hoffman. If you can't, get the boat camouflaged again."

Reigel stood up, masking his irritation, and acknowledged Ludtke's suggestion with a stiff salute and an even stiffer "Aye, aye, sir." The son-of-a-dog, he said to himself. He left the cottage and a short distance down the path met Dr. FitzGerald and Nora Berkeley, plodding upward. The doctor gave him a malevolent stare and Nora tried to look the other way as they passed. Undismayed, Reigel bade her a good afternoon and made his most punctilious, heel-clicking salute. He watched her legs appreciatively as they climbed the path. She was a lot more woman, he told himself, than Hoffman deserved.

When Dr. FitzGerald and Nora entered the Beg cottage, Ludtke was agreeable to both. With an effort, he stood up and made stiff little bows.

"We are very grateful, fraulein, for your help in locating the cable and acid. Please sit down." The captain indicated stools and offered the physician a cigar, which was curtly refused.

"Well, Doctor, what can you tell me about my boys?" Ludtke asked jovially. "Can you patch them up by tomorrow? We'll be underway for France tomorrow."

Dr. FitzGerald scowled. "There are sick men down there," he said shortly. "At least two of them should be in a proper hospital."

"We've done what we could for them, Doctor Fitz," Brede said. "Of course, it wasn't much, but we've tried to make them comfortable."

Dr. FitzGerald glared at her, his eyebrows joined in a heavy, uncompromising thicket, his eyes sharp as ice and his lips compressed.

"Aye, you've done very well by the Germans," he said. "You've lied for them about Lady Maudie——"

"Not at all, not at all," Dermod Beg said feebly. "That wasn't a lie. We had to have you here, Doctor Fitz."

The physician did not appear to hear.

"And what of poor Shelagh?" he asked softly. "And she as witless as a sparrow. Och, the shame of it, the terrible shame of it."

The Begs stared at the floor, saying nothing. Presently Dr. FitzGerald spoke again.

"I'd like some penicillin for the lad with the amputated hand, Captain. There's a stock of it in my cottage at Ballykerry. Could we send a curragh for it?"

"No," Ludtke said. "We'll be sailing tomorrow. Oberteuffer will make it."

"They could go tonight, with a couple of your sailors. I'll give them directions——"

"I'm not taking the chance, Doctor," Ludtke snapped. "Here, take a look at this leg of mine. I'm sure it needs something more than morphine and cognac."

Dr. FitzGerald grunted and washed his hands. Then he hitched his stool to Ludtke's side and opened his bag. He cut away the bandages and sniffed them with distaste. When he peeled the last layer of gauze away, Nora was white-faced, Brede sucked in her breath as though she had been physically hurt, and her husband gave a little groan.

Ludtke's right leg was badly swollen from the ankle to above the knee. Most of it was a pasty white, but around the jagged, four-inch wound itself, the skin was hideously discolored. Barndt had done what he could. The smashed bone had been splinted and sulfanilamide used generously. But it was obvious that the leg was in poor condition. There was some suppuration, and the physician swabbed it away with alcohol, conscious of the pain he caused his patient. He studied the wound intently and, after an injection of morphine, probed gently at the bone and tissue for several minutes. He carefully resplinted the bone, dusted the wound with sulfa, and gently bandaged the entire leg. This done, he took Ludtke's temperature and his blood pressure. All this time he said nothing, although a good half hour had elapsed before he finished his task. No one else talked much. Brede helped the physician, skillfully anticipating his desires. Nora watched with a sort of stunned fascination and Dermod took the first opportunity to slip outside. The sailor with the radio-telephone watch returned and made himself as small as possible by the set. Ludtke kept his teeth clenched on a dead cigar, careful not to betray his pain.

After he had washed his hands again, the doctor spoke curtly and to the point.

"I don't have to tell you it's serious, Captain. Very serious. You need penicillin, too." And when Ludtke shook his head, "The leg's septic—how badly I can't say. We may have to take it off. But we won't decide that until tomorrow. In the meantime, you'd best go to bed and let Mrs. Beg nurse you."

Ludtke started to protest and changed his mind. Despite the drug, his brain was icily analytical. The next step was up to Hoffman. If he could repair the motors, they would sail tomorrow. Even if he failed, Grand Admiral Doenitz would not. In the meantime, there was no reason for him not to rest.

"Very well, Doctor," he said. "I'll follow your advice. Thank you." He lit the cold cigar and watched the doctor pack his little bag. Then, as Dr. FitzGerald and Nora rose to go, Ludtke spoke again.

"If you please, fraulein, a word with you."

"As you will," the girl said. Frowning, the doctor paused at the door.

"Thank you again, Doctor," the captain said coldly. There was a little pause, two or three seconds perhaps, and then Dr. FitzGerald slammed his way out. Brede went into the best room to prepare the bed for the captain.

Ludtke drew deeply on his cigar. "I want you to know, fraulein," he said slowly, "not only am I grateful for your assistance in the past three days; the German Navy and the German Reich are grateful. I shall recommend that our ambassador in Dublin present you with the Reich's highest civilian award, the Golden Badge of Honor."

"I couldn't accept that," Nora said sharply. "I didn't really help, you know."

"Lieutenant Hoffman reported you were a great help."

Nora said nothing.

"I trust Lieutenant Hoffman treated you properly?" Ludtke asked politely.

"Of course. Lieutenant Hoffman is a gentleman—and a very efficient officer."

Ludtke blew out a long blue plume of smoke.

"He is that—gentlemanly, efficient, and very charming. Did you notice he wears a gold locket around his neck?"

"Why, no. Not a locket. I think I noticed the chain."

"The locket contains a picture of his wife. Her name is Erika. Did he talk to you of Erika and their children?"

The girl said nothing. She was very pale.

"No reason he should, I suppose," Ludtke said lazily. "He may be planning to sleep with you."

Nora's face flamed with sudden anger. "I'll not listen to talk like that," she snapped and turned to go.

"Thank you again, fraulein," the captain said. "You will be hearing soon from our Embassy in Dublin."

The door cracked behind her and he sat thinking for a minute. Then he called for the watchstander's assistance and hobbled to his bed. Brede had made it comfortable and had a couple of Dr. FitzGerald's pills ready for him. Ludtke took them, relaxed, and closed his eyes. A few hours' sleep was a good idea. In a few hours, the boat would be ready for sea. He thought of his conversation with the girl. Reigel was right. There had been some hanky-panky between her and his engineer lieutenant. Had been. Watching him, Brede saw his lips curl slightly, as though he were amused, and she shuddered. It was only a little more than four days since the Germans had landed, but it seemed like an eternity. She went to the little light of perpetual adoration in the kitchen, knelt, crossed herself, and began silently to pray.

Nora trudged up the hill slowly. She felt stunned and sick. It was hard to realize Peter Hoffman was a husband and father. He had said he had no family. Other than that, during their long talk the night before, Peter had said nothing about himself. He's probably very experienced in these tactics, she thought bitterly. A regular girl-in-every-port type. This morning, aboard the steamer, he had gulled her into kissing him. Nora's pride was outraged. She had looked forward to something that had never existed, and she felt horribly cheated. The more fool you, Nora Berkeley, she told herself.

She found Lady Maud propped up and playing two-pack Patience before the kitchen fire. The old invalid greeted her warmly and insisted they have a cup of tea. Nora accepted, but her manner was distracted, and Lady Maud thought she knew the reason.

"Now, Noreen, pay no mind to what Doctor Fitz said about Lieutenant Hoffman. It makes the doctor mad as a wet cat to be fooled. Och, the black face of him," Lady Maud chortled, "when he came here expecting me dying and found two great sailors instead."

Nora responded with a weak smile and her grandmother changed the subject. "The lovely thing is that the sub will soon be repaired, Nora. Thanks to you."

The girl started to protest, but her grandmother, pouring the tea, did not notice. "And you went all the way to Limerick City for the acid and wires," she said gaily. "Right under the nose of Tommy Sassenach!"

Nora's face was dark with anger. "I didn't want to help the Nazis," she protested. "Look what they've done to poor Shelagh and Padraig."

"Och, indeed yes," said Lady Maud, suddenly serious. "That's a dead bad thing."

There was a long pause. Nora got out a Sweet Afton and lit it with trembling hands.

"It could be worse, though," Lady Maud said slowly. "When you put sailors near a good-looking, dim-witted girl like Shelagh, something's certain sure to happen. The islanders, I know, think this is a great crime, worse than murder, but Sheleen'll get over it—we'll all get over it."

Nora shook her head sadly, and Lady Maud, changing the subject again, spoke agreeably of the engineer lieutenant. Mr. Hoffman, she thought, was a nice young gentleman.

Nora drank her tea, finished her cigarette, and agreed in monosyllables. To be sure, she thought dully, Peter is a gentleman. A gentleman who wants to repair his ship and get home to his family and is ready to do anything—steal, rescue a drowning man, or, like Reigel, make love to a dim-witted girl to attain those goals.

Nora stood up and flipped her cigarette into the fire. "I'm dead tired, gran," she said quietly. "May I excuse myself for a nap before supper?"

"Of course, of course, my dear. Forgive me for nattering on so." The old lady accepted a peck on the cheek from her granddaughter and, with concern, watched her leave the room.

Far below the Wynne cottage, the submarine basked in the late afternoon sun. Like Gulliver overrun by Lilliputians, her weather deck was busy with sailors spreading and staking out the camouflage nets. Below decks, in the boat's maneuvering room and battery compartment, other work went forward, more quietly and infinitely more important. There, Lieutenants Hoffman and Reigel, the petty officers, Albrecht and Kreisler, and the engine-room ratings struggled with the electric motors. Word had spread that the rescue mission would not be flown from France that day, and the news sharpened their efforts.

Their first obstacle had been the generation of power. With the battery cases and the zinc plates thoroughly dried, this was relatively easy. On the weather deck rainwater was mixed with the sulphuric acid and taken below in well-scrubbed buckets. It was slow work. Leading Torpedoman Muller, supervising the gang, discovered that veterans who were fatalistic about depth charges were mortally afraid of the searing burn of acid.

Difficult, but not insurmountable, was the job of connecting the batteries with the turbines. The conduits had been jarred loose by the collision and corroded by seawater. No one was familiar with the new cable, the proper tools were lacking, and it took a seemingly interminable time to rig it. At four o'clock Reigel came aft from the battery room and inquired as to progress.

"We've tested the new battery acid, Chief. It will work perfectly. The camouflage topside is completed. I'm going up now to report to the Old Man. What can I tell him about the cable?"

Hoffman wiped his hands on a bit of waste and spoke warily. "Too early to tell, Number One. So far, so good. We're installing the cable now to hook up the batteries with the dynamotors. I think we'll be able to know in another four hours—by the end of the dog watches. Of course, it'll be another eight hours before we can fully charge the batteries from the diesels."

Reigel grinned and held up crossed fingers on both hands. He left the boat and climbed to Dermod Beg's cottage. When he learned Ludtke was asleep, he wrote a brief progress report, and left it with the sailor on duty at the radio-telephone set. For a while, Reigel reflected, his time was his own. But he was dirty from his work in the battery compartment, and it was getting close to supper time. Not the best time to seek out Nora Berkeley. He went back to the U-boat to wash, shave, and change into a clean shirt.

That evening, at Lady Maud's, Kelly set out her best culinary efforts, preceded by a festive gin-and-Angostura. After all, Kelly reasoned, the two persons in all the world closest to Her Ladyship were under her thatch tonight. But the two guests were unhappy and there was nothing Kelly or Lady Maud could do to make the meal a success.

Dr. FitzGerald had had an unpleasant morning, and his afternoon had been even more so. It had been difficult examining Shelagh; she was still frightened and given to long bursts of nervous, bitter weeping. But, he told Lady Maud, she would be better in a few days. He was discouraged by the condition of most of the German wounded, including the captain, and depressed by the captain's refusal to allow a boat to go for medicine.

Lady Maud shook her head in sympathy. "And how is Padraig?" she asked.

"He'll be fine in a week or so," Dr. FitzGerald said. "His cheekbone isn't fractured. The boy took a terrible thrashing, though, and he's that low in his mind."

"Poor Paddy," Lady Maud said, "and poor Maura Mor. This is a terrible time for all Spanish."

When Nora joined them, Dr. FitzGerald mumbled an apology to her for his remarks to Hoffman at lunch. Lady Maud was pleased by his words and dismayed by Nora's reaction.

"Ah, don't fret about it, Doctor Fitz," the girl said. She had been unable to sleep and looked flushed and unwell. "The lieutenant means naught to me. They're all the same, those Nazis."

They drank their pink gins and dispiritedly chewed at their meal. As it drew to a close, the physician again voiced his concern about the German wounded. "If there were only someone to spell the sick berth attendant," he said. "Maeve and Maura won't have a thing to do with those poor devils. Nor will Peg or Kathy O Ŕuiarc."

Reluctantly, Nora volunteered to resume the chore of nursing. It was decided she would stand the watch until midnight. The doctor would relieve her for four hours, and then Barndt could take over.

Dr. FitzGerald was grateful to her. "Are you sure you can handle this?" he asked. "It shouldn't be difficult, mind you, but you must be awfully tired."

"Not at all," she said. "It's you that has the hard spot, Doctor Fitz. Why not let the German petty officer relieve me?"

The doctor rejected this; Barndt was exhausted, he said, and needed eight hours of sleep. Dr. FitzGerald's mind was made up, and presently he took Nora down to the sick bay, inspected the patients, gave her a few instructions, and left her to herself. It was then nearly eight o'clock. By that time, in the maneuvering room of the U-boat, Hoffman and the petty officers had begun to worry. The storage batteries were charging, and current flowed through the cables. But the motors refused to turn over. The power that could drive U-324 submerged was still stifled in the inert machinery. Until it could be liberated and put to work, the boat would not leave Spanish Island.

Nora found that the wounded did not require much attention. Oberteuffer moaned softly but she had seen Dr. FitzGerald give him a shot and knew there was nothing more she could do. Of the other patients, three slept easily and naturally. Another, a petty officer with both legs in splints, was conscious and lucid. He wanted to talk, but she understood no German and their conversation was not profitable. The sixth man lay in a coma. The doctor had examined him carefully and told her nothing could be done until morning.

Nora had been on duty less than two hours when the door creaked open and Hoffman entered. Both were genuinely surprised to see the other.

"Good evening, Nora," the engineer officer said.

"Good evening, yourself," the girl said coolly.

He spoke for a few moments with the wounded petty officer and then crossed to where Nora sat. In the dim light, she could see that his face was lined with fatigue, but she resolutely stifled her sympathy.

"I thought I'd get a breath of air," Hoffman said. "We've the cables hooked up and the batteries charging. The first lieutenant is fussing with the motors now."

Nora said nothing.

"It's good of you to take over the nursing. You must be very tired."

"Not at all," Nora said. A glint of the locket he wore caught her eye. She arose, turning her back on him, and needlessly straightened the blankets on a sleeping sailor.

"For God's sake," the engineer officer burst out irritably, "you don't believe what that damned ass of a doctor said at lunch, do you?"

Nora remembered Dr. FitzGerald's insistence on staying up from midnight to four to nurse the German sailors and anger bubbled inside her.

"I think you'd best go, Lieutenant," she said over her shoulder. "You'll wake the patients with that rude, loud talk."

Hoffman protested, Nora ignored him, and after a moment Hoffman left, out of sorts and softly blasphemous. Nora felt nervous and unhappy. She had routed him, and undoubtedly Peter was a fraud, but he was also brave and gentle, and she could easily remember his slow, lovely kiss in the cuddy of the *Kerry Queen*. She dabbed at her eyes with a handkerchief. Don't blub, you simpleton, she told herself crossly, the lieutenant is married and a father—he's not worth blubbing about.

As it turned out, the girl did not have much opportunity to dwell on her problems. Shortly after ten the comatose sailor emerged from his stupor and began to cry out irrationally and struggle in his blankets. His face was hot and feverish and Nora spent nearly an hour by his side, applying damp cloths and trying to soothe him. She was very conscious of her inadequacy, as she tried to keep the sailor from throwing off his blankets and to keep his face cool. Eventually, he slipped off into a deep sleep, groaning a little, and for a time her watch was again uneventful.

About eleven thirty, the door creaked open and she saw a flashlight's beam. For a moment she thought it was Peter, come back to make things up, and her heart sang; then the newcomer spoke. With a little quiver of alarm, she recognized Lieutenant Reigel's voice.

"I was sure you'd be bored in here, Nora, with no one to talk to. I thought I'd keep you company for a bit."

Graceful as a panther, the first lieutenant came into the building and sat on a lobster pot. In the fitful light of a kerosene lantern, his shoulders seemed very broad.

The girl said coldly she was not bored. She had plenty to do. Reigel chuckled mockingly, his strong white teeth glistening in the lantern light.

"Don't try to fool me, my dear. Everyone is bored on this revolting island. Everyone but myself. I'm not bored."

"Why not?" Nora asked, without thinking.

"Because, for the first time in a long, long while, I'm talking with a lovely young lady."

"Och, you do lay it on with a trowel," Nora said scornfully. "That's a rather obvious technique for a lady-killer."

"Lady-killer?" Reigel repeated in a questioning voice.

"You know whom I'm talking about. Shelagh."

"So-o-o," Reigel said slowly. "That's what you mean." His voice was very serious, all trace of mockery gone from it.

"I never touched that girl, Nora," he said. "She got herself into trouble with one of our crew. I know who it was, but he's a good man and we need him. If I were to turn him in, the captain would have him shot."

"Everyone knows it was you——"

"The old lady accused me, and I won't betray the man who did it."

"Well, why did Maura accuse you?" Nora asked sharply.

He shrugged his powerful shoulders. "Who can say? Perhaps because I was kind to Shelagh. I think old Maura is as cracked as her daughter."

Nora was silent. Everyone knew the first lieutenant had violated Shelagh, but there was no real evidence. Shelagh herself had said nothing. Nora gave a slow, shuddering sigh.

"Ah, I don't know. It's a dreadful, dreadful business, whoever's guilty. Now, you'll have to excuse me."

"I never touched the girl, Nora," Reigel said again with slow earnestness. "I hope you will believe that."

There was another long pause, broken only by the soft snores of the wounded.

"It doesn't matter who's guilty and who's innocent," Nora said heavily. "What does matter is poor Shelagh."

167

"It matters to me whether you believe me or not," Reigel said.

"I don't know what to believe," the girl said, her voice muffled and agitated. "You'll have to leave now, Lieutenant. I don't want to discuss this further."

"Ah," Reigel said in his easy, mocking voice, "you prefer married men like Hoffman to a poor bachelor, eh?"

"Get out," Nora said tensely. She repeated the words, her voice sharp and desperate. A couple of the wounded stirred and muttered.

"Very well," Reigel said silkily. He knew he had found a soft spot in the girl's defenses. But the sick bay was the wrong place to exploit it. With punctilious formality, he bade her good night, and walked down the quay to the gangway.

Nora watched him leave the building and sat down, trembling with anger. Apparently, she told herself, everyone knows that Peter Hoffman is married and that you're soft on him. Damnation, she said softly, double bloody damnation for all the Nazis. Captain Ludtke may have been right about his men, when he warned they were sex-starved. His officers, she decided, were a lot worse. Lieutenant Hoffman was a bit more subtle, but just as dangerous as Lieutenant Reigel. She remembered films in which the U-boats torpedoed tankers and cargo ships, and she swore softly. The U-boat that lay alongside the jetty must not go back to sea, she told herself, and she began to cry. When Dr. FitzGerald relieved her at midnight, Nora was dry-eyed, but her resolve had hardened. The German submarine, she told herself, and the men who manned her, were enemies of civilization. The simple people of Spanish realized the first lieutenant was an evil man. They did not know, as she did, that the captain and the engineer officer were just as ready to cheat and lie to get their U-boat home. The islanders wanted U-324 to leave, but Nora was convinced that that was morally wrong. You'll not let the U-boat go back to the war, she told herself fiercely. You'll do anything in your power to stop it.

Chuckling to himself, Reigel went aboard the boat and down the hatch. There was a murmur of voices from the maneuvering room, and he walked aft to see if anything had developed. Hoffman was holding a midnight council with the chief machinist's mate and the electrician's mate.

"We'll never get those dynamotors to turn over," Albrecht was croaking again as Reigel entered the compartment. "It's a Navy Yard job."

"We're not in a Navy Yard, damn it." The engineer lieutenant's eyes were red-rimmed with exhaustion.

"He's right, Peter," Reigel broke in. "Let's be realistic and get some sleep. The Luftwaffe will get us out of here tomorrow."

"That's right, sir," Kreisler said with instinctive deference to his seniors. "Of course, it's possible that with new brushes for the armatures . . ."

Albrecht was scornful, but there was a pin prick of hope in Hoffman's tired brain. He barked questions at the electrician's mate and the hope grew. Reigel said the idea was ridiculous and went off to his bunk. The two petty officers enviously watched him leave. Albrecht was completely pessimistic and Kreisler's comments full of guarded qualifications, but Hoffman was not to be put off. He got them to agree there was no failure in the storage batteries or the wiring. Cautiously, they admitted the armature might be the faulty link in the complex series of operations needed to turn the dynamotors. It was possible, Hoffman wrenched from them, the armatures would function with new brushes. Finally, it was agreed the brushes probably could be found in Limerick. "At Ryan's" Hoffman said slowly. "They'll be at Ryan's if they're anywhere in Ireland."

It was nearly 0130 when the engineer lieutenant made up his mind to go back to the mainland. Albrecht might look as though he thought him crazy, but for Hoffman there was no other alternative. He set down his coffee mug with finality and rubbed his eyes.

"We'll leave at three," he said. "Kreisler, you'll go with me. Get yourself some rest. Albrecht, tell the messenger of the watch to break out Dermod Beg and Eamon Og. They'll do the rowing. Have some sandwiches cut for us."

Albrecht looked incredulous and Kreisler unhappy. Simultaneously they mumbled protests, but the lieutenant cut them short.

"I'll tell Mr. Reigel our plans," he said, getting to his feet. "Then I'll grab a nap, too. We'll shove off at three. Albrecht, make sure they wake us at ten before the hour."

He went forward, shook Reigel awake, and told him of his decision to return to Limerick.

"It's bound to be a defect in the armature brushes, Number One. We've eliminated every other possibility. It must be the damned brushes."

Reigel grunted dubiously. "Perhaps it's more than that, Chief. I know these motors." He reached for a cigarette. "Look, Peter," he said, "why not wait a day? The Luftwaffe will be here tomorrow. We can send a signal about new brushes."

"True. I'd have to get the Old Man's approval to break radio silence, though."

"You won't get that tonight. The doc gave him some pills today. The Old Man won't surface until morning."

"The hell with it," Hoffman said wearily. "The Luftwaffe may not make it. I'm going at three. I've got to go." He stood up and pulled off his outer clothes.

"Good luck," said Reigel, stubbing out his cigarette and composing himself for sleep. Hoffman grunted and climbed into his bunk. He thought briefly of Nora with mingled irritation and tenderness. Then he was asleep.

TUESDAY

It was closer to three thirty than three when Lieutenant Hoffman again left for the mainland. This time Dermod Beg was at the oars with Eamon Og. Tomas Mor, Hoffman knew, would have refused to go, and Hoffman could not blame him. Dermod was not the boatman that Tomas was, but he would be more help ashore. He was glib of tongue and claimed to be familiar with the mainland, and those qualities might well be more valuable than seamanship. Electrician's Mate Kreisler was an asset, too; Kreisler knew no English—a serious handicap—but he was armed and dependable.

The night was black and the sea smooth with long, slow swells and a quiet, onshore wind. Hoffman estimated they could make Ballykerry shortly after dawn. After a few hours' sleep in Mick's barn, they would take the lorry and drive to Limerick, arriving there after dark. They would raid Coyle and Ryan's about ten or eleven, drive back, and put to sea again before daybreak on Wednesday.

Tired as he was, Hoffman felt his spirits rise as he sat low in the stern and admired Eamon Og's dexterity with the heavy oars. It was not like the first expedition; Hoffman knew where he was going and had complete confidence in his party.

He thought of Nora a good deal during the crossing to Ballykerry. With bitter clarity, he recalled her coolness in the sick bay, and he tormented himself with thoughts of Reigel. The handsome Nazi would charm and beguile her, he told himself, just as he had poor, childish Shelagh. No wonder the enlisted men called him the Tomcat.

Hoffman was annoyed at himself for this concern over Nora. He had a job to do. With the Old Man incapacitated, ultimate responsibility for the repair of the electric motors rested with him. He couldn't be a guardian for every young woman who came into Reigel's path. Nora Berkeley would have to look out for herself. He glanced at his fluorescent pocket compass and barked at Eamon Og:

"A point to starboard, Eamon, and put your back into it. We have to be ashore by daybreak."

The two islandmen brought him to the beach at Ballykerry when the eastern sky was still rosy mother-of-pearl. Behind them, as they crossed the dark, dew-wet pasture to Mick's cottage, Spanish Island was slowly coming to life. For most of the people on Spanish—Germans and Irish alike—it was to be a day of waiting and hoping. The sailors, discouraged by Hoffman's failure, would put their faith in the Luftwaffe. The islanders would pray for some miracle of intervention from the mainland. For all of them, except for the little children and the badly wounded men in the sick bay, there would be only the anxious waiting.

Ludtke awoke late, refreshed by his deep sleep. As he breakfasted, Reigel told him about the failure to turn over the dynamotors and Hoffman's decision. The captain was momentarily depressed, but at ten o'clock, with the weather fresh and fine, he was confident the Luftwaffe would soon be overhead. He gave Reigel a short signal requesting spare armature brushes. He enjoyed his breakfast, read the meteorological signals reporting clear weather over Brittany, suffered the doctor to inspect his leg, and heard the reports of his subordinates. The reports were routine and increased his optimism. The boat was well camouflaged, Reigel reported, and Albrecht was still hard at work on the dynamotors, tearing down each part and checking it. There was a great deal of operational traffic, Dietrich told him, but the signals were clear; if a message was addressed to U-324, they would have no trouble copying it. The six wounded men, he learned from Barndt, and then the doctor, were resting comfortably. Even Oberteuffer, who had received his fifth pint of blood that morning, seemed to be holding his own.

"How's the Mor girl coming along, Doctor?" he asked once, in his most casual manner.

Dr. FitzGerald's reply was short but not unhappy. "Shelagh is improving," he said, "thanks be to God."

"And her brother—Padraig?"

"He's all right, physically," Doctor Fitz said, "considering the awful smashing he took. But he's broody in his mind."

Ludtke was silent, watching the doctor's hands. He was not really concerned with the Mors. He was wondering, like the rest of his crew, which would come first, a signal from Headquarters or a search aircraft from Coastal Command.

The signal came first. Marked "Urgent and Most Secret," it arrived just before noon. Decoded, it informed U-324 the airdrop would be made between six and seven that evening. Reigel personally took the dispatch to his captain, who smiled thinly and told the first lieutenant to make sure all the crew, including the wounded, heard the good news. Reigel had just read the signal in the sick bay, where the patients raised a ragged cheer, when the messenger of the watch entered to report a boat approaching the island. It was a curragh, the watch at the Norseman's Tower had reported, a couple of miles offshore, and making for the cove. Two men were in it.

Reigel was mildly annoyed, but not surprised. Visitors were to be expected. He left the sick bay and went to arrange for a reception committee. Once the stranger entered the cove and saw the U-boat, he might try to run. Petty Officer Muller and a loader were ordered to stand by the port-side Oerlikon, ready to fire a warning burst. A curragh, with Sean and Timmy at the oars and two armed Germans at bow and stern, was put in the water, ready to pursue the intruder. The messenger was sent to notify the captain.

From the Norseman's Tower, the signal lamp flashed almost continuously. The curragh was making straight for the cove. One man was rowing, another in the sternsheets. Sailors came on deck and stared curiously at the entrance to the little bay. There was no alarm signal, but the islanders trickled down to the quay. There was a low buzz of speculation. The minutes dragged by. Reigel stood on the bridge reading the Morse messages from the tower. Hoffman could have been taken, he thought, and it would be the police; or it might be only casual visitors. Regardless of their identity, they could not be permitted to see U-324 and then depart.

Abruptly, there was a little murmur from the islanders on the jetty. The curragh had appeared in the entrance. It came on steadily until it was well inside the cove. Then its oarsman shipped his oars, twisted around to stare at the U-boat, and back to confer with his passenger. Muller sent the first twenty-millimeter shell clicking into the firing chamber of the Oerlikon. Reigel stared through his glasses and said slowly, "I think that's a priest in the stern, Torps. It looks like a Roman collar he's wearing."

The oarsman began to row again—straight for the quay. "It's a padre all right, sir," said the petty officer of the watch beside Reigel, and behind them on the jetty, they heard words of glad recognition from the islanders.

"It's Father Healy come to visit us."

"Aye, Father Healy is come to celebrate the Mass."

"That will be Liam Curran rowing him."

The curragh came steadily on. In a few minutes, it was alongside the quay, and a young priest, puzzled but smiling, climbed out and shook hands with the people of Spanish. His boatman, muscular and middle-aged, followed with a battered gladstone. Reigel watched them with cold, scornful eyes.

Father Healy was sturdy and very young, ordained for only three years. It had been long customary for the Bishops of Tralee to assign young men to Ballykerry, a poor parish and one that required strenuous trips over rough water, rocky roads, and steep footpaths. Father Healy had proved an admirable selection. Now, despite his surprise and vague alarm, he chatted briefly with the men and women who clustered around him and patted the heads of the children. When Reigel came down the gangplank and advanced, the priest broke off and gave him a firm hand-clasp.

"I'm Father Healy," he said briskly. "Sorry to hear of your trouble. I've come out because the people here couldn't get to Mass Sunday. The storm, you know. I'd have come yesterday, but there was a bury-ing."

Reigel stiffly identified himself. When the priest instructed his boat-man to take the bag up to the Beg cottage, the German interrupted. "That won't be possible, I'm afraid. Our captain is at the Begs'. He's ill and I don't want him disturbed by your service."

"Certainly," said Father Healy. "We'll have the service at Mrs. Mor's, Liam, at one o'clock. That'll give everyone time," he added, turning to Reigel, "—and leave us the light to get back to Ballykerry."

"You won't be leaving the island today," Reigel said bluntly, and when the priest protested, "No one leaves this island until the U-boat is repaired and ready for sea."

He turned and ordered Father Healy's curragh taken out of the water and placed on the submarine's fo'c'sle with the others. The smile left the priest's face.

"Och, Lieutenant, don't be that hasty. I won't breathe a word of your being on Spanish, and I can vouch for Liam. We'll keep your secret, sir, but I have business on the mainland. Parish business, sick people to visit——"

"You and your man are forbidden to leave—on pain of death," Reigel said coldly. He turned, but the priest took his arm.

"You mean," he asked very seriously, "you mean if I were to leave the island, you'd fire on me? On this cloth?"

"I do mean that." Reigel gave him a sour smile. "I'd kill you as quickly as I would Winston Churchill." He spat and walked down the quay to the gangway.

Father Healy looked stunned. "Did you hear that, now?" he asked Sean.

"Aye, Father," the old islandman said. "I heard him, all right. He's a hard, godless man, Lieutenant Reigel. The worst of the lot."

Together they walked off the jetty and started up the path. Sean did the talking. Succinctly, he told of the ban on leaving the island. He told of the false message to lure Doctor Fitz to the island. Of the censoring of the post, the beating of Padraig, and of the guards at the tower, at the radio-telephone set, and over the curraghs. Finally, he delivered the bombshell:

"But the worst, Father, Shelagh Mor has been violated—by that same Lieutenant Reigel. Yes, sexually violated." He turned away, as though ashamed of his next words, and said, "She was raped, Father."

Young Father Healy was visibly shaken. In his three years in Bally-kerry Parish, he had never heard of such a crime.

"He had carnal knowledge of the girl? When? Where? Did he admit it?" The questions tumbled over one another in stuttered horror.

"Two nights before last—Saturday night. No, he wouldn't admit it to us—or to his captain—but I'm told he joked about it to his sailors. He's the man, all right. Where? Why, in the old Conor cottage, Father."

The young priest crossed himself and murmured a few words of prayer. He seemed to gain strength from this and spoke with decision.

"We cannot celebrate the Mass in Maura Mor's cottage, Sean. Not under the roof where there is so much grief. Can we hold the service in Lady Maud's?"

Sean said he was sure of it. Every island woman, he knew, was proud of the opportunity to have an altar set up in her kitchen. He called to young Tim Mor and sent him racing ahead to tell Liam Curran of the shift. The chalices, vestments, and wine were to be repacked and brought up to Lady Maud's.

"Tell Liam the Mass will be at half after one, not one, Timmy," Father Healy said gravely. "I'll need that extra time," he said to O Ŕuiarc, "to hear the poor girl's confessional."

A few minutes later they entered the Mor cottage and shortly there-after Sean led Mrs. Mor out. She looked flint-hard and bitter. Tomas followed them, his face twisted and crushed with grief. They did not see Shelagh or Father Healy again until the Mass began in the Wynne kitchen, with all the islanders present. Both Shelagh and the priest were very pale. He stammered a good deal during the service and occasionally forgot to give directions to Timmy Mor, who served as acolyte.

When the Mass was over, Nora went down the rocky path to the sick bay. Despite Dr. FitzGerald's arguments, the island women still refused to nurse the wounded. Father Healy was not so obdurate, how-ever, and at four he relieved her.

The girl told him what she could about the patients and went out into the sunlight. Timmy Mor was waiting for her. Earlier that day she had promised to go for a walk with him. She felt very sorry for the little boy who, without understanding the details, was aware he had brought some strange tragedy down on his aunt and his family.

Fortunately, there was no discussion of that. Eight days before, Nora had brought the boy Howard Pyle's book on King Arthur and he talked about it as they went up the path, past the moldering, gull-haunted Norseman's Tower and across the shallow saucer of the island's summit. It was a lovely day, with the sea blue-green all about them and the mainland clearly visible to the east. Timmy had dozens of questions about his book—so many that Nora could hardly begin to answer. Yet it scarcely mattered. The exercise, the exhilarating scenery, and the questions themselves combined to give her a feeling of escape from the reality of the past few days.

Once across the plateau, Nora and the boy threaded their way down a trace of a path that led to the south end of the island. Timmy led the way, his pink upturned face constantly twisting back to ask some question about Merlin or Sir Mordred or Uther Pendragon. The questions came so fast and Nora knew so little that she burst into laughing protest.

"Indeed, Tim, I don't know what you're talking about. It's much too complicated. I'll read the book, if you'll let me, and we'll start again."

He laughed with her, enjoying himself greatly, and Nora was pleased. The walk was good for both of them, she told herself. At the foot of the path, they turned back toward the cove and the settlement of Spanish Island. The going was awkward, but in a quarter hour they were close enough to see the thatches of the cottages. Their route took them along the shore, a hundred yards or so beneath the shell of Seamas Conor's cottage; because of Timmy, Nora wanted to give the ruin a wide berth. They were picking their way over rocks and boulders below it when Kurt Reigel hailed the girl.

"Halloo, Nora! I see you're out for a hike."

Tall, debonair, and supremely confident, he bounded down the hill like some lithe mountain lion. The girl stood frozen still, Uther Pendragon forgotten, as all the awful troubles of Spanish flooded back on her. Timmy Mor, alarmed, afraid, and uncertain, came back to her; automatically, she pushed him from her.

"Go on, Tim, go home. I'll see you after tea."

The boy gave her a puzzled, doubtful look, Nora repeated her command, and he scampered off toward the settlement. Reigel ignored his departure as the boy clattered down the hillside.

"I've been looking for you, beautiful," he said directly. "Where have you been, counting the goats?"

Coldly, Nora told him she had been walking.

"*Zum Teufel!*" the first lieutenant cried gaily. "There are better things than walking for a girl like you."

"Excuse me," Nora said. "I've things to do. I must be getting back."

"Now, wait a minute. Let's sit down and talk this over."

"There's nothing to talk over."

"We could talk about Peter and his trip back to the mainland,"

Reigel said with jovial sarcasm. "Maybe he'll find another girl who thinks he's a bachelor."

The girl whitened and bit her tongue. She looked at Reigel as he stood blocking her path, a gay, mocking smile on his handsome face. She knew she wasn't safe with Reigel, but the mention of Peter reminded her how little she knew of the Germans' plans.

"Let's sit a minute, then," she said, choosing a boulder only big enough for one. "I knew Lieutenant Hoffman went back but I wasn't sure what he needed. There's something still wrong with the engine?"

Unsuccessful at getting Nora to join him on a spur of rock where two could be comfortable, the first lieutenant smiled. "We need new armature brushes. The chief has gone back to get them. Probably, though, they'll be parachuted in this evening."

"Oh? A plane is coming?"

"Yes." Reigel glanced at his wrist. "A Condor is due in about two hours. But let's not worry about that."

"Then the submarine will soon be off," the girl said. For a moment she was silent, gazing at the faraway cliffs of Ballykerry Head and thinking of Peter Hoffman. She was wondering whether they would repair the submarine and leave without Peter, when Reigel slid onto her boulder and put his arm about her. In a flash of panic, Nora realized her brief reverie had trapped her.

"It's a terrible shame you'll not see something of Ireland before you go," she said desperately.

"I'm sure I've the loveliest girl in Ireland with me now," he said, drawing her toward him.

She ignored that and began asking him questions. Did he like to ride? To fish? Reigel did not care to admit he had grown up in a city slum, and when he answered in the affirmative, she launched into a lyrical description of the Irish sporting life. She spoke of steeplechasing, flat racing, and horse shows, of hunt breakfasts and balls, and the loveliest trout fishing in all the world in the Lee and the Blackwater. Not daring to pause, she told him of hunting pheasant and deer, of Dublin's restaurants, where you could eat steaks three inches thick, and dance halls filled with pretty, unattached young women. Some of her descriptions were highly imaginative, but she could tell Reigel was impressed. Two or three times he began to interrupt, but she merely talked faster and more extravagantly of the charms of Ireland.

Finally he laughed, a rolling boom of a laugh, and when she stopped to look at him questioningly, he swung her into his arms and kissed her violently. She was frightened by the urgency of his action, the strength of his hard-muscled arms, and the passion of his lips. She struggled and cried out and he gently returned her to her seat. He looked at her and grinned broadly.

Nora breathed deeply for a few moments. "Oh, my God," she said weakly. "Oh, my God. Give me a cigarette, please."

Reigel took his arm away then and she scrambled to her feet and started walking. The lieutenant swore good-naturedly, and followed her, begging her to stop and enjoy a smoke. She kept walking, saying she must be back at her grandmother's, and presently she turned the conversation into a safer channel: "Poor Peter Hoffman. I have a feeling he won't get back from Limerick this time."

"Why not?" Reigel asked.

"The Guards will be watching Coyle and Ryan's this time. They'll have found his note, you know, signed by a German Naval officer, and they'll be checking the ports and watching the roads from Limerick to the sea."

"The gear will soon be here by parachute," Reigel said callously.

"Yes, of course," the girl said. "Actually, internment in Ireland is a lovely thing. It's not like being in a prison camp. I've seen lots of R.A.F. types wandering about Dublin. They were forced down in Ireland, you know, but their pay comes regularly and they keep their uniforms, and there's no discipline to speak of."

Reigel was amazed. "You mean they're not locked up?"

"Not at all, not at all. Saving to report now and again, they have the run of the city." Nora smiled. "Perhaps by this time next week, Peter and his petty officer will be watching the racing in Phoenix Park." She could see Reigel was impressed, despite himself.

After a minute's silence, Reigel asked, "When can I see you again, Nora? What time this evening?"

"Och, not this evening," the girl said. "You'll be that busy after the plane gets here and I'll be on duty with the wounded." You'll have to know, though, what their plans are, she told herself, and she spoke again. "Tomorrow, when we'll have more time."

The first lieutenant was not satisfied with this vague promise. He had spent over an hour with the girl and accomplished nothing. She was ripe, he knew, ripe and ready. But she had talked so much about her damned Ireland, he had let the minutes slip by. Next time, by God, when she began to chatter, he'd slap her once or twice. Reigel was fond of postulating, "Treat a duchess like a whore and a whore like a duchess," and extensive experience had confirmed the effectiveness of this. Obviously, Nora Berkeley was a duchess and should be treated accordingly.

He was still irritated at his failure when they came back to the little settlement. Less than a hundred yards from the sick bay, Timmy Mor ran up with the fateful news:

"The airplane isn't coming, Nora. The airplane is shot down in the sea."

Reigel raced down to the jetty, knowing it was no use. The watchstander on the bridge of the U-boat corroborated Timmy's report.

"That's right, Mr. Reigel. We got the signal half an hour ago. They shot her down in the Bay of Biscay." The sailor still seemed stunned by the news.

Reigel walked back to where Nora stood. His face was hard.

"It's true," he said. "I'll go up and see the captain, I guess." Stiff-legged, he began to climb the hill. A few paces away, he turned with a trace of his old panache. "I'll be here tomorrow, it seems," he said. "Our date still holds."

Ludtke was alone in the cottage with the radio-telephone watchkeeper. His face was ashen and impassive. He stared at his first lieutenant and said dully, "Sit down, Number One. Make yourself comfortable. Did you hear the news?"

"Yes, sir." Reigel sat down by the fireplace. Ludtke silently handed him a flimsy and he studied it thoughtfully.

FW-200 VP12 CARRYING GEAR FOR U-324 REPORTED SIGHTED BY BEAU-FIGHTERS AT 1410 GMT. LAT 4930 N LONG 0915 W. DISTRESS SIGNAL MADE 1413 GMT, NO SUBSEQUENT REPORTS, PRESUMED LOST. WILL TRY AGAIN EARLY TOMORROW, ADVISING ETA.

"God damn those limeys," Ludtke said heavily. It was not an oath but a supplication. He bent over and picked up a brandy bottle from the floor. Another effort and he had a tumbler. He poured three inches of liquor and savored the drink briefly.

"Where you been, mister, out with that skirt from Dublin?"

"I talked to her for a few minutes, sir."

"You're determined to get your court-martial, aren't you, mister?"

"No, sir."

Ludtke took a gulp of the brandy. "Don't worry," he said thickly and fell into a brooding silence. After a bit, he roused himself and made uncomplimentary remarks about the Luftwaffe and the failure of the High Command to permit the Navy its own Fleet Air Arm. He summed up the genealogy, masculinity, and patriotism of Reichsmarshal Goering in a few terse sentences. Then he commented, briefly and unfavorably, on the decision to send aircraft instead of a U-tanker to Spanish Island. He finished his brandy and stared at the fireplace.

"We'll give them another day. If a Condor doesn't come by then, we'll try it ourselves, on the surface."

Reigel was startled, and a little shocked, by the perceptible change in Ludtke since morning. Then, the captain's face had been white and lined with suffering. But the face had been lit up and the eyes had flashed with optimism. Now Ludtke's whole visage seemed tinged with gray. His cheekbones seemed more prominent and the yellow eyes were hooded, revealing only an occasional glitter.

Later, at a dismal supper aboard the U-boat, Reigel expressed his concern to Barndt.

"The Old Man doesn't look well at all, quack," he said in a low voice. "That signal about the Condor shook him badly."

The sick berth attendant glumly assented. He looked old and dispirited.

"What's the croaker say about him?"

"Doc says he needs medicine from the mainland. I don't know all he says, but Doc thinks the Old Man's going. It's gas gangrene, Mr. Reigel."

Reigel said nothing.

"Oberteuffer needs help, too," Barndt added. "He was hemorrhaging a lot about five. Doc gave him some coagulants and more sedation. Bleeding's stopped. But I think *his* number's up, sir."

Reigel growled that Oberteuffer was a weakling and got up. The sailors in the mess looked at him dully as he left the compartment and walked forward.

After Reigel had left her to report to the captain, Nora climbed the hill to Lady Maud's cottage. The girl was thoughtful. She was vaguely sad at the thought of a German air crew shot down in the ocean, and, at the same time, pleased the supplies would not be parachuted. She thought of Peter Hoffman—driving to Limerick and back in a country crawling with Guards—and, despite herself, she was dejected. If he were captured, she told herself, there would be no easy internment, watching the racing at Phoenix Park. Instead, he and his petty officer would be digging turf on the desolate moors of County Mayo.

Nora came to the Wynne cottage precisely at six. Predictably, Kelly bustled about the kitchen and Lady Maud and Dr. FitzGerald sat before the fire. But, unpredictably, Lady Maud did not respond to her granddaughter's kiss; instead, the old lady stared at the fire. Her physician grunted the barest response to Nora's greeting and regarded the girl as though she were unclean.

"Now, what in the name of Holy Heaven's the trouble?" Nora demanded, her hands on her hips. But even as she spoke, she knew the cause of the trouble. Whatever happened on Spanish, Lady Maud seemed to have immediate knowledge of it. Obviously, Her Ladyship knew how her granddaughter had spent the last hour and a half. Even more obviously, she did not approve.

"Och, gran," Nora said protestingly. "There'll be nothing wrong in taking a harmless walk with the German lieutenant."

"There's everything wrong with it," snapped Dr. FitzGerald. "I'm amazed at you, Nora, walking out on the strand with that blackguard."

The girl turned furiously to the doctor, but Lady Maud intervened quickly. "We'll not discuss it further, not under this thatch. Nora, wash your face. Kelly, serve the supper."

Dr. FitzGerald offered thanks for the meal as though he were angry with the Almighty, and addressed himself silently to the barley soup. Sausage from the U-boat, potatoes, bread, and jam and tea followed, but nobody enjoyed the meal. Nora had been ravenous when she entered the cottage, but the silent fog of disapproval dampened and destroyed her appetite. Her temper mounted and finally she flashed out:

"Granny, for the love of God, say something. The lieutenant may be a blackguard, but he's important to know. Through him, we can learn what the Germans are planning. He likes me——"

"That's just it," Lady Maud snapped. "You're not safe, Nora."

"I'm not a helpless child," the girl retorted. "At home I go dancing or to the flicks with lashings of men, some of them regular D.O.M.'s. I can cope with Kurt Reigel."

"This man is a pirate, child," Dr. FitzGerald said angrily. "Can't you understand that? The Germans have broken all the rules here, just as they break them at sea. They've lied, they've robbed, they've made hostages of us all—even Father Healy. And Reigel is the worst of the lot."

Kelly began to sob. Lady Maud stared stonily at her plate. Doctor Fitz glared about the room for a moment, pushed back his chair, and asked his hostess' pardon. He was going out, he said, for a breath of air. After a bit, Nora also excused herself. She went to the room she shared with Kelly, applied some scent, picked up her handbag, and left the cottage and its implacable air of disapproval.

She climbed to the heights of Spanish Island, avoiding the Norseman's Tower. It was dusk and the sea was purple. She sat down on a rock, fished out a Sweet Afton cigarette, and tried to think. She hated to have

Lady Maud and Doctor Fitz displeased with her. But, she told herself, her relationship with Kurt Reigel was the one link the islanders had with the Germans. It was important to maintain that link. It was the only way to keep abreast of the Nazis' plans and progress.

The sea and the sky grew darker and the wind tousled her hair. She watched a detail of German sailors plod up the path with a lantern to relieve the watches at the Begs' and the tower. She could see them quite plainly as they came; on their return trip only the bobbing lantern was visible.

There was another reason, Nora told herself, to maintain the liaison with Reigel. It was far more important than getting information. She had blundered into it, with that line-shoot about the delights of internment, but Reigel had partially swallowed it. If she were smart, the girl thought, she could hook him—induce him to surrender. With Ludtke crippled, and probably dying, and Peter Hoffman in Limerick, or in jail, there would be no question of the first lieutenant's authority. If he could be persuaded to give up, the submarine would be out of the war, as irrevocably lost as if it were sunk in mid-Atlantic.

She thought about this solemnly, reviewing her strategy and finding no loophole. In the morning, she decided, she would make herself available to Lieutenant Reigel. He was a clot and a swaggering bully, but she would talk to him, make up to him, tell him lies about the size of the steaks and bosoms in Dublin.

Nora put back her head and inspected the sky and the dim, fast-moving clouds. She tried to identify some stars and constellations, as Sean O Ŕuiarc had once taught her, but she was unsure of them. At the thought of Sean, she considered confiding her plan to him. He wasn't brassed-off at her, like Lady Maud and the doctor. Sean was an old friend, and understanding. It would do her good to talk to him.

Slowly, she made her way down the path. A few yards above the O Ŕuiarc cottage, she was conscious of faraway, alien noises, a series of muffled reports. She first thought it was a lorry backfiring, and then she realized she was miles from any lorry.

There was a moment's silence, and then it came again—a rattling, staccato drumfire from the jetty. The door of the O Ŕuiarcs' cabin was flung open, and she heard Sean sing out, "They're shooting," and then Nora began to run down the path. As she ran by them, lights appeared in Eamon's and Padraig's cottages; she could see torches and lanterns moving on the weather deck of the submarine, and a rectangle of light at the door of the sick bay. From the jetty, there was no more gunfire, but a confused, excited babble of voices. God and Mary, thought Nora, perhaps the Guards have arrived.

She reached the jetty and encountered Barndt. He was wild-eyed and frightened. When she questioned him, he only rattled incomprehensible German phrases.

When the shooting began, it was only a few feet above Reigel. The first lieutenant was relaxing in his bunk with a bottle of Dortmund Union beer. Unlike Nora, he recognized the first report as a pistol shot. His feet had hit the deck plates before the second shot was fired. He was going up the conning tower ladder when he heard the deafening bursts of a Schmeisser machine pistol. When he reached the bridge the firing was over and he quickly ascertained what had happened. Someone had come aboard the submarine and, unnoticed by the bridge watch, had eased one of the curraghs over the side. The intruder had then silently entered the water and begun to push the curragh away. The watchstander had heard swimming noises and had used searchlight and pistol in quick succession. Muller, the petty officer of the watch, had been in the conning tower. At the first shot and cry of alarm, he had come onto the bridge with a machine pistol and had squeezed off three bursts, riddling the thief as he tried to hoist himself into the little boat. Two sailors quickly manned one of the rubber rafts and paddled out to the curragh. From the fo'c'sle, Reigel watched them tow it back to the submarine. In the glare of the searchlight, the badly smashed curragh was very low in the water. A man's body was draped over one gunwale, head and chest inboard, legs trailing awkwardly. The body looked like a small, water-soaked scarecrow.

Once alongside the U-boat, they got a line under the scarecrow's arms and with difficulty hoisted him aboard. It was Padraig Mor. His body was cruelly smashed and blood was trickling from his mouth, but he was still alive and his eyes burned with hatred.

"Mother of God, it's Padraig," Reigel heard someone cry out in a high, shocked voice, and there was an incredulous, many-throated groan. For the first time Reigel was aware that nearly every adult on the island was on the quay or the topside of the submarine.

"Clear the deck," he shouted irritably. "All you damned Irish off the boat. *Raus!* Doctor Fitz, lay up here. Doctor Fitz, move your stumps!"

There was momentary confusion around the gangway and then Dr. FitzGerald, nightshirt tucked into his trousers, was kneeling beside Padraig. It was obvious to the doctor he could do nothing. In a second he raised his head and said bleakly to Reigel,

"The boy is dying. Ask Father Healy to come."

"Get the priest here," Reigel snapped at Albrecht. He was disgusted.

Father Healy came aboard and administered the last rites of the church. He was about to apply holy oil when Padraig raised himself briefly on one elbow and tried to speak. Blood bubbled from his mouth and nostrils and he fell back, his head cracking sharply against the steel deck. He was dead.

On the jetty, there was another drawn-out groan. Maura Mor tried to board the submarine and was held back by a young blond sailor at the gangway. She began to curse him. Mechanically, Father Healy went on with the Sacrament. When he was done, he gently thumbed the lids down over Padraig's eyes and stood up. A louder groan welled up on the jetty. Barndt came up with a stretcher, and they put the corpse on it, covered it with a blanket, and carried it down the gangway.

Proudly erect, Sean O Ruiarc came up to Lieutenant Reigel.

"Can we have the body?" he asked grimly. "It's customary, you know, for the family——"

"Take it," Reigel said. "I don't give a damn what you do with it."

Old O Ruiarc gave him a look of hatred and the Irish took over the poles of the stretcher. A stunned, unbelieving Tomas Mor from Stoker Schirmer. Liam Curran from Seaman Kramer. Sean, himself, from Barndt, who muttered an uncomprehended word of sympathy. And Dr. FitzGerald from Stoker Scheutze. They left the jetty, Father Healy with a lantern striding behind them. After him, in the first stages of shock, walked the dead man's wife and mother. Shelagh followed them, gnawing her knuckles, and then came the rest, Peigeen Og, Brede with another kerosene lamp, old Kelly, and Nora Berkeley.

Reigel watched them off the jetty and into the darkness. He grew progressively irritated as he watched the bobbing lanterns climb the hillside. When the lights reached the dead man's cottage, he rasped at Barndt to get back to the sick bay, and Muller to have the fo'c'sle swabbed down. Then he walked up the path to report to Ludtke.

The captain looked old and shrunken. He had sent the watchstander to investigate the shooting and he didn't like what he heard. He listened to Reigel and grunted. There was nothing to say and, in fact, nothing to do. After a long silence, Ludtke dismissed his first lieutenant and resumed his somber brooding.

Back in the privacy of the wardroom, the beer tasted flat and Reigel poured himself a stiff peg of Navy rum. He sipped it slowly, darkly contemplating the future. The shooting had not altered their chances appreciably, he told himself. Tomorrow, there would be an airdrop, and, with luck, the boat would be ready for sea on Thursday. The shooting would eliminate any assistance from the islanders, but that was no longer important. Padraig's death, however, might make it more difficult for him to bring Nora to bed. That *was* important. The girl was certain to be upset tomorrow, and after tomorrow it would be too late.

The lieutenant had another drink, undressed, and climbed into his bunk. He was furious with his luck. It had only been bad since they landed. First, the commotion about the redhead, and the Old Man's threats of a court-martial. Then Nora's coolness and inaccessibility. She was delicious, that one, and he wanted her badly.

Despite the rum, sleep would not come to Reigel. The vision of Nora's parted lips and heavily lashed blue eyes crowded into his consciousness and made him squirm. He had missed his opportunity that afternoon and he couldn't be sure there would be another. He wanted another opportunity desperately. All the women he had known—Hitler girls in Hamburg, strapping blondes in the Norwegian ports, dark-haired Frenchwomen in Lorient and on the Riviera—they seemed drab beside this girl from Dublin.

Reigel forced himself to think of other things. He considered that for the first time since they had arrived at Spanish, the captain's truculence seemed dulled and his confidence blunted. Item two. Hoffman was due in the morning, but he had failed once, and probably would again. As Nora said, the police would be out in force. Why should the engineer lieutenant, Reigel asked himself, come back to Spanish Island at all? It was a disquieting question.

A few minutes before midnight, Dietrich knocked on the bulkhead and handed him a pink flimsy. It was a signal to the effect that another Focke-Wulf Condor would leave France before dawn with equipment for U-324. ETA SPANISH ISLAND: 0700 HOURS. Reigel grunted. There was no reason to wake Ludtke with this intelligence. He ordered the watch at Norseman's Tower to be informed and that he be awakened at six.

The interruption made sleep even more unattainable. He recalled Nora's easy, limber stride along the shore, her flashes of temper, her bubbling laugh, and her obvious delight in the fishing and horses of Ireland. He was mildly surprised to realize that his yearning for the girl transcended physical desire. He thought of her body and the delights of taking her to bed, but he was also impressed by her knowledgeable descriptions of Dublin and her cool, poised dignity. Reigel had not known many ladies, but he recognized one in Nora. She had a mind of her own, he admitted, and she represented a civilized, rational way of life. He decided it must be very pleasant to live in Dublin. The Dubliners knew nothing of war or of the specter of defeat that hung over Germany.

At this point, the first lieutenant propped himself up and lit a cigarette, considering the fate of the Reich. With the collapse of Italy, Germany stood alone in Europe. Her cities were bombed day and night. Russia was advancing and Eisenhower's armies were ready to open the Second Front. Even the U-Waffe knew the depression of defeat. When U-324 left Lorient, it had been estimated that two out of five boats putting to sea would not return. In the Officers' Club at the Prien Barracks there, they had talked incessantly of the increasing efficiency of the English airborne radar, of the new hunter-killer groups, and of the sabotage by the French dockyard workers.

Recalling the talk at the Officers' Club, Reigel drew deeply on his cigarette. The Allied leaders were calling for unconditional surrender. Stalin had vowed to level Berlin and sow the ground with salt. The Jew Roosevelt was pledged to turn all Germany into farmland. The French Resistance was bringing scores of diseased prostitutes, parachuted by the R.A.F., into Lorient to infect the ships' companies of the Second Flotilla.

These had been the conversational staples of the Club in February. Reigel was convinced they were true. Since the Shark Boat had been at sea, he had not changed his mind. Like everyone aboard, he ignored the boasts of the Propaganda Ministry's daily broadcasts; but he could not ignore the operational radio traffic—the reports of U-boats missing and convoys too strong to attack—and this increased the gnawing awareness that Germany was going down to defeat.

Reigel ground out his cigarette butt on the deck. He thought of the yarns he had told Maura Mor and Lady Maud about the successful progress of the war and snarled derisively. They were lies. The war was lost. The Luftwaffe had lost it over England. The Army had lost it in Africa, Russia, and in Italy, where its allies had crumbled like so much dry spaghetti. The U-boats were the Reich's only hope, but the U-boats couldn't do it all.

The transition from Germany's problems to those of U-324 was an easy one. We can't get back to Lorient, Reigel told himself savagely. Even if the morning's drop is successful and the boat can submerge, the odds are overwhelmingly against us. The Old Man and half the crew are casualties. If the English haven't D/F'd our signal, the islanders will betray us as soon as we've cleared the quay. He lit another cigarette and stared at the blackness of the bulkhead. In his imagination's eye, he could see the green fields of Ireland, the gay paddocks and the color of the Dublin Horse Show. The backgrounds were vague, but in each one, very clearly, he could see himself, sometimes with another girl, usually with Nora. Why, he asked himself, why go back to Lorient?

The first lieutenant smoked nearly a package of cigarettes during the long middle watch. At first, he put it from him, but his mind kept creeping back to the thought of internment. Internment meant disloyalty to the Reich. But the alternatives were even more disquieting. If they did get back to Lorient, the best he could hope for was his own boat— a command in a war already lost. The worst was the court-martial Ludtke had threatened and sentence to a penal battalion. Internment meant Nora would be near. Reigel twisted in his narrow pipe-lined bunk, ravaged by his hopes and fears. He wanted Nora. Somehow, he identified her with happiness—and with internment. Nothing stood in his way of attaining those goals, he told himself, except the captain.

Up in Padraig Mor's cottage, Nora Berkeley felt depressed and frustrated, but she was afraid to slip away; every man and woman on the island, except Lady Maud and the children, was in the cottage, and she knew her absence would be conspicuous. So she stayed with the men in the kitchen, smoking nervously, listening to them speak of Padraig.

"Och, he was a grand boy with the nets—quick and skillful," Sean O Ŕuiarc said, the smashed look still on his face.

"He was thinking of us when he took his leave," Dr. FitzGerald said sadly. "Padraig wanted to be helping us."

"Shot down like a dog, he was," put in Liam Curran.

"Aye," said Tomas Mor thickly. "May the devil choke the man who shot him."

Whiskey was passed around, the conversation grew harsher. Nora went into the back room, where the island women were preparing Padraig's mortal remains for interment. The corpse was spread on the bed, washed clean of its clotted bloodstains, but looking as though a shark had chewed its torso. With occasional sobs, Peigeen and Brede were busily preparing a shroud from the best Mor sheets. The new widow, Maeve, and Shelagh Mor knelt by the bed. Behind them, in the shadow, old Mrs. Mor watched from a stool. Father Healy knelt in the other corner, silently praying.

Nora knelt unobtrusively and made a prayer. There was little to choose between the rough, violent talk of the kitchen and the bitter, tortured grief of the bedroom. With all her heart, she wanted to leave the cottage, but she knew it was next to impossible. As she prayed, she thought of the dead man. Padraig had always been kind and good to her. She remembered watching the birds of Spanish with him, puffins, fulmar petrels, and the lovely kittiwake gulls. Recalling her desperate attempts to escape from Peter, she felt a particular affinity for this small, battered body. Nora had seen little of death; she had been only to a handful of funerals in the last ten years. But violent death, she was aware, was no stranger to Spanish Island. Even in her lifetime, the population had been reduced by half. Even without help from the outside world, she thought bitterly, it was a difficult life that Spanish Island offered, hard on the men who fished the ocean, hard on the women who struggled to make a life ashore.

Presently, the shroud was sewn up under Padraig's chin and the body was carried out of the bedroom and tenderly laid on the big kitchen table. Homemade tallow candles were lighted and placed at his head and feet. Crucifixes and rosaries were put on the table, and Padraig's wife and sister knelt by the table, alternately sobbing and praying. His mother, wearing her fringed black shawl, took a chair near the head of the bier. Her eyes were dry, and in the light of the candles her deep-lined, bony face seemed frozen with grief. Occasionally, Nora could hear the clicking of the wooden beads in Maura Mor's hands.

Father Healy said a Hail Mary, all the company kneeling, and shortly after excused himself. Kelly went with him. Peigeen and Brede remained with the Mor women beside the bier. Behind them the men talked in guarded, vindictive tones. The bottle went from hand to hand and blue pipe smoke curled under the low rafters. Nora sat in a corner, occasionally smoking a Sweet Afton. Tomas brought her a tumbler of whiskey and water; she accepted it gratefully. She wanted to leave, to return to the Wynne cottage, but she felt obliged to stay. She felt desperately sorry—not just for the Mors in their bereavement—but for all the people of Spanish. They were doomed—no, they wanted—to stay on this storm-swept, eroded island, turning their backs on all the outside world. Now, as though to mock their isolation, they were caught up in a war between alliances of great nations. Only a handful of the combatants—the crew of one tiny ship—had come to Spanish, but the island was already stained with the hate and misery of the twentieth century.

Kathy O Ruiarc was kneeling at the foot of the table, her hands knotted in prayer. Presently she started a sort of rhythmic, singsong wailing, equally compounded of prayer and eulogy. The other women joined in. As the ancient chant grew, Maeve and Shelagh occasionally twisted their kneeling bodies in a frenzy of despair. The men behind them tapped their toes on the hard clay floor. Mrs. Mor stared with unseeing eyes at her son's head; only her fingers moved, clicking the beads in her lap.

There was a peremptory rap at the door and the keening slackened and died. Tomas opened the door and Lady Maud, seated in a chair, was borne into the room by Dr. FitzGerald and Liam Curran. Kelly followed them. Everyone, even the three Mor women, stared at Lady Maud. Lady Maud hadn't left her cottage for years. More remarkable, she held a double-barreled shotgun upright, its stock resting on the seat of the chair.

"God bless this house," Lady Maud said in her high, clear treble. "May He hear the prayers and know the sorrow in it." In the sudden silence, Nora heard someone suck in his breath. Everyone stared with surprise at the tiny old woman and the shotgun. Then the girl heard a strange voice. It was the first time Padraig's mother had spoken since the tragedy.

"Lady Maudie," Maura Mor said, "God stay with you. Tomas, fetch Her Ladyship something to freshen her."

Lady Maud's chair was set down, close to the bier. She declined Tomas' offer. Conscious that all eyes were on her, she said:

"A great wrong has been done this night. A lovely lad has been cruelly murdered." She paused and there was a responsive groan from the kneeling women.

"I knew Paddy Mor when he was a little boy, gathering the kelp and hunting birds' eggs," Lady Maud said slowly and distinctly. Maeve uttered a long, low moan of despair.

"I have no use for the English," Lady Maud went on. "And with good reason. The English are like wolves. But they are fat, complacent wolves, sated with blood. There are other wolves abroad today—the Nazis—but they are starving and bloodthirsty."

She paused, and there was an angry growl in the kitchen.

"Padraig Mor sought only to help—to lift the Nazi yoke from around our necks," Lady Maud said. "He has failed. But in another sense, he has succeeded. He has brought home to us the bestiality of these invaders. These bold, godless men . . ." She choked and looked up to Dr. FitzGerald, behind her chair.

"These bold, godless men," echoed the doctor grimly, "have held us prisoners. They have stolen and lied and raped. Now, they have murdered."

Again, the angry sound welled up in the throats of the islandmen.

"I am an old woman," said Lady Maud. "Older than most of you. Like you, I welcomed the German submarine and hoped we could help its crew. They have betrayed our help and our trust. I say to you, men of Spanish, drive them into the sea. That is not easy, I know. They outnumber us and they are armed. But I have a shotgun here that may help to make the battle more equal. Sir Laurence said it was a good gun—it's a Purdey. It has not been used since we came to Spanish."

There was another noise in the kitchen. This time it was almost a cheer.

"A shotgun is not much use against a submachine gun," Lady Maud said. "But it can help avenge Padraig. It can be used, for instance, to kill a German officer."

There was a blaze of approval, with cheers and applause. A few shouted "the Nazi captain," and more, "the first lieutenant." The noise was deafening in the smoky kitchen. Everyone, except Lady Maud, Nora, and Maura Mor, was on his or her feet.

After a minute, the tumult ebbed. Lady Maud rapped for attention and, eventually getting it, said in a tone of stern reproof:

"My friends, forgive me. We cannot go on this way in front of Maeve and her mother. Let us first give Padraig a Christian burial and then discuss avenging him."

There was a murmur of assent, broken by Tomas' fierce growl: "Avenged he will be, the good Christ willing."

Lady Maud paid her respects to the two widows and asked to be excused. She put a copper penny beside the corpse, to keep him through Purgatory, and was carried out by Liam and Dr. FitzGerald. Nora put her penny on the bier, excused herself, and followed them into the night. She was exhausted and drained of emotion. The islanders, she thought numbly, were usually individualistic, but they were fiercely united now, desperately vengeful, and they had a weapon. Inevitably, they would use the shotgun and there would be bloody reprisal. The girl shuddered as she followed her grandmother up the path.

WEDNESDAY

No day begins auspiciously for a man who has had less than two hours' sleep. When he was called at six, Lieutenant Reigel was tired and depressed, despite all his youth and vigor. The Condor, he knew, was due over the island at seven. He washed, shaved, and made a hasty breakfast of *Kommissbrot*, cold sausage, and coffee in the galley. Then he went ashore, and, with three sailors, trudged up the path to the Norseman's Tower.

The island was still shrouded in mist, but the sun had made its appearance over Ballykerry Head and was beginning to burn the haze away. All the cottages of Spanish, except one, were silent and sleeping. Bluish smoke still curled from Padraig Mor's chimney, and as the Germans approached, a dog barked at them insistently.

When they were abreast of the cottage, the half-door opened and Maeve Mor, Padraig's widow, stared malevolently at them. Framed by a black shawl, her face was old and harsh. She said nothing.

"B-r-r-rh," said Stoker Scheutze with an exaggerated shudder. Able Seaman Kramer gave a short, nervous laugh. Signalman Koenig swore and threw a stone at the dog. They walked past the Mor cottage, each of them feeling the cold hatred of Maeve's eyes boring into the backs of their heads. When they were nearly to the Norseman's Tower, Reigel turned and looked down. The tiny figure in black still stood in the door of the Mor cottage, staring up at them.

At the tower, Reigel was coldly aloof while his sailors laid out brightly colored signal flags in a square to guide the Condor pilot. Then they waited, smoking, watching the mist disintegrate under the morning sun, straining to hear the sound of aircraft engines.

By 0715 the mist was almost gone and wisps of smoke were coming from every chimney. Spanish Island was breakfasting. The sea was a shining cobalt, banded with strips of turquoise at the horizon. In the cove, around the submarine, the water was more green than blue. Reigel stared down at the Shark Boat, idly trying to identify the tiny figures on the bridge and forecastle. Occasionally, he cursed Reichsmarshal Goering and the Luftwaffe.

He was watching the U-boat when its signal lamp began to wink. "Koenig," he snapped, "the boat is calling us up." But he could read the signal as well as the petty officer. Message just received, the bridge blinked up at them, Condor intercepted, presumed lost by enemy action.

"Acknowledge," he shot at Koenig. "Gather up the flags," he ordered the sailors. "There'll be no drop this morning."

They looked at him dumbly, their shoulders drooping. Trembling with irritation, Reigel blazed at them: "That's what I said, damn your eyes. There'll be no drop this morning. The Condor was shot down."

There was a curious, high-strung quality in his voice, but the enlisted men did not notice it. They were too shocked by this latest setback. Stoker Scheutze thought of his nineteen-year-old wife in Augsburg. Seaman Kramer cracked his knuckles. "Jesus, we haven't a chance, now," he said.

Reigel marched down the path, thinking hard. He went past the Command Post, down to the quay, aboard the U-boat, and into the radio shack. He read the signal carefully. It was from the Admiral Commanding U-boats and addressed to U-324.

FW-200 VPI2 REPORTED INTERCEPTED AT 0620 GMT. 4952 N 0930 W. NO FURTHER REPORTS PRESUMED LOST DUE ENEMY ACTION. WILL FLY ANOTHER MISSION LATER TODAY ADVISING YOU ETA. ALSO U-741 LEFT BREST 0600 TODAY TO ASSIST YOU. ETA 0800 SATURDAY. KEEP UP YOUR COURAGE. VON FREIDEBURG.

"I'll just copy this and take it up to the Old Man," Reigel said to P.O. Telegraphist Dietrich. He reached for a pad of message blanks. "That way you won't have to make the trip."

He copied the first two sentences of the signal in block capitals. He ignored the rest, but printed two additional sentences so that the new message read:

FW-200 VPI2 REPORTED BEING INTERCEPTED AT 0620 GMT. 4952 N 0930 W. NO FURTHER REPORTS PRESUMED LOST DUE ENEMY ACTION. DUE PREVIOUS COMMITMENTS REGRET UNABLE FLY OTHER RESCUE MISSIONS. VON FREIDEBURG.

He folded the forgery carefully, and put it in his pocket. He had a cup of coffee in the galley and left the boat.

In her kitchen Brede Beg was breakfasting with the watchstander. She was dressed in her Sunday best for the funeral and obviously not pleased to see Reigel. The watchstander reported all was quiet. The captain, he said, was awake. He seemed to be in considerable pain and had refused breakfast.

Reigel went into the bedroom. Ludtke was covered with a heavy quilt. His face was gray and lifeless, but the yellow eyes were glittering.

"Good morning, sir."

"Morning, Reigel. What's the news?"

"Bad news, I'm afraid, Captain. Another rescue plane has been shot down. We just got the signal."

Ludtke closed his eyes for a moment. "Has the Grand Admiral said when they'll try again?"

"They're not going to try again, Captain." Reigel took out the folded square of paper. "It's not from Admiral Doenitz, sir. It's from the Admiral Commanding U-boats. Here, I'll read you the signal."

When he had finished, Ludtke snarled an oath and with an effort sat up. He took the signal from Reigel, studied it, and crumpled it into a ball. "That doesn't sound like the Grand Admiral, mister. The Grand Admiral never abandons a U-boat. Never."

Reigel ignored the captain's irrelevance. He sat down on a three-legged stool. "I'm afraid there's no hope, sir. There's not much left for us but internment."

"Surrender to these damned people? Don't be a fool, Reigel. We're going back to Lorient——"

"Captain, Captain, listen to reason. The Grand Admiral has given us up. You're a very sick man. You need medical attention——"

"I have medical attention," Ludtke snapped.

"Not any more, sir. The doctor won't come near you—or come to the sick bay—since Mor was killed last night."

"Mor? Ah, the fisherman." Ludtke made a gesture of annoyance. "Well, bring the doctor here, mister, with a gun at the back of his head."

"That won't work, Captain. He's a stubborn man. If I brought him here against his will, he might give you an overdose—or poison you. He could kill you, Captain."

Ludtke hissed a violent obscenity. "I don't need the damned doctor, anyway," he said. "The chief will be back with the armature brushes today. We'll be out of this hellhole tomorrow."

"Hoffman was due back last night, sir," Reigel said in the even tone of an adult addressing an overwrought child. "He told me before he shoved off that if he couldn't locate the armature brushes he was going to give himself up——"

Ludtke repeated his obscenity. "Hoffman is *one* officer I can depend on."

"I think Hoffman has surrendered, sir."

Ludtke hugged his knees and rocked back and forth for a moment. His eyes glittered wildly. Reigel could not be sure whether it was mental anguish or physical pain that caused the rocking. When it stopped, the first lieutenant pressed the attack.

"You need a proper doctor, sir. So do the others. We can't go to sea and we can't stay here like this. There's one thing left, Captain: scuttle the Shark Boat and give ourselves up."

Ludtke lowered at him balefully. Scuttle was not one of the captain's favorite verbs. It was a word associated with shame and defeat. It reminded him of the High Seas Fleet opening its seacocks in Scapa Flow after the first war. It recalled *Graf Spee*'s inglorious death after the Battle of the Plate. Two years ago, the Admiralty in Berlin had promulgated a new code word—"Rainbow." If "Rainbow" were ever signaled to the fleet, it meant every ship was to scuttle herself. Ludtke was still furious when he thought of it. "Rainbow," to him, was symptomatic of a dangerous, defeatist philosophy in Berlin. And here was one of his officers thinking in the same cowardly fashion.

"We'll not scuttle, mister, or surrender," the captain said at length. His voice shook with anger. "When we get back, I'll have you court-martialed for thinking we should scuttle. You'll never have a boat, you bloody scuttler. Now, I'm going to signal the Grand Admiral again. Take this down—" Reigel produced a notebook and a stub of pencil and copied down the dictated words.

PERSONAL FOR ADMIRAL DOENITZ. URGENTLY REQUEST YOU NOT GIVE UP ATTEMPTS FURNISH ME ARMATURE BRUSHES EITHER BY PARA-CHUTE OR U-BOAT. U-324 STILL FIGHTING UNIT THAT NEEDS ONLY THIS GEAR TO BE FULLY OPERATIONAL. LUDTKE.

"Send that off right away, mister," the captain growled. "Top priority. And tell Barndt to come see me. Tell him to bring another bottle of brandy."

"Aye, aye, sir," Reigel said, stowing away his notebook and pencil and picking up his cap. He had no intention of sending the dispatch. Instead, he considered composing another signal, one that would report U-324 about to surrender. Walking down the hill, he decided that was too dangerous. It would probably mean the Admiral Commanding U-boats would redouble his efforts to complete the rescue. There would be signals in reply, too, and Dietrich might smell a rat.

Reigel stopped at the sick bay to tell Barndt the captain wanted him. He was surprised to find Nora there, helping the sick berth attendant to change Oberteuffer's dressings. Barndt reported Oberteuffer much improved and Nora gave Reigel a tentative smile. He grinned back with newly kindled desire and chatted with Schiller while Barndt and Nora finished their job; then, as Barndt climbed the hill to the Beg cottage, Reigel suggested to the girl they go outside and talk.

"Och, I couldn't do that," Nora said. "The funeral procession starts at ten." But the patients were comfortable and she went outside with him; to get a few minutes' privacy, she consented to go to the leeward side of the sick bay.

"I'm sorry about last night, Nora," Reigel said.

"It was a sad affair," the girl said gravely. "Poor, poor Padraig."

"He shouldn't have tried to steal the boat and get away," the lieutenant said. "We have our orders to shoot anyone who tries to leave Spanish, and everyone knows it."

"I feel so sorry for Mrs. Mor and Maeve—what with Shelagh and all. And now this." Nora stared out at the cove. She was so quiet and disconsolate that Reigel, sensing an opportunity, took her arm. As though a wasp had stung her, Nora jerked away and retreated toward the windward side of the sick bay.

Reigel caught up to her before she had reached the corner.

"Wait, Nora," he said and took one of her hands. "It's going to be all right, *Liebchen*," he told her. "Ludtke is a very ill man, and a little crazy. I've been trying to persuade him to surrender to the authorities. He doesn't like the idea of internment, but I think he will listen to me before nightfall."

Nora's heart leaped up. The U-boat about to surrender! This made all the fear and torment of the last seven days worthwhile. The submarine would be out of the war! But before she could savor this incredible, glorious news, Reigel reached for her again; she fended him off with the first question she could think of:

"You were up at the Norseman's Tower this morning. Were you expecting another aircraft?"

"Yes. The R.A.F. shot it down."

The girl shook her head. "Och, the sadness of it all."

"It's going to be all right," Reigel said again. They stared at one another for a moment, and then Nora said, very clearly and distinctly: "You must surrender, Kurt. You know that, don't you?"

"Yes," Reigel said slowly. "But before I go to a prison camp, I want a few hours alone with you."

Nora disengaged her hand. "Saints above, I must go. The funeral is at eleven. The procession starts at ten." She looked at her wristwatch. "I'm late now."

The lieutenant was completely unconcerned with the corpse that lay in the Mor kitchen. "Do you have to go?" he asked. "We have so much to talk about."

"Of course I must go. The whole island will be there, even Lady Maudie. Let me know when you convince your captain."

She left him, going around the corner of the sick bay and starting up the hill. Reigel got out a cigarette. He lit it and sat down on a boulder. She loved him. He was sure she did, though she might not know it herself. His problem, now, was to get Ludtke to surrender. This afternoon, very likely, the Luftwaffe would try again. Reigel frowned as he concentrated. Ludtke was a stubborn man. Perhaps the only way was to get rid of him for good.

When Nora reached the Mor cottage, most of the islanders were in the kitchen paying a last farewell to Padraig. Eventually the women came out, Maeve and Shelagh in tears and Mrs. Mor dry-eyed and grimly proud. They heard the last of the coffin being nailed down and presently the bearers brought it out and started up the hill toward the Norseman's Tower and the cemetery. Sean O Ŕuiarc and Tomas Mor carried its front, Liam Curran and Dr. FitzGerald the rear. Ahead marched Father Healy, wearing his vestments, his lips moving in prayer. Behind them came Padraig's mother, Padraig's widow and sister, and then the rest of the islanders—Brede, Peigeen Og, old Kathy O Ŕuiarc, the children, and Nora herself.

The coffin was a small and necessarily shallow affair. Sean had made it that morning from the Mor kitchen table and some planks given him by Lady Maud. It was covered with flour sacks, dyed purple with seaweed, which masked the crudeness of its construction. While Sean had built it, Tomas Mor and Liam, assisted by Timmy, had dug Padraig's grave.

The little procession struggled up the hill slowly. There was a tradition on the island that a burial party should not go in a straight direction to the grave, but on this day, the tradition was ignored. The going was difficult for old Sean, even though Tomas Mor had more than his share of the weight. From the rear, Nora anxiously watched the bowed back of the old man. If Liam and the doctor had not been there, she thought, to take the place of Eamon and Dermod Beg, it would have been difficult to give Padraig a Christian burial. Poor, poor Spanish, she thought. When death came to the island, there was barely enough wood to make a coffin, barely enough people to carry it, barely enough earth for a grave.

From the crumbling doorway of the Norseman's Tower, a German sailor watched the modest cortege pass. Stoker Schirmer had the forenoon watch and he had the grace to take off his forage cap. None of the mourners looked at him, not even the children. It seemed to Nora the women drew their shawls tighter around them and looked even straighter ahead.

When they passed the tower, they crossed the ridge of the hill and reached the plateau, which ran slightly downhill toward the west, a sort of shallow saucer. Centuries ago, the top of the island had been mountain pastureland, but the wind and rain had long since eroded most of the soil away. To the north, where the protection was greatest, there was a patch of earth, mostly clay and sand, where the islanders buried their dead. It was a tiny cemetery, with barely a score of lichen-rimed headstones and Celtic crosses. There were remnants of earlier monuments, too, some inscribed with Gaelic runes, and traces of stone circles and prehistoric shell mounds. In this ancient burial ground, by a shallow trench, Lady Maud waited in her chair. Kelly, with a parasol, stood by her mistress' side. A half hour before, Father Healy and the indefatigable Liam had brought Lady Maud to the graveside.

The service was a tedious one. The prayers, whether in Latin, Gaelic, or English, were lengthy, and Father Healy's sermon was half fulsome eulogy for the departed and half condemnation of the invaders who had shot him down. To Nora, there seemed to be little Christian charity in his remarks. Looking about her, she decided there was little charity left on Spanish Island for the Germans. Maeve and Shelagh still wept and Kelly sniffled periodically, but most of the islanders were flint-eyed and tight-lipped.

Nora remembered something Lady Maud had once remarked about the islanders. "They have a great capacity for sorrow," Lady Maud had said. "They have endured so much, they have become stoics." Looking at the harsh, gaunt faces about her, Nora thought the description an apt one. There was also a vengeful, Old Testament look about them. The girl remembered Lady Maud's dramatic appearance with the shotgun the night before and she shuddered. Once Padraig was buried, the islandmen would have more time to think—to plan their retribution. They would be tempted to use the shotgun, she knew, and if that happened, if Kurt Reigel or his crippled, half-insane captain were shot down, anarchy could quickly follow. Without their leaders, the desperate sailors might seek revenge. The islanders would be shot, their women desecrated, and their cottages looted and burned. The girl shuddered again. Reigel, she told herself, must persuade the captain to surrender.

The priest finally sprinkled a symbolic handful of dirt on the coffin. Liam and Tomas began to shovel the sand and clay back into the grave. Maeve Mor broke into fresh sobs and continued them until the soil had been frugally packed around the coffin. Timmy Mor brought up the crude wooden cross—" 'tis only until we can get a proper one from Dingle," he assured Father Healy manfully and then burst into tears and ran to his mother. Tomas hammered the cross into place with a spade. The priest mumbled a few Latin phrases and the service was over. Clutching his chasuble, Father Healy led the procession back across the plateau, past the tower, and down the hill.

There was the usual approving comment on the sermon, but Nora did not hear it. Liam and Tomas carried Lady Maud. The sun was almost at its zenith and it made them sweat. But Nora felt chilled—chilled with a dreadful foreboding.

Reigel was eating in the wardroom when the bridge messenger reported the islanders returning from the burial ground. He grunted an acknowledgment and continued his meal, chewing with thoughtful deliberation. He was sure he could predict the islanders' next move. Now Padraig was buried, they would be hungering for vengeance—vengeance best satisfied by killing the captain or himself. But there were two good reasons why they would choose Ludtke. In the first place, Reigel himself was safe aboard U-324. Secondly, the islanders would want to do more than kill an officer; they would also want to capture the radio-telephone set and report the U-boat's presence to the mainland.

The first lieutenant smiled slowly. He did not know how they would try it, but it should not be a difficult job for the islanders. The Old Man was groggy. He and the sailor on watch would not be suspicious if, say, Brede and Liam came into the cottage. It would be easy for Brede to snatch up Ludtke's pistol while she served him some food; easy for Liam to get behind the watchstander with an open clasp knife. There were lots of ways they could do it, Reigel thought to himself. Once they had Ludtke out of the way and warned Ballykerry, he would simply wait for internment and the end of the war. It wouldn't matter then if the Luftwaffe dropped all the armature brushes in the world.

He finished his meal in good spirits and climbed to the bridge. Koenig, the petty officer of the watch, reported most of the islanders had come no farther than the Wynne cottage.

"All of the men, I think, and most of the women are in there, sir." He ventured a grin. "Probably speeding the departed soul with a drop or two."

They chuckled together. Reigel hoisted himself up into the captain's conning chair. He swept the island with his Zeiss glasses. Timmy Mor was at the well, gathering some water. The little Og girl was feeding the chickens. Except for a couple of dogs and some grazing sheep, there was no other sign of life. Reigel grunted with satisfaction. He could wait all afternoon if he had to, but he was confident it wouldn't be necessary.

Reigel knew nothing of Lady Maud's shotgun, but up in the big kitchen of the Wynne cottage, events were proceeding along the lines of his conjecture. There were eight persons seated around the table and on the chest under the window: Sean O Ŕuiarc, of course, presided. On his left hand sat Dr. FitzGerald, and on his right Father Healy. Opposite them bulked Tomas Mor, agitated and impatient, and Liam Curran, who said nothing. Brede Beg, Maeve Mor, and Peigeen Og were ranged on the chest. The bedroom door was open. Lady Maud sat up in her bed, propped by pillows, with Nora and Kelly at her side.

The meeting began informally. The noonday sun had been hot at the graveside and the men enjoyed a bottle of Her Ladyship's stout, as they opened the question of revenge.

"We have Lady Maudie's shotgun," Sean O Ŕuiarc said in grave preamble. "There, in the chest you ladies are sitting on. It is not much against the German rifles and machine pistols. But we might be able to use it in ridding Spanish of these devils. The question is how best to use the shotgun."

"Sean, Sean, I beg you to listen to me," Nora broke in. "The Nazis are ready to surrender. Lieutenant Reigel told me. He's trying to get the captain to call up Ballykerry."

The news startled the company, but they greeted it with skepticism. They were too polite to say so, but everyone knew that Nora had walked the strand yesterday with the Hun lieutenant. He had beguiled her, their looks seemed to say, just as he had charmed poor Shelagh.

Desperately, Nora pleaded for time. Use of the shotgun, she argued, would lead to bloody retaliation. Ignoring her, Tomas Mor demanded that the gun be used to eliminate Lieutenant Reigel. Father Healy objected, citing the Sixth Commandment. Doctor FitzGerald compromised, condemning Reigel but calling attention to his impregnable position aboard the submarine. Sean O Ŕuiarc, regaining control of the meeting, suggested consideration of strategic points rather than persons.

"Nora is right. If we start shooting just to shoot people the Nazis will kill us all," Sean said soberly. "We can't stand against them. It seems to me our job is to get possession of the R/T and let Ballykerry know what's going on here."

"Then let's kill the bloody captain," Tomas mumbled with thick anger.

"Och, no, man," Father Healy said.

"—And the sailor with him," Tomas said bitterly. "We can do it."

He glared at the priest, who looked back steadily. Sensing trouble, Sean O Ŕuiarc laid down his pipe.

"Now then, Tomas. Mayhap we can do it without bloodshed."

They turned to him blankly, and he went on; "Mayhap we can surprise the captain and his sailor—get their weapons—and bring them up the hill. We needn't harm the Nazis, we only want to reach Ballykerry."

Tomas sizzled with contempt. "Indeed, Sean, you're mad. The guard at the tower would pick us off afore we'd gone twenty paces. Even he missed, he'd watch us and signal the sub."

There was a grumble of agreement, and a long silence.

"Could you not surprise them," Father Healy asked apologetically, "and hold them prisoners while you warned Ballykerry?"

"Aye, Father, that might work out," Sean said slowly.

They considered the priest's suggestion, almost out of courtesy. Tomas thought it would take too much time. Sean argued it might work, but his voice lacked conviction. Finally Dr. FitzGerald spoke, tentatively at first, but gathering strength as he developed his thesis:

"Perhaps it's not necessary to use the gun. There might be another way." There was a silence, full of question and protest, and then the physician went on: "Captain Ludtke is a very sick man. He's suffering. He needs medication. If I could give him a sedative"—his blue eyes gleamed at them—"he wouldn't be bothering us for hours."

"What about the sailor?" Tomas asked triumphantly.

"Surprise him," Doctor Fitz said sharply. "He'll be in the kitchen, Ludtke in the bedroom. Once we've given the syringe to Ludtke, we'll take care of the sailor. A knock on the head and give *him* a syringe. That's no problem, Tomas."

"Then we can call up Ballykerry," Sean O Ŕuiarc said, "and let the Guards know about these bandits."

"You'll be able to leave the cottage in a few minutes," Father Healy said jubilantly. "No one will know it wasn't just a medical call—there'll be no bloodshed. . . ."

"It's a grand idea," Sean said. "Let's agree we do it. Now, there are some small points to work out."

The plan certainly did not fulfill Tomas Mor's concept of vengeance, and Nora considered it foolish and dangerous. But the majority carried and the details were quickly organized. About two o'clock most of the islanders scattered to their cottages, and thirty minutes later, Brede and Dr. FitzGerald, carrying his dusty bag, left Lady Maud's and walked down the path to her cottage.

They said very little as they came down the hill, past Padraig Mor's, the Ogs', and the O Ŕuiarcs', as well as the shells of older dwellings. From the windows of the occupied buildings they were furtively watched and prayers were said for them. Far below, on the bridge of the U-boat, Lieutenant Reigel put down his glasses and smiled to himself.

As soon as they had crossed the threshold, Brede and the doctor knew their job would not be easy. The sailor on watch was glad to see them.

But Ludtke was seated beside the fire and he was obviously hostile. The captain's skin seemed to have darkened since morning and his facial bones were more pronounced. He said nothing, but the quartzlike eyes glared venomously at them. His wounded leg rested on a three-legged creepie before him, the morning's gauze and tape already fouled with pus. More disconcerting was the Luger pistol cradled in his hands.

The physician made nervous small talk and got no response. He approached the captain and was motioned back by a flicking gesture of the pistol. It occurred to the doctor that he had never seen a mortal closer to death and, at the same time, never more dangerous. Ludtke, he thought, resembled a cobra—hooded eyes and all.

"Now then, Captain," Dr. FitzGerald said, "time to change the dressings on that leg, eh?" He opened his bag and began to arrange his gear on the kitchen table.

"I'm all right, damn you," Ludtke grunted. His words were muffled and indistinct. Saliva oozed from his mouth but he seemed unaware of it. His yellow eyes were feverishly bright.

"Indeed you are, Captain," the doctor said in his best bedside manner. "Indeed you are. I just want to change the dressings. Then Brede'll give you some lovely hot broth and you'll be even better."

Ludtke mumbled incoherently. Brede set the kettle on to boil and the doctor fussed briefly with his bandages, vials, and instruments. His plan called for a triple-strength injection of morphine. In minutes Ludtke would be unconscious and the sailor would be eating Brede's soup. Then he would pick up the captain's Luger and slug the sentry.

He loaded the syringe and straightened up from the table.

"What's that?"

"Just a little morphine, Captain Ludtke. It will be painful when we take the dressings off."

"No, by God, no!" Ludtke snarled thickly. The yellow eyes gleamed wildly and the pistol barrel stabbed jerkily at the physician. "You're not going to knock me out."

Dr. FitzGerald remonstrated and Brede tried to reason with the captain.

"Dear God, Doctor Fitz is trying to help you. You need the doctor, man. You want to get well, don't you, and sail your ship back to France?"

Ludtke glared at her and snarled something in German. He sounded irrational and tortured. The doctor and Brede exchanged frustrated glances and the sailor looked helplessly from one to the other.

The captain checked his incoherent gutturals and there was a long pause. The doctor, the woman, and the seaman watched him with fascinated apprehension. Ludtke glared back at them. He was breathing stertorously and the saliva dribbled down his stubbled chin. The knuckles of his pistol hand were white-clenched. When he spoke, it was in German, an order to the sailor, but the meaning was clear even without a translation.

"Get Barndt. I want Barndt here before they start giving me dope."

The rating saluted and left the cottage with alacrity. Dr. FitzGerald shrugged his shoulders and sat down. They still had time, he speculated, to knock Ludtke out and alert Ballykerry. With the same thought, Brede moved fearfully toward the kettle behind the captain. At one side of the hearth stood a blackened poker and a heavy wooden potato masher. But Ludtke was alert to the danger. He rasped a warning and thumbed off the safety catch on his pistol. Brede was a brave woman, but she retreated, white-lipped, and sat down on the creepie by the door. The doctor got up and approached the table, hoping he might inconspicuously reduce the dose in the syringe. But Ludtke told him to sit down and waggled the pistol at him. Dr. FitzGerald obeyed. Checkmated, he thought dully, checkmated.

Ten minutes inched past before the sailor was back with Barndt. Words were exchanged in German, questions by the sick berth attendant, harsh, angry answers by the captain. Barndt examined the syringe and the vial of morphine and reported, shaking his head nervously. Ludtke used violent language at some length. Dr. FitzGerald tried to explain to Barndt, arguing that the captain was critically ill and needed maximum sedation.

"Dear God, man, that leg is septic," he shouted at the German. "We'll probably have to amputate."

Barndt couldn't understand him but Ludtke's anger mounted at the word "amputate." He began again to snarl incoherently and to wave his pistol. Bubbles of saliva flecked his lips and his eyes glittered malevolently. Even FitzGerald grew frightened. Behind him he heard Brede whisper, "Mother of God, it's crazy mad he is," and the two German sailors were obviously in agreement. The physician was no coward, but when, with choking fury, Ludtke told him to get out, he dumped his gear hastily into the bag and obeyed, Brede scuttling before him.

In the path before the cottage, he shook his head. "It doesn't matter, Brede. In his condition, I doubt the morphine would take effect."

"Aye, Doctor, he's raving mad. I doubt he'll last the night."

They plodded up the path toward the Wynne cottage, but there was no need to make a report. The islanders watching from behind their shutters knew by their faces that the plan had gone wrong.

On the bridge of U-324, Reigel also sensed they had failed. From the moment Barndt was summoned from the sick bay, he had known something was wrong. He waited impatiently for the sick berth attendant to return, and then sent for him. Barndt dolefully reported the skipper was worsening.

"He's like a lunatic, sir, cursing and yelling, even frothing at the mouth. The surgeon wanted to give him a big shot of morphine but he wouldn't let him. He's more afraid of the morphine, I think, than of amputation. He's afraid of blacking out."

Reigel grunted and dismissed him. The islanders had failed, but he was sure they would try again. Probably they would wait until dark. Then, if some created a diversion at the door and others entered by the bedroom window, it would be almost impossible for them to fail. He told Koenig to call him if any activity developed, particularly around the Command Post, and went below. He checked the radio shack, examining the broadcast schedule closely. There was no sign of a message that might concern U-324 and the transmissions from France were numerous, loud, and clear. Satisfied, the first lieutenant walked aft. A halfhearted game of Skat, the ratings' favorite card game, was in progress in the After Torpedo Room and a few off-duty hands slept in their bunks. It was stuffy and very quiet in the boat. In compartment after compartment, the machinery was inert. Engines, motors, compressors, rheostats, dynamotors, pumps, blowers, motors, dials, gauges—all were idle, awaiting the armature brushes.

Reigel climbed into his bunk and tried to relax. There's nothing to worry about, he told himself. There had been no signal about an airdrop and not enough daylight left to try one today. Up the hill, the rustics would be planning another scheme to seize the radio-telephone set and sound the alarm. They were bumpkins, but they had the advantages of surprise and superior numbers. Inevitably, they would succeed.

The long afternoon dragged itself along. It was hot in the boat. Reigel dozed fitfully. Once he was awakened by the faint sound of voices above him. Four o'clock, his wristwatch told him, and he knew the bridge watch was being relieved. He pushed the button for the messenger of the watch, remembered there was no power to sound the buzzer, and got to his feet. He climbed to the topside and studied the eastern slope of Spanish. From the sick bay to the tower, no human moved.

"The Irish are sticking close to their cabins, sir," Albrecht, the new petty officer of the watch volunteered. "Been that way all afternoon. Seems funny, don't it?"

"Probably getting drunk," Reigel said. "They always get drunk after a funeral." He paused. "I'll be in the wardroom, Chief. Let me know if any of them come near the Command Post. And when the watchstander comes back from there, have him report to me."

A few minutes later, in the tiny wardroom, he questioned the sailor who had witnessed Dr. FitzGerald's visit to Ludtke. The captain, faltered the rating, was a very sick man. Out of his head most all the watch.

"How is he now?"

"He sits by the fire, very quiet for a while, sir, you'd think he was asleep. Then he'll start mumbling and swearing and waving his pistol. He's got his cognac bottle beside him and he drinks pretty steadily. Of course, his leg pains him a lot, sir."

Reigel dismissed the man and stretched out in his bunk again, wishing night would come. He was dozing once more when there was a rap on the bulkhead, and Chief Machinist's Mate Albrecht pushed aside the green curtain and entered. Behind him, P.O. Telegraphist Dietrich squeezed into the wardroom. Both were very grave. Albrecht was apologetic but firm.

"Begging the lieutenant's pardon, but I'm worried about the captain."

"Oh? What about him?" Reigel asked warily.

"We'd like to suggest bringing him back to the sick bay, sir. Where the quack could keep an eye on him. The Irish might make trouble tonight, sir."

"Nonsense," Reigel said irritably. "We have to guard the R/T set, Chief."

"Yes, sir," Dietrich cut in, "but I could put the set out of commission for tonight, sir. Just take a relay out. The Irish couldn't use it tonight but we could operate it first thing in the morning."

Taken off balance, Reigel began to argue. The captain was too ill to be moved. Lieutenant Hoffman might call Spanish from Ballykerry. The Irish might be able to repair the set. As he talked, he sensed the two petty officers were skeptical, and that increased his vexation.

"The Old Man's off his rocker, damn it. All afternoon he's been drinking cognac and waving his pistol around. He's delirious. It's not safe to go near him."

There was a silence. Albrecht and Dietrich stared with disapproval at the deck.

"All right, boys, all right," Reigel said finally. "I'll talk to him about moving." He glanced at his wrist. "It's five thirty now. I'll go up after supper. There's plenty of time before dark."

Satisfied, they thanked him and turned to go. They were barely in the companionway before Reigel heard the watchstander in the radio shack, a dozen feet away, calling for Dietrich. A priority signal was coming in, addressed to U-324.

Dietrich, as the senior radio rating in U-324, normally did all the decoding and encoding. He had already taken the lead-weighted top-secret cipher book from its cabinet and was watching the radioman copy the encoded signal, when Reigel pushed his way into the shack. Reigel held out his hand.

"I'll break this one down, Sparks," he said easily. "Let's have the book."

Dietrich was surprised. Decoding was slow, arduous work. He couldn't remember the first lieutenant doing it since he joined U-324.

"Yes, sir."

As he took the heavy volume, Reigel realized Albrecht was in the doorway, looking puzzled; behind him curious sailors clogged the companionway. Everyone wanted to hear the latest from Headquarters; everyone expected to hear it from Dietrich.

Reigel clamped his jaw shut and watched the coded groups of letters formed by the typewriter's clacking keys. In a minute or so, the radioman looked up at him and said nervously, "Signal finished, sir."

"That is good," Reigel said coldly. He tore the paper from the typewriter and turned to Dietrich. "I've been thinking about our talk, Sparks. Maybe you're right, you and the chief. I want you to go up to the cottage and check the R/T. Make sure you can dismantle it for the night. But don't dismantle it and don't tell the Old Man what we plan to do. That's important. Don't tell him anything. Just say you're checking the set. Understand, Sparks?"

Dietrich repeated his instructions. He was obviously puzzled by the lieutenant's orders. "You're sure, sir, you don't want help with the signal?" he asked.

Reigel's temper flared. "Damn you, Dietrich, don't be impudent. You've got your orders. Get out of here and carry them out!"

His face stained with anger, Dietrich went out of the shack and up the conning tower ladder. Reigel shouldered his way past Albrecht and the others, back to the wardroom. He lowered the hinged desk top over the wash basin, produced a pencil, and set to work. Sweat from his fingers soiled the cipher book and he realized his forehead was damp with nervousness. Since boyhood Reigel had not believed in any god, but he prayed now—that he could decode the signal quickly and that its contents would be favorable.

The first part of his prayer was answered. After only a couple of false starts, the signal decoded smoothly:

ACTION U-324 REPEATED ADMIRALTY, SECOND FLOTILLA, NAVAL AT-
TACHE FUEHRER HQ, LUFTWAFFE RECCO GROUP THREE, AIR COMMAND
PARIS FROM ADMIRAL COMMANDING U-BOATS . . .

But the signal was not favorable for Lieutenant Reigel. As he worked,
he cursed and sweat beads glistened on his brow.

DISPATCHING FIVE REPEAT FIVE FW-200 RECCO PLANES TONIGHT
ABOUT TWENTY ONE HOURS GMT. EACH PLANE FULLY LOADED AC-
CORDANCE YOUR REQUEST INCLUDING ARMATURE BRUSHES HAS NIGHT
FIGHTER COVER FIRST 200 MILES. EACH HAS PARASURGEON. EACH
ROUTED DIFFERENTLY. ETA OF ALL BETWEEN TWO THIRTY AND THREE
TWENTY HOURS GMT. SUGGEST YOU ILLUMINATE DROP ZONE AND
GUARD LUFTWAFFE VOICE CIRCUIT. WHEN TWO DROPS ARE SUCCESS-
FUL, ORDER OTHER AIRCRAFT RETURN TO BASE. VON FREIDEBURG.
MSG. ENDS.

Reigel stared at the decoded signal for a full minute. True, the moon
would set shortly before midnight, but a circle of flares on the island's
plateau would guide the pilots beautifully. Of five Focke-Wulf Condors,
one was almost certain to get by the routine patrols of the R.A.F.
Stripped of nonessentials, the signal meant everything U-324 needed
would almost certainly be on Spanish by four thirty in the morning. A
few hours later, the submarine would be able to proceed submerged.

Now that he knew the worst, Reigel's nervous sweat disappeared.
Coldly the lieutenant analyzed his position. It was essential, he decided,
that Ballykerry be alerted immediately, and Headquarters be told U-324
was about to surrender. If they knew that, the five Focke-Wulfs would
not take off. But Reigel could not use the U-boat's radio to alert Ballykerry, and he could not depend on the Irish to seize the radio-telephone.
They would storm the cottage, yes, but it would be late at night, too
late to prevent the rescue planes from becoming airborne.

The odds against the first lieutenant were great. He was marked for
death by the islanders. He had been promised a court-martial in Lorient.
He could not confide in any member of the crew. And time was running
out on him. In four hours, the Condors would leave Brittany. The signal
that would cancel their mission must be sent by eight o'clock.

In the next two hours, then, he must take over the radio-telephone and
alert Ballykerry. Would the post office there believe a strange voice
telling a yarn about a crippled U-boat? It seemed unlikely, but Reigel
felt he had the answer.

The lieutenant looked at his watch. It was exactly six o'clock. Quickly, he paraphrased the Headquarters' signal on a message blank, so that it read:

DISPATCHING FIVE REPEAT FIVE FW-200 RECCO PLANES TOMORROW AT ELEVEN HOURS GMT. EACH PLANE FULLY LOADED ACCORDANCE YOUR REQUEST INCLUDING ARMATURE BRUSHES AND HAS FIGHTER COVER FIRST 200 MILES. EACH HAS PARASURGEON. EACH ROUTED DIFFERENTLY. ETA OF ALL BETWEEN SIXTEEN THIRTY AND SEVENTEEN TWENTY GMT. VON FREIDEBURG. MSG. ENDS.

He folded the coded and correctly decoded messages and put them carefully in his pocket. He buckled on his pistol and scooped up his cap. With the bogus signal in his hand, he opened the curtain and made for the conning tower ladder, ignoring the questioning looks of the enlisted men in the companionway.

On the bridge, he showed the bogus message to Albrecht. The chief machinist's mate read it and was guardedly optimistic.

"At least they haven't forgotten us," he said. "That's something. Out of five planes, one ought to get through."

"I'll take this up to the Old Man, Chief," Reigel said. "While I'm there, I'll persuade him to move down to the sick bay. Dietrich back?"

"No, sir."

"He's coming down the path now, sir," broke in the messenger of the watch. "He just left the Command Post."

"Good," Reigel said, packeting the false signal. He climbed down to the main deck, saluted the colors perfunctorily, and left the boat. Going up the path, he was completely concentrated on the job ahead. Ballykerry must be alerted. If Ludtke would not leave the R/T set, Ludtke must be eliminated. It was as simple as that.

When he met Dietrich on the path, he regarded the P.O. telegraphist with suspicion.

"Well, can you close down the set so it can't be operated?"

"Yes, sir. No trouble at all."

"Did you talk to the skipper?"

"Just to say good evening, sir," Dietrich said uneasily. He wanted to ask about the contents of the signal but he was afraid.

"Very well," Reigel said, "carry on," and ignoring the petty officer's salute he continued his way up the path.

When he came to the door of Dermod Beg's cottage, he took a long look around. Above him, there was no sign of a human being. Below, Dietrich's tiny figure walked along the quay to the gangway. He caught a late-sun glint of binoculars on the U-boat bridge. They're watching me, he thought; probably the Irish are watching me, too. He gave a short, humorless laugh and entered the cottage.

Very obviously, the sailor on watch was glad to see another visitor, and Ludtke was not. The captain had visibly worsened since Reigel's interview with him that morning. Huddled by the fire, he seemed shrunken and his face was shock-gray. His crippled leg rested on its creepie and on a small keg to his right were a cognac bottle, a tumbler, and the pistol.

"Well, where you been?" he demanded querulously. "Chasing the women again?"

"No, sir," Reigel said evenly. "I've been aboard the boat all afternoon." He glanced at the watchstander. "Go down and get your supper, Kramer. Bring a ration back for the captain. And when you come back, bring Barndt with you."

"Aye, aye, sir," said Able Seaman Kramer, happy at the chance to get away from Ludtke. He saluted and went out quickly. It wasn't too bad when there was someone else in the cottage, like P.O. Dietrich or the first lieutenant, but it was scary to be alone with the Old Man.

Reigel expected the captain to object to his order, but Ludtke only helped himself to brandy. His hand shook as he raised the glass and the rim clicked against his teeth. He put the glass down and wiped his mouth with the back of his fist. "Well, mister," Ludtke said finally. "What's Grand Admiral Doenitz have to say?"

The question threw Reigel off stride. He had planned to persuade the captain to come to the sick bay for the night. That way he could call Ballykerry. Only if the captain refused did he intend to use the bogus message to distract Ludtke's attention. But obviously Dietrich had told Ludtke a signal had arrived.

"I've got it right here, Captain," Reigel said, with an instant's hesitation. He fumbled in his pocket, produced the bogus message, and unfolded it.

"Shall I read it, sir?"

"Give it here," the captain croaked, extending his right hand.

Reigel took two paces forward, the message in his right hand. As the captain took it, Reigel seized his hand, took another step, and snatched up the Luger with his left. He moved so quickly that almost before Ludtke started to wrench his hand free, Reigel had disengaged his grip and had retreated to the other side of the kitchen. He tucked the pistol into his belt.

"Excuse me, Captain. That pistol makes me nervous."

Ludtke's voice was low and guttural, half-strangled with fury and saliva. "God damn you, mister, you mutinous, puking pimp——"

He tried to get up, failed, and fell back. His face was contorted, livid, and glistening with sweat. His head shook, as if consumed by an enormous spasm of fury. For a few seconds incoherent obscenities poured out. Reigel stared back at Ludtke, revolted, fascinated, and, even with two pistols at his belt, a little frightened. He's like a mad dog, the first lieutenant thought.

With an obvious effort, the captain checked himself. The yellow eyes glowing with hatred, he said, "Consider yourself under arrest, mister. Get back to the boat. You're confined to the wardroom and relieved of all duties."

Reigel laughed shortly. Intended to be easy and mocking, it was a hollow, nervous bark of a laugh.

"Easy, Captain, easy. You're a sick man, Captain. Let us take you down to the sick bay for the night. Barndt will look after you, and we'll put the R/T temporarily out of commission."

"Don't give me that, mister," Ludtke grated. He stopped and looked at the crumpled ball of paper in his hand. He spread the torn message blank out on his lap, picked it up, and studied it carefully. His hand shook as he read it. Across the room, the lieutenant licked his dry lips.

"Tomorrow, eh?" Ludtke said with an icy bitterness. He looked up. "What did the signal really say, mister?"

"What do you mean?"

"I mean this message is too short, much too short. Dietrich told me there were ninety-odd groups of coded letters. You've juggled the signal, mister. Now tell me what it said."

Reigel took his Walther pistol out of its holster and clicked off the safety. He was coldly furious at being discovered. He said: "They're coming tonight, Captain, not tomorrow." Then he shot Ludtke.

The crash seemed to shake the kitchen and there was a bitter smell of explosive. Fired at close quarters, the impact of the heavy slug knocked Ludtke and his chair back a good six inches. The captain tried to rise and fell back again. His left hand clawed at the chair arm. His right seized the cognac bottle and shattered it on the other arm, so that he held only the neck with its razor-sharp shards.

"I'll see you on the gallows, Reigel," Ludtke snarled. He started to rise again, the yellow eyes gleaming. "God damn you to hell, you mutinous, scuttling, mother-sucking bastard——"

Lieutenant Reigel, compressing his lips, brought the Walther down deliberately and fired again. Halfway to his feet, Ludtke was smashed violently backward, upsetting and breaking the chair. His head hit the hearth like a ripe squash.

Reigel stood stock still for an instant, his mouth twisting. He took the captain's Luger out of his waistband, fired it into the wall behind him, and then tossed the pistol toward the hearth.

Dust was everywhere in the kitchen—dust, silence, and an evil, acrid odor. Reigel put up his own pistol and walked to the radio-telephone set. He flicked on the switch. "Hello, Ballykerry, hello, Ballykerry," he said in a cold, conversational tone. "This is Spanish, this is Spanish. Come in, Ballykerry, come in. . . ."

Within a minute, Ballykerry answered, and he gave his message:

"There's a German U-boat here—ready to surrender to the authorities. That's right, a U-boat, here at Spanish. The Germans have kept Dr. FitzGerald and Father Healy prisoners, but they're ready to surrender them now. Send soldiers or policemen as quickly as you can."

Reigel knew the atmospherics would distort his voice. They could not, however, disguise the shock and incredulity of the Ballykerry postmaster. Finally, Ballykerry asked the identity of the sender of this amazing message.

"Tomas Mor," Reigel said unhesitatingly. "This is Tomas Mor of Spanish Island." There was a squawky pause and then Ballykerry acknowledged. The postmaster might know Tomas, Reigel thought, certainly know of him, but the chances were good that Tomas rarely spoke on the radio-telephone and that his voice was unfamiliar.

He switched the set off and thought for a moment. His watch read six thirty-three. He walked to the door and looked out. As was to be expected, the firing had alarmed the bridge watch. Albrecht was puffing up the path toward him; strung out behind the chief were nearly a dozen other sailors.

Reigel waited for them calmly. When they arrived, his story was smooth and plausible. The captain went out of his mind, he said, when he heard the rescue planes would not leave France until morning. Ludtke had decided then and there to surrender U-324 to the Irish authorities. He had called Ballykerry up, told about the boat's presence, and asked the police to be sent. When Reigel protested, the captain had tried to kill him. In self-defense, the first lieutenant had fired back.

They trooped solemnly into the cottage, removing their caps, and looked with respectful interest at the smashed and twisted body. There seemed to be no doubt that Ludtke's death had occurred as Reigel had reported it. Everyone knew the Old Man was half crazy. The news that the rescue planes weren't coming until tomorrow had obviously pushed him around the bend. No one had liked Ludtke, but everyone had trusted him. The Old Man had always gotten them out of tight spots before. They seemed to ask themselves, who will look out for us now?

Reigel gave his orders crisply. Slowly, as though they were in a state of shock, four sailors put the corpse on a shutter, covered it with a blanket, and carried it down to the quay. The captain, Reigel said, would be buried tomorrow morning. Then he turned to the P.O. telegraphist.

"We won't need the R/T any more, Dietrich. Take out that relay so the set can't be used."

"Aye, aye, sir." Dietrich produced a small screwdriver and crouched by the set. Watching him work, Reigel speculated how suspicious the P.O. telegraphist might be. Dietrich had lied when he told Reigel he had had no conversation with the captain; that in itself made him dangerous. It would not do, Reigel told himself, to show Dietrich the bogus Headquarters signal. From its length, he would know it for a fake.

When the petty officer was finished, Reigel took the relay and put it in his pocket. He satisfied himself the set was inoperative. Then he spoke again to Dietrich.

"All right, Sparks. Let's go back to the boat. I want to send a signal to France."

Outside the cottage a group of Irish waited curiously. Nora Berkeley was there, looking pale and exhausted. The doctor was with her, and Tomas, Brede, Peigeen, Sean, and Liam Curran. The lieutenant spoke briefly to them:

"Captain Ludtke is dead. He attacked me and, in self-defense, I had to shoot him. Shortly before that, the captain informed Ballykerry Post Office of our presence here. I imagine soldiers will land on the island tonight to accept our surrender."

Sean O Ruiarc removed his cloth cap and his lips moved in brief, perfunctory prayer. Tomas glowered truculently at Reigel. The others, for the most part, managed to look both solemn, as befitting the demise of a man they had known, and pleased, with the realization they would soon be free. Dr. FitzGerald asked if he might communicate with the mainland—he had been away from his patients for three days—and was told the radio-telephone was out of commission. Liam asked when the funeral would be—Father Healy would want to know—and Reigel told him the captain would be buried in the morning.

There was no more to be said. Brede, Peigeen, and Sean went into the cottage. Dietrich started down the path. Turning to follow, Reigel spoke urgently to Nora.

"I have to send a signal to France now, but I must see you soon. Where will you be in an hour's time?"

"I'll be in the sick bay after supper," the girl said.

Reigel went down the path buoyantly. As soon as he went aboard, he wrote out a signal in the wardroom and took it to Dietrich in the radio shack.

"Code this up, Sparks, and get it off as Top Priority," he said. Dietrich read it through carefully. His eyes were troubled, but he said nothing and sat down with the cipher book to begin his work.

ADMIRAL COMMANDING U-BOATS FROM U-324. REGRET REPORT CAPTAIN LUDTKE DEAD. BEFORE DEATH LUDTKE SURRENDERED TO IRISH AUTHORITIES. IN VIEW OF THIS SUGGEST MISSION DESCRIBED YOUR 061652 WILL BE USELESS. REIGEL, COMMANDING. MSG. ENDS.

Reigel lit a Gauloise and watched the encoding of his signal. When Dietrich had finished and begun to transmit, Reigel sent word to the bridge to have the ship's company fallen in on the fo'c'sle. Then he waited, drawing deeply on his cigarette and watching Dietrich's practiced hand on the radio key. The electric clock in the compartment was stopped, but Reigel's wristwatch read seven thirty when Dietrich reported the signal sent and acknowledged.

"Very well, Sparks. We'll secure the wireless watch now. Give me your key to the shack."

The petty officer started to protest and thought better of it. He handed over the key and followed Reigel into the companionway. Reigel closed the door and locked it. There were two keys to the radio compartment and he had them both. For the first time since she was commissioned, U-324 was cut off from Headquarters. With the keys and the electrical relay from the radio-telephone set in Reigel's pocket, the boat and her crew were completely sealed away from the outside world.

Followed by Dietrich, who looked puzzled and unhappy, the lieutenant climbed to the bridge. Chief Petty Officer Albrecht saluted.

"Ship's company present, sir. All hands except for the wounded and the watchstander in the tower."

Regiel looked down on the fo'c'sle. Of the forty-eight officers and men who had sailed from Lorient, twenty-three ratings were present. Uneasy and dejected, they waited for the first lieutenant to speak.

"Sailors of the Shark Boat," Reigel began in a solemn voice, "we have just sustained our greatest loss. The captain went insane and I had to shoot him. Earlier this afternoon the Irish doctor wanted to amputate the captain's leg. The captain wouldn't permit it and refused to take morphine.

"When I visited him a little while ago, I tried to persuade Captain Ludtke to let us bring him down to the sick bay. I told him the islanders might rush the Command Post. I also told him the Luftwaffe planned another rescue mission—but not until tomorrow afternoon.

"When I told him these things, the captain went out of his mind. He went to the R/T set and before I knew what he was doing, he told the mainland a U-boat was here, ready to surrender."

Reigel paused and there was a little groan from his audience.

"I protested what the captain had done. That infuriated him and he tried to kill me." He paused again, apparently struggling to control his emotion, and then went on, his voice strong and confident.

"The Irish authorities will arrive on the island sometime tonight to accept our surrender. We can resist them, of course, but not for long. To prevent useless bloodshed, I am going to surrender. I have notified Headquarters of this and suggested the rescue planes not fly tomorrow. If they do, the R.A.F. will be waiting for them.

"That's all I have to say, comrades. Half your shipmates are dead or wounded. I don't want any more suffering. The war is over for us. Internment in Ireland will be *gemütlich*. Pretty girls. Good food and beer."

He turned and said, "That's all, Chief. Dismiss ship's company and pipe hands to supper."

Albrecht gave him a strange look, half accusing, half baffled. Then he said, "Aye, aye, sir," in a low, strangled voice.

Reigel ate his supper in the tiny wardroom, avoiding the eyes of the sailor who served him. At 2230, he saluted the somber Dietrich, now petty officer of the watch, and left the boat. He walked up the quay, wearing his melancholy like a tightly wrapped boat cloak. Behind him, on the deck of the boat, he heard a few off-watch sailors softly singing the sentimental favorite of the U-Waffe, *"No roses bloom on a sailor's tomb."* When he came abreast of the captain's body lying on its shutter under Brede Beg's blanket, Reigel stopped and removed his cap. He knew this gesture of humble respect would be marked by Dietrich, the bridge messenger, and the other sailors on the topside. He held his cap against his heart and looked gravely at the lumpy mound of blanket. Well, he thought, you were tough and smart, ready to sacrifice every man aboard to bring the boat home and collect your Oak Leaves. But you ran up against someone tougher and smarter than you. He replaced his cap, clicked his heels to attention, and formally saluted the remains of Gerhard Ludtke. Then, whistling under his breath, he walked purposefully toward the sick bay.

Nora was there, her patients quiet after their supper. She had nothing to do for them and, after some urging, consented to go outside with the first lieutenant. Now that the Guards had been summoned, she wanted no part of Reigel, but violence could still erupt on the island, and it was important to know his plans.

Once more, Reigel led her to the seaward side of the sick bay. The sun was low on the western side of the island and Spanish was beginning to take on its twilight tones of darkening purple. It was very still, broken only by the sound of the sea and the faint cry of gulls hovering over the U-boat. Reigel lit cigarettes for them and they sat together on a grassy ledge, their backs to the wall. For part of a minute they smoked quietly.

"It's so lovely and peaceful," the girl said softly, although every nerve of her body was tense. "So peaceful."

"It's going to be that way always for us, Nora," Reigel said. "No more fighting, no more killing. The war is over for us."

"I'm glad," she said. "Very glad."

"Pretty soon the police will be here to accept our surrender. Tomorrow we'll be taken to some internment camp. There probably won't be a chance for us to be alone again. That's why I wanted to see you this evening."

Reigel flipped away his cigarette. It was time to play his trump card. "You must know, *Liebchen*, that I love you very much," he said earnestly. "I want you to wait for me. I want to marry you when the was is over."

"Oh," Nora said in a small, surprised voice. She had met Reigel to learn if he planned to resist the police; suddenly she had a proposal of marriage to cope with. The man who offered his hand was highly dangerous, an accused rapist and admitted killer. He was a bloody sod. At the same time, he was the most handsome man she had ever seen, and aflame with desire for her.

"Oh," she said again, weakly. "Oh, the war is apt to go on for years and years."

"Not that long, Nora. Once Germany has to fight on two fronts, the end will come quickly."

The girl did not answer and Reigel spoke again.

"We're beaten, Nora. The fact the Luftwaffe couldn't make a drop here proves it. The limeys and Yanks control the sea and the air. They're getting stronger while our strength is bled away on the Ostfront. The war is nearly over."

He fell silent, brooding, and Nora waited for him to continue. After a bit, she spoke.

"Did Captain Ludtke believe that?"

"Captain Ludtke believed in nothing but medals and G.R.T. sunk. He was insane."

"But if he called Ballykerry to surrender——"

"He didn't call Ballykerry, Nora. I did. Because I want to marry you."

"Is that why the captain tried to kill you, Kurt?" the girl asked in a small voice.

"No, I called Ballykerry after he was dead."

"I mean, did he attack you because you wanted to be interned?"

The lieutenant grunted an affirmative and they sat without speaking. Reigel was annoyed by her questioning. *Zum Teufel!* He was trying to get an answer from her. Beside him, Nora reflected that Captain Ludtke could not be blamed for objecting to his first lieutenant's desire to surrender. That, she supposed, was mutiny. She turned to look at Reigel, but he was staring at the ground and the twilight had deepened so that his features were blurred. She started to speak, but he sandwiched her hand, squeezed it, and said urgently:

"This is the right way, *Liebchen*, for you and me. The men are happy about it. They know the Luftwaffe has failed us. Even if we had the armature brushes, they know we could never cross the bay. The men are glad of internment, glad the war is over for us."

His voice was oddly high-pitched and in the gathering darkness, it helped give the girl the peculiar feeling that a stranger was speaking to her. Reigel sounded almost desperate and she was certain he was not speaking the truth. There had been no gladness in the sick bay when she had relieved Barndt thirty minutes before. The conscious wounded had seemed broken and crushed. They had not talked much, but Nora heard the words, *"Herr Kapitan"* in nearly every exchange. Barndt had said nothing, as he went from patient to patient, but she could see he had been crying. No, the sailors were not glad about internment.

Again Reigel asked his question, "Will you wait for me, Nora?" Again she demurred.

"Kurt, I hardly know you. You're asking me to wait for years——"

"Months," he broke in. "Maybe weeks. *Liebchen*, I did this for you. I want to stay in Ireland, with you, for the rest of my life."

Nora said nothing. She thought of the wounded sailors and the red-eyed Barndt, of the deranged and dying Ludtke, and of shy, cheerful Peter Hoffman going back to Limerick. None of them wanted internment. Only the man beside her, the superbly endowed, supremely arrogant first lieutenant, wanted asylum.

Furious at her silence, Reigel abruptly stood up, wrenching Nora to her feet and into his arms. He kissed her with sudden, brutal passion, and felt her tense and unyielding in his arms.

"God damn it," he said thickly, holding her at arm's length. "I'm going to show you what loving is. You asked for it and you're going to get it, by God. You may be too good to marry me, but you're not too good to come up to the Conor cabin with me——"

"Kurt, Kurt," the girl said quickly. "I'm flattered, believe me. But I need time to think."

Reigel relaxed his grip and she stepped back, badly frightened. It was now so dark she could barely see his face. There was no sound except for the rustle of the wind and the boom of the surf.

Then, abruptly, there was a new sound, muffled yet close at hand. It was a man's voice and it was calling, *"Fraulein, Fraulein, kom ist hier."*

Almost instantly, Nora realized the cry came from inside the sick bay. "It's one of the wounded, I must go," she said. She tried to wrench herself free but Reigel's hold on her wrist was like a manacle. "Please!" she begged, but he swung her against him and kissed her violently. For a moment Nora knew complete terror. Then the lieutenant released her and stepped back.

"Very well, little nurse," he said sardonically. "Let's go see what the kike wants."

She did not know what he meant and did not care. She turned and fled, still badly frightened. In a few seconds she was in the musty-smelling building. Only then was fear replaced by relief, which, in turn, was preempted by a new fear that something had gone wrong with one of her patients—that she had let down Doctor Fitz.

It was Oberteuffer who had called for her. He had improved greatly during the past twenty-four hours, but now he groaned horribly and thrashed about on his mattress. Nora ran to him and knelt by the pallet, trying to soothe him. She took his elbow and examined the heavily taped stump. She felt his forehead and took his pulse. Despite the sailor's agony, everything seemed completely normal. Nora was aware that most of the other patients were awake and watching Oberteuffer and that the first lieutenant had followed her into the building.

"Ah, Kurt," Nora said desperately, "I haven't a clue what's causing this. Fetch Barndt, please."

Reigel stood over the pallet, looking down at Nora and her patient. In the dim lantern light, the lieutenant looked enormous.

"There's nothing wrong with the malingering son-of-a-dog. He just feels sorry for himself."

The sailor moaned piteously, and the girl said angrily, "Please fetch Barndt," and Reigel, with a final word of contempt, wheeled and left the building.

Oberteuffer twisted and groaned for another minute and, then, as

Nora was preparing to take his temperature, he did a very surprising thing.

He winked at her.

Nora almost dropped the thermometer. She goggled and a slow smile spread over the sailor's young face.

"Good God," the girl whispered, shocked and indignant, "what's the meaning of this?"

Still smiling, the sailor spoke briefly. At first, she could not understand him but when he said "Herr Reigel," pointed his finger at her, and then at the leeward side of the building, Nora had a sudden flash of comprehension. Oberteuffer had been concerned at her absence with Reigel, had heard Reigel when he lost his temper, and, by crying out for help, had saved her.

She smiled down at the sailor and said, *"Danke, Herr Oberteuffer, danke."* In the dim light she noted that the other conscious patients were grinning at her. Tears of gratitude sprang up in her eyes and she busied herself with the brewing of tea.

After the tea, the next hour passed quietly. Barndt did not appear and Nora knitted as the patients dozed or slept. About ten o'clock, a new sound, clamorous and imperative, shattered the night. It was U-324's Action Stations klaxon and the wounded were suddenly tense and listening.

Nora ran to the door. It was dark outside, with a few stars visible. Some lights winked on in the cottages above her, but no light showed on the quay or the U-boat. The gangway lantern had been extinguished and she could barely make out the vertical silhouette of the boat's conning tower. She stood at the sick bay door, listening to the rattle of the klaxon, thoroughly alarmed.

There was a tiny report and, from the U-boat, a brief streak of flame arched seaward, over the cove. Nora ran out a few steps to follow its flight. A hundred yards above the water, there was a soundless burst of white light, like a rocket, and then a parachute flare began to descend. Nora looked at the surface of the little harbor and sucked in her breath. There was a boat there, a curragh, just inside the entrance and making slowly for the submarine. She stared at it for nearly half a minute— until the flare was quenched and everything was inky black. She went back into the building and tried to answer her patients' questions.

"It's a curragh," she said. "It must be the Guards. You know, police. *Polizei. Polizei.*"

They understood that and they groaned. Oberteuffer began to cry.

． ． ．

Everyone on the U-boat's bridge thought it was the police. Reigel had not expected them so quickly and he was startled at the sight of a curragh. But when the flare went out, he realized the Irish had no gunboat in these waters. It would have to be a curragh, with a few rustic constables to take the surrender.

A few minutes later, the intruder was clearly illuminated by the submarine's searchlight and the first lieutenant swallowed hard. It was not the police. In the sternsheets of the curragh, and easily identified, was Lieutenant Hoffman. He waved, acknowledging the shouts of welcome from the U-boat. Reigel, putting down his glasses, felt a sour knot of foreboding in his stomach.

The curragh made its approach, slowly and awkwardly. The four men who had left Spanish in it, two nights before, were still aboard; Eamon Og and Dermod Beg at the oars, Electrician's Mate Kreisler in the bow, and the engineer lieutenant. Their movements were cramped with weariness. From the moment it had been illuminated, the curragh seemed to handle clumsily, and as it approached the U-boat, the cause became apparent; it was towing two long cylindrical objects, about the size of telephone poles, and almost entirely submerged. The forward ends of the metallic cylinders were lashed alongside the little boat, and their ends barely broke the water's surface some forty feet behind the curragh.

The German sailors lined the submarine's port rail, shouting welcomes and questions. Reigel joined them and cupped his hands to his mouth:

"Ahoy there, Chief! What the devil have you brought us—the Loch Ness monster?"

Hoffman waved back, but delayed his answer until the curragh was nearly alongside. Then he shouted up at the first lieutenant, "We couldn't find the armature brushes. We brought these gas pipes instead."

He waited for an interval, listening to the mingled groans and questions from the U-boat. When the curragh was secured alongside, he raised one hand for attention and spoke again.

"We couldn't get the armature brushes to let us run submerged on the electric motors—this way, we'll run submerged on our diesels."

Hoffman paused for a moment, grinning up at the baffled faces.

"You've heard of the snorkel, boys. Well, this is the Shark Boat's snorkel. We'll rig it tomorrow, and test it. God willing, we'll be able to sail on Friday."

From the darkness of the shore, Nora and a few of the islanders watched them come aboard, stiff with fatigue. She couldn't understand the questions and answers—the important thing was that Peter and the others were safely back. She offered a little prayer of thanks as the engineer officer and his party went below, followed by Reigel and every sailor not on watch. She went back to the sick bay and reported that it was Lieutenant Hoffman, not the *Polizei*, in the curragh. Her patients cheered at that and until she was relieved, at midnight, the room buzzed with optimistic talk.

All the German sailors wanted to ask about the snorkel, but the first thought of Hoffman's little expedition was for food. Hoffman himself had something else uppermost in his mind. At a mess table in the after torpedo room, he asked the question that had scourged him throughout the five-hour trip from Ballykerry:

"What's all this about surrender? On the mainland we heard there was a U-boat at Spanish ready to surrender. Has the captain changed his mind?"

"The captain is dead, Chief," Reigel said in a sudden hush. "He attacked me and I had to kill him in self-defense. Just before that, he called Ballykerry on the R/T and told them to send the police— that he was ready to surrender."

Hoffman seemed stunned. "The Old Man ready to surrender? My God. He must have been delirious."

"He was out of his mind, Chief."

"And you killed him?"

"I had to, Chief, I had to. He fired at me first."

Hoffman shook his head like a boxer who has just sustained a heavy blow. Thick meat sandwiches and steaming mugs of coffee were set down on the mess table and Kreisler and the Irishmen began to eat ravenously. The engineer officer scowled at his food.

"That makes me skipper of the Shark Boat," he said slowly. "Well, here's my first order. There won't be any surrender. The police won't leave Ballykerry until morning—probably on the *Kerry Queen*. We'll work tonight. If we can get the snorkel rigged we ought to be able to sail right after breakfast."

The compartment rang with cheers. About to protest, Reigel thought differently and said nothing. Acting Captain Hoffman began to eat, listening to the excited buzz of voices around him. He wanted to inquire about Nora, but before he could phrase the question, Albrecht and the others were asking about the expedition. How had he happened to bring back the piping?

"Things went well—at first," Hoffman said between enormous mouthfuls. "We got to Ballykerry before daybreak yesterday and we slept all morning in Mick's barn. We took his truck and got to Limerick just after dark. We went to the warehouse we'd been to before—Coyle and Ryan's—and two others as well, but the armature brushes weren't to be found."

He chewed for a few seconds and had a sip of coffee. "It was four in the morning and we had found nothing. There were police in the streets and we were scared. We were ready to come back. Then, behind Coyle and Ryan's, in the gas utility's storage area, we saw the piping and I thought, why not a snort for the Shark Boat? We can't get the armature brushes, but we can try this."

There was an appreciative murmur from the sailors jammed into the compartment. No one knew exactly how a snorkel worked, but everyone knew Headquarters believed it would win the war and that it was already operational in the Atlantic.

"Kreisler estimated it's about twenty-five feet from the main deck to the top of the periscope," Hoffman said. "The piping in the courtyard was eight inches in diameter—in lengths of about forty feet. So we took two lengths and brought them here."

He chewed slowly on his sandwich, thinking *that* was a bit of understatement. We took two lengths and brought them here. The simple sentence encompassed a great deal. Once the decision was made, in the dim half-light of early dawn, one hundred and ten miles from Ballykerry, it had not been easy to implement. To begin with, the dull-gleaming lengths of pipe were much too long for the truck to handle. Kreisler and Dermod reconnoitered and within the hour produced a two-wheeled milk cart. With much effort, they got the end of one pipe onto the truck and the other aboard the cart. Another length of pipe was similarly emplaced and the two were lashed together and made fast. It was difficult to get the long, improvised truck-and-trailer out of the yard and around the corners of the Limerick intersections. Of necessity, Kreisler rode on the trailer, helping to guide it around the corners.

There were few persons abroad, but those stared curiously at the odd rig as it slowly rattled along the streets. Miraculously, none of the *Guarda Siochana* appeared. Halfway through the city, they passed a sewer excavation and, at Dermod's suggestion, appropriated two signs which they fastened to the piping. The lettering on the signs—Gas Service Dept., City of Limerick—gave them an appearance of legitimacy and might forestall questions. By half past six in the morning, they were out of the city and headed for the Dingle Peninsula.

On his earlier return from Limerick, Hoffman had been careful to avoid towns and villages. Then there had been nothing unusual about the truck. But the long pipes were sure to attract attention and comment, and, after consulting his map, Hoffman decided to return by an even more obscure route. They went south of Adare, skirted the town of Croom, and drove westward, detouring around the villages of Ballingarry, Kilmeady, and Glenquin. West of Glenquin, the road became progressively hillier. The grades were steeper and the turns abrupt. Well up into the mountains, a wheel of the improvised trailer broke. For more than five miles, they had to drag the pipes along the tortuous road, manhandling them around sharp corners. In the bog country south of Castle Island, they found a turf-cutter's cart, lashed the pipes to it, and made better time. By one o'clock, they had reached the Dingle Peninsula and were following the shore road to the west.

A policeman stopped them in the village of Inch and Hoffman reached for his pistol. But the policeman was merely curious and Dermod's explanation that the pipe was for the Dingle gasworks seemed to satisfy him. Hoffman drove on, apprehensively transiting Dingle. Dingle was the last town of any consequence on their route, the last place they might be halted. Nothing happened, and by four in the afternoon they were at Mick's, on the outskirts of Ballykerry. They plugged both ends of the pipes to give them buoyancy and Hoffman backed the truck and trailer down to the beach and into the water. Waist-deep in the swells, they lashed the pipes to the curragh and cut loose the turf cart. The lines that fastened the pipes to the truck were also cast loose and the truck turned over to Mick. Mick stared at the pipes but he asked no questions. He did volunteer the information, however, that there was a German U-boat at Spanish Island. Tomas Mor had called up Ballykerry two hours before and asked that the Guards be sent. The U-boat wanted to surrender. More than that, Mick knew nothing. The news, he supposed, had been sent to the barracks at Dingle. There were no policemen at Ballykerry, God be praised.

Hoffman had been alarmed. He could not guess what had happened on the island, but obviously something had gone wrong. It was essential they return as quickly as possible. They would not stop, even for the evening meal. Shortly after four, they had embarked and the islanders were straining at their oars. It had been hard going, towing the pipes into the slow, heavy swells, but perhaps, Hoffman kept telling himself during the long journey, perhaps there was still enough time.

Lieutenant Hoffman finished his meal and reflected that there still was enough time. He thanked Eamon Og and Dermod Beg and sent them off to their wives. He learned of Padraig's death and the irrevocable hostility of the islanders. The news was all bad, Hoffman thought grimly, but perhaps it would not affect the U-boat's sailing. There was no need for any member of the crew, save the watch-standers at the tower and himself, to go farther than the sick bay. The watch at the tower would be maintained, and he must see Nora before they sailed. He had thought of her often in the last two days. But, first, there was the snorkel.

Hoffman asked for pencil and paper, motioned to Albrecht, Kreisler, and the engineering ratings to come closer, and began to explain his plan. Essentially, he began, it was necessary to place one length of pipe vertically over the air induction valve and the other over the exhaust vent in the engine room. A hole must be cut in the pressure hull to accommodate the pipes. The tops of both pipes should be cut off, level with the periscope shears. Both should be welded at the pressure hull and to the superstructure. If the job were done properly, Hoffman said, with a confidence he did not entirely feel, U-324 could submerge to periscope depth off Spanish and steam back to Lorient at fifteen knots. It was true, he admitted, that enemy radar might pick up the snorkel, but it was unlikely. If they were picked up, they would have to come to the surface and fight; they could not dive below periscope depth.

They asked him about rough weather, and Hoffman shrugged his shoulders.

"The regular snort is fitted with some sort of baffle," he said, "which admits air and keeps out the seawater. I imagine we could work out some sort of shutter valve. Eh, Chief?"

Albrecht nodded. "Aye, sir. We could rig a valve on the pipe, balanced so it's open when above the surface, but closing automatically with the weight of the seawater."

As Hoffman answered questions and drew his diagrams, Reigel slipped out of the compartment and walked forward. Any moment now, he said to himself, Hoffman will want to reestablish radio contact with France. He's just been too busy to think of it since he came aboard. The first lieutenant unlocked the radio shack and entered. He knew enough of the equipment to put both transmitter and receiver out of commission, and this he did, swiftly and thoroughly.

He paused in the wardroom, buckled on his pistol belt, and folded a blanket over his arm. Then he went up to the bridge. As his head poked up through the hatch, Reigel saw there was a new petty officer of the watch. He looked at his wrist—twelve twenty. A new day had come to Spanish Island.

THE SECOND THURSDAY

For the rest of the night, the Germans struggled with their improvised snorkel. The hardest job was to cut a hole for the two eight-inch gas pipes in the pressure hull. Work began with the cutting torch shortly after midnight and was not completed until the morning watch took over at four. At the same time, Chief Machinist's Mate Albrecht and his ratings fabricated the connections between the intake pipe and the air holes of the diesels, and the exhaust pipe and the engines' exhaust vents. While these operations proceeded, Leading Torpedoman Muller and the deck force, using the after torpedo crane, winched the two pipes up on deck. They were cut to the proper length, and a crude shutter valve was constructed and installed at the end of the intake pipe. They tested this and were satisfied it would close when a few inches under the surface and open when the water's weight was removed. A block and tackle was rigged halfway up the attack periscope, and the two lengths of piping were slowly hauled to a vertical position just abaft the conning tower. They were lashed in place there, awaiting the time when they could be lowered into the hull of the boat.

At first, Hoffman was everywhere, encouraging the hands with the cutting torch, Albrecht's people, and Muller's deck force. He supervised the tests of the shutter valve, studied the dog-eared pages of the Navy manuals on diesel engines, and continually tried to recall what he had read about the snorkel. Twice he asked for Reigel but no one seemed to know where the first lieutenant was. On both occasions, Hoffman shrugged; he had more to worry about than Reigel. There were two main dangers about the snorkel, for instance, dangers as deadly as a full pattern of Torpex depth charges. The first was concerned with the intake pipe. If the top of the snorkel went below the surface, and the air was cut off for even a few seconds, the diesels would suck in air from the interior of the boat. The eyes of the crew would bulge out of their sockets and their ears would pop painfully until the snort broke surface again and the shutter valve opened. It was a very real danger, he thought, but exceptional vigilance by the man at the conn and the diving planes could avert it. He reminded Albrecht that the emergency bottles of compressed air must be prepared for instant use.

The second danger concerned the exhaust. Hoffman had read of tests in the Baltic where the outlet pipe was submerged and the diesel exhaust was reversed. When that happened, the ratings in the engine room would drop like flies from the carbon monoxide. The only protection was a man alert enough to shut down the engines instantly.

He shrugged his shoulders again. If every man on watch stayed on his toes, the snorkel would work. He was confident they would. The insuperable problem was that U-324 would be completely vulnerable. It could not submerge below periscope depth. If a ship or plane spotted the diesel exhaust or the wake of her shears and snort, the boat had only one recourse—to surface and fight with her Oerlikons. Also, if they were spotted, they would probably be attacked without warning. Low in the water, the periscope had a very limited range, and the noise of the diesels would prevent the sound operator from hearing propeller noises.

Hoffman grimaced. The boat could not submerge more than a few feet. She could not hear and she was nearly blind. Her captain and nearly half her crew were dead. Nearly four hundred sea miles lay between her and Lorient. Yet, despite the odds, Hoffman believed they could make Lorient, and his conviction transmitted itself to the enlisted men. Around him, the crew worked with enthusiasm and confidence. When he approached, sailors would grin at him. Spirits were running high in U-324. It had taken some time, the grins seemed to say, but the Shark Boat, at last, was going home. Hoffman smiled to himself. He needn't worry about morale. The work was progressing well. The best thing he could do, he told himself, was to pray for overcast skies, poor visibility, and a slightly choppy sea.

Shortly before two in the morning, Albrecht came up to him, smiling in his dour phlegmatic fashion, and wiping his hands on a piece of waste.

"Why not turn in, Mr. Hoffman? You could use a little sleep."

Hoffman demurred. He felt fine, he told the chief petty officer.

"Kreisler says you haven't slept for thirty-six hours. Once underway, you won't get your head down for a minute. We'll need you then, sir. Better turn in now."

Hoffman considered this advice and decided it was good. "All right, Chief," he said quietly. "Call me in a couple of hours, will you, please?"

He walked forward to the wardroom and lay down. The other three bunks in the tiny compartment were empty. The two uppers, of course, had belonged to the torpedo officer and the midshipman, but he wondered again about Reigel. He hadn't seen Reigel since midnight. For a few minutes he speculated, and then, despite the noise in the boat, fell into a heavy, dreamless sleep.

•   •   •

Albrecht awakened him with a cup of coffee at six o'clock. Hoffman was annoyed at being permitted to sleep so long, and made some mock-acid comments.

"They only cut through the hull at four, sir," Albrecht said placidly. "It took time to lower the pipes, weld them to the conning tower, and connect them up with the diesels."

"All right, all right," Hoffman said. He felt greatly refreshed, but his pride was pinched by the realization the job had been done without him.

"Permission to pipe to breakfast, sir?" Albrecht asked. "When we get that over with, we'll be ready to test the snort."

"Very well, Chief," Hoffman said. "Carry on." He took a sip of coffee.

"Another thing, sir," Albrecht said with glum imperturbability. "The wireless shack has been smashed up. Receiver and transmitter are both out of commission."

"My God! Did the Irish——?"

"No, Mr. Hoffman."

The lieutenant put down his cup and began to wriggle into his boots. "Where's Dietrich?"

"He's right here, sir. Come in, Sparks."

The P.O. telegraphist squeezed into the wardroom.

"What's this all about? We'll want to send a departure signal."

Dietrich made a wry face. "Mr. Reigel took my key yesterday, Mr. Hoffman, and locked up the shack. Seeing as how we're going to sea today, I thought I ought to get the early morning Met Report. When I couldn't find Mr. Reigel, Albrecht and I took the door off its hinges. We found the set had been damaged. We can't transmit or receive, Mr. Hoffman."

"Can it be fixed?"

Dietrich shook his head and the engineer officer sat silent for a moment, stunned by this development.

"Where do you suppose Mr. Reigel is?"

The two petty officers shook their heads again.

"He left the boat just after midnight, sir," Albrecht said. "No one has seen him since. We've checked the sick bay, and the Norseman's Tower, but they've seen nothing of him."

"The islanders must have captured him," Hoffman said. "Maybe killed him." He got to his feet and buckled on his pistol. "Pipe the hands to breakfast, Chief. I'm going ashore."

The two petty officers wanted him to take an escort, but Hoffman refused. As he went up the path, the sun was emerging from behind the mist-shrouded mountains of the mainland. Seven days before, almost to the minute, he had climbed this hill with the luckless Oberteuffer. They had been, Hoffman reflected wryly, a busy seven days. He stopped first at Mrs. Mor's cottage. The Widow said she knew nothing of the first lieutenant; she hoped he was dead—dead without a prayer for him. Tomas joined her at the door and seconded his mother's remarks. There was obvious honesty in the Mors' vindictiveness and Hoffman continued up the hill.

Dermod Beg came to his door and wished the lieutenant the luck of the day. He had always liked Hoffman. Things would have been different, he said later, if Hoffman had not made his two trips to the mainland.

The postmaster's eyes hardened when asked about Reigel. No, he'd not seen him.

"I expect the Guards will find him, Lieutenant," Brede added from behind her husband, "when they come to take over the submarine."

"They're not taking over the submarine, Frau Beg," Hoffman said decisively. "We're sailing for home this morning. If the police get here first, we'll blow them out of the water."

He went on his way then, but at each successive cottage the answer was the same. Maeve Mor, her eyes red, and Eamon Og curtly disclaimed any knowledge of Reigel. Sean O Ŕuiarc said he had not seen the first lieutenant and hoped he never would again. At the half-door of the Wynne cottage, Dr. FitzGerald was equally emphatic.

"I've not seen the wicked man," he said bluntly. "I hope the villain is dead. Good morning to you, Lieutenant."

Dr. FitzGerald turned back into the Wynne kitchen as Hoffman plodded up toward the Norseman's Tower.

"What were you saying, Doctor Fitz?" Nora Berkeley asked, coming into the kitchen from Lady Maud's bedroom. The girl had slept badly and felt out of sorts.

"Lieutenant Reigel is missing. That was the other officer—Hoffman —looking for him."

"Missing? That's odd."

"The coward probably thinks he can hide from the Guards," the doctor grunted as he sat down to his breakfast. "Och, they'll find the bloody man," he said to Nora. "Have no fear of that, now."

Nora went to the door and looked out of the open upper half. She could see Hoffman making his way slowly to the top of the hill. She came back to the table, her face troubled, and began to pick at her food. Reigel did not want to hide from the Guards, she thought. He had summoned the Guards. Something must be very wrong. She listened dully as the doctor told how the Germans proposed to ventilate the submarine with the long pipes from the mainland, how they planned to sail submerged under diesel and not electric power.

Nora was confused by the doctor's remarks, perplexed by Reigel's absence. When the doctor and Kelly were busy, she opened the chest under the window and satisfied herself that the shotgun was there. It seemed to eliminate the theory that someone had shot Kurt Reigel.

Presently she left the cottage and climbed up the path. Her timing was good. At the top of the hill, she encountered Lieutenant Hoffman. When he saw her, his face brightened and he gave her his shy, tilted smile.

"Ah, good morning, Nora. I've been looking for Lieutenant Reigel."

"Good morning, Peter. Doctor Fitz was telling me. What could have happened to him?"

"I don't know," Hoffman said slowly. "He's completely disappeared. I thought maybe one of the islanders had captured him—held him as hostage—but I don't think that's very likely. Do you?"

Nora agreed it was not likely. She sat down on a boulder. "Perhaps," she suggested, "he fell somewhere last night and hurt himself."

"That's possible," the lieutenant said dubiously. "I'll organize a search party when I get back." He sat down beside her. "We'll need Number One badly if we're going to get away this morning."

"You're leaving? Those pipes you brought back are going to work?"

"I hope so," he said, pointing at the submarine below them. Faint traces of exhaust gases were coming from the snorkel. "See that smoke? That's from the diesels. They're testing them now. If there's no hitch, we'll go back to Lorient at periscope depth."

He explained the principles of the snorkel and admitted its dangers. "We've got to try it, though. The men are for it. They understand we can't sit here and surrender the boat to the first few constables who come along."

Nora asked about the second trip to Limerick and learned they had not found the armature brushes. He said little about the expedition, but the girl was impressed once more by Hoffman's ingenuity and by his determination. She caught a glint of the locket chain around his neck, and felt a tiny ache of envy. Peter was kind and resourceful, she told herself, and he had a tough, obstinate courage. All those qualities—compassion, intelligence, courage—belonged to a girl named Erika. Nora wanted to know about Erika, but not in a hundred years would she have asked about her.

Hoffman gave her a cigarette and they sat, companionably smoking and talking in the early-morning sun, and looking down over the eastern slope of Spanish. It was going to be a grand spring day, Nora thought, but she felt the sting of defeat. The U-boat was about to sail. All her attempts to take it out of the war had failed. She had persuaded Kurt to surrender, but she knew there was no chance with Peter.

"Just think," she said in an attempt at lightness. "It's been seven days since you lectured us, in front of Dermod Beg's. I never thought I'd spend the next three nights with my leg shackled to yours."

He gave her his shy grin and then a quiet chuckle. "Ah, Nora, I had to do it. I know it's been like a bad dream for you, but we'll soon be gone."

Nora drew thoughtfully on her cigarette. A bad dream, she told herself, was a fleeting thing, ephemeral and hard to remember. The events of the last week were indelibly fixed in her memory. Many of those events had been senseless, cruel, and tragic, but she had met Peter Hoffman. On the beach at Ballykerry and in the steamer's little cabin, she had had fragments of happiness with him.

"You know, I'd like to come back here after the war," Hoffman said. "I like these people—I'd like to try to help them."

"They like you, Peter."

"We've brought a lot of misery and grief to Spanish. I'd try to make it up to them."

They were both silent. Hoffman was searching for the right way to say he wanted to see Nora after the war. The girl wanted to ask if he would bring his wife to Spanish, but she was afraid to phrase the question.

After a moment reality returned. The U-boat was still due to sail that morning. Almost casually, Hoffman told Nora about the smashed wireless shack and answered her questions as best he could. No, there wasn't a chance of repairing the radio. Yes, its destruction would jeopardize their return to Lorient. And no, he had no clue as to the identity of the saboteur, except it must have been one of the crew.

"Oh, Peter," Nora said earnestly, "this makes the trip even more dangerous. You won't know about weather, or changes in mine fields, or reports of British warships. You mustn't go, Peter," she burst out. "You'll never make it. It's suicide." She no longer wanted to keep the submarine out of the war. She wanted only to save Peter Hoffman's life.

"We have to try it, Nora. We can't just sit here and surrender the boat." He stared down at the submarine and after a bit, he said softly, as though to himself, "I can't figure out who could have done it. None of the islanders could have come aboard and I was sure all the crew were with me."

They fell silent again. In her own mind, Nora was certain no Irishman or German sailor had sabotaged the radio. It had to be Reigel. He was the one who wanted to surrender. And realizing the submarine would sail anyway, he had hidden himself somewhere on Spanish. It all fitted together.

Hoffman, on his part, was also thinking about Lieutenant Reigel. Not about Reigel's possible connection with the smashed radio or about his mysterious absence. Instead, he thought about the first lieutenant and Nora. Hoffman had been gone nearly forty-eight hours on his second trip to Limerick. When he left, Reigel's desire for Nora had been very obvious. Plenty of time for an affair, Hoffman thought, deliberately lacerating himself. No one had remarked on the subject since his return, but something must have happened. Hoffman wanted to know, desperately, but an obstinate pride prevented any question. It's none of your business, he told himself savagely, if she flirted with Reigel or even slept with him. She's old enough to have a mind of her own. Whatever happened, Hoffman thought grimly, it makes no difference. U-324 was going back to Lorient.

"We have to find Kurt," Hoffman said slowly. "Besides myself, he's the only one left who has stood a deck watch. And we need him to navigate. We need him badly, if we're going to bring the Shark Boat home."

Hoffman stood up and the girl felt a great rush of sympathy for him. Quiet, modest, and physically unimpressive, so completely unlike Reigel, there was still something wonderfully strong and indomitable about him. Ah, she told herself fiercely, there's no point in these silly comparisons. Peter is a happily married German Naval officer.

She walked down the path with him, as far as the Wynne cottage. At its door she gave him her hand. "This is the last time I'll see you, Peter. I'm sorry I was rotten to you Monday night—in the sick bay."

"Ah, you had a perfect right. I was very rude. Doctor FitzGerald's talk made me angry."

"Doctor Fitz was foolish, Peter. Of course, I paid him no mind." She wanted to add something, but the glint of the chain around Hoffman's neck checked her. Hoffman, in turn, wanted to say more. He wanted to take her in his arms and shout, "I love you, Nora, my dearest. If I survive this madness, I'll come back and spend the rest of my life making you happy." Instead, he stood holding her hand, with the tilted smile on his lips.

"I was foolish, too, Peter," the girl said, very soberly. "If we could have seen more of one another . . ."

"The war won't last forever," Hoffman said, still smiling. "One of these days I'll come to Dublin and look you up."

Nora smiled, too, although she was sure he was lying. Her eyes shone with tears. "Do that, my dear," she said softly, "do that, please."

They stared at one another for a moment. Then Hoffman saluted her and plunged down the path, and the girl entered the cottage and went to her room.

It was after eight when he returned to the U-boat. At the gangway, Albrecht reported the snorkel tests had been successful. With the boat buttoned up tight, the diesels had functioned smoothly. Some minor leaks had been discovered in the connections between the exhaust pipe and the engines, but these had been put right.

Hoffman bolted his breakfast and gave orders to his petty officers.

"Be prepared to slip at eleven thirty hours," he told them. "We can't risk waiting longer. Bring the captain's body aboard. We'll bury him as soon as we leave the cove. I think he'd like to leave here on the bridge of his boat, and be buried at sea." There was general assent and he continued:

"Now, as to the search party for Mr. Reigel. I don't think the Irish hold him prisoner, but every cottage and outbuilding will have to be searched. Kreisler, you take a detail of four men and handle that. Koenig, you and Muller take four hands each and search around the island. Koenig's party will go clockwise and Muller's counterclockwise. When you meet on the other side, climb the hill and fan out so as to cover the plateau on your way back. Tell your people to keep an eye on the Norseman's Tower. If I want to recall you, we'll fly the Blue Peter from the tower. Everybody understand? Then let's get at it."

Hoffman had Schiller brought out of the sick bay and the crippled boatswain's mate piped Captain Ludtke aboard for the last time. Then Kreisler, Muller, and Koenig mustered their search parties and set out. Hoffman gave other orders. Water was to be brought down from the well and ammunition placed in the watertight ready boxes on the bridge. The air bottles were to be made ready, and the wounded berthed in the wardroom. A sea chest was set out on the quay and filled with gifts for the islanders—binoculars, first-aid kits, cutlery, soap, sheath knives, and some canned delicacies from the wardroom pantry. In addition, there were all the hundreds of routine checks necessary before a submarine is ready for sea.

Hoffman was the epicenter of this activity, answering questions and receiving reports. He approved Dietrich's watch list, dismayed as he realized only half the crew were fit for duty. It would be watch-and-watch all the way to Lorient. He got out a roll of charts and, working at Haas's tiny desk in the conning tower, began to lay off his courses. His plan was to submerge outside the cove, steer southeast until well past Galleon's Point, and then alter course to 190 degrees, so as to give the Skelligs plently of searoom to port.

A hail from the bridge interrupted him. He went to the topside to find a large group of Irish at the gangway—Sean, Tomas, Timmy Mor, the Begs, the Ogs, the doctor, the priest and his boatman.

"We understand you've not found Lieutenant Reigel," old Sean said directly. "Your sailors are searching our cottages now. They'll not find him there, but he must be somewhere on the island. We'd like to help root him out."

Hoffman formally gave his thanks and told them the routes of his search parties. Sean considered this information and disposed his own forces accordingly. When he had finished he turned back to Hoffman.

"When we find him and turn him over to you, Lieutenant, you'll be leaving Spanish?"

"Yes. But if we don't find him by eleven thirty—less than two hours and a half from now—we'll be underway without him. The police will be here by noon. Maybe sooner."

"Aye. Do we have your word Lieutenant Reigel will be punished for his cruel debauchery?"

"You have my word that charges will be preferred. Yes. But if we do get back to France, Lieutenant Reigel probably will be largely responsible. He may be court-martialed, and also recommended for the Knight's Cross."

Sean considered this for a moment. He was about to speak when Tomas Mor blurted: "Och, let's find him, Sean. They'll not make it to France. I'd liefer he'd take his chance on the submarine nor be cutting turf on a prison farm."

O Ruiarc grunted and the Irish filed off the quay. Hoffman watched them with a little smile. There were ten of them, with their dogs. Time was running out and Spanish was a rocky, mountainous island, full of caves. But there were twenty-five searchers now, many of them familiar with the island's six square miles. Inevitably, Reigel would be found. Hoffman stared up at the Norseman's Tower for a second or two, unnecessarily advised the watchkeeper on the bridge to keep alert, and cheerfully swung down the ladder to his charts.

Spanish *was* a small island. The twenty-five searchers covered it well that sunny June forenoon, but they found nothing.

Nora Berkeley spent a miserable morning. She was irritable and nervous and smoked incessantly. Once, when Lady Maud asked her to help Kelly air some bedding, she answered with an abrupt impatience that surprised the old lady and caused Kelly to regard her with concern. Nora was ashamed of her shortness but too irritated to make amends. She performed her part of the chore with ill grace and hurried back to her bedroom to pace the floor. For a week now she had struggled to protect the people of Spanish and to take the U-boat out of the war. She had failed to stop Peter Hoffman—to make it worse, she had fallen in love with him. She had succeeded with Reigel. But, at the eleventh hour, Peter had returned to retrieve his victory and to plunge her into sad, baffled confusion. Damnation! She wished she had never seen him after he stamped out of the sick bay Monday night. She thanked God she had seen him for a few minutes Thursday morning.

At breakfast, when Doctor Fitz told her the first lieutenant was missing, Nora had been puzzled. Later, when she found the shotgun in its place, she felt even more perplexed. It would be possible, she thought, for an unarmed Tomas to ambush Kurt, but it was not likely. The night before, when she had last seen Reigel, he was nervous, high-strung, ready to reach for his pistol at the slightest noise. It was difficult to imagine him being taken by surprise.

Then, during the half hour she spent with Peter Hoffman at the top of the path, Nora had become convinced Reigel was unharmed. He had hidden himself, she was sure, to avoid sailing in the submarine. She saw the German search parties leave the jetty and a little later watched the smaller but more experienced group of Irish fan out in both directions over the eastern slope of Spanish. With Lady Maud's brass-bound telescope, she could see them working to the north and south of the island, the dogs exploring ahead, as excited as if they were after a rabbit. Germans and Irish together, two dozen men and women, were engaged in the manhunt. Most were armed and many knew every square foot of the island.

As the girl watched with the glass from her window, she prayed inwardly that Reigel would not be discovered. He was a detestable sod, she told herself, but if they found him, there would be shooting. Intuitively, she knew he never would be taken alive, and others would be shot down—perhaps Sean, the doctor, or Timmy. Somewhere on

Spanish, the first lieutenant had gone to ground like—the analogy suddenly struck her—like a frightened, dangerous ferret. Somewhere on Spanish he was hidden. He might be in her field of vision, or on the plateau. He might be on Galleon's Point on the southern tip of the island, or in one of the caves on the western coast. Somewhere Kurt Reigel crouched, his hand at his pistol, ready to fight like a cornered animal.

Nora put up the telescope and went into the kitchen. She had a cup of tea and another cigarette, conscious of Kelly's disapproving look. When she had finished her tea, the girl went back to her room, annoyed with Kelly and disgusted with herself.

Like a cornered animal, she thought again. She remembered Reigel last night behind the sick bay. There had been something terrifying about him when he crushed her in his arms. His teeth had gleamed as he shook her and snarled, "You're not too good to come up to the Conor cabin."

The Conor cabin. The thought struck her brain as sharply as an explosion. She stared through the telescope at the ruins of Seamus Conor's cottage. It was half-hidden by the rise of the hill, with only one triangular stone gable and a crumbling side wall visible. It was about one hundred and fifty yards from the shore line and she recalled that the first search party—the German sailors—had passed along the shore. The Irish—she was convinced of this—had been well above it as they moved toward the south end of the island. For more than a minute, she carefully studied what she could see of the ruin. Nothing moved in the telescope's field, yet her excitement mounted. This, the girl told herself, was completely absurd. And yet there was something very logical about it. She knew there was an enormous chimney place in the west wall. Reigel had not been on the island long enough to know the caves on the western shore, not well enough, at least, to find them by night. Probably, too, he realized the far side of the island and the tangled rocks of Galleon's Point would be the natural targets of any search party; the hunters would hardly think of a crumbled cabin so close to the jetty. The islanders might, because of Shelagh, but they'd assume the Germans had searched it. And there was something else. If the first lieutenant was taken by surprise, his proximity to the U-boat might indicate he had never tried to hide. He could always claim he had left the noise of the submarine-under-repair to get a good night's sleep.

Nora lit another Sweet Afton and derided herself for an overactive imagination. You're insane, she told herself, absolutely starkers, a bloody mental case. The cigarette tasted vile. She snapped it out of the window and picked up the telescope again. The slope below her was almost devoid of life. Directly below her, Kathy O Ŕuiarc fed three stringy hens. Nearly a mile away a couple of goats moved slowly on the northern arm of the cove. A single sailor moved about on the U-boat's bridge. Nora felt like laughing—a shrill, humorless laugh. She was suddenly convinced. All the hunters were out of sight —on the other side of Spanish—and their quarry was right below her.

Nora fixed her glass on the U-boat. She wished Peter Hoffman would come up on the bridge. She wanted to see him again. He was a little crazy, yes. If it weren't for Peter, they would never have rigged those weird breathing pipes and decided to take the submarine back to France. It was an insane idea—and yet the sailors were behind him. He's daft, the girl told herself, Reigel is the smart one. The first lieutenant is a practical man who recognizes the incredible recklessness of this adventure. But, somehow, Nora was not sure she was right. On an impulse, she put the telescope down and went into Lady Maud's room.

Lady Maud was propped up on her pillows, playing two-pack Patience. She gave the girl a sharp, inquiring look and said nothing.

"How do you feel, gran?"

"Very well, my dear," the old lady said with some acidity. "Kelly looks after me most carefully. My physician has inspected me this very morning. And this wretched pastime teaches me tolerance. How do you feel, child?"

"Wizard, simply wizard," the girl said. She sat on a creepie and produced her packet of Sweet Aftons. The old lady gave her a steady birdlike look. Nora lighted a cigarette.

"Curious word—wizard," said Lady Maud dryly. She flipped over several cards, eyeing them grimly.

The girl did not respond. She concentrated, rather ineptly, on blowing smoke rings. When she spoke, her voice was harsh and strained.

"How long did you know grandfather before you married him?"

The question caught Lady Maud unprepared. The bright blue eyes blinked several times, and the tone of her voice altered perceptibly.

"My dear, that was so long ago."

"You must remember."

"It was a quick courtship, Nora." The old lady was silent, remembering, but not volunteering any detail.

"A year, two years?"

"Och, not at all, not at all, my dear. It was four days, it was."

Nora looked impressed and the old lady's blue eyes twinkled.

"There were whirlwind romances, my dear, even in Victorian times. Even in Ireland."

The girl considered this for a few moments. Then, remembering the yellowed photograph of the late baronet that stood on the kitchen mantel, she ventured, "Grandfather must have been a fast worker."

"Fast? Och, not at all, not at all," Lady Maud chuckled. "He wasn't witty or clever, not a bit of it." She paused and said quietly, "But Laurence was kind and he knew how to make me happy."

"At least, he was very brave," Nora said stoutly. "One doesn't get a gong like the D.S.O. for hiding in a shell hole." The word "hiding" slipped out, she realized, because she was thinking of Kurt Reigel.

"No, I don't think he was really brave," Lady Maud said gravely. "I saw him frightened, more than once. He admitted it. What Laurence had was—ah—integrity. He had a sense of honor."

"But the gong——?"

"Laurence didn't win the D.S.O. for making a great whooping cavalry charge, Nora. He won it because he refused to surrender his company when they were surrounded at Montoen Kop. I'm sure I've told you this story, my dear. They were cut off for three days. Laurence said he was terrified. But he had taken an oath to the Queen, and he refused to surrender. He was a man of honor. Honor, my dear, is more important than bravery."

"Of course, gran."

"When we first came to Spanish, you know, Laurence and Sean O Ruiarc hit it off from the start. They had very little in common. Laurence was a knight, even if he was on the run, and a man of some education. Sean was a poor fisherman. Even today, he can hardly read the Bible. But they were thick as two tinkers. I believe the reason was they were men of honor."

The old lady got out her pipe and loaded it carefully.

"Sean must have been handsome then," Nora said.

"That he was. And, like the other island folk, kind and generous to the people on the run." Lady Maud lit her pipe and puffed energetically for a few seconds. "Just as they've been kind and generous to those poor devils, the Germans."

They smoked in silence for a few moments.

"God knows, the Germans have not exactly reciprocated," Lady Maud said. "Och, the sadness they have brought to Spanish."

Nora sighed heavily.

"You know, Noreen, one of the Germans is a man of honor. Lieutenant Hoffman. In that way, he reminds me of Laurence. Not really a brave man——"

"He *is* a brave man," Nora said. "The odds are a hundred to one he can't sail the submarine safely back to France. But he's taking the risk."

"It's a question of honor, child, not bravery. I'll wager the lieutenant is afraid right now—but he's sailing because he feels he owes it to his country. That's what I mean by honor."

"I think I see what you mean," Nora said thoughtfully. She looked at Lady Maud's clock. The hands pointed to half after ten—an hour before the U-boat's sailing time.

"Now, on the other side of the sixpence, Noreen, there's Lieutenant Reigel. Indeed, he's stronger and handsomer, but he's a cruel man, and he's a coward, skulking in some cave now, while his ship goes to sea."

"Boat, not ship," Nora said, and before her grandmother could ask her to explain *that* curious statement, she added in a low unhappy voice: "They're all of a sort, those Nazis. But at least Lieutenant Reigel wants to marry me."

"Arrhh." The old lady made a sound of disgust. "And what of Lieutenant Hoffman? I saw how he looked at you, under this very thatch."

"Lieutenant Hoffman is married and a father."

"Claptrap," Lady Maud snorted. "Complete and utter twaddle."

"It's true enough," Nora said dully. "He has a wife named Erika."

"His wife is dead. Killed in an air raid. Your friend, Lieutenant Reigel, told me so himself."

"What are you saying, now?"

Her Ladyship repeated her words and the shrewd, china-blue eyes gleamed as she watched their effect. Nora's own eyes were suddenly bright with tears, her cheeks were flushed, and she smiled uncertainly.

"Och, what an idiot I've been," she said weakly, and asked to be excused.

Lady Maud agreed in her forthright fashion, and gave permission for Nora to withdraw. "There's time, Noreen, to make it all come right as eggs."

Nora went into the kitchen. She was trembling with emotion. She remembered Ludtke's sly phrases, Peter's angry profanity in the sick bay, and Kurt's confirmation of Hoffman's marriage. Peter, Peter, she muttered, I'll make it up to you, my dear.

The upper half of the kitchen door was open and she heard voices on the path. She went to the door and saw a handful of German sailors descending. She could tell from their faces the search for Reigel had been unsuccessful. At the top of the hill, the blue-and-white recall flag flew from the Norseman's Tower.

Behind the sailors, Father Healy and Liam Curran came down the path, the priest holding his skirts above his ankles.

"They've sighted the *Kerry Queen*, Nora," he shouted gaily, as they passed the Wynne cottage. "The sub will be leaving very soon. Up Spanish!"

The girl did not answer. She went back to the hearth, lit a cigarette, and paced back and forth for a few moments, thinking hard. She desperately wanted to run down the path and aboard the submarine, to apologize to Peter and let him take her in his arms. But she knew this was not the answer. She wanted Peter, but, above all else, Peter needed Kurt Reigel. Intuitively, she knew Reigel was hidden in the Conor cottage. He would stay there until the U-boat sailed. He would not surrender to Hoffman. If she told Hoffman of her presentiment, Kurt would be flushed out with bullets. Kurt would be killed—others probably —and nothing would be accomplished. Whatever you do in the next few minutes, she told herself fiercely, will stay with you for all of your days. She sank to her knees and tried to pray, but it was no use. Very distantly, she heard the Action Stations klaxon of the U-boat sounding the recall.

"Nora, Nora," Lady Maud's shrill, imperious voice came from the bedroom. "Are you still here? What ails you, Noreen? Get down to the submarine and see him off properly."

The strident questions acted like a catalyst on the kneeling girl. Suddenly she knew what she had to do. She got to her feet and went to the chest. She opened it and took out the Purdey shotgun. The agitation in her face was replaced by implacable resolve. Carrying the piece, she went out of the cottage, down the path, and then started across the rocky pasture behind the O Ŕuiarcs'.

Kathy O Ŕuiarc saw her and called to her with alarm. Nora did not answer. The old woman was frightened at the sight of the white-faced girl, the shotgun cradled in her arm, moving swiftly and determinedly in a diagonal direction down the hill. A knot of German sailors, hurrying down the path, was puzzled. The sight of the gun startled them, but there was no time to investigate, and they continued their descent.

Less than ten minutes after her decision, Nora Berkeley paused. She was a dozen yards from the Conor cottage. She could see the stump of the chimney protruding a yard above the sloping terrace on which she stood. At right angles to the chimney place the triangular gable of the north wall extended down the hill. She looked around her. Above and behind her, a small figure watched from the garden of the O Ŕuiarc cottage. That would be Kathy. Almost every other soul on the island was on the jetty, three hundred yards below and to her left. There was much activity there and on the weather decks of the U-boat. There was no sound except, as always, the boom of the surf and the cries of the seabirds. It was about ten minutes after eleven.

The girl moved cautiously down the slope to the chimney. She could see into the interior of the roofless cottage and was not surprised that it was empty. She looked down the chimney but could see nothing. This, she thought briefly, was an absurd wild goose chase. There were thousands of places to hide on Spanish. But she remembered the knowledge the islanders had of the caves and she knew somehow she was right. She cocked the unfamiliar hammers of the shotgun.

"Kurt, Kurt, are you there?" she called softly. "This is Nora."

There was no answer, no sound at all except for the muffled boom of the waves, the distant clamor of the gulls, and the tiny shouts from the U-boat, part of the routine of preparing her for sea.

"Kurt," she called again. "Everything's all right. I'm alone. The submarine is ready to sail."

There was no reply and she said to herself, he's not here. I've let my imagination run away with me.

Then, suddenly, there was a noise directly below her, a slight scraping rattle. Nora leaned forward tensely. Ten feet below her a man's head and shoulders cautiously appeared. She held her breath and then the first lieutenant stepped out of the chimney place, flexing his cramped muscles. He turned, glancing upward for Nora, and found himself looking into the twin muzzles of the shotgun.

"Hands up, Kurt," the girl said in a small, strained voice. "Put up your hands, please."

He obeyed slowly, his jaw slack with surprise. For a few moments they stared at each other, Nora uncertain as to how to proceed, and Reigel, recovered from the initial stunning shock, weighing his chances. For the present, he decided, the odds were against him. The girl was protected by the chimney and her elevation. It would be almost impossible to draw his pistol and hit her with a hip shot. On the other hand, with the shotgun, she couldn't miss her target.

"For Christ's sake, Nora," he asked, "is this a joke? Where did you get that?"

"Keep your right hand in the air, Kurt," the girl said, tense and frightened. From some long-forgotten film of the American West, the words came back to her. "Now, with your left hand, unbuckle your pistol belt. Don't lower your right hand, Kurt. I don't want to shoot, but I will."

The lieutenant brought his left hand down very gradually. His mouth was working. *"Um Gottes wegen, Liebchen,* what's this about?" he stammered. "What do you want?"

"Go on," she said implacably. "Don't move your feet. Keep your right hand up in the air."

With his left hand, Reigel pulled the belt free of its buckle. Belt, holster, and Walther automatic fell at his feet.

"Now," Nora instructed him, "move slowly to the eastern wall. Both hands up, please. Outside, now, and slowly down the hill."

He obeyed, thinking hard. "Nora, what's this all about?" he asked again. "You know why I've hidden here. There's only one reason. I love you. I want to marry you."

The girl paid no attention. She rose and came down the slope, outside the crumbling north wall of the ruined cottage, with the shotgun covering him at every step. When they were both in the open, her directions were explicit:

"Walk slowly down to the jetty. Keep your hands up. Don't talk, don't look back. I'll be right behind you."

They went down the hill toward the quay, the lieutenant desperately searching for some avenue of escape, and the girl following, her eyes fixed on his back, praying inwardly she would not stumble on the rocky ground. Once, when she thought he might be trying to put the sick bay between them and the jetty, she ordered him to alter his direction. Twice he started to speak and she ordered him to be silent.

The crumbled ruin was only a few hundred yards from the jetty and they were spotted from the bridge of the U-boat before they were half-way to it. U-324 was ready for sea, her mooring wires singled up, the gangway taken in. Of her crew, there were only a few men on the bridge, and a couple of line-handlers on the fo'c'sle and stern. The jetty itself was crowded with Irish. Only Lady Maud and Maura Mor were absent. A few minutes before, it had been a glum group, vaguely disturbed that the U-boat was escaping, bitterly resenting Reigel's failure to be aboard, and irritated at their failure to find him.

Now, here he came, his hands raised, and the grins spread among the islanders. Behind him marched Nora Berkeley, the shotgun at her waist, her face twisted with strain and concentration, looking neither right nor left. As they moved onto the jetty, the islanders wanted to cheer her, to question her, but they were silent before her look of fierce resolve.

When they came abreast of the conning tower, Reigel hesitated. Nora gave a short command and he leaped across to the submarine's saddle tank. He did not look back. Hoffman, who had come down from the bridge, helped pull him aboard. The acting captain of U-324 grinned broadly.

"Welcome aboard, Number One. Now, we're ready to make Lorient."

He looked at Nora across the gap between the weather deck and the quay and saluted.

"Bless you, Nora. Remember what I said about coming to Dublin."

The girl lowered the shotgun and smiled weakly back at him. She wanted to cry out that she would wait for him, but her lips moved soundlessly. She felt ill and exhausted by the strain. She wanted to tell Peter he was an honorable man, and that honor was the most important thing of all. She wanted to wish him luck, the great amounts of luck he would need to bring U-324 back to safety. But she could do nothing but smile feebly, even when Dr. FitzGerald relieved her of the shotgun, carefully uncocked it, and told her how brave she was.

At exactly eleven thirty-five, U-324 slipped her cables and proceeded to sea. Once outside the cove, she paused briefly to bury her first captain and then submerged on a southeasterly course. Some of the islanders, who had climbed to vantage points to observe her, said that when last seen, she was proceeding smoothly. The diesel exhaust was visible, of course, if one knew where to look, but it was not obvious. Not as obvious, for example, as the smoke put up by the *Kerry Queen* as the steamer approached the island.

From the moment the U-boat was outside the cove, Nora Berkeley was smothered by congratulations.

"Och, that was a grand thing, Nora," Sean O Ŕuiarc said, shaking her hand. "My love forever, Nora." He solemnly kissed her cheek, and noted it was wet with tears.

The others gathered round, praising, with flights of hyperbole, her wisdom and courage.

"Glory be to God, Noreen, you have saved the honor of Spanish," Dermod Beg grinned, and he bussed her soundly.

"You have the truth of it, Dermod," Tomas Mor boomed, pumping her hand. "Indeed, Nora, I'd never have slept easy if that devil had gone to a soft prison farm."

They wanted to know, of course, how she had discovered Reigel, and she made up some story about seeing his head emerge briefly from a cluster of rocks. She knew they wanted to please her and she seized her opportunity.

"Thank you, thank you all. Now, I have a favor to ask of you. The Guards will be here shortly. If we tell them the submarine has just left Spanish, they'll tell the R.A.F., and the Coastal Command will sink the U-boat before she's past the Skelligs. She won't have a chance."

"Indeed, she won't," cried Maeve Mor. "You can see the sub's exhaust, and we know she's making south. If we tell the *Kerry Queen,* she can track her easy and wait for the planes."

"I beg you," Nora said earnestly, paying no attention to Maeve. "I beg you to tell the Guards the U-boat left early this morning—at seven o'clock. It's a bit of a story, I know, but it will give those poor sailors a fighting chance. That poor boy who lost his hand, the boatswain's mate who made toys for the little ones, Lieutenant Hoffman—they deserve a chance."

All the islanders looked at Sean O Ŕuiarc, knowing the old man's respect for the truth. There was a second's hesitation and then the blue eyes gleamed in the crinkled mahogany face.

"If Nora wants to give them a chance, then a chance they'll get. Is it agreed the U-boat left Spanish at seven o'clock?"

There was general assent and when, some twenty minutes later, the *Kerry Queen* came alongside the jetty, the Guards were told the submarine had a five-hour start. The police had installed a radio aboard the trawler and a message was quickly sent off to Dingle. Within an hour, the Admiralty would be deploying its ships and planes.

There were close to a dozen of the Guards and a young man who identified himself as a reporter for the *Kerryman.* They were very busy, inspecting the sick bay and the inoperative radio-telephone set, asking questions, and taking down statements in their notebooks. Nora noticed no mention was made of Shelagh's violation. Instinctively, the islanders were protecting one of their own against the outside world. When she realized this, the girl smiled to herself, proud of the people of Spanish.

"Now, sir," the tall sergeant commanding the detail finally said to Sean. "One question again, please. Where was the submarine headed?"

"I'd not be knowing that, Sergeant," the old man said uneasily, and Nora thought what a poor liar he was.

The policeman thought so, too, and tried again. "Surely you'd be knowing the submarine's home port?"

"Indeed, I forget those foreign names," Sean O Ŕuiarc said. "One of the French ports, I'm thinking."

The sergeant made a note. "Och, indeed, they're going the wrong way then," he said, closing his notebook.

"What do you mean, Sergeant, the wrong way?" Nora asked quickly.

The policeman looked at her and smiled. "I'm forgetting, miss, you've been cut off from the world. Tuesday, the day before yesterday, General Eisenhower landed in Normandy. Och, there were millions of soldiers with him. Likely the Yankees and Tommies will be in St.-Nazaire and Lorient and those places before the submarine gets there."

Nora's knees went weak. She smiled mechanically and walked slowly and unseeing up the jetty. Her thoughts were filled with Peter—Peter struggling to get the cable and acid to Spanish, failing with them, failing again with the armature brushes, and rigging the gas pipes as a snorkel. Peter struggling with Tomas and Eamon in the sea, Peter consoling her in the barn and angry with her in the sick bay. His captain dead, his first lieutenant a traitor, half his crew casualties, Peter had taken the U-boat to sea in the face of almost certain destruction. And now the ultimate irony—he had no port to return to. She was sick with the mockery of it—yet instinctively she knew that after the wound had scarred and healed, and she had married, she would always be grateful she had known this man, this quiet, obstinate man with the finely developed sense of honor.

Near the sick bay, she encountered Maura Mor.

"Glory be to God, it's a grand day, Nora Berkeley," the Widow said, almost smiling. "I'm hearing you're quite responsible for it."

"Don't thank me," the girl said dully, and began the long slow plod up the path to Lady Maud's.

ABOUT THE AUTHOR

William Gage was born in Detroit
and educated at Yale University.
He was a Naval officer for five
years, chiefly in destroyers. In
February, 1942, escorting the first
American troop convoy, he went to
Ireland, and found it delightful.
Since the war, Mr. Gage has
worked in an advertising agency
in Detroit, but he goes back to
Ireland as frequently as possible.
The Cruel Coast is his second
novel.

DATE DUE
